Royal Again.

By
Iain Benson

For
Adam and Thomas
and
Elaine, always.

Royal Again   **Iain Benson**

Royal Again

Copyright December 20th 2022 by Iain Benson
Cover Design by Iain Benson.

No part of this book may be reproduced in any form or by any electronic or mechanical means, including information storage and retrieval systems, without permission in writing from the author. A reviewer may quote brief excerpts in their review.

This book is a work of fiction: Names, characters, places, and incidents either are products of the author's imagination or are used fictitiously. Any resemblance to actual persons, living or dead, events, or locales is entirely coincidental.
One thing this book taught me is: People change. The question is whether to embrace the change or lose them.

First published December 20th 2022 on Kindle (www.amazon.com)
First printed edition December 20th 2022 on Amazon (www. amazon.com)

ISBN: 9798356171116

By Iain Benson

Dorking Review (contributor)
App World!
Fakebook.con
The Watcher
Protean
Yesterday Pill
Royal Again

The Women Trilogy
Loosely Women
Sparkly Women
Legally Women

James London Series
It's a Kind of Magic
2000 Lightyears from Home
The Man Who Sold the World
Everybody's Happy Nowadays
Spirits in the Material World
Here, There and Everywhere
London's Burning

Louise Sargant Series
The Case of the Half-Baked Mummies

Royal Again **Iain Benson**

Iain Benson **Royal Again**

1
Pippa: Perfect storm

On the day everything changed, nobody could accuse Pippa of being unreasonable for vacuuming the Main Hall at eleven in the morning.

But she knew what it meant.

It meant she could exert a minor act of vindictive, passive aggressiveness. Her slight revenge for dozens of recent complaints.

The sun streamed through the tall windows that ran down the Main Hall, creating stripes of shadows on the lush red rug covering the marble flooring. It cast the portraits on the wall opposite into bands of light. Between the portraits, ornate double doors into the Royal Apartments gave no clues who lived in each one.

The flex from the dumpy red vacuum cleaner ran behind one of a dozen Rococo chairs. Annie had told her they had a value higher than her yearly salary, making Pippa careful around them.

As the grand grandfather clock struck eleven, a crash heralded Prince Harrison emerging to glare at her. Framed by the wooden panelling, he wore a single-breasted suit in charcoal grey. With his coiffured dark hair and velvety brown eyes, he gave a regal impression, despite the clouds of thunder in his expression.

Pippa stabbed at the off switch on the vacuum, unable to hear the crown prince's words.

"Sorry!" Pippa cocked her head to the side.

"I said, why are you making this cacophony?" Harrison had an edge to his voice. Pippa may have gone a little far. She couldn't risk more complaints.

"Sorry, sir!" Pippa felt the need to explain. "Annie told me to vacuum the hall today. Sorry if I disturbed you."

Stepping forward, towering over her, Harrison fixed her with a brutal expression. She wilted a little. Harrison enunciated each word, his breath warm on Pippa's face. "I am working. Do your cleaning later!"

Attempting to return to his apartment, he got his expensive tan brogues wrapped in the vacuum wire, almost falling back inside.

Wishing she'd been able to film that, Pippa nibbled her cheek, waiting for a vitriolic diatribe that never came. Instead, he muttered

Royal Again   Iain Benson

expletives and slammed the door.

"What a jerk." Pippa gesticulated after him. What did he know about working? Dogs in handbags worked harder than him.

She disliked Horror-son, but it would push her luck if she finished vacuuming the hall. She depressed the button to recoil the flex inside the happy-faced vacuum cleaner.

Pulling it along by the hose, she headed for the staff quarters, greeting other staff members as she went.

"I can't vacuum the Main Hall," she told Annie, her supervisor, leaning into her glass-walled office.

Annie pushed her reading glasses up onto her head, through the thick mop of dark curls, and looked up from her screen.

"What's the excuse this time?" Annie didn't sound cross, instead resigned to Pippa's failure.

"His Royal Pain in the Butt." Pippa needed to return the vacuum to the storage room, but sensed Annie's stern demeanour crack and paused by the door.

"Was diddums napping?" Annie's voice held a smile.

Checking her boss had smiled, Pippa tapped her lips. "Probably."

Annie sighed, gazing into the distance. "It's not like he needs beauty sleep, though, is it?"

"Oh, god!" Pippa said with a squeal. "You don't fancy him, do you?"

"What's not to like?"

"Uh? Apart from his entire personality?" Pippa mentally flicked through her interactions with Harrison. "I can't think of a single time he's ever been nice to me in the month since he's been back."

"You don't need to be nice when you're rich and handsome." Annie returned her focus to work, pretending her computer screen contained something important, brushing away imaginary dust. "Anyway, take an early lunch break. Prince Harrison is entertaining Lady Isabella later. Make sure you clean his rooms before that happens."

"Will he be there?"

Annie ran her finger along the computer screen. "According to this, he is visiting a school this afternoon to congratulate them on getting an Outstanding Ofsted report."

"How long was the report outstanding that they require a prince to be there when they get it?"

Annie's eyebrows collided as she pursed her lips to one side for a moment. Understanding dawned. "Outstanding as in very good, not very late."

"Oh, fair enough." Pippa had a sudden thought. "When is he back?"

"After six." Annie ran her finger down the roster.

Pippa folded her arms. "I'll give the room a thorough clean. With any luck, Isabella will move up the wedding and Harrison will leave!"

Annie harrumphed. "Go get your lunch."

"See you later!" Pippa headed off down the corridor towards the staff cafeteria.

Annie's hand flew to her lips as she gasped, re-reading the roster. She called after Pippa. "Pippa! Not six, four! He's back at four!"

Pippa missed the shout entirely, thinking about lunch.

Wiping her forehead with the back of her arm, trying to keep the toilet brush and rubber glove away from her face and hair, Pippa heard the apartment door open.

Puzzled, she considered checking who'd entered. It couldn't be much past four, so Harrison's arrival would be unlikely. She finished cleaning the toilet, wondering who it could be.

It'll probably be Tim with some nibbles for His Nobbles. She tried not to let panic set in. Harrison surely hadn't returned early? The prince took punctuality to a level only observed in the military and on first dates.

The sounds coming from the sitting room reminded her of a coat taken off and dropped untidily onto a chaise longue.

I'm sure it's Tim. Pippa glanced at the bathroom door. *He'll be setting up for Harrison's dinner with Isabella.*

Her surety faltered when she heard a muffled voice.

"What do you mean, she's here?"

Pippa realised the voice had more timbre than Tim, and a lot less Liverpool twang.

"Crapola," Pippa muttered, packing away her cleaning cart.

While she tried to be quick and quiet, the bottles and cans started clinking and clanking like they were trying to mate. Pippa winced with every sound, considering ways to sneak from the apartment without Harrison seeing her. She listened to Harrison stomping around. He sounded annoyed. She'd never seen him any other way. She pictured the apartment layout: the short corridor from the bathroom to the sitting room. The bedroom and dressing room were opposite the bathroom. She could creep across the

Royal Again   Iain Benson

corridor into the dressing room, the room Harrison would be less likely to go into. When he went to the loo, she could leave.

Any choices vanished as Harrison entered the bathroom.

"Good god!" His face kept the thunder from earlier. An expression she equated with him. "You! Again!"

Pippa reached her limit for pussyfooting around his ego. "I'm trying to do my job. They tell me what to clean and when. It's never been my intention to be in your way. Quite the opposite. You can report me if you like, but I will not stand to be treated like this!"

Her vitriol spat at the prince, making him take a step back into the corridor. She realised she'd been gesticulating with the toilet brush.

Well, serve him right. She put the brush behind her back as though that might make him forget she'd waved it at him.

"I will not tolerate your insolence." Harrison's tone had lowered to dangerous steel.

Realising speaking to the prince in such a way meant she'd be out of work in the morning if he had his way, she unleashed all the pent-up frustration he'd built in her since his return. No point holding back now.

"My insolence? You're rude, obnoxious, and entitled. You treat the staff working here like so much dirty laundry to kick aside. Ignoring us until you need us."

Harrison hissed. "What?"

"You were the same before you left five years ago. Your bloodline doesn't make you better than me. Just richer. I can't wait until you get married to Isabella and I never have to see you again."

"Out!" Harrison pointed at the sitting room with a quivering finger.

"That is the first instruction you have ever given me, which I will obey with relish!"

Pippa tossed the brush beside the toilet and marched past Harrison with her chin up, pulling her little cart behind her, trying to keep her quivering stomach from betraying her in her face or gait.

The prince followed her into the sitting room, watching her head for the tall double doors and, Pippa hoped, freedom.

Five steps from sweet release, her hand already reaching for the handle, somebody knocked on the main apartment doors with a rat-a-tat-tat.

Pippa paused.

"Who is it?" Harrison demanded, almost shouting.

"Lady Isabella Eldredge, your majesty," said Ben's voice from the hall outside. The butler's distinctive baritone carried through the flimsy wood with ease.

Pippa gestured with a "what-now?" at Harrison. He kept glancing at her and the door, unsure, hesitant.

"Change of plans," he snapped. "Go into my changing room and make yourself comfortable. You are going to be there for quite some time."

"I finish at five," Pippa said, any pretence at reverence abandoned.

"If you walk out of that door, I will have your employment terminated."

"Sir?" Ben's voice came again.

"One moment," Harrison replied. Quieter, he glared at Pippa, stopping short of grasping her by the shoulders, though his hands moved in that direction. "Dressing room."

Pippa flicked her hair and returned up the corridor, turning left into the dressing room instead of right into the bathroom. Hiding in the dressing room was her idea originally, but it smarted when instructed to do so. However, if it meant she could keep her job after giving the prince a piece of her mind, she felt a winner in a reasonable exchange. How wonderful to tell the prince what she thought about him. Sitting on the chair beside the vanity, she allowed herself a little momentary smile.

Even with an entire room full of beautiful clothes, Pippa got bored after an hour. She paraded before the mirror with Harrison's dress uniform held up to herself, pretending to be on a state occasion. It felt too coarse on her skin, so she hung it back up and slipped on one of his jackets instead. The jacket smelled of expensive cologne and a musky odour that she found quite enticing.

Pippa wished the palace rules allowed her to have her phone with her. She could have played a game or rung a friend. With her phone in her locker, she instead passed the time rifling through his jewellery, marvelling at the amount of money contained within one drawer. No expert, but she imagined one wristwatch might be worth her yearly salary.

"How the other half lives," she muttered.

After a while, she cracked open the dressing room door a little, trying to listen to the conversation in the sitting room. She justified the eavesdropping by telling herself she only wanted to work out how much longer her incarceration might last. Whilst sitting with her back to the wall,

Royal Again   Iain Benson

earwigging, Tim arrived with food for the couple. Their evening meal smelled heavenly, wafting through the slight crack to make her stomach rumble.

Quietly, she closed the door and sat in the window seat. She watched the last light vanish from the world, a storm moving in. The clouds roiled with purples and blues, bruising the sky, lit by lightning flashes that seemed to skit across the heavens. A little shiver made her wrap her arms around herself in the face of nature's ferocity. Rain beaded on the window, chilling the air further. She added a scarf to Harrison's jacket that created a dashing look in the mirror, even if the jacket swamped her. Pippa twisted and turned, making model pouts and using her fingers as guns to click at her reflection.

In a pompous singsong voice, she stuck her nose in the air. "Oh, I'm the dashing Prince Harrison. All bow before me!"

Remembering the instruction to stay quiet, she shrank into the jacket and listened intently, hoping Isabella didn't discover her.

Harrison and Isabella argued in the sitting room, their voices difficult to distinguish. She reopened the door, curiosity getting the better of her. From the odd parts she could discern, they discussed a dinner at Eldritch mansion to be followed by dancing. Harrison announced he had a busy afternoon that day, watching a film premiere.

Busy? Pippa's disgust mounted.

"My grandparents will be there." Isabella's high-pitched voice carried easily.

Harrison's deeper reply only became audible when he raised it. "I can meet him at the wedding."

One thing Pippa worked out, neither entered the union with any love or desire. Pippa felt sorry for Isabella. Forced to see Harrison every day and pretend to enjoy it. *Poor girl!*

At least they didn't need to decide the venue, the wedding guests, or any details that most people discussed ahead of a wedding. Pippa struggled to come up with anything they could control. Someone else decided everything for them, from the flowers to the honeymoon destination. While she waited, Pippa idly fantasised about their honeymoon. Sailing around Caribbean islands on a private yacht. She shuddered, thinking about them creating progeny to continue the royal lineage.

"Definitely poor girl!" Pippa gave a quiet chortle.

With rain lashing the window, creating small haloes where the lightning flashed, the voices in the sitting room quietened for a few moments before a full-blown argument began with both shouting simultaneously.

"Well!" Pippa guessed Isabella spoke, as her voice lacked Harrison's baritone. She did, however, have Harrison's temper. "There is nothing more to discuss! I am leaving. Your father will make you come."

Hearing Isabella's vitriol, Pippa felt a little less sorry for her. Realising she'd be leaving soon, she unknotted the scarf, placing it back into a drawer.

They sound like they deserve each other. Pippa grinned. *Great timing, too! She'll be leaving in the pouring rain.*

As she left the apartment, the expensive double doors refused to slam behind Isabella. From the sounds of it, she'd given it an excellent attempt.

Moments later, Harrison yanked open the dressing room door before Pippa could remove the jacket. His square jaw clenched. He impatiently gestured for her to leave.

Pippa needed no encouragement. She stormed past him, stopping in the sitting room.

"Take off my jacket," he instructed.

Pippa shrugged out of it and placed it neatly over the sofa back. Her fingers trailed across the smooth material. "Remember our deal. I stayed really quiet for the whole time, so you don't get me sacked."

His fists clenched, but he grunted and nodded. "Fine! Now get out."

His firm grip on her arm steered her towards the apartment's door. They both reached for the handles at the same time.

The lights went out.

2
Pippa: Switched

From the floor, the ceiling receded into the distance. Especially in the intermittent dark, only lit by the full-blown lightning storm raging around the palace. Pippa blinked, trying to clear the stars swimming around her head. She could smell toast. In the back of her mind, she had a vague memory that smelling toast signalled a horrific medical condition, but couldn't remember what.

Something felt wrong.

Her body felt wrong.

Heavier.

Her breath came in ragged bursts, her heart thumped with an irregular rhythm, and she had a raging thirst.

A woman spoke to her left. "What happened?"

Pippa froze. Harrison had been to her right; nobody had been over there. She wondered if Isabella had returned to find her future husband on the floor with a cleaner.

Harrison!

She turned to look for Harrison.

Momentary illumination from a brief flash lit the chaise longue by the occasional table. No sign of Harrison.

She relaxed. He had to be all right.

The woman spoke again. "Oh! My god!"

Pippa twisted toward the voice.

In the dark, she saw a woman's shape lying next to her. Confusion befuddled her mind. Her heartbeat and breathing were not her own.

"Who?" she asked. She stopped after one word, hearing her voice. Everything had the wrong timbre.

The room flooded with light as whatever had extinguished it got repaired by a palace electrician.

Her twin lay on the floor next to her.

They sat up at the same time.

As though looking into a mirror, she confused the doppelgänger with herself. Events had scrambled her mind. She couldn't make sense of anything. When her reflection developed a mind of her own, patting bits of her body, Pippa's confusion grew, grappling with the discordance between her mind and eyes.

Her hands flew up to her face, feeling the rasp of a day's beard growth. Her hands explored her face, abhorred at cheekbones and aghast at losing her hair. Opposite her, the person wearing her face did the same, tentatively touching her chin.

Pippa stammered her words out. "Harrison?"

"That's Prince Harrison to you or sire!" Although fierce, she lacked the baritone. *He* lacked the baritone Pippa associated with him.

Pippa smirked. "Princess Harrison."

"No!" Harrison's hands flew to his chest.

"Get your hands off my breasts!" Horror welled up in Pippa's stomach.

Harrison sneered. He twisted Pippa's face into a parody and squished her breasts maliciously. "Ow!"

"Serves you right!"

"What have you done to me?" His tone came across as plaintive in Pippa's voice.

"To you?" Incredulous, Pippa stared at the prince. "Seriously? You think I did this?"

"Well! I certainly didn't do it. Why would I want to be a servant?" Harrison almost choked on the word 'servant'. "Never mind a girl!"

"And why would I want to be an obnoxious jerk?" She could say anything, he could hardly fire her!

Moving from a sitting to a standing position sent her head spinning. Her limbs hung awkwardly in the wrong places. Lurching, she moved to the chaise longue and fell into the chair, miscalculating the distance. Nausea swelled, mixing with chills in her cheeks and a tightness in her chest, utter dread throbbing through her veins. Panic symptoms hovered, ready to leap into action if she dwelt too long on their predicament.

The last time she'd been this terrified, she'd been opening her exam results as a teenager.

Breathing purposefully, Pippa closed her eyes and tried to think, but the absurdity of being dumped into Harrison's body, and him into hers, kept forcing itself to the forefront of her mind. She hardly felt consoled by Harrison's struggle. He'd remained on the floor, swaying slightly.

Perhaps he got a handle on it faster than her, as he asked: "What happened? Put us back this instant."

Royal Again   Iain Benson

Scowling, Pippa shrugged. "How would I know? It's not like I'm an expert on this. Whatever this is. You're the one with private education. You figure it out."

"You can forget our deal. Forget being fired! For doing this, I'll see you thrown in jail!" She could hear him breathing, anger coming from lips that were hers. "I can't imagine what trick you're pulling, but it is not funny. I will not sit here and let you think you can get away with it."

A tear leaked from her eye. She wanted to go back to being Pippa. She slumped a little. "It wasn't me."

"Then explain this!"

"I, I can't."

Harrison snorted. "Is it hypnosis? Mirrors? Prosthetics?"

"I don't know."

"Is there a secret camera recording this for some sick and twisted reason?" Harrison searched around the room, peering into the corners.

"Why do you think I have answers? I'm you! I don't want to be you! Life's already hard enough without being a gigantic jackass!"

Any hope that Harrison could help vanished. He slumped on the floor, his hands limp in his lap, hanging his head. His pained expression was more despondent than she felt. His eyes glistened as he sighed, chest heaving.

Pippa needed something to drink; her mouth felt parched. Tempting as she found it to leave that for Harrison to deal with, a water jug on the side table found its way into her hands. Flitting around at the edge of her whirling thoughts, Pippa could almost touch an idea. She poured water, needing two hands to hold the shaking jug, splashing onto the polished wood. The switch on repeated replays swamped any thought of wiping it away.

"We touched the handle together," Pippa said, speaking slowly, trying to keep the glass from spilling as she sipped the water.

Harrison's head snapped up; his lips parted slightly as though about to speak.

After a few moments, slightly breathless, he said: "That is what we will do again, then. Let's get started."

Pippa's stomach flip-flopped. It had to be worth a try.

Standing came easier this time. She had a better grasp of Harrison's leg length, but she still needed to clasp the chaise longue, her fingers digging into the plush velvet. She offered a hand to Harrison, helping him to his feet. A surge of strength she'd never experienced before surprised her as she pulled him to his feet. Harrison's muscles tightened under her shirt.

Together, they each grabbed a door handle.

The brass felt cool under her fingers, but nothing happened.

Harrison sniffed. "Nothing. What a terrible idea."

Pippa felt a growl growing but choked it down, determined to end the nightmare before it became a bigger problem. "Then we start from the beginning."

"The beginning?" Harrison's flinty words made Pippa want to slap him.

She again had to choke down a sarcastic response. "The beginning. Unless you have a better idea?"

"I'll call somebody."

Pippa gave a half laugh. "Does your family have a witch on staff? Perhaps your royal doctor can perform a brain transplant? And who is going to believe you? Hi, I know I look like a cleaner, but I'm the crown prince! That person who looks like me is the maid! We'd both like gender reassignment surgery, please."

Harrison began several responses, eventually conceding defeat. "I'm not sure I can remember everything from the beginning."

"We start at the dressing room."

They took the short corridor to the end. Harrison folded his arms. "You should be in here. I am you, after all."

"If this doesn't work, we'll try that." Pippa kept her tone authoritative and opened the door for the prince, ushering him to the dressing room.

Reluctantly, Harrison went inside and closed the door.

Pippa violently opened it and gestured down the hall, though inside, she giggled at the reversed role.

"Ah," she said. "Wait here."

Harrison paused halfway from the room. "We didn't do that. I remember that much."

"No." Pippa tilted her head. "But I wore your jacket."

"Yes, you did."

She found the jacket where she'd left it and brought it to Harrison. He slipped it on. Far too big, sagging around the shoulders, ridiculously ill-fitting, but slightly sexy. Pippa quashed that idea immediately.

Once more, the door closed before Pippa angrily opened it again

Royal Again   Iain Benson

and gestured down the hall.

Showing less surety than Pippa had displayed, Harrison trudged back into the sitting room.

"Take off the jacket."

Harrison slipped from the jacket, putting it over the back of a chair. Inwardly, Pippa scolded Harrison for not folding it, but simply dropping it into a charcoal puddle on the sofa.

Tilting his head back, Harrison paused for a moment. "Remember not to sack me."

"Fine. Get out."

They grasped the handle simultaneously.

"Nothing." Harrison snorted. "You should have gone into the dressing room, like I said."

"Okay," Pippa replied. "Perhaps I can get my lines right. Did you even do drama at school?"

They retraced their steps, Pippa standing in the dressing room. The jacket fit perfectly. In the mirror, she admired Harrison's silhouette, feeling his biceps. Harrison didn't open the door immediately, so she surreptitiously felt his crotch, fully expecting to get caught. Considering his royal status, it could have been bigger. She snatched her hand away, disgusted. *What are you doing, Pip?*

The moment she thought Harrison had gone to bed leaving her in the dressing room, he barged into the room. His angry face almost made Pippa laugh. She wondered if she'd always had creases on her forehead when she got angry.

In the sitting room, Harrison told her to take off her jacket. She folded it neatly and laid it across the sofa back.

"Remember our deal. Don't get me fired."

Harrison narrowed his eyes. "Fine. Get out."

With a lighter grip than their first iteration, he led her to the door.

Together, they grabbed a handle each.

Once again: nothing.

"This is ridiculous. It's never going to be the same." Harrison's voice caught slightly.

Pippa sat on the couch while Harrison remained by the door.

"I'm out of ideas," Pippa said. "Perhaps it will wear off?"

Sitting beside her, Harrison's glum expression told her the prince did not believe it.

"I think I'm dreaming," Harrison said. "It's the only explanation."

"In that case, we're sharing the dream."

"There is a simple test." Harrison tweaked her arm. It hurt.

"How does hurting me prove if you're asleep?" Pippa tweaked Harrison's arm back in response.

"Ow!"

"You're not dreaming." Pippa frowned. "And neither am I."

"This is all your fault!" Harrison said.

Harrison's vehemence astounded Pippa. "How is this my fault?"

"If you'd not been in the apartment when Isabella came, you wouldn't have stolen my body!"

Pippa tried to bite back her vitriol, because he had a point. She couldn't. "You are a jackass even when you're me."

"What do you mean?"

"There is no point blaming me when we need to figure out how to change back, preferably before you have to go to work in the morning."

"So, you admit it's your fault." Harrison stumbled to a stop. "Wait! I cannot go to work like this. People are expecting a prince."

"Not your job. Mine."

"What? What do you mean, I have to do your job in the morning?"

Pippa shrugged, half a smile forming on her lips. "I'm on the list for polishing the floor in the Grand Ballroom tomorrow morning."

"I'm a prince. I don't do the cleaning."

His pout made Pippa laugh out loud. "At the moment, you're a cleaner."

"We need to turn back! You did this. You undo it!"

Pippa gave a heavy sigh. "I'll explain slower for the hard of thinking at the back: I did not do this. If we don't get this fixed in the next –" Pippa checked Harrison's chunky watch, "- nine hours, you're cleaning the ballroom floor and I'm doing whatever it is you have to do tomorrow."

"I'm going to a dedication for the Centenary Wood," Harrison said, sounding desultory. "After that, I have lunch with friends from the law society. In the afternoon, I'm going to the stables to select horses for the wedding carriage. Finally, the President flew into the country and is attending the wedding dance and I must be my most charming."

Making no attempt to hide her derision, Pippa said: "I think I'll be able to manage that heavy workload. After the floor's polished, you'll have to speak to Annie in scheduling to see what's next on the agenda."

Royal Again   Iain Benson

"You don't know what you'll be doing?" Aghast, Harrison gave an audible gasp.

"Nope. We have a general rota, but your royal highnesses announce things late on and we juggle it all around."

"I know what I'm doing for the next six months!"

"How dull. The only thing I know I'll be doing over the next six months is heading to Albufeira for an all-inclusive holiday. Hopefully, *you* won't be going on that in my place because *I* saved up for it. I have been looking forward to sitting on a sun lounger in a bikini drinking mojitos brought by a tanned Portuguese waiter."

"Oh! God!" Harrison suddenly hyperventilated slightly, as though the idea of heading for an all-inclusive holiday with two other women ranked as the worst vacation ever.

"What? Don't you like mojitos?"

"My wedding is in five days!"

"Got to love a deadline." Pippa raised her eyebrows. "Trust me. I no more want to marry Isabella than you do."

"I want to marry her."

Pippa chuckled. "I'm sure you do."

"I do!"

"Your dad told you to marry her. Nothing to do with want. Anyway, I don't fancy girls."

"We'd better get this fixed before you have to." Harrison frowned. "My dad would have a heart attack if he had a gay son."

"Then I'd be a gay king." Pippa laughed. "Hey. I could be king!"

"Over my dead body!"

"I don't think it works that way." Pippa gave him a reassuring smile. "Don't panic. I have absolutely no desire to be anything other than me."

"On this, we agree."

"Then put that private education to good use and think of something."

They sat in silence for a few minutes. Pippa's mind had gone blanker than the day she took her maths exam.

Harrison moved to a different chair. "Your breathing is annoying."

"It's your breathing, so now you know how the entire world feels."

"You're doing it wrong."

Pippa over-exaggerated her breathing until she felt lightheaded.

An unusually bright flash of lightning cast a momentary shadow across the ceiling. Pippa went to watch the storm for a while in search of inspiration. Rain lashed against the window, the cold seeping through. Her reflection gave her no comfort, gazing upon Harrison's face.

"Maybe the lightning caused this," she said, more to herself.

Although only a musing, it perked Harrison's interest. "We need to jolt ourselves back into our bodies!"

Pippa seriously considered running high voltage through herself to get back to her own body. Reservations crept in. "Sounds deadly. I don't want to switch back, only to have a dead prince lying next to me."

"I'll write a note!" Harrison scrambled across to the writing bureau.

He got as far as writing his name when Pippa spotted an issue.

"You have my handwriting."

Harrison paused. "Oh."

Pippa took the pen from him and scrunched up the top sheet of paper, dropping it into the bin beside the desk.

"It's pointless writing a note."

"What will you do if I die?"

"Hold a party, probably." Pippa rolled her eyes at his hurt expression. "We'd both die. Anyway, I don't know the first thing about getting a shock the size of a lightning bolt, never mind surviving it. Or even if that's what caused it originally."

"We could stand on the roof with a metal rod." Harrison seemed intent on seeing how crispy he could get.

"I'd rather not. We're not in a DeLorean."

"What are your suggestions?"

Pippa opened the lid on Harrison's laptop. "We could check on the internet."

The laptop booted up to the password screen.

"Let me," Harrison went to turn it around.

Pippa pulled it back. "What's your password?"

"I can't tell you that."

"If we cannot undo this, I will need to know it."

Harrison mumbled.

"Pardon?" Pippa exaggerated a listening movement.

"Prince dot charming eleven," Harrison said. "Capital P, eleven as numbers."

"Prince Charming?" Pippa raised an eyebrow. "I would never have guessed that one. Prince dot repulsive eleven, maybe."

Royal Again   Iain Benson

After a few seconds, Harrison's browser came on the screen. He had over thirty tabs open. The first few contained news articles about Harrison. Pippa shook her head and closed them all.

"I hadn't finished reading those."

"If you were so drunk you need to work out where you've been by reading the *Daily Royal*, you have a problem."

Harrison crossed his arms and stood up straight. After a moment, he recrossed his arms under his breasts. "I'm keeping tabs on my public profile."

"About thirty tabs, it seems." Pippa searched for 'body swap'.

"What have you found?" Pippa knew he could see the screen as well as she could.

"Several pages," Pippa replied, clicking on links and skim reading. "It seems we need to find a mystical fortune telling machine and wish or perhaps lift a magical hourglass."

"Anything else?" Harrison's desperation came through as his voice squeaked.

"Touching a magic skull, peeing in a fountain or getting into Yale."

"No lightning?"

"I've not found any yet."

"Where are you getting this information?"

"A list of body swap films."

Harrison dismissed the comment with a wave of his hand. "That's the movies. What about in real life?"

Pippa searched for real-life examples. "It doesn't happen in real life."

"It does. We did it."

Pippa conceded that point. With a slight lift of her chin. "In that case, if it happened to somebody, they never talk about it again. I can understand that."

"What about that?" Harrison jabbed his finger at the screen, leaving a smudge.

"That is mumbo jumbo that talks about souls and gurus."

"It might be right."

"I don't think *KidsKwestions* is a reliable news source."

"It *might* be right."

Pippa rested her head in her hands momentarily, sighing. She added gullible to his list of negative traits. One day, he'd get something in his positive trait column. "Did you smell incense or see a guru earlier?"

"No." Harrison dipped and immediately brightened. "I did smell toast."

"So did I," Pippa admitted.

"I thought I was having a stroke."

That's what the smell means! "I'm not sure how to use that information."

"Eat toast?" Even Harrison sounded like he didn't believe that idea.

"Face it," Pippa said, her heart heavy. "For the time being, we're stuck like this."

3
Harrison: Late night talks

Slumping back onto the sofa, Harrison buried his face in his hands.

"I am not cleaning toilets." The thought of the smell made his stomach convulse. How did this maid steal his body and his life? He needed to make her switch them back.

"You'll be polishing the ballroom floor first." Pippa's evil smirk created a knot of anger in Harrison's chest. "Whereas I'm cutting a ribbon on a woodland and eating lunch with stuffy lawyers."

He wanted to beat his fists against her chest, but she had his strength. "It's harder than you make it sound."

"I've used scissors before," Pippa gestured the idea away.

Her dismissive hand wave reminded Harrison of his own gesture. "You won't know what to say or who anybody is!"

Despite the gesture, there was no way she'd be able to convince anybody that the real Prince Harrison stood before them. His life ended with the switch.

What were the alternatives?

"What do you suggest? A job-swap? Prince Harrison is going to be a royal cleaner for the day, while the cleaner takes his royal duties?" Could she read his mind? Harrison considered the idea worth pursuing. His face lit up. He crashed back down, shaking his head.

"Nobody would go for it. It's not in the plan."

"What was the last spontaneous thing you ever did?"

That was one of Harrison's favourite memories. The day he broke with his security plan to check out a market in a village he'd once spotted when returning home. "A farmer's market trip about six years ago."

Pippa's mouth dropped open. "Six years ago?"

"Spontaneity isn't in the job description. I'm expected to perform certain tasks exactly when scheduled. I need a security detail every time I leave the palace. They must know where I am going, the exact time, and who will be there."

"That sucks." Pippa gave a small downturn of her mouth, commiserating. Harrison considered Pippa free. Her every waking minute appeared disorganised, unscheduled, and unplanned. She quickly returned to taking charge as though she'd become him. "You'll have to walk me through what I need to do tomorrow, and I'll walk you through polishing the ballroom floor. I'll go first. You get the polisher from stores after checking it out with Annie, wheel it to the ballroom, plug it in and walk backwards and forwards to cover the entire floor before the furniture guys arrive at twelve."

"There are a few problems I see already." Harrison's hackles went up. He needed to regain the upper hand. He started ticking off a list on his fingers. "I don't know where the stores are. I don't know Annie from Adam, and I wouldn't recognise a floor polisher if I tripped over it."

"Oh dear. I might literally have to walk you through it."

A cascade of thoughts about heading out of the room swirled through Harrison's mind. "Now?"

Pippa lifted Harrison's watch, staring at it for a long time, as though too uneducated to read an analogue face without numbers. "It's past midnight. We should be okay. There won't be many people about. And if they say anything, I'm the prince!"

"Can't we do it in the morning?"

Pippa shrugged. "The castle is already busy when I get in."

"When is that?"

"Just before eight."

"Eight?" Harrison grimaced in horror. "In the morning?"

"Yes. What are you doing at eight?"

Being civilised! "Getting dressed ready for breakfast with my family."

"Well, tomorrow, you'll be getting up at six, showering, getting dressed, and putting on makeup. Hopefully, you'll have time to dry your hair."

"Hopefully?" Her life sounded horrendous.

"Sometimes, I must leave it wet. Although to be fair, this time, you'll already be here. So, you should have time."

"Makeup?" Nausea welled up in Harrison's gut.

"I always wear some. The last time I didn't, people thought I was ill. Annie nearly sent me home."

"I'm not wearing it." She couldn't make him.

"Yes, you are."

"I don't know how to apply makeup." Harrison had an endless supply of excuses.

Royal Again　　　　　　　　　　　　　　　　　　　　　Iain Benson

"I learned how to do it at eight, practising with my sister. You're a grownup." She took a sharp breath in through her nose. "We'll cross that bridge when we get to it. Right now, you need to learn a bit about the place you've lived most of your life."

She thought she knew the palace better than *him*? He grew up here!

Opening the door a crack, she peered out.

Silence mingled with darkness in the Main Hall. The only light came from the storm raging outside. Lightning made the people in the portraits move as though alive and spying on them.

"It's clear, come on." Pippa waved to Harrison.

The prince froze in place. There might be people out there. No. There *would* be people out there.

Sighing, Pippa closed the door again. "What's the matter?"

Harrison had a tiny voice. "What if somebody sees?"

Pippa's eyes actually rolled towards the ceiling. "What if somebody sees you, the crown prince, in a woman's body?"

Harrison fumbled around for his response before saying: "Yes."

"They will think you're me. They'll think I'm you. How could anybody think differently? The same is true tomorrow morning. You might as well get to grips with it now."

"I could ring in sick." Harrison felt sick, so he'd be telling the truth.

"I don't get paid if I don't work," Pippa said. "Your father had us all put on zero-hour contracts. If we're not here, we don't get any money."

"It's just a day." Surely, she could miss a day's pay so they could get this issue sorted out. *This is far more important to me!*

Pippa put her hands on her hips and spread her legs, unmoving on the subject. "You're going to work tomorrow. My bills need paying, so I can't afford to miss a single day. If I don't work, my rent doesn't get paid, and I'm sleeping in your changing room for the foreseeable future."

Harrison's shoulders sagged, his chin sinking. "Okay. Lead on. Let's get this over with."

The Main Hall remained dark and empty. Pippa gestured for Harrison to follow her. As the door closed, motion detectors turned on the lights.

"So much for being sneaky," Pippa said, shaking her head slightly.

Harrison pushed past her and headed down the hall towards the large double doors onto the ornate royal staircase. Halfway there, Pippa called after him.

"Where are you going?" Pippa's amused smile irritated him. Which one of them lived here?

"To the staff quarters."

She laughed. She laughed at him!

Harrison stormed back up the corridor towards her, his face reddening in anger. "What are you laughing at?"

"When was the last time you saw a servant on the royal staircase?"

Harrison held a finger up, thinking. "Okay, but that doesn't mean that's not the way."

"Come on." Pippa headed in the opposite direction.

She really didn't have a clue. "There's nothing down there but the royal bedchambers. Don't you know where to go?"

Between portraits of his great-grandfather astride a horse and his great-great-grandmother sitting by a fire, Pippa pushed the wall. The entire section swung back.

"A secret passage?" Why didn't he know this existed?

After nearly three decades, Harrison now discovered the servant's corridor paralleling the Main Hall like arteries running through the palace. Making the staff red and white blood cells.

"No," she said as she closed the panel behind him. "Staff access."

The servant's corridor lacked the Main Hall's ornate opulence. Constant fluorescent strip lighting replaced chandeliers. Antiseptic replaced the scent of jasmine they used in the royal suites. No windows or portraits adorned the walls, but they got health and safety posters reminding them to never leave boxes unattended and to always return equipment to the stores. A utilitarian staircase led down, with a black enamel handrail and unadorned stone steps wrapped around a plain metal service elevator.

Pippa peered down the stairway.

Harrison also looked, unable to see what she searched for. "You said there will be nobody around."

"Apart from the night porters, the kitchen staff, security and a skeleton maid crew in case one of your highnesses decides they would like their potty emptying."

Harrison bit his tongue and followed her to the ground floor.

She held a finger to her lips. "That's the security lodge."

Through an archway into the security lodge, Harrison saw a man in a pale blue shirt and dark trousers, his shiny boots propped up on the desk, eating rehydrated noodles and watching monitors. Pippa tugged his sleeve,

Royal Again   Iain Benson

leading him down a well-lit corridor. They passed a glass-walled office.

"This is where Annie works." Pippa barely paused. "Go here to get the polisher and when you've finished."

"I'm not planning on doing any polishing."

Pippa fixed him with a hard glare. "If you get me fired, you're never getting your body back. My rent is due in a fortnight, so you'll be broke, jobless and homeless. I might have to pretend to like Isabella, but I'll be living the high life."

That remark hit home. He had to keep her onside. He had to keep her close. "Right. I'll be polishing floors."

Pippa set off again, touching doors, announcing them as the server room, a shower room, and the staff toilet.

Harrison paused again. He shuddered, thinking of the loss of his penis. Also, he desperately needed to go. He hoped Pippa's bladder control wouldn't let him down. Lights and sound from farther up the corridor distracted him from his urination needs. He wanted to put off that distasteful task as long as possible. Hopefully, until after they switched back. Idly, he wondered at the female equivalent of "putting a knot in it."

Pippa had reached a side room, waiting for him to catch up.

"This is the locker room." Pippa waved into a side room filled with tall metal lockers. The dark blue paint peeled from them; names scratched into doors with bored fingernails.

"Which is yours?" Harrison asked, entering.

"Fourteen." Pippa followed him in, going habitually to her locker halfway along the back wall. A combination lock kept it fastened. "I guess you need the combination?"

"That would help."

"Fourteen, fourteen," she said. Harrison's incredulity made it to his face, making Pippa defensive. "What? It's easy to remember."

Harrison flicked the combination to double fourteen and opened the locker. Pippa's coat and handbag hung inside, a pair of low courts on the floor, beside a tin of deodorant.

"Nosey!" Pippa closed the metal locker, reopened it, and grabbed her phone out of her handbag. "We might need this."

"Is having it with you against the rules?" Harrison snatched it off her.

"Of course," Pippa replied. "Plus, it could get broken."

Harrison traced his fingers along the cracks in the screen. "You should get a new one."

"I can't afford a new one. Anyway, it still works."

Harrison turned back to the locker. Under the faded stencil identifying it as number fourteen, the small card slotted into the holder said "Pippa".

"Pippa? That's your name?"

"What? You didn't know my name?"

Did she think he memorised the names of the servants? Harrison shook his head. "Of course not. Why would I?"

"I work here. It's basic manners."

"Is it Philippa?"

"Penelope."

"Why not Penny?"

"My mum called my Pippa Longstocking."

"That was Pippi."

Pippa shrugged. "I know. Something I found out years later. My mum made the mistake. Call my mum and tell her. Oh, and before I forget. You saw the security guard back at the stairs?"

"Yes. Eating something from a plastic pot that smelled of feet."

"That was George. He's nice. He has a wife called Janice and two kids called Jack and Oliver. Both are still at school. If he's not on, it'll be Simon. Simon can be brusque and a letch, but he's harmless enough."

"I won't remember all that."

Pippa shrugged. "As long as you remember to put your hand on the scanner as you come in or go out, that should be enough."

When he developed an unhealthy fixation with the names on the lockers, Pippa pulled him across the hall to the stores. The room went back a long way, with a fire door at the far end. Pippa's nose wrinkled; disgust etched across her face. He sniffed. A vague smell of bleach hung in the air. Perhaps Pippa had become nose-blind to cleaning products. Lucky for him! Much less olfactory offence. Shelves of cleaning products, spare bulbs, mops, and buckets filled the room. Halfway along, two industrial polishers waited for the morning. Pippa rested a hand on one.

"When you come for a polisher, check it out with Annie first."

"Even though they've already told you to do it?" Harrison shook his head. "That seems stupid."

Pippa agreed with him. The machines mystified Harrison. He came to stand by her, resting his hand next to hers.

Royal Again   Iain Benson

"You'll need to get the parquet fluid from the shelf over there." She pointed over her shoulder straight at the shelving filled with thick plastic bottles. "Two capfuls go in this hole here."

She knew her stuff, but would never make a teacher. Harrison strained to see where she pointed. "I can't see."

Pippa flicked the wheels down and pulled the heavy machinery from the bay. She touched various parts as she explained. "This cap lifts. Remember two capfuls. If you put too much in, you'll be cleaning away excess foam. Too little and you'll be filling it up every five minutes. A beeping tells you when it needs topping up."

"How do you use it?" Harrison touched the handle with the trigger.

"Tilt it back, and while holding both handles, pull the trigger. It will try to drag you off your feet."

"I've ridden horses." If she could use this machine, Harrison knew he could. It couldn't be as hard as she made out. "I can control this."

Pippa scratched her chin, smirking. She looked like she'd burst into laughter at any moment. "Take it slow to start, sweep side to side and walk backwards, not forwards. If you can't remember that, make sure you get it videoed to earn some cash from a television clip show."

Harrison shrugged, blasé. "Whatever. It can't be that hard."

Pippa quickly went through where other common cleaning products lived. Harrison stopped listening. He wouldn't need to know where the caustic soda lived.

She prodded his shoulder. "Are you listening?"

"Sure."

"You'll have to work the rest out for yourself."

"Whatever. I've got a law degree. I'm sure I'll figure it out."

"I don't think I can show you more." She turned to leave. "The canteen is through there. That's where you can get lunch. It's the same kitchens that supply the food to the great and good, so meals here are excellent. It's a perk."

"About the only one." Harrison followed Pippa into the corridor.

Halfway up the staircase, Harrison trudging behind heard the words that made his blood run cold as a strong Yorkshire accent drifted up the steps.

"Oh hi, Pippa. Are you working nights now?"

4
Pippa: Bedtime

Pippa paused at the switchback, one hand on the railing. Behind her, she heard Harrison's footsteps also stop.

Pippa turned to see George in the lobby by the stairs. Hopefully, she'd be in enough shadow for him not to wonder why he'd found a maid sneaking around with a prince.

Harrison turned slowly. "Oh hi, George!"

Pippa took a mental step back. Harrison slipped into the role with a grace of a Hollywood actor, sounding sunny and warm.

Instead of leaving the conversation there, he carried on, to Pippa's surprise. "Oh, no, I'm helping tonight. What with the President coming for that big shindig tomorrow."

"Tell me about it." George sucked air through his teeth. "You know his own security is coming in. They're going over everything!"

"No!" Harrison almost sounded shocked. Pippa guessed he knew.

She edged around, further out of sight. Harrison, instead of simply bidding George goodnight, seemed to be on a roll.

"Are you on nights, then?"

"Aye. Four days, four nights, then four rest. It's always the same for us."

"I bet Janice loves the space in bed on nights like this."

George laughed, chortling. "Aye, lass."

"I must get on, George, or I'll be working mornings, too!"

Pippa almost heard George's nod. Harrison came up the stairs.

She held the panel open for the prince, only exploding into laughter as it swung shut. Harrison smirked, leaning against the panel, folding his arms.

"Oh my god, Harrison, that was awesome."

"I think we got away with that one. Being you is easy, so far." Harrison headed back to his apartment. "Time to take you through my day tomorrow."

"Get up at eight, waltz around until they take me to cut a ribbon, go for lunch at some swanky restaurant, then off to the stables."

"Your speech about the woods?"

Royal Again   Iain Benson

Pippa pushed out her chest, tipping back her chin. "I declare these trees now a wood!"

Harrison's face clouded over, erupting into a grin as he realised she'd needled him. Holding the door for Pippa as they went inside his rooms, she wondered if he was mellowing.

"Thanks."

"Don't thank people for opening doors." Harrison's tone reverted to curt. "Ever. It's expected. I wasn't being nice. I was teaching you your first lesson."

So much for mellowing.

Harrison turned on his laptop and brought up his schedule. Pippa loomed over his shoulder. Every day for the next week, Harrison had events on; he even scheduled exercise. The woods, a film premier, dinner at Isabella's home, the royal gala tomorrow. One week of his calendar matched Pippa's year planner. On Sunday, one big all-day event: his wedding; with every hour scheduled: from the wedding breakfast to a Freedom Lunch, culminating at the big event itself. Most events had breakdowns within them, including his bachelor party. Clay pigeon shooting, a posh dinner and opera. It sounded like Pippa's idea of hell.

"You've planned your own bachelor party?"

"I had to."

"You realise, if we can't undo this, I'm going on that and will hate every second."

Growling, Harrison clicked on the first appointment later that day.

"Each appointment has all the details I need." He prodded the screen aggressively. "I wrote the speech for the woods, interrupted by a vacuum cleaner. These are notes for discussion with the President during his brief visit to our country. He'll be coming straight from the airport and will be jetlagged. Bear that in mind."

"What about other speeches?"

"Hopefully, you won't need any." Harrison's brusque tone brushed away questions. "If you do, they have to be written and emailed to the speech editor." Harrison brought up an email. "He makes sure that I don't say anything stupid."

"I bet he has his work cut out."

Harrison ignored the remark. "Once you've memorised this speech for the Centenary Woods, there is a list of people you will meet, with pictures and a little snippet of information my previous aide compiled."

"Previous aide?"

"I sacked him. You'll need to memorise those snippets."

"Sounds dull." Pippa flicked through the reams of information.

"Talking to people is what I'm good at."

"That's funny. You never seemed to manage it with me."

"Harsh."

Pippa shrugged. "But true."

"Anyway. That's this morning." Harrison opened the lawyer's lunch appointment. "These are the lawyers you'll be having lunch with. These two are Curtis and Alex Monroe, twins. I went to Magdalen with them."

"I'm never going to remember all this." She realised as she said it, that's exactly what Harrison had said. Although remembering the names and information snippets for fifteen people plus two pages of speech seemed more information than where to find the floor polisher. And George's wife's name.

Harrison came to her rescue. "Print off the speech and the same information is available on my phone. That will help you with what you need. You can brush up on them right ahead of meeting them."

Harrison passed her his phone. Pippa clutched the phone she'd grabbed from her locker to her chest. Reluctantly, she passed it to him.

Together they unlocked each other's phones using their thumbs and swapped numbers.

Harrison immediately went to Pippa's camera folder.

Pippa gulped. She had to hope he didn't read the text messages she'd sent to her mum about the prince.

"Let's make a deal," she said. "I won't judge you on your phone contents if you do the same for me."

"There's not a lot on mine," he said.

"You don't text your parents?"

Harrison shrugged, making a face. "To say what? When I'm home for dinner?"

"Photos?"

"I have an official photographer."

"Sexting with Isabella?"

Harrison laughed. "No. All communication is between her people and my people."

"In that case, I won't judge you for having nothing on your phone."

Harrison flicked through pictures. "You take a lot of selfies."

Blushing furiously, Pippa snatched the phone from him. "No."

Harrison snatched it back before she could delete anything. Maliciously, he swiped through and stopped. "Ah. You are aware if I want to see you naked, I only need to get undressed."

To emphasise the point, he took off his apron in the style of a stripper.

"Okay, I get it." Pippa scowled. "You can stop now."

Harrison gave a massive yawn. "I think we need to get some sleep."

Admittedly, Pippa felt tired. She'd had a long day and would have an early start to at least read through Harrison's speeches.

"I agree." Having cleaned the apartment more times than her own flat, she knew the layout better than Harrison. She could have found the bedroom in the dark, blindfolded, and turned around until she became dizzy.

"Where do you think you're going?" Harrison snapped.

"The bedroom."

"I only have one bed." Harrison folded his arms.

"There are spare bedrooms in the guest quarters. Your valet is going to find it odd to have a cleaner in the room."

"You seem to have forgotten that this is *my* apartment. You might look like me, but you're still a cleaner. And I sacked my valet a week ago for being useless."

His remarks made Pippa's hackles rise. "You could sleep on the couch."

Narrowing his eyes, Harrison managed about as much fierceness as he could ring from Pippa's face. "*You* could sleep on the couch."

"You're smaller!"

"I don't care. It's my bed."

"For a prince, you're not very chivalrous."

Harrison strode to his bedroom, pushing past Pippa, shocked into immobility.

Seeing him almost reach the bedroom spurred her into action. The door had a lock.

Harrison tried to lock her out, but Pippa's greater strength pushed the plain white door open. Harrison, defiant, glared at her. Exhibiting her sudden, unwanted masculinity, Pippa realised his vulnerability. She took a step back, palms out.

The double bed didn't need making, Pippa knew because she'd

made it earlier. The sheets remained pristine. A large, scrolled headboard rested against the far wall. She knew how comfortable the mattress would be, having lain on it more than once.

One last envious staring competition and she capitulated. "Okay, you can have the bed. The man is supposed to offer to sleep on the couch. I guess that's me. For now."

Harrison's eyes widened in surprise, his hands dropping to his sides. "Oh. That makes sense. Don't let me stop you."

"I don't want to sleep in this suit. It will crumple."

"I have nightshirts in -"

"I know." Pippa opened the top drawer of Harrison's dresser, seeing her reflection in the mirror. Behind her she could see Harrison starting to get uncomfortable, sitting on the bed, feet dangling over the end.

She extracted a striped blue nightshirt. It smelled delicately of primrose. She held it up and inhaled the scent. It made her smile. Harrison remained on the bed; the corners of his mouth turned down.

Sitting near, but far enough away to stay out of Harrison's personal space, she twisted her head to see herself the way others saw her. Pippa realised she had a tiny nose.

"What's up?" She didn't have to be a genius to know her own miserable expression.

"You're me."

There had to be more. "And what else?"

"I'm not getting undressed."

Understanding came as Pippa considered removing her clothes. "I know what you mean. When you see it, it becomes real. I've needed the toilet for a while now. I don't want to go. It means, well, touching."

"Now you've said that I must go right now. It's urgent."

An idea came to her. "It might help us get to grips with ourselves."

"You'd better not get a grip of yourself."

Eyes rolling, Pippa went to the ensuite bathroom. Reflective onyx panels surrounded the shower cubicle with small halogen lights in the ceiling, creating a starburst effect on the walls. Everything glimmered with cleanliness.

"I need to go too!" Harrison told her.

"The other bathroom is clean," she said. "I know. I cleaned it."

Harrison paused, before admitting: "I don't know what to do."

Pippa returned to the bedroom and glared at a belligerent Harrison.

"My god! Work it out as you go. If my nephew can pee in a toilet at two, I'm sure you can figure it out. I'm going to have to, so you can."

"Your nephew hasn't suddenly lost his peepee."

"Peepee? Seriously?" She stood aside to let him into the ensuite. "I'll be right here in case you can't figure out how to sit down."

Harrison skulked past her into the bathroom, not locking himself in.

After a few moments, the prince encountered the first of his problems. "Your zipper is on the other side."

"If that's confusing you too much," she said, "Perhaps you could wear a skirt."

"Absolutely not. No way."

The splashing of water accompanied the prince sigh of relief. The tinkling noise only increased her urgency. She took to pacing.

"When you've done, wipe yourself with toilet paper," Pippa said, suddenly wondering if he'd known to do that. "Front to back."

"Why?"

"Why what? Wiping?"

"No, why front to back?"

"Because, when I get my body back, I don't want a urinary tract infection." Did Harrison have any experience at all with female plumbing? The virgin Prince? Waiting for Isabella? Pippa giggled.

She heard a flush like a waterfall. Washing his hands with the tap constantly running left her hopping from foot to foot. At least he knew to wash his hands.

The bright orange tee shirt hung outside of his work pants. He'd washed his face, with smudges of eyeshadow and a wet fringe betraying the attempt.

"How am I supposed to take your makeup off?"

"Go down to my locker, get my handbag, and bring it back."

"Me?"

"Well, I can't do it."

Harrison made an uncertain squeak, his head shaking slightly. "On my own?"

Pippa used her nose to point at the bathroom. "I need to go there. I'll help little diddums get ready for sleepy time when he gets back."

He stared at her, hands automatically going to his hips. "And if I run into anybody?"

"Chin up, shoulders back, and brazen it out. Tuck my uniform in before you go, though."

Pippa placed a hand on the doorjamb, waiting as Harrison left the apartment. The need to go to the toilet now occupied the majority of her attention. It focused her mind wonderfully.

"You've seen a peepee before," she told herself. "It must be like watering a garden with a hose. A short hose."

With a deep breath, she went into the bathroom. Licking her lips, she wondered if she should stand or sit. Her bravado abandoned her. She turned, putting the toilet behind her. Although she'd ridiculed Harrison for complaining about having the zipper on the opposite side, it *was* more awkward than she'd expected, as was unfastening his belt in reverse. She sucked up the inconvenience to use the convenience.

Sitting with her trousers around her ankles, she had to see the little prince. She pushed it away, out of sight, closing her thighs as the flood gates opened and she felt blessed relief. Harrison's hairy legs made her feel a little ill, but she put it down to tiredness. Alone for the first time since the switch, she felt a heaviness inside her and gave a little heaved sob.

"I don't want this anymore." Pippa wiped herself down with toilet paper, discovering that she would have to direct the stream next time, given where she'd to wipe and wash. She'd reached some extraordinary places and she'd been sitting down!

She refastened her trousers, vowing to put the belt on the right way when she got dressed in the morning.

Pippa had almost finished washing her hands and face and had started cleaning her teeth when an angry Harrison returned, thumping the apartment door closed.

Without checking to see what stage she'd got up to, he came into the bathroom, handbag held tightly in one hand, her coat in the other. "Tall guy, dark hair, sounds Italian and needs a shave."

"Are we playing describe our ideal date?"

"He was in the locker room. He knows you. I've never seen him before. He said I looked like I'd been in a rainstorm and he liked it!"

"What uniform did he have on?"

"Dark blue."

"That sounds like Michael. I'd advise you to stay away. He's tried it on with just about every female member of staff, married or not. What happened?"

"I got your bag and was about to leave when he put his hand across the exit. He wanted your number. I grabbed your coat, so he thought I was going home."

"I hope you didn't give him my number!"

"I don't have it memorised. I ducked under his arm and escaped."

"Not too bad, then? You got away easily."

Harrison paused and stared at Pippa. "Easily? That was very intimidating."

Pippa shook her head sadly. "You and I will need a conversation about how to negotiate the world. It can be so much worse than that."

"I didn't know."

Pippa shrugged. "Most men don't. Come on, let's get your makeup off."

From her handbag, she extracted her wipes and passed one to Harrison.

He held it limply. "What do I do with this? I thought you'd do it."

"You really are hopeless." Pippa worried about the state of her skin when she got her body back.

Pippa took a sheet of toilet paper and held it flat in her palms, up to her fingertips. Standing close to him, so they could share the mirror, she showed him how to wipe around the eyes, nose, and cheeks. For the first attempt, he made a reasonable job.

"The rest will wash off. But don't use the white towels."

"Why not?"

"If you want a rumour to fly around the palace that you've had a woman over who left makeup all over the towels, use a white one."

Pippa knew how the rumour mill worked below stairs. She'd known of Katy's pregnancy before her husband. A towel coming down from the prince's room plastered with makeup would be in the newspapers by morning. Having the press crawling over her private life would make this entire issue doubly troubling, and it had already surpassed complicated. She handed him a brown hand towel from the linen cupboard as he finished washing his face.

Skin glowing, he picked up the electric toothbrush she'd finished with. She stopped his hand. A list of things he'd need of hers flashed across her mind. Toothbrush, clothes, makeup. Underwear! *I hope we get switched back before he needs sanitary products! That could get messy.*

The further she went with this, the more the little details became insurmountable problems.

"Not today. That toothbrush is for this mouth."

"Ah, yes."

In the bedroom, Pippa almost laughed. They both faced each other like the most awkward first date sleepover ever.

"It doesn't matter if we get undressed in front of one another." Harrison made no move to remove any clothing. Pippa grabbed the nightshirt she'd taken out earlier and handed it to the prince. She took out another with a thin, pale blue pinstripe.

Taking a deep breath, she removed his shirt, getting an eyeful of a tightly toned body. A small relief flooded through her that the only hair she could see formed a downy softness on her arms.

"Have you seen enough?" Harrison asked, a smirk in his voice.

Pippa realised she'd lingered rather too long. Flushing a little, she slipped her trousers down.

"You have to shake after urinating," Harrison told her, pointing at a small damp patch.

"Thanks." She couldn't keep the sarcasm from her voice. "Perhaps they should teach male urination at school, so we all know."

She slipped into the nightshirt and placed carefully folded clothes on the chest of drawers.

Harrison removed the stiff canvas pants the cleaners wore. Pippa felt quite proud of her legs. She considered them her best feature. He tossed the trousers on the bed and started to pull the tee shirt off by grabbing the neck behind his head.

"Woah," Pippa said, putting her hand on his.

"What's wrong? This is how I take off a tee."

Pippa shook her head. "That was before you had a ponytail. It'll get stuck."

"Right, sure." Harrison tried anyway, the tee-shirt neck catching on his hair. "Ow."

Pippa sighed. "Like this."

She crossed her arms, grasping the nightshirt material. In a smooth motion, she lifted the garment over her head, uncrossing her arms as she did so.

"Damn, I've got a good body." Harrison nodded, almost lasciviously.

With a tut, Pippa put the nightshirt back on. "You do that."

On the first attempt, Harrison's left elbow caught up in the crook of his right arm, but after a little untangling, he removed the shirt, standing in front of her wearing only his underwear.

My underwear, Pippa reminded herself. She vowed to burn this set the moment she had her body back.

Harrison grabbed the nightshirt. Pippa stopped him again. "Woah!"

"What is it this time?" Harrison propelled the nightshirt back onto the bed with a growl.

"Bra."

"Don't you sleep in it?"

"Absolutely not! That would be so painful by morning."

Twisting his shoulders, Harrison tried to reach around to the fastener. "Why is the fastener on the back? That makes no sense."

Pippa shrugged, barely containing a chuckle. "Probably designed by a man. Turn around."

The prince faced away from her. With a practised flick, she unfastened the bra.

"Oh, that actually feels good." Harrison slipped the bra off, eyes closed. "Wow. Oh. You should be able to bottle this feeling."

He put on the nightshirt. It swamped him, hanging below his knees, the sleeves flopping past his hands. He rolled them up and headed to the bed.

"Hair." Pippa beckoned him back. "You need to take out the scrunchy and brush it."

Harrison tugged and pulled, releasing waves of long brunette hair. "How do you deal with this amount of hair every day?"

"Familiarity," Pippa said, handing him a brush.

With a whole series of muttered curses, Harrison did a half-decent job of brushing. Eventually, Pippa's frustration overflowed, and she snatched the brush to finish the job properly.

"I used to put a nightshirt on and go to bed. Why make your life more complicated?"

"You're lucky. At home, I'd be putting on moisturiser and night cream. You've had the sleepover version." She put the brush back on the vanity, picked up her clothes and hung them next to Harrison's shirt and trousers. "I'll be on the couch if you can't figure out how women sleep."

She'd almost left the bedroom when Harrison coughed. "The bed's big enough for two."

"This is the reason they call them a double bed."

"You can sleep with me." He paused, frowning. "As long as you don't try any funny business."

Pippa shook her head. That would never happen. "Do you know how far beyond weird it would be for me to even *think* that?"

"Yes, I do."

"Good."

They climbed into bed, deliberately as far from one another as possible. Harrison set the alarm for six thirty, a mere three hours away. Pippa lay facing away from the prince.

She could feel him, a warm presence behind her. *God, I hope you don't snore, Pip.*

5
Pippa: The morning after

An unfamiliar alarm dragged Pippa from a strange dream. She could feel a body moving in the bed beside her. Having somebody in bed dragged her back to reality to relive the previous evening.

Her hands immediately flew to her face, hoping, praying fervently, that she'd feel her own features.

Instead, they felt a rasp of night's beard growth.

Great. The alarm went quiet after a thump. *Shaving a face. Another new skill to learn.*

Needing the toilet, she padded into the bathroom and found it easier and less messy this time. Wrinkling her nose and looking away, she gave Little Harrison a little shake. Her heart felt heavy. The day stretched out ahead of her. She had no illusions. Today would be hard for them both. Harrison's face staring back from the mirror at her made her release an expectant breath she'd held, hoping she'd see her own face. She cleaned her teeth, holding the electric toothbrush while opening the mirrored cabinet to find Harrison's shaving equipment.

Rinsing, she washed and picked up the safety razor.

I'm going to slice my face open. She tried to turn her gloom away from the situation and concentrate on the practicalities. Shaving gel became foam as she slathered it on her face and gingerly used the razor. Her chin and under her nose were the hardest areas to do, and seemingly where Harrison's hair grew the coarsest. A small nick where her jaw turned a sharp corner bled far more than expected. Though there had been a momentary heat, she found she could let it bleed while finishing the rest, gliding over unfamiliar contours. Finished, she checked she'd got everywhere and held the towel to the slight gash.

No harder than shaving my knees.

In the bedroom, Harrison sprawled on the bed, his face in the pillow.

"Harrison," she said, shaking his shoulder.

"It's too early," he told her, grumbling.

"You need to get ready for work."

Harrison rolled over, his eyes puffy, wild hair cascading around his face. Rumpled sheets gave Pippa pause. Although she'd barely moved while sleeping, the signs of two people in the bed screamed from the dents and rumples.

"Get in the shower." Pippa instructed. "I need to do something with the bed."

"Why?"

Now she knew how her mum felt on a school day. "Just do it."

Muttering complaints, Harrison thudded into the bathroom like a petulant teenager. Pippa checked he didn't enter autopilot and clean his teeth or shave. He had enough wherewithal to squirt toothpaste straight onto his tongue and use a finger to remove the night's taste from his mouth. He vanished behind the door, steam soon billowing out of the bathroom from the shower. With him occupied, she partly made the bed, making sure she gave the pillows a good fluff to remove any trace of two heads. Somebody would be in to make the bed. She doubted Harrison knew how to do a hospital corner, so she left one side crumpled.

"As I mentioned last night," Harrison said, as the water shut off. "You'll need to have breakfast with Mother and Pa."

Had he mentioned that? Pippa's eyes widened as she felt ice seep through her body, making her fingers tingle. "Breakfast?"

"Nine, sharp."

"Where?"

Harrison entered with a bath towel wrapped around his waist, rubbing at his hair with another. "The Sun Room," he said.

He spoke as though everybody knew that.

She'd have said something sarcastic back, but he got weird. "You have a lovely body. Do you work out?"

"No, I don't have time," she snapped. How could Harrison ask that while her thoughts windmilled around the idea of breakfasting with the head of state? "I eat healthily and have an exhausting job."

With a small, assertive nod, Harrison dropped both towels on the floor and picked up yesterday's clothes.

"Weird question," he said. "You don't have more underwear, do you?"

Pippa bit her bottom lip. Discordant feelings made her mind go blank, seeing her own naked body holding up yesterday's underwear.

She got a grip on herself and shook her head. "Of course not. Turn the knickers inside out."

Royal Again — Iain Benson

It took the prince three attempts to get the knickers inverted before putting them on. If the knickers caused issues, the bra became an insurmountable problem for Harrison. One cup somehow became reversed as he put the straps over his shoulders. Pippa wanted to let him work it out, but as he tried to fasten the twisted strap, she sighed and went over.

"Let me."

He removed the bra and passed it over. With deft twists, she straightened it out and held it up. He slipped his arms through the straps and turned around for her to fasten it.

"I don't know how you cope with these hanging off the front of you."

"Men haven't complained about them before," she said. "I'm sure you can manage the rest of my clothes. They work the same as yours, after all."

In the changing room, she ran her fingers through the array of suits. "What do you wear for breakfast?"

"Polo shirt with slacks," he called.

Pippa selected a pale blue polo shirt and charcoal slacks. She took them to the bedroom. "Is this suitable?"

Harrison nodded, pulling the bright orange tee-shirt down.

Dressed, Pippa passed Harrison a brush.

"Argh!" he said as he brushed through the knots. "You should shave your head."

"Absolutely no way."

The clock told her Harrison had twenty minutes before he was due to start work.

"I'm only two minutes away," Harrison reassured her.

She remained a little jittery and anxious, rummaging in her handbag like a thief with ill-gotten gains. She extracted makeup and Harrison's shoulders slumped like she'd wounded his very soul.

"Don't be a baby."

"Intellectually, I know you need to put that slop on me." Harrison cringed away from the mascara wand. "An irrational part of me thinks, once that goes on, I'll be a girl forever."

Pippa put a hand on her hip and cocked her head. "That's dumb. Now hold still. You'll have to learn to do this yourself, but there's no time right now."

"Leave it."

"You can't go to work without mascara, eyeliner, and lipstick. People will think you're ill."

"Not a bad thing. I get a day off."

"It is a bad thing. Hold still, close your eyes."

Harrison's eyes closed. She'd not applied makeup to another's face since childhood and hoped she wouldn't poke his eye out as she traced the line of his eyelids with the liquid eyeliner. Brief brushes on his lashes plumped them up, further defining his eyes. She finished with a vibrant pink lipstick wand that she knew really suited her.

Harrison faced up to the mirror. "Okay. That looks better."

Without prompting, he picked up a brush and ran it through his hair, sorting out the knots and snarls.

"I normally dry it and put it in a ponytail for work," Pippa said, running through his hair with fingertips, gathering it up, and feeling the silkiness slide against her fingers almost sensuously. She knocked those feelings on their head and picked up the scrunchie from the night before, tying his hair up in a high pony.

Breathing through his nose, his tongue darting across his lips, Harrison placed both hands on his knees. "I don't think I'm ready."

"Ready or not, you need to go. I'm depending on you."

That pushed the right button. Harrison's one certainty in life was his duty.

He took a deep breath, climbed slowly to his feet. His hesitant steps strengthening as he walked out of the apartment.

"Good luck," Pippa whispered to the closing door. Hopefully, by the evening, she'd still have a job.

She read the information Harrison had shown her, hoping that at least some would stick before she read it out. Butterflies twisted her stomach as the clock reminded her to head to the Sun Room for breakfast. The King and Queen had to know the prince better than anybody. She didn't know what to say to them or how to make small talk with a monarch.

In her absent musings, she almost took the staff route to the Sun Room. Everywhere, she got constant reminders of being Harrison; from the staff turning and appearing busy or vanishing entirely. Except for Ben, the butler. As Pippa approached, he inclined his head and stepped into the room, holding the doorknob.

"Prince Harrison, your majesties." His deep baritone created musical waves of resonance in the corridor.

Royal Again   Iain Benson

Pippa reminded herself several times approaching the door that she could not, would not, say thank you. Even with preparation, her lips formed the words.

The table in the Sun Room followed the orangery's ceiling to maximise the morning sun along its length. Pippa had to walk to the table's far end to reach the set places. Already seated at the table's head, King William and Queen Charlotte. *No. Mother and Pa*, Pippa reminded herself. The Queen's mother, Elizabeth, sat to her daughter's left. Pippa supposed she should consider this an honour. Elizabeth rarely made any public appearances these days. Two remaining places to choose from, both with a single egg in an ornate golden cup. Pippa's breath caught. She did not know where to sit. They all had assigned places, and she didn't know hers! Her pace slowed.

Fortunately, Princess Tiffany arrived, the whirlwind of energy that embodied Harrison's sister.

"Out the way, slowcoach!" Tiffany pushed past, knocking into Pippa's elbow, despite plenty of room to avoid her. Harrison had five years on his younger sister, but she acted as though she had not left her teenage years behind two years previously.

That left Pippa with one choice at the table.

"Manners, Tiffany." The King twitched his paper to one side to give his daughter an unamused glance.

The glance hardened as he turned his attention to Harrison.

"Good morning, Pa, Mother." Pippa wished Harrison had given her some tips for dealing with his family. She had no idea how to greet the Queen's mother or his sister. She guessed. "Grandmother."

"Harrumph," said William, taking his paper, folding it neatly and placing it on the table corner.

Tim, the other butler, came and removed the paper, tucking it smartly under one arm, before retreating to his spot beside the tall French doors overlooking the garden.

The King wore similar clothing to Pippa, though he'd opted for a white polo. Queen Charlotte wore a sunflower print dress, her hair and makeup already perfect. Pippa wondered what time she'd awoken to get ready. Elizabeth still wore a dressing gown over a frilly nightdress, long past caring what others thought, whilst Tiffany wore the previous evening's mini-skirt and tank top, her hair piled up, makeup smudged. *I guess somebody has had another night of partying.* Pippa had heard the rumours, though her makeup looked deliberately smudged.

"You look a bit peaky, Harry," Elizabeth said, her gaze steady.

Pippa lowered her eyes from that piercing stare, sure Harrison's grandmother could see straight into her feminine soul. "I did not sleep well."

"Are you worried about the wedding?" Charlotte's concern creased the wrinkles above her nose.

More than you can know! She gave a tight smile. "It feels as though it's approaching quickly, but the storm kept me awake."

"Go with the flow. That's my advice." William picked up his spoon, lifting the lid on his egg. "Even have some fun!"

"I hope you're not referring to that ridiculous Freedom Lunch before the wedding." Charlotte opened her egg, her tone flat.

"Ridiculous? It's a centuries-old tradition!"

"It's the twenty-first century, Willy." Charlotte almost scolded her husband, stopping just short using her tone. "Women are not objects!"

"Harrumph." William turned away from her and ate his egg.

Glad she had not dived into her egg on sitting down, Pippa watched the conversation, mystified. They ate, so she ate.

Her aim to say as little as possible stumbled at the first hurdle when Charlotte sent a beaming smile her way. "Are you all ready for the day?"

Pippa stopped, the spoon halfway to her lips. She gave a half-shrug. She could never replicate Harrison's response, deciding to give her honest opinion instead. "The woods this morning is a lovely jaunt to the countryside, but I am more looking forward to lunch with the law association."

The King gave a grunting laugh. "Careful that they don't eat you!"

"I meant the wedding, dear." Charlotte's sympathy came through her smile.

Am I ready for the wedding? Not really. "I can't wait for it to be over."

Elizabeth cackled. Casting the older woman a sideways glance, she chewed her boiled egg as though trying to blend it with her teeth.

Pippa's heart thumped in her ears. She forced her breathing to return to normal. Her booming heartbeat elicited no gasps or sudden exclamations. Pippa caught Elizabeth's eyes boring into her again. The older woman knew something, insufficient to level an accusation, but Pippa could tell from the silence. She gave a slight smile to Harrison's grandmother. This mollified her enough to let Pippa eat her egg. Pippa skipped the toast.

The second she'd emptied the eggshell, Tim came and removed it, replacing it with a bowl of granola, blueberries, and yoghurt. Pippa suppressed her natural urge to turn and thank him. Instead, she picked up the next spoon in line. Two knives and a fork still lay on the table, telling her that more breakfast would follow. Most days, her breakfast was a cereal bar and a banana on the bus. Working out in the gym had to be Harrison's attempt at avoiding piling on the weight like his father, whose corpulence had flourished over the years. Charlotte had somehow stayed slim.

"Done," Tiffany announced, standing. "If you need me, it'll be a miracle."

"Sit down," the King told her. "We have not finished."

"I have. See you later, pops." She almost skipped from the Sun Room, Ben, expressionless, opening and closing the door for her.

Breathing through his nose, William regained his equanimity. "That girl is wild. After you're married off, Harry, she's next."

Pippa had the feeling Tiffany would simply abscond at the altar. Something she wished she could do. Mindlessly, she crunched her way through the granola. Barely had she returned the spoon to the table, and Tim came to swap the bowl for a plate of ham and cheese with a chunk of crusty bread. Everybody had something different. William had a fried breakfast, whilst Charlotte had a choc-au-pain and Elizabeth had porridge. Tim placed a small pot of butter next to the plate.

Again, decorum stumped her. Should she butter the bread and tear off chunks with her teeth? Make a sandwich? Use the knife and fork to cut small chunks and take tiny bites? Instead, Pippa placed her knife and fork on her plate. If Tiffany could escape without a third course, perhaps she could do the same.

"Something the matter, Harrison?" Elizabeth asked, once again scrutinising her.

"I'm not hungry."

The older woman sniffed. "It's not like you to lose your appetite. You should be ravenous after your nocturnal activities."

That gave Pippa cause for concern. What did Harrison's grandmother know?

"I'm not sure I follow?"

"Really?" Elizabeth spooned porridge, keeping her eyes on Pippa. "I must be mistaken."

Elizabeth's casual dismissal of her questioning freaked Pippa out. The words held an innocence, which drew no attention from either the King or Queen and her tone remained convivial.

"Harry," William said, snapping Pippa's attention away from the heart-stopping words of Elizabeth.

"Pa?"

"Have you remembered that it is the Presidential soiree this evening?"

"I have." Forgetting something so important seemed unlikely. She wondered at the direction of his conversation.

"Isabella is attending. I trust you will be attentive, yes?"

Ah, Pippa understood. "Of course."

"Marvellous. I will allow you to leave and begin your duties for today."

"Thank you, Pa. Mother. Grandmother."

Pippa gratefully left the table, neatly folding her napkin and placing it beside the full plate of food.

"Keep hydrated, Harry!" Elizabeth called.

Pippa paused as she left, nodding. Elizabeth had reached across to examine the fold in the napkin. The older woman gave a slight smile to Pippa, tapping her nose. With relief, Pippa left the Sun Room and returned to the apartment. Ordinarily, Harrison would head to the gym, but she needed a rest before the next exhausting interactions at the wood.

6
Harrison: The morning after

As the door closed behind him, Harrison momentarily leaned back against it. Pippa had chosen the extract phrase to manipulate him perfectly. Prodding the one part of him he couldn't control: His sense of duty.

He took a deep breath in through his nose.

How could I share a bed with a maid? With a maid*!*

He'd really wanted to clean his teeth. Harrison ran his tongue over his teeth. They felt small. He felt small. All the windows soared higher, and the disproportionate furniture loomed over him. The morning stretched out ahead. Cleaning. He clenched his unbrushed teeth. The thought of him, the Crown Prince, cleaning floors made him seethe. Worse, she'd made him wear the same underwear as yesterday. And wear makeup. Unseemly barely covered his aversion. And her hair! His hair. All that brushing. *Though I liked that part!* The memory sent a shiver down his spine.

"What are my options?"

Cleaning the floor or running away.

Cleaning held the only chance of getting back to into his body and not having to shower and see her breasts. *His* breasts.

It meant interacting with people who knew Pippa. They'd see straight through him.

Without further thinking about what lay ahead, he headed down the staff staircase to the various staff areas. As he descended, warm cooking scents drifted around him. From the meaty smells, he decided they were making his father's breakfast and taking the opportunity to give the staff the same. He'd have loved a bacon sandwich, but Pippa had said she ate healthily. Instead, he let the aroma caress his nostrils, leaving his mouth to salivate.

"Pippa, you're here, great," said an olive-skinned woman with a mass of black curls and small round glasses. She held her office door open to speak to him.

"Morning, Annie," Harrison said, hoping he had guessed correctly.

"Somebody mentioned you'd been working nights," Annie said, speaking at a hundred miles an hour. "I didn't think that could be right, what with you on floor-polishing duty this morning. I'd certainly have known. I'd not put you down for any overtime."

Harrison took a step back and held up his hands defensively. He sidestepped the inquisition.

"Talking of which, I need a floor polisher."

"Of course, I'll book it out. At least you shouldn't bump into Harrison. He's out for most of today." Her head tilted back, a slight smile flitting across her lips before she returned her focus to the very person she daydreamed about. "They're moving the furniture in at noon. You'll need to finish before then."

"I'll do my best."

"Too right! No excuses this time, Pippa!"

A perplexed Harrison wandered down to the stores. Pippa had seemed worried about her job. While Annie seemed friendly enough, she'd signed off with a passive-aggressive threat, giving Harrison pause. He wondered if it had anything to do with the complaint he'd put in yesterday morning about vacuuming. In his defence, he was trying to put together his speech for today. A previously unfelt stab of guilt hit him in the chest.

He shook his head.

Once they'd swapped bodies back, it wouldn't matter.

He might put a good word in for her.

Probably not. She knew too much.

Manoeuvring the polisher proved harder than it should. Why make it so difficult? Pippa's ease the previous night told of her experience with the cumbersome device. Eventually, he remembered the small wheels she'd clicked into place. Muttering about his stupidity, Harrison found it wheeled much more easily. He grabbed a polish bottle and a rag, wheeling everything into the corridor. He paused, trying to orient which way he needed to go. Above stairs, he could find the ballroom with his eyes closed. He'd done that as a child.

"You look lost, Pip." A butler carrying a tray with breakfast dishes startled Harrison. Harrison tried to remember his name. He recognised him as the one from breakfast most mornings. He tried several names, settling on Alan or Chris. Eventually, he'd learn it was Tim.

"I didn't sleep well," he replied, glad he could use a little honesty for a moment. "I'd completely forgotten which way to go to the ballroom."

Tim's eyes flicked down the corridor past the cafeteria. He blew out his cheeks. "You are dizzy sometimes."

Harrison gave him the head tilt and sneer Pippa had given him

Royal Again   Iain Benson

shortly before they'd switched. Chortling, the butler left, shaking his head. Harrison headed into the canteen. Several members of staff ate around cheap plastic tables. Harrison recognised most, but could name none. The kitchens opened straight onto the tables, two chefs currently putting together breakfasts for his family and Pippa. He saw a chef sawing at a ham joint. His stomach rumbled.

On the table by the double doors leaving the canteen, he found a full and tempting bowl of fruit. The yellow of a banana stuck out. He paused and ate it, dropping the skin into a bin under the table.

"Jeeze! Pippa!" a woman in a similar uniform to hers said in passing. "You must be starving."

"I am. I didn't have time for breakfast."

"Next time, maybe don't eat the banana like you're eating your boyfriend. You had Michael salivating."

The other cleaner pushed through the double doors. Harrison's mind raced. How should he have eaten a banana? When did they teach women the correct method? Did girls' schools have a special lesson listing all the special rules boys would never know? Did Pippa have a boyfriend?

That last idea set off a whole new runaway train of thoughts that he had no time to analyse now. His breath caught, and although unsure how he felt about the news of Pippa's boyfriend, he had to save her job. Saving her job meant she'd be close enough to switch back when they figured out how, so although he fulfilled his duty towards her, altruism remained a long way off.

He pushed through the doors and onto a cross corridor that had to run from the ballroom to the grand dining room. Mentally laying what he knew about the palace over the staff corridor layout, he turned left at the end, pushing through a tall door into the ballroom.

Harrison allowed himself a brief congratulatory mental fist pump and wheeled the polisher out into the room.

With all the furniture removed, the ballroom overwhelmed him with its vast floor space, the high ceiling dominated by the four corner chandeliers. To his untrained eye, the floor sparkled already, reflecting the lights into a thousand diamonds. Somebody had decided it needed doing again, so he set to the task. As Pippa had instructed, he put two acrid ammonia-scented measures into the machine and spent five vital minutes searching for a plug socket. He eventually found it behind the long red velvet curtains that overlooked the gravel driveway sweeping around the palace's façade.

Gingerly, Harrison squeezed the trigger on the polisher handle.

It immediately dragged him forward, switching off as he pitched face first onto the floor, the handle flying from his grasp.

He dusted himself down and checked nobody had seen. He still had the enormous ballroom to himself. The only sound came from the polisher's ticking. Taking more care, Harrison again squeezed the trigger. The machine veered off to the side as before, but he expected it, letting go as it twisted him around. Finally, he found the sweet spot, but again lost his footing as he stepped onto the freshly polished floor and the machine pulled him around and onto his backside. Growling, he grabbed the handles and pulled the polisher backwards, ensuring he stepped on unpolished areas.

After polishing a section, Harrison saw the difference. The newly polished area held a deeper, more liquid sheen. A sad sigh accompanied him looking at the rest of the ballroom floor.

"Best get to it," he muttered, pulling the polisher with an aggressive jerk.

The job became an autonomous task, giving him plenty of time to contemplate his fate.

His thoughts circled, centring on how to reverse the swap, how the swap happened in the first place, and what the passing comment about Pippa's boyfriend meant for him. If he couldn't switch back into his own body, would he now have a boyfriend? Although he inhabited the body of a woman, this didn't mean he suddenly wanted to sleep with men. He could make an exception for Pippa. While she inhabited the body of a man, of him, her soul remained female. An annoying soul, but a feminine soul. Did she have a boyfriend? That notion kept coming back to him. He pushed it aside. A palace maid would never be a suitable suitor for a prince.

The only reason I'm doing this is to get my body back.

He knew if they were separated, living each other's lives would become problematic. They'd end up stuck.

"And how would we switch back then?" Harrison gave the polisher a violent shove. It responded by giving a series of high-pitched beeps, Harrison stared at it like a forgotten sculpture by Michelangelo, worried he'd broken it. Closing his eyes and mentally slapping his forehead, he remembered Pippa mentioning the machine beeped to communicate its need for more polisher fluid.

At some point in the morning, he saw a car pull up outside and

Royal Again   Iain Benson

Pippa crunched across the gravel to get in the back. Harrison watched her set off; she'd chosen a crisp navy-blue suit. He'd have gone with forest green, but he guessed the colour didn't matter. The frown on her forehead told him how worried she felt. On the positive side, she had survived breakfast with Mother and Pa, and especially Grandmother. As the car pulled away, he released his breath in a long stream.

"I won't tell if you don't," said Michael arriving silently behind Harrison.

"Tell what?"

"You, pining for the prince."

Harrison shook his head. "Did you want something, Michael?"

"Letting you know, the furniture van is on the way, you've got twenty minutes to finish up." With a sinister grin, Michael swept his arm over the third Harrison had yet to polish. "You'd best stop lusting after Prince Charming and get moving."

Another growl escaped Harrison's lips. "Don't walk across the bit I've just done."

Michael's grin widened. He took a malicious step onto the polished section.

His foot went out from under him. After windmilling on the way down, he ended up on his back.

Harrison gave a playful smile. "I wish I had my phone. I tried to warn you how slippery it is."

Sheepishly, Michael skulked from the room. Laughing to himself, Harrison resumed polishing, trying to go a little faster. He'd nearly finished as the doors at the far end opened. Harrison concentrated on the last two strips. "Wait there," he said. "I've nearly finished."

The two men ignored him, crossing the floor.

"Penelope Palmer?"

Harrison mentally noted the surname. He studied the two newcomers. They didn't have any furniture and their accent told him they were foreign.

"Yes? Are you bringing in the furniture?"

"We need you to come with us."

Would Pippa know who they were? He'd never stopped to learn the names of the staff. He had an excellent memory for faces, and these two looked unfamiliar.

Another row remained of polishing. If he left now, Pippa would be in trouble. He held up two fingers. "Give me two minutes."

He restarted the polisher and completed the row.

"Finished?" the man on the left asked, cocking an amused eyebrow.

Harrison surveyed the results with pride. He had done a good job. "I need to take the polisher back to the stores or Annie will have my head."

"That's fine," the left-hand man said. "We're going that way."

Harrison appraised the pair in their black suits and ties. They had the physiques of athletes and the height to match. Both hung their arms loose by their sides, as though expecting him to suddenly bolt so they could chase him down like beagles finding the fox. Only the one on the left spoke, his voice calm and measured. The way the other glanced around constantly reminded Harrison of his own family's security detail. They'd be incognito in the background wherever he or his family went. He didn't recognise this pair. Harrison nodded to himself. These two came from the President's detail.

Wrapping the cord, Harrison casually asked: "What's it about?"

"We need you to clear up a discrepancy, that's all."

Discrepancy sounded like a euphemism. He wondered if he'd somehow got Pippa fired, even though he'd shown up and polished the floor in time. He wheeled the polisher to the tall staff doors halfway down the ballroom. Outside, he saw the furniture truck pull up. Annoyance crept in as he realised he had no way of getting to the ball.

I'm Cinderella!

Except he wouldn't waste his wish with his fairy godmother to go to a party. Cinders might have got her prince, but she showed a distinct lack of ambition.

Both men waited at the entrance to the stores as he secured the polishing machine. He could hear their steady breathing without turning. They didn't talk to each other; they didn't talk to him. He could almost feel their stares on his back with palpable pressure.

"Pippa!" Annie's voice came. She pushed between the two security guards, disregarding them. They ignored the afront.

Pippa straightened.

"I got the floor polished in time." He hated that his voice sounded plaintive, pleading to keep a job he didn't want.

"Well done! Amazing what can be accomplished with a little bit of focus. Anyway, the furniture people are here, and I want you and Katy to start polishing up the platters.

Royal Again   Iain Benson

"This will be unlikely," Harrison's more talkative minder told Annie.

Annie placed her hands on her hips and ensured that Harrison could see nobody but her. "Why are Tweedle Dumb and Tweedle Dumber here?"

Harrison shrugged. "No idea."

"There has been a security incident," Tweedle Dumb said. "Penelope will be accompanying us for questioning."

Annie turned to face them, switching from a picky supervisor into a fiery protector. Though the speed she spoke barely slowed, Harrison got the impression Annie had gone into fight mode. "I don't think so. You're not part of our security, so I'm guessing you're the President's men. Pippa has worked here for over ten years. I can vouch for her."

"Ma'am." Tweedle Dumb inclined his head, acknowledging her tirade, but still interrupting it. "*Pippa* did not log out last night and did not log in. Until we get answers, she will be with us."

"That?" Harrison could not keep incredulity from his voice. "Please, speak to Prince Harrison. He can explain everything."

"Until Prince Harrison returns, you will remain with us."

A speechless Annie got brushed aside by Tweedle Dumber as he collected Harrison, leading him from the stores.

"Get Harrison," Harrison begged Annie as he left the stores, wishing he'd come up with an excuse instead of invoking Prince Harrison.

Annie remained motionless, her mouth an 'O'.

7
Pippa: To the rescue

Dillon drove. Since he'd started, Pippa daydreamed about Dillon asking her out. Now she occupied the limousine's back seat while he drove. It would surprise her if he asked her out now!

Fortunately, the soundproof darkened privacy glass had created a cocoon and Pippa didn't have to see Dillon's smouldering brown eyes under that peaked cap of his. Nor could she see Reece, her security chief, sitting beside Dillon.

Only her attempts to maintain a stiff upper lip prevented her from breaking down and crying on the back seat. She'd thought a shop mannequin could perform Harrison's duties. Having been Harrison for only part of a day, she now knew he did more than she thought. She stared through the window, watching the trees pass by in a flickering blur, trying to push the disastrous lawyer's dinner from her mind. In an unexpected turn for her thoughts, she couldn't wait to get back to the annoying, grating Harrison.

She defocused her eyes to see his reflection in the glass. Lawyers! Blokey, crass men, with their crude and misogynistic remarks, expecting Harrison to reciprocate the banter. Two had been the prince's personal friends, people he'd gone to university with. She'd never felt so uncomfortable. That had to come across when the conversation stuttered to a stop. She could hardly contribute to memories of Oxford.

"Do you act like that with them?" Pippa asked her reflection. She answered for him, pretending he had the other seat. "Of course, it's just banter."

She found it difficult to shake the blokey feeling. It left a knot in her stomach that weighed heavily.

Only around Harrison did she feel the most like herself.

"It's because you don't have to pretend," Harrison said from the reflection.

"True." She pressed her fingers to the window like she could touch him.

The car swept into the palace grounds through the high gate posts. She could see more activity than when she left. Two large trucks had

Royal Again   Iain Benson

deliverymen flitting about like ants around a boiled sweet, carrying the contents into the palace ballroom through the French doors. She hoped they'd put cloths down, as Harrison would have spent the morning polishing that cavernous room. Also in the yard, she could see black Range Rovers with black-suited security nearby. She guessed they belonged to the President, checking out the location of his visit. A little insulting, considering a head of state's security lesser than their own.

The car crunched to a stop by the columns and Grand Entrance steps. She knew better than to open the door herself and waited for Dillon to come to her side. Bright light flooded in as Dillon let her disembark. It grated not to thank him. Reece stayed a few steps behind her, wary of the strangers swarming around the grounds.

"Thank you," she muttered once she reached the steps out of Dillon's earshot.

According to the schedule, she now had three hours to prepare for the gala later. *Does a nap count?* Rolling her eyes, she entered the palace. They'd probably have to spend that time trying to find some way of swapping back. Preferably before the President arrived so that Harrison, not her, could dance with Isabella. Perhaps sticking their fingers in a plug socket would switch them back. After her calamitous lunch, she decided even a heart attack was a reasonable alternative to another day as the prince.

As she headed to the main staircase, the repetitive padding of somebody running attracted her attention. She saw Annie coming down from the ballroom.

Annie stopped, panting, her cheeks flushed, face tilted down, hidden, until she could regain composure.

Pippa waited, puzzled.

"Prince Harrison, sire," she said in panting breaths, giving a little curtsey once she could.

Remembering their roles were reversed, Pippa drew herself up, holding back a smile. Her eyebrows unintentionally proclaimed her amusement.

"Annie, isn't it?"

She saw Annie stifle a giggle. Prince Harrison *knowing her name*, would be a story she'd regale everyone with for at least a month.

She gave another curtsy. "Yes, sire."

"What can I do for you?"

"Pippa has been arrested!" Annie's words came in her usual gush.

"Two presidential security men took her away. She's not talking, she'll only talk to you! It's not like her. Really it isn't. She said you could explain why she's skipped sign-in. I don't know what's got into her. Why can you explain and not her?"

Inside, Pippa's heart pounded, her mouth went dry, and her palms turned clammy. She tried to hide this on the outside, halting Annie's gushing flow with a raised hand.

"Annie. Slowly. Deep breaths and take me to her and tell me what happened."

Talking a deep breath, Annie led Pippa into the staff area. She spotted a marked difference from when she usually traversed the corridors. Instead of greetings and small talk, the staff stopped, bowing their heads to examine the floors as she passed. She held back the increasing urge to yell her identity and tell them to all stop being so subservient. She caught the edges of whispers, the origins of a rumour that would sweep the staff. The day Prince Harrison came when Pippa called.

Pippa knew she'd be intrigued if she saw a member of the palace staff arrested by the secret service.

She could only imagine the evolution the rumours would take over the next few hours.

Let them ruminate on what happened. They would never get close to the truth. Tweedle Dumb and Tweedle Dumber had put Harrison in the only room they could guard: the staff toilets near the kitchen. Much to the staff's annoyance, as they could no longer use them. Conversations ceased as Pippa entered the kitchen, the cooks all stopping to stare, those eating in the cafeteria pausing, food halfway to their mouths.

"Your majesty." Tweedle Dumb inclined his head slightly in an acknowledgement of the heir to the throne, but coming from a republican who felt no need for a constitutional monarchy.

"Where is Pippa?" Pippa tried to inject contempt for both the men.

"We put her in the restroom." Tweedle Dumb opened the door to reveal Harrison sitting on a chair. "It saved having her ask to go."

"Pippa, we're leaving."

"I'm afraid not, sir." Tweedle Dumb had the grace to at least project a little contrition.

"You do know who I am, correct?"

"Sir. Yes, sir. Ms Palmer is a security risk. Until we understand why she failed to sign out last night and did not sign in this morning, we cannot allow her to have access to the building with the President coming."

"She is a trusted member of staff at the palace."

"I am informed of this by several people, sir. She told us you could explain to our satisfaction."

"Can you two stop yapping and get me out of here?" Harrison demanded. "I'm starving. And need a drink!"

Pippa's mind raced. Annie hovered nearby. The entire canteen craned in a little to listen. She needed time to produce some reason, any reason.

"Annie, could you get Pippa a sandwich or something?" Pippa asked, careful to avoid using 'please'. She laid a hand on Tweedle Dumb's shoulder. "Can we go somewhere to talk, away from prying ears and wagging tongues?"

"I would prefer to remain to guard the suspect," Tweedle Dumb said.

Pippa pointed to Tweedle Dumber. "She's a waif of a girl. Surely, it only takes one of your highly trained security personnel to make sure she stays in there. Follow me."

Without waiting to see if Tweedle Dumb followed, Pippa headed to the stairwell up to the Main Hall.

"Hey! Come back!" Harrison called.

Pippa held a single finger up over her shoulder, hoping the prince would understand to wait.

As she passed with a plate of sandwiches and a water bottle, Annie's gaze flicked at Pippa. She handed them quickly to Tweedle Dumber and scurried to catch up with Pippa and Tweedle Dumb.

"As Pippa's supervisor, I need to hear this, too!"

And me. Pippa wondered what she would say. Her mouth felt dry as various excuses ran through her mind. She discarded most as failing to cover all the evidence.

She stopped at the stairs, resting one hand on the rail. Both Tweedle Dumb and Annie hung on her every word.

"It's quite simple." Pippa wondered how to concoct a simple, plausible story when she had the answer. The truth! You can't get tripped up if you tell the truth. "Pippa was cleaning my room last night when Lady Isabella arrived early. Rather than embarrass me by having a maid leaving my suite as my betrothed arrived, she graciously agreed to spend the time in my dressing room."

"Pippa agreed to that?" Annie's pitch rose three octaves.

Pippa licked her lips. "Unfortunately, Isabella and I talked far longer into the night than I thought we would."

"Lady Isabella left about twenty-two hundred, according to the logs," Tweedle Dumb announced, telling Pippa he had information to validate whatever story she concocted.

"You will also know, in that case, that there was a terrible storm last night."

"Oh! Yes, it was bad. Lightning and lashing rain!" Annie performed the actions of lightning and rain. Pippa decided it was how Annie supported her in the face of Tweedle Dumb.

"With the hour's lateness, I allowed Pippa to sleep in my bed." Pippa paused long enough to let both Tweedle Dumb and Annie think salacious thoughts before adding the only lie, if she didn't count the omission of swapping bodies: "I slept on the couch."

"You are such a gentleman, sire." Annie clasped her hands together and beamed a wide smile, adding in a curtsy for good measure.

"This explains why she did not sign out last night. As for signing in, I can only assume some oversight. I know how eager she seemed this morning to help get the palace ready for your President's visit later."

Tweedle Dumb stroked his top lip with his index finger before nodding with deliberation.

"I believe you."

"Fabulous," Pippa said. "Now please have Pippa released from a bathroom. It is quite undignified."

"You have no cells."

Pippa gave a condescending smile. "Sadly, we had the dungeons converted into a wine cellar some years ago."

"She stayed all night?" Annie asked. She needed more information to sate her curiosity.

"She did."

"She shouldn't really have done that." Annie's face hardened into a frown. "She is skating close to the wire, that one. This is all so irregular."

Pippa started walking back to the bathroom, accompanied by Tweedle Dumb, who spoke into his earpiece by holding one finger to his ear like a petrol pump.

"Perhaps she is in the wrong role?" Pippa cocked a half smile to Annie.

"How do you mean?"

"If I would like her to be my personal aide, could you make that happen?"

Several expressions flitted across Annie's broad features, settling on suspicion. "That is possible, if your majesty requests it."

Pippa raised her eyebrows at Annie. "Well, I do need a new one."

They reached the cafeteria, and once again, conversations hushed as Pippa entered. She could see the nudges and nods, pointing and surreptitious looks. Tweedle Dumber opened the door.

"Do you know how degrading this has been?" Harrison said, leaving the room. "Four hours I've been in there. Four!"

Harrison squared up to Tweedle Dumb's chest, drawing himself up to his full height so he could nearly glare at Tweedle Dumb's chin.

Tweedle Dumb looked down to her, his face impassive. "I'm happy with the explanation. You're free to go."

"No apology?" Harrison stepped back, waving his hands up and down Tweedle Dumb's body, incensed. "Thank god I was innocent. If Harrison hadn't been here, no doubt you'd have thrown me in the back of a blacked-out van, never to be seen again."

Pippa took Harrison's elbow. "They're not going to apologise. Come on."

Annie stopped Pippa from taking Harrison away. "Pippa?"

Both turned. Harrison tilted his head. "Yes?"

"A word before you go, please?" Annie's demeanour softened as she turned to Pippa. "If that is amenable to your majesty?"

Pippa shrugged. "That'll be fine. Send her up when you've finished your chat."

8
Harrison: Dancing lessons

Eventually, Harrison entered the apartment. His face clouded with a mix of relief, anger, and indignity.

Having expected this, Pippa handed him a glass of white wine. She'd already poured herself one.

"I prefer red." He took it anyway.

"It's my tongue, trust me."

Pippa sipped her own and sat on the couch. Harrison slumped next to her.

He unloaded the day's events on her to let her know how much he'd hated his first day. "What an awful day! How can it get worse?"

"Your lawyer friends might not be speaking to you anymore."

Harrison paused, sipping his wine. He twisted on the couch to face her, trying to imagine what she could have done to upset the brashest men he knew. "What did you do?"

"Well, you know how they are complete jerks when they talk about women?"

Harrison gave a politician's reply. "I'd not noticed, but in retrospect, I think I see how they might come across that way."

"I told them what massive pricks they are, and they should treat women with more respect. They intimated I might be gay, so far from the truth as to be hilarious. I suggested they might want to rethink their attitudes towards sexuality, as well."

"Politely?"

"No." Pippa drained the glass. "I may have used the phrase 'Check your privilege'."

"That will be an awkward conversation when I get my body back." Harrison's tone deadened as he contemplated the alternative. "If I get my body back."

"I've asked they make you my personal aide."

"Annie told me. Thanks."

"Wow."

Harrison's eyebrows furrowed. "What?"

"You said 'thanks'," Pippa gave him a playful smile. "I think that's the first time."

"I thank people all the time!" Harrison's indignation came through loud and clear. "Just not for stuff they should be doing."

"Do you though?"

He changed the subject. "I finished polishing the floor."

"Well done," Pippa told him, totally sincere. "How was it?"

"I wish I'd been detained sooner, so I didn't need to do it." Harrison finished the wine. "I don't know how you do that sort of thing every day."

"And I don't know how you stand in a muddy field and wax lyrical about how forests will help us save the planet and then go for lunch with clots without smacking two around the head and poisoning the rest. Never mind calling them friends."

"Did anybody have anything to say about my wedding?"

"I forget the name, but a gawky one with a beard regaled everybody with his exploits with a bridesmaid after the rehearsal."

"Curtis Monroe." Harrison's mind drifted. "What was lunch?"

"Barbecued beef brisket," Pippa answered. "Too chewy for me. Tasted like an ashtray."

Harrison heaved a sigh; he loved that dish. "Anything else to report?"

Pippa was about to say 'no' until she remembered something. "Your grandmother."

"What about her?"

"She was very weird at breakfast."

"In what way?" Harrison felt irrationally affronted by Pippa disliking his grandmother.

"She seemed to imply she knew something happened last night. Nothing overt, but enough to let me know she knew something."

That did sound odd, making Harrison wonder if his grandmother had been speaking to the staff. "What did you do?"

"I pretended not to understand what she meant."

"Probably for the best." Harrison poured more wine for them both.

"Not too much for me," Pippa said. "I need a clear head at this party tonight. Isabella will be there."

"Ah, yes. Part of our discussions last night. She insisted we needed to be seen together more before the wedding. This could be problematic." Although he kept his tone light, inwardly, his heart sank.

Pippa placed her glass on the table and got to her feet, holding out

Iain Benson — Royal Again

her hand for Harrison. "You need to teach me to dance."

"You can't dance?" Harrison's lip twisted in surprise. "But you're a girl."

"I can sway my hips in a nightclub and do a little boogie without breaking an ankle in heels." Pippa gestured with her fingers that Harrison should take her hand. "But that stuff you see on *Strictly Celebs Dancing*? I have no chance."

Harrison placed his glass on the table and took her hand, allowing her to pull him to his feet. He placed his hand around her waist, keeping hold of her left hand with his right.

"I'm used to leading," he said. "It's how my dance teacher taught me."

"You have two hours to get me up to a level where Isabella isn't going to notice."

Harrison's face wrinkled up. "I had fifteen years of dance lessons."

Pippa waggled her eyebrows at him. "Condense it."

He considered the stupid idea for a moment, hoping she learnt quickly. "Push off on your right foot, sweeping your left forward."

"Show me."

Harrison buried his forehead in Pippa's chest. He put all his weight onto his right foot, swinging his left forward. "Now you."

Pippa repeated the movement, with Harrison stepping back onto his right foot, leaving his left behind. Pippa avoided stepping on his toes, grinning at her achievement.

"I did it!"

For the next half an hour, Harrison led her through several basic dance steps. Most came naturally when he led, but having to follow taxed his memory and physical control over Pippa's slender frame. Either Pippa was a perfect student, or the notion of muscle memory held merit, as she picked up the basics quickly.

Harrison decided she could move on to the next stage. "Let's try music."

He went to the wall, activating the room's smart speakers. Selecting some common waltzes that they might play.

Music suffused the room.

Pippa's jaw dropped. "I didn't realise you danced to popular music. I figured you'd dance to Mozart or Bach or something."

Pleased, Harrison smiled at her. "The monarchy might be stuck in the Middle Ages, but the people in it are not."

Keeping in time with the music proved more difficult for his dance partner. She repeatedly trampled his feet. Fortunately, Pippa's stout footwear protected his delicate toes. Slowly but surely, Pippa picked up enough for Harrison to throw her a curveball.

"What did you tell the President's security people, by the way?"

"The truth." Pippa's smile ghosted around her lips, but talking, listening to music, and dancing proved too much. She trod on his toes. "Damn! Multitasking with a boy's brain is *hard*."

Harrison let go and took a step back. "You told them the *truth?*"

"To a point." Pippa laughed. "The look on your face is priceless. I said I'd stuffed you in the dressing room because you were still here when Isabella came. When she'd gone, it was late. I said you slept in my bed and I took the couch."

Harrison considered that. As excuses went, it contained mostly truth and would pass any level of inspection. She thought on her feet; he had to give her that.

"I can't stay two nights." Harrison suddenly realised that the whispering heads in the cafeteria would have been discussing a maid and a prince. He winced.

"No." Pippa took his hands, slipping a strong arm around his waist. A slight electric spark caused him to catch his breath for a moment. He gazed up at Pippa's face, at his face, hoping she'd not noticed. She didn't seem to have. The corners of her mouth dipped in a lip shrug.

"What is it?"

"When I go to this thing tonight, you will have to go to my flat and come back in the morning."

Pippa let him go and headed to the table where she'd put her handbag the night before. She wrote her address on a slip of paper and took out her keys.

"This is the apartment block fob." She held up a small triangular piece of plastic. "Put it on the pad by the call buttons. I live on the third floor, number thirty-nine. Straight from the lift, four doors down on the left. It's this key."

Harrison held the key in his open palm and paused. "That's well and good. How do I get there? Do you drive?"

Pippa laughed. "I can, but I can't afford a car."

"In that case, how do you get home? Be as detailed as you can."

Iain Benson **Royal Again**

Harrison didn't want a repeat of not knowing how to find the door to the ballroom.

"You get the palace staff bus to town, then take the number fifteen bus from stand F. When you see Bernie's Chicken Shack on the left, get off. Walk down the road in the same direction as the bus to the first corner and turn left. You'll see a tall white block of flats on the right. The entrance is by the potted plants, past a line of half-dead bushes. If you carry on past the door, there's an entrance around the back, but you'll only need that if the druggies are out front."

Harrison inwardly groaned at the way she described her home. It sounded positively awful. "Where do I get the staff bus?"

"Outside the door by the security lodge." Pippa's tone indicated he should have known that. Some bosses knew their staff. He couldn't see the point.

"Anything else?" Her life sounded dull. He tuned out as she described how to work the television and microwave.

She wrote the alarm code for her flat and the computer password on the paper. "Try to keep that out of the wrong hands."

"I'll guard it with my life." She must think him an imbecile with a remark like that.

"If you make a mess, clean it up."

He resisted the urge to roll his eyes. "I'll treat your flat as my own."

"I'd rather you treated it as if it belonged to somebody who scares you."

"Point taken. Is there anything you'd specifically like me to do?"

"Try to find something on the internet to get us to change back." A long sigh interrupted Pippa's words, her chin dropping and her glum expression returning. "We've only got two full days before the wedding. I don't want to marry Isabella."

"Right." Harrison tried to sound convivial, but he felt the same way. Both in wanting to switch back, and not wanting to marry Isabella. That revelation to himself came as something as a little shock. He'd accepted the marriage as inevitable and his duty.

Pippa straightened, her jaw clenching. "Now, back to dancing."

He cocked his head to the side and gave her a half smile. She annoyed him, but she was at least committed to maintaining the fiction of being him. "Remember, only dance if you hear the dum, de dah dum in the beat, or the waltz won't work. Isabella might want to foxtrot or worse, jive.

Royal Again   Iain Benson

If she does. Say no."

"Got it." Pippa stepped back, spinning Harrison around. Despite himself, Harrison joined in.

"Don't get complicated!" He'd felt a giddy thrill as she turned him.

Pippa's smile dropped off. "I need to get ready. As my aide, what do you suggest I wear?"

Harrison sucked his teeth and nibbled the inside of his cheek, an affectation he'd not had before. He wondered briefly if Pippa's mannerisms were seeping into his own. "I'll select something."

He took her into the changing room and critically analysed the suits. He selected a mid-grey double-breasted suit with a maroon lining and a pink waistcoat. Pippa held onto it as Harrison pulled out a pair of shiny black brogues with a smooth sole.

After Pippa dressed, Harrison checked her over as critically as he would when he'd dressed himself. "You've done the tie wrong."

"How do you do a tie *wrong*?"

Unfastening the monstrosity Pippa had created with the pale pink tie, Harrison explained: "Each event has a different knot. Get the wrong knot and they'll immediately know you're not me. For something like this, I'd do an Oriental knot, for its smoother, symmetrical lines. At a push, a Milanese knot would do, but they'd know I'd been in a hurry."

Harrison had never done the knot backwards, but he found being face on, while he flicked and slotted the material, easier than fastening it in the mirror.

He stood back. "You'll do."

"I'll see you in the morning." With her shoulders slumped, Pippa left.

Harrison suddenly felt the apartment's quietness. He'd never noticed it before her arrival.

He sniffed and made sure he put everything back into her handbag. Slinging it over his shoulder, he became indistinguishable from millions of women returning home from work. Slightly bedraggled from the day, tired lines around his eyes. He took a deep breath, trying to dispel the disparity, before heading out.

"Good night, Pippa," George said as Harrison left the building for the first time as Pippa.

"Good night, George," he replied. The daunting, darkening sky chilled him. He pulled his coat tighter.

Iain Benson   Royal Again

By the door, a white minibus, already half full, waited. He climbed the tight steps, letting his eyes adjust to the dingy interior. He saw three other maids and Annie, along with two men. He'd have to sit next to somebody. Either a maid, whose name he didn't know, or Annie.

Annie solved the problem by patting the seat.

Another maid gave him a broad smile. Harrison returned it, but sat next to Annie. The maid turned in the seat, her grin getting wider.

"Is it true, Pip? Did you sleep with Prince Harrison?"

"Katy Williams!" Annie said in a scolding tone.

"What? Jill heard it from Carl, who was in the café when the police came."

"Word for word, that's what I heard." said Jill, another maid, sitting on the opposite side.

"No!" Harrison replied. He did not need to pretend indignation, he felt it.

Annie shuffled in her seat. "But you did stay the night in the royal bed?"

Harrison glanced at her, blushing slightly. He chewed his cheek. "I'll admit to that."

The bus set off, the women onboard leaning in. While the men pretended not to be listening, Harrison knew they covertly earwigged.

"Was it comfortable?" Katy asked.

"It was okay." Harrison delved into his childhood books of fairy tales. "I'd have thought a royal bed would be super soft. You could have put an entire bag of peas under that mattress."

Katy gave a dreamy moan, clasping her hands. "I'd have invited him into the bed."

"Oh, yes!" Jill joined in. They looked at each other and laughed lewdly. "He's so handsome."

Harrison felt himself blushing. "He's not."

"Have you changed your tune?" Annie pressed in on him. "You always called him a jerk. But now?"

"Okay, he's not a complete jerk." Harrison's sense of self disassociated as he spoke in the third person. "But I wouldn't *sleep* with him! Would you?"

"In a heartbeat," said Katy.

"You're married!" Jill grinned triumphantly. "So, he's all mine."

"He'll be married on Sunday." Harrison felt this was worth

Royal Again   Iain Benson

mentioning.

"Somebody's doing a countdown!" Jill said.

"One less eligible bachelor." Annie sighed.

"Did you see him in his underwear?" Katy asked. "I bet he's ripped."

The minibus arrived in the town centre, saving Harrison from further interrogation. He stepped into the bus station, the light fading from the sky.

"I want to know *everything* tomorrow!" Katy yelled over her shoulder, running for a bus already at the station. The passengers dispersed to different stands. Harrison turned. He'd never felt so alone, so small, and so unsure. No security detail, no adoring crowds. His shoulders sagged.

"Stand F," he said to himself. A dozen bus stops sheltered a range of people; each stop had a letter on a pole. He spotted F and headed for it, joining a huddled group dressed mostly in dark colours, his clothing standing out like a red balloon on a Banksy.

A youth in a black hoody leaned on the bus timetable. Harrison didn't feel comfortable asking him to move, not that it mattered anyway. Whether five or ten minutes, it would take how long it took. A vulnerability he'd not experienced before settled on him, making him wary of taking out his phone as a distraction. Instead, he stared at a spot in the middle distance, the other passengers in the station fading into a peripheral smudge. Only buses arriving pulled him from his trance. Eventually, he saw the number fifteen, allowing him a deep-seated relief from the chilled air.

He watched passengers tapping their bus passes on the driver's contactless machine. He followed suit, taking a seat on the left near the front, where he could see from the window. Following her directions, he congratulated himself for getting off the bus at the right spot and finding Pippa's flat.

He turned the alarm off and the light on, leaning on the front door, surveying a flat that, from the bathroom to the kitchen, took up less space than his sitting room. A chill ran up his spine at standing in the strange room. Harrison walked around, picking up Pippa's possessions and photos. He stared for a long time at one with two women standing with Pippa. They both looked like her. He guessed a sister and mother. He didn't have photos in his apartment.

Several future events already loomed large in his mind's eye. He'd have to make something to eat, sleep in somebody else's bed, and get up early to put on makeup.

Put on makeup.

He closed his eyes, running his fingers down his face, trying to push that thought from his mind.

His reverie smashed as the phone rang, making him jump. Harrison saw the answerphone light flashing on the kitchen counter. Thirty messages. An inner voice told him not to answer the phone. He could not look anywhere other than the handset, though.

The message ran through. Harrison heard Pippa's voice saying she couldn't get to the phone. Her cheerfulness in the recording brought a smile that fell when the man's voice left his message.

"Ms Palmer, we understand you slept with the prince last night. My name is Mark Sporco. I represent the *Daily Royal*. We're willing to offer a quarter of a million for exclusive rights to your story."

"Oh, crap." Harrison slid the bolt shut on the door.

9
Pippa: The dance

Pippa slowly walked down the stairs. She'd given a confident front to Harrison. Inside, her stomach twisted into knots. She had to force her way through the molasses of fear to reach the grand staircase.

Already, the Great Hall thronged with elegantly dressed people. She spotted movie stars, TV personalities, and sportsmen and women. Around the edges, she saw black-suited security personnel. These would be the ones intended for the guests to see. Tweedle Dumb and Tweedle Dumber had the post by the door, watching everybody enter.

Pippa could not resist approaching. It gave her a focus, something to exclude the hubbub surrounding her, compartmentalising away her predicament for a moment.

"Evening gentlemen." Pippa's eyes twinkled.

"Your highness." Although he turned his head to Pippa, his gaze constantly scanned the people entering.

"Locked anybody in a bathroom yet?"

"There has been no need, sir. Yet."

"Keep up the good work." Pippa deflated, her little bit of fun and joy sucked away by the humourless vacuum of Tweedle Dumb.

"Sir," Tweedle Dumb replied.

Left with no more delaying tactics, Pippa headed into the ballroom. She checked out the floor, silently praising Harrison for a job done well. She barely heard Ben announcing her to the room, due to the wall of sound created by scores of people milling around talking. Along the wall with the tall windows, cocktail tables and high stools offered the weary a temporary seat too uncomfortable to sit in for any length of time. They gave those in heels a chance to change which discomfort to feel. Dignitaries and celebrities mingled around the central area, the dance floor left clear, waiting for the bravest soul to initiate the dancing. Music came from a chamber orchestra in the corner, fighting against the sound of conversation. A rotund, balding man Pippa recognised as a comedian waltzed across the floor with his drink as a partner.

Serving staff moved around with finger food and drinks. Pippa didn't recognise anyone serving, suggesting they came from an agency. Had

Iain Benson — Royal Again

Tweedle Dumb vetted them all?

Lording over the party, Pippa saw the King and Queen occupying the room's focal point. Easily visible from everywhere, but especially at the entrance.

Pippa headed over to them, smiling and nodding greetings to people she did not know. The gnawing feeling deep in her core refused to go away. Although she feigned confidence, she doubted she'd be able to eat due to the churning inside.

"Harry, my son," William said as Pippa reached them.

"Pa." Nervously, she glanced around, scanning for Isabella.

"I understand you slept with a maid." The king gave a jovial guffaw.

"Willy!" Charlotte said, lightly punching her husband's arm.

"Do you have the entire story, Pa?"

"I read the briefing. We got ahead of it in the papers."

"The papers?" Pippa added horror to her anxiety. Her mum would see the papers.

"The tabloids are running with salacious headlines in the morning," William said. "Those gentler towards the monarchy are leading with your gentlemanly heroics. In both cases, the actual story is largely a non-story. But you know how the press is. Especially the *Daily Royal!*"

Thinking of Harrison, if the papers worked out his involvement, they may well go hunting for him. A disaster in the making.

Casually, she shrugged. "Between you and me, she didn't really volunteer to go into the changing room for hours. I might have strongly insisted. The papers haven't got hold of who she is, have they?"

William clasped Pippa's shoulder. "Unfortunately, yes. She's still in the palace, though, isn't she?"

Pippa swore under her breath, feeling the urge to vomit. "No. She went home."

"I'll send a car to get her." William beckoned over one of his security people and whispered in his ear.

"Thank you, Pa."

"It's self-preservation, my boy." William patted Pippa's back. "The tabloids will offer a considerable sum. I'd expect most people would say anything for the cash they'll offer. We can't have this derailing the wedding. Even if you slept with her."

"I've not had sex with any maids, Pa." She could think of nothing more to say without lying. If she mentioned they were so intimate they'd become each other, William would respond with derision and a trip to the royal therapist.

Taking her phone out, she texted, letting Harrison know rescue would be coming. Seconds after sending it, a hush fell at the ballroom's far end.

Isabella had arrived.

Standing under the balloon arch, she wore a long, shimmering silver dress. Her hair fell in soft waves around bare shoulders. Pippa knew Harrison and Isabella's wedding would be a world-watched event. The papers billed the couple as the public's darlings. The papers cast Isabella as the most beautiful woman in the world and Harrison as a handsome eligible bachelor. Pippa had to admit Isabella *was* beautiful, and while she grudgingly admitted Harrison was handsome, she reminded herself she disliked his personality. His friends didn't help with liking him, either.

"The press is watching, Harry." William pushed Pippa slightly. "Make sure you put those tabloid rumours to bed."

With a slight nod, she walked from her position to the dance floor's centre. Pippa gave a slight, stiff bow towards Isabella.

"Isabella, you look ravishing." Pippa hoped Harrison would say such a thing, especially with dozens of people within earshot.

Isabella offered a cheek. Feeling a blush form at the base of her neck, Pippa leaned in and kissed both Isabella's cheeks, following it up by taking Isabella's hand to brush her lips lightly over Isabella's knuckles. She'd read that in a romance novel as a teenager and had always wished somebody would do it to her. Like a wish fulfilled by a sadistic genie, she had become the one doing the kissing.

"Harrison." Isabella gave him a playful smile. With the skill of a ventriloquist, she added: "Tell me you've not been screwing the help, or I am walking."

Anger shoved Pippa's anxiety to one side for a moment. "I did not sleep with the maid."

Isabella's smile became wider. "Good. Although, if it was the cute one, I could have understood, if not forgiven. Now, are we going to stand as the centre of attention, or are you taking me to your parents?"

Raising her hand for taking, Pippa realised what Isabella asked of her, taking the proffered hand to lead her to meet the King and Queen, somebody Isabella had met more than Pippa had.

"Isabella, my dear, you are a picture," William said.

"Your royal highnesses," Isabella curtseyed.
"Is that a McNair?" Charlotte asked, appraising Isabella's dress.
"You have a good eye, ma'am."
"Oh, please," Charlotte said. "Call me Lottie. You're almost family."

Wishing she could be anywhere but the ballroom, Pippa gave a vacuous smile at the interchange. Although Isabella's outfit garnered envious and appreciative glances, Pippa could not see any future with her. She felt no attraction to the woman. Isabella played the role of fiancée flawlessly. Her tinkling laugh at the king's bon mots, while elegantly holding a champagne flute, created the perfect image of a future queen. She greeted several people as they came over to speak with her and an increasingly uncomfortable Pippa.

"Are you not taking anything to drink?" Isabella asked as the greetings died down.

I can't risk starting drinking. I won't be able to stop until I'm blitzed.

She kept her internal monologue to herself. "Not tonight."

Isabella's eyebrows rose. "No drinking and telling your lawyer chums they are a bunch of sexist asses? What has come over you?"

Pippa examined the floor. Isabella's smile remained, nodding and raising her glass to people almost constantly. She decided how to defuse the line of questions. "I'd had enough of sexist comments."

Squeezing Pippa's arm, Isabella reached up to peck him on the cheek. "Well, keep it up. It's an improvement."

Another hush fell, announcing the President's arrival, along with his entourage.

Impossible to miss, they filled the entrance, both in numbers and personality. The President himself, though short, made up for it in sheer superstar celebrity. He waved and greeted people as he crossed the floor, warmly shaking people's hands and flashing the trademark smile that had swept him into the top job. Forming a flying goose formation, his aides, security, wife, and children drove a wedge through the crowd until he came to rest directly before the royal family.

"Your royal highnesses," he said, brilliant teeth glaring against a tanned face. "Lady Isabella."

"Mr President," William said, before stepping forward and clasping the shorter man in a bear hug. "So good of you to come, Thomas."

"Like I'm going to miss the century's biggest wedding!" The President turned his fake smile to Pippa and Isabella. "Your wedding is filling our papers every day. I'm sure the spectacle will be," he paused before amping up the smile, "spectacular!"

Although subtle, Pippa noticed the First Lady took a champagne flute from a passing server, downed it, and placed it on the next passing tray, taking a fresh one. Thomas's children shuffled impatiently, stuffed into ill-fitting clothes. The boy, nearly twelve, in a dinner jacket and bow tie that seemed more like a garotte than a neck adornment, constantly pulled at with a finger. The girl, two years younger, in a flouncy white dress with more ruffles and frills than a bridal show, kept pressing the frills and flounces down. The boy's hair had been slicked back; the girl's primped to a point where it defied gravity. The girl's beauty pageant makeup made her appear doll-like.

William and Thomas briefly chatted before Thomas had to drift off and interact with other guests.

"Odious little man," William muttered to Charlotte.

Pippa couldn't believe she'd met Thomas Cruz.

With the brilliant Presidential arrival, the orchestra picked up the volume, encouraging people to the dancefloor.

Charlotte touched both Pippa and Isabella. "Be a dear and start the dancing off."

"And remember." William's tone hardened. "Convince the press you two are in love."

Pippa blew out her lips and gave a resigned nod. She offered her hand to Isabella and led her onto the dance floor. Milling people parted to allow them some space. In Pippa's head, she listened to the music's beat, hearing the dum de dah dum of a waltz. Silently, she thanked the musical gods for taking care of her tonight. Isabella's slim arm slipped around Pippa's waist and she placed her arm on the small of Isabella's back.

On the musical beat, Pippa pushed off. She counted in her head as per Harrison's instructions.

"You seem stiff," Isabella said.

Pippa's mind raced to find a reason she couldn't dance. It drew a blank.

Fortunately, Isabella filled in the gap. "Is this about last night?"

"My act of gallantry backfiring and leaving me mostly sleep-deprived after taking the couch, you mean?"

Isabella scoffed. "I meant my remark that our wedding was a mere show wedding, that I could never love you and your touch made me recoil?"

Internally, Pippa's eyebrows rose. "Having thought about it, you might be right. As my father says, we must maintain appearances."

"Duty is all. What I'd give to fall in love like ordinary people. Perhaps one day, we could learn to love one another." Isabella's movements sashayed under Pippa's grip.

Privately, Pippa thought: *No chance!* But vocally she conceded: "Perhaps."

The act of talking allowed Pippa to relax into the dance. Intellectually, she had fifteen years of practice to make up, but physically, Harrison's body took control, allowing her to pull off something she'd not considered possible: She led Isabella through the whole dance, noting about halfway through that the floor partially filled up. Most couples eschewed formal dancing in favour of more casual movements.

The music rose to a crescendo. Pippa released Isabella's waist and turned her with their clasped fingers raised over her head, bringing her back into a clasp, bent backwards over a strong forearm.

Polite applause rippled among the closer observers.

"Kiss me," Isabella whispered.

Pippa hesitated.

From the corner of her eye, she saw a photographer. Steeling herself, she leant in and kissed Isabella lightly on the lips, a chaste kiss, but one which drew gasps of admiration from the crowd. Pippa held Isabella in her powerful arms for what felt like an eternity, eventually releasing her to an upright position.

Flushed, Isabella's fingers went to her lips. She glanced shyly away from Pippa's face, showing Pippa the first genuine emotion she'd ever seen from Harrison's fiancée.

Pippa held out her hand, taking Isabella back to the King and Queen.

"Loving you might be a lot easier than I thought," Isabella murmured as they walked, giving him a slight smile. "I've never felt such an electrical tingle from a kiss before."

Pippa swallowed her urge for a sarcastic reply. *Probably a static charge.*

Clasping her shoulder, William beamed at Pippa. "Outstanding performance, my boy. That photo will be on the front page of every paper tomorrow."

Pippa forced herself to smile at the king. She felt Isabella's fingers entwine with hers. With her free hand, she rubbed at Harrison's chiselled

Royal Again   Iain Benson

chin.

What had she done? President Cruz broke them apart, sliding between them and facing Isabella.

"Can I borrow your fiancé?" The President's personality made up for the twenty centimetres Pippa had on him. He turned like a dancer on the ball of his foot and grabbed Pippa's arm, steering her away.

Pippa wondered what she'd done now. Why Thomas wanted to talk to her, she didn't know. Nor had she found enough time to read Harrison's notes on what to discuss with the President.

As alone as they could be, Thomas leaned in conspiratorially. "Tell me, man-to-man, are you boning the hired help?"

Sighing, Pippa shook her head. "No. Don't believe everything you read in the tabloids. I indeed allowed a maid to stay in my room, but that was more down to her being unable to get home and in staying quiet and out of sight while Isabella and I discussed our wedding."

Thomas's hundred-watt smile faltered. Pippa noticed he smiled only with his mouth. His eyes barely crinkled under the onslaught of enforced civility. "Gotcha. Loud and clear. Between you and me, with a stunner like Isabella, you don't need to be doing the help. Congrats on the wedding, man. It's going to be awesome."

"Yes," Pippa said, inwardly glum. "Awesome."

10
Harrison: The dance

Amid the constant phone ringing, Pippa's message almost went unheard. Fortunately, Harrison still held Pippa's phone, clasped in his hands, curled up on the sofa.

"Thank god," he muttered.

Staring down a night alone in Pippa's flat brought home his plight, his future and his own behaviour. The silent dark surrounding him acted as an echo chamber to his self-reflecting mind dwelling on a future without privilege. He vowed to be better. He would listen to those around him and learn.

Pippa's text said a driver called Dillon would pick him up and he could hide out at the palace. The irony hit hard. He could hide at home.

Fabulous. He hunted through Pippa's flat for something to put clothes in. He'd already worn this underwear for two days. He didn't think he could turn knickers inside out twice. Once already made him feel unclean.

Harrison could almost touch the opposite walls in Pippa's bedroom. She had a three-quarter bed squashed up under the window, a single wardrobe, and a chest of drawers under a large mirror surrounded by lights. Accompanied by the soundtrack of a ringing phone, he found a wheeled suitcase stuffed atop the wardrobe. It still had the price tag on.

The dresser contained a selection of makeup. He considered momentarily leaving it, but he put it into the suitcase along with underwear, two clean uniforms and non-work clothes. Pippa had very few clothes. Two pairs of skinny jeans and loose blouses. Three pairs of shoes had to do the work for whatever situation she found herself in. The suitcase barely had space left, but he could fit her laptop into it, so he did. He left the skirt hanging up, shuddering at it.

Fastening the suitcase, a flash of light from outside made him glance up and see a man at the window.

An intrepid paparazzo had brought a cherry picker.

He slammed the curtains closed. Momentarily blinding, the camera flashed with a stroboscopic effect. Jittery, he hurried from the bedroom into the bathroom to get ablution products. Especially Pippa's toothbrush. He ran his tongue over his teeth.

A knock on the apartment's door made him drop the shampoo bottle into the bath. His hand shook slightly as he picked it up again. Had the paparazzi got into the apartment block? Creeping, he peered through the peephole. The fisheye lens distorted the corridor. A single, tousled-haired man waited. Harrison recognised him as his driver. Pippa had told him the driver's name. Daniel? David? Dillon? Definitely Dillon.

Harrison pulled the door open, yanking the driver into the apartment like an amorous triste.

"Wow, Pip." Dillon said with a broad smile, his back going into the wall, taking his breath from him. "I'd normally suggest dinner first."

He had smouldering brown eyes, but with a slight twinkle that mirrored the playful smile.

"Thanks for coming, Dillon." Harrison let him go, as he had the wildest urge to plant a kiss on his lips. "I'd take the dinner right now. I'm starving. All I've had today is a banana and a sandwich."

"I'll see what you've got in and rustle something up, while you get changed."

"Changed?"

Dillon raised his hands, exasperated. "There are a billion photo-gropers out there. You leave in a bright orange top, and they're going to see you. More importantly, they'll recognise you."

Grimacing, holding his temper in check, Harrison lifted the case onto the bed having packed most of Pippa's clothes. As Dillon headed for the kitchen, Harrison opened the suitcase. He nibbled the inside of his cheek wondering if he could extract some clothing without unpacking the whole thing. Hanging in the open wardrobe, a knee-length skirt and skin-tight top announced themselves. He shuddered, but held it up, his eyes following the skirt's length, seeing how far down his legs it fell.

"That'll be good," Dillon said from the doorway. He held up the remains of a block of cheese. "All you have in the way of edible food is half a block of cheese, a tin of tomato soup and some stale bread. You up for my outstanding gourmet cheese on toast with nuked soup?"

Harrison wondered why Pippa had no food in. He made up a plausible excuse. "I've not been shopping yet."

"Don't sweat it." Dillon's smile held no condescension. "I'm the same. I eat my big meals at the palace. It's better food."

Harrison gave a shrug. "It is. Cheese on toast sounds like nectar right now."

"I'll let you get dressed."

Dillon pulled the door closed. Harrison changed outfit, including underwear, trying not to check the mirror at Pippa's naked body. He failed. In only underwear, Harrison stood critically by the mirror. When she said she ate healthily, she didn't eat enough. The waistband of the skirt gaped a little, but he luxuriated in the way the material swished around his legs. He swayed his hips to let the material caress his calves. The silky sensation gave him a little thrill. The skin-tight top proved harder to put on than the skirt. After one aborted attempt that left the long sleeves corkscrewed, he twisted his arms before putting it on and spent a couple of minutes untwisting the body and armpits.

The outfit suited him. As a final part of his temporary disguise, he pulled the scrunchy out of his hair and onto his wrist, shaking out the long locks. He ran his fingers through to give a bit of body and mask at least some of his face. It wouldn't fool anybody for long.

Dillon toiled over a hot microwave as Harrison entered the kitchen area behind the lounge.

The driver gave him a flirtatious grin over his shoulder. "I can see why you turned the prince's head. You scrub up good."

"I've only put clothes on." Harrison felt secretly pleased with the compliment. "Anyway! Nothing happened. Really. It's all a rumour."

"I believe you. Honest, I do. It's completely convincing that you spent the entire night in Horror-son's quarters and absolutely nothing happened."

Harrison parked the nickname for the moment, suppressing the urge to snap at Dillon. "It didn't."

"Nothing didn't happen?" Dillon could barely suppress a laugh. "That's a double negative."

"In the curious case of the maid and the prince, absolutely nothing happened." Harrison's earlier vow to be a more likeable person and maintain Pippa's friendliness came close to breaking.

Dillon shrugged. "I'm teasing."

He removed the bowl of soup from the microwave, splitting it into two and pulled the tray out from under the grill, dropping two slices of cheese on toast onto plates.

"Do you have a table?"

"I, I, no. I usually eat standing at the counter or, if it's a special occasion, sitting on the sofa."

"I think having guests makes this a special occasion."

Dillon took the plates around the couch, which formed a division between the two areas. Harrison sat beside the driver he'd previously sat behind. The couch accommodated them both. Snuggly. Harrison nearly drank the soup straight from the bowl, his stomach shouting for more.

The phone rang again.

Dillon twisted to locate the jarring sound. "Are you getting that?"

"It's the press." Harrison crunched the toast, the cheddar melting across his tongue. His eyes closed of their own volition, holding the toast under his nose to inhale the cheese's scent.

True to form, another monetary offer to fabricate a titillating story about the prince, recorded onto an already overflowing machine.

"Quarter of a million is a lot of cash." Dillon's eyebrows went up. "That has to be tempting."

"It would destroy him," Harrison said, knowing exactly what would happen if the press ran stories of infidelity before he even married.

"But you'd be extremely *rich!*"

"You think I should answer the phone?" Harrison's pitch went up in disbelief at Dillon's suggestion.

Dillon shook his head. "Absolutely not. Morally, it's totally wrong."

"That's what I think." Harrison wondered if Pippa would have taken the money. Seeing how she lived, she'd be a fool to keep quiet.

"I'd hold out to the day before the wedding and sell your story then. You'd get three times that easily!" Dillon burst into laughter. "No, seriously. I'm impressed with you."

They finished eating, forcing Harrison to imagine what Pippa would do now. *She'd tidy up!*

He took Dillon's plate and bowl off his lap and into the kitchen. Washing up liquid and a sponge lived beside the sink, so he washed the crockery and cutlery, slipping them onto the draining board. He figured they would be totally dry by the time Pippa returned here. Pride swelled his chest at washing up for the first time. Pippa had pilfered the washing up liquid from the palace. He could almost forgive her.

"Ready?" Dillon had her suitcase.

Harrison grabbed Pippa's coat, slipping it on. "I guess so. Where are you parked?"

"I couldn't park outside the front door," Dillon told him as Harrison locked up the apartment. "Too many paparazzi. We'll have to go out the back and walk around to the side."

Mouth dry and trembling slightly, Harrison let Dillon lead him down the stairwell.

At the bottom, Dillon peeped out. "They're all by the front door, look."

He stood aside to let Harrison see down the corridor for himself. The big glass doors beside the post boxes had every millimetre covered by faces and lenses. Lifts and a back door were in the opposite direction. The front door had a good view of the lobby.

"They will see us." Harrison shook slightly, his breathing sharp.

Dillon's grin told Harrison the driver had a plan. He slipped his arm around Harrison's shoulders. "Come on, put your arm around me."

A little unsure, he slipped his arm around Dillon's waist. They fit together easily and well, calming the quivers. Although the paparazzi flashed as they left, the stroboscopic light ended as they moved away. The photographers assuming they'd got the wrong woman. Outside, the night air chilled Harrison, his breath visible in short bursts.

A path between bushes led to the property's rear, past tall metal bins in a shelter overflowing with rubbish. Harrison let Dillon steer, as he didn't know where to go. Two photographers turned the corner ahead of them. Harrison's eyes widened, drawing a deep breath. Dillon turned and cupped the back of Harrison's neck, tipping him back slightly, leaning in.

"Trust me," he whispered, pressing his lips onto Harrison's.

A surge of heat ran down Harrison's body into his toes. His breath caught and his eyes closed. The two paparazzi walked past, but the kiss lingered.

"Um," Harrison muttered as they parted.

"Sorry, it was all I could think of."

Harrison struggled for words at first. "As plans go, it was the best. But don't get used to that!"

Sitting in Dillon's car, Harrison felt the heat from the kiss drain away. Replaced by ice from driving past the mass of photographers crammed around the entrance, hoping to glimpse the maid that could bring down the monarchy. The heat had gone, but the tingle of Dillon's kiss reverberated on his lips. Despite reservations, he'd happily experience it again. He didn't think he'd become gay. Instead, Pippa's female body responded to the charged sexual tension. He licked his lips, almost tasting

Royal Again
Iain Benson

Dillon still there, a slight smile curling his lips into a cupid's bow. Dillon concentrated on driving through the darkness back towards the palace. His profile was lit by a soft staccato glow from the streetlights. Harrison could think of worse ways to spend his life if they couldn't reverse the swap.

Glancing at Harrison, Dillon smiled. "Are you okay? You're quiet. You're not upset by the kiss, are you?"

Shaking his head, Harrison returned the smile, feeling the warmth return along with happiness. Strange, it took losing every privilege to find such comfort.

"Not at all," Harrison replied after a moment.

"I've wanted to do that since the day I first saw you," Dillon said. "If I'm being totally honest."

Not knowing how Pippa felt about Dillon, Harrison wanted to keep an option open for Pippa. "When this all blows over, ask me again. It's not a good time right now."

A half-smile from the driver and that delicious twinkle brought an unfamiliar feeling to Harrison's tummy.

They swept through the palace's rear gates, more photographers hanging out, hoping to catch celebrities in compromising poses away from the palace's public parts. Their car attracted attention, but the journalists looked for celebrities. They'd not considered Pippa might return. Dillon came around to open the door. Almost clambering out in his usual way, Harrison remembered at the last second how he'd seen his mother exit a car. He swung his legs around to slide out more gracefully. Dillon offered his hand to help him stand, even though he'd mastered that skill as a toddler.

"I need to let the King and Harrison know you're safe," Dillon told her as they signed in at the security desk.

Harrison didn't want to admit he had his number on Pippa's phone.

"Good idea." He pulled the handle up on his suitcase and trundled after Dillon to the staff door leading onto the ballroom.

Dozens of staff members used the doors, one side for coming in, the other for going out. Empty trays returning, heading for the kitchens, laden trays of booze and food going the other way. He'd never seen the organised chaos that operated behind the scenes at these events, concentrating more on drinking and socialising.

At the doors, Harrison sighed at the number of feet trampling over a floor he'd spent all morning cleaning. Including Dillon, who headed into the crowd. Harrison's breath caught in his throat as he saw Pippa dancing with

Isabella. Pippa spun Isabella and bent her backwards to place a seductive kiss on her lips. In his mind, Harrison knew a publicity stunt arranged by his father when he saw it, but in his heart, Harrison felt a pang of jealousy.

And he didn't know who the jealousy targeted.

Did he envy Isabella for being kissed in such a way, or Pippa for kissing Isabella?

"I am going to need therapy after this," Harrison muttered. "A lot of therapy."

11
Pippa: Revelations

The sofa squeaked alarmingly as Pippa landed on it, exhaling as much air as the sofa.

She felt emotionally drained.

The deception and duplicity ate away at her. She didn't know how much more she could take.

Adding to her tiredness, the kiss with Isabella gave her additional worry. Pippa couldn't say she felt anything from the kiss, but Isabella's reaction and subsequent actions told Pippa Isabella felt the opposite. Pippa struggled to reconcile that with her feelings, concluding she was contemptible.

She didn't like the person she had become, even if it meant she could return to being herself.

Duty sucked. If not for the need to stay close to Harrison, the temptation of vanishing into obscurity might overwhelm the slight feeling of duty being Harrison instilled.

As though thinking about him summoned him, Harrison's head poked into the apartment.

"Good, you're here." He sat beside her. "Your stupid idea of telling people you'd stayed the night backfired big time."

"It seems like a good idea," Pippa said.

"No. It wasn't." Harrison stared into the middle distance. "Your answerphone is full."

"Full?"

"You're getting constant calls from the press to rat me out as a love cheat. Photographers have blockaded your building."

"They're going to run stories, aren't they?"

"They already are." Harrison showed Pippa her phone on a news page.

"Could I borrow my phone?" Pippa asked.

Silently, Harrison passed it over. Pippa tapped on it for a few seconds, paused momentarily, deleted what she'd typed, and put a new message.

"Who are you texting?"

"My mum," Pippa replied. "I'm letting her know nothing happened and to ignore anybody from the newspaper. She might ring. My mum doesn't do texting."

"What do I say?"

"She'll do the talking. You'll occasionally have to say '*uh-uh*' and '*really?*'. If she asks about a boyfriend, say she can meet him one day. But don't get drawn on anything. If she asks how you're eating, say 'well'. That's it. Conversations with my mum are ninety percent about the illnesses of her friends."

"Do you have a boyfriend?" Harrison's question threw Pippa sideways.

"Are you applying for the role?" Pippa's patience threshold had reached rock bottom.

"Of course I don't want the role. I'm serious. I need to know."

Yawning, Pippa turned to Harrison. "No. I've not got a boyfriend. Why do you ask?"

"Dillon kissed me."

"Dillon? As in your driver?"

Harrison's sheepish smile and how the tension drained from him told Pippa she'd guessed correctly. He confirmed it. "Yes."

Pippa's jealously rose. "That's so unfair. I'd love to have kissed him."

"You kind of did." Harrison's reply made her jealousy worse.

A few moments of silence followed, broken wide open by Pippa's increasing annoyance with Harrison. "Are you two dating now? It's going to be really awkward when this is over. I'm not going to know anything you two do. Have you slept with him?"

"No!" Harrison's hands came up, defending himself from her onslaught. "He told me he'd wanted to kiss you from the moment he saw you."

"Not helping."

"And I told him to try again when everything had died down."

Pippa's bottom lip stuck out as she considered that. Harrison, it seemed, had done her a favour. Should she switch back, she might get a chance with Dillon. Did she want that? She felt split. Harrison huddled there, opening his mouth to speak, and holding back. If they switched back, he'd be with Isabella, so being with Dillon would be okay.

Pippa paused. She'd relegated Dillon to a consolation. Part of her mind stomped around her brain, yelling at the part that decided she had a chance with Harrison for even *wanting* to have a chance with Harrison. Harrison the jerk. Harrison the jackass. Harrison the quite thoughtful and sexy when you got to know him.

When had her emotions decided that the last part was an option?

Pippa's lips compressed.

A tiny part of her mind took centre stage and pointed out that if they couldn't switch back, at least Harrison would be happy.

"Did you like it?"

"Like it?"

Pippa rolled her eyes. "Yes. When Dillon kissed you, did you like it?"

Harrison's pause spoke more than his words when they finally came. "Yes. I think I did. Does that mean I like guys now?"

"Probably not," Pippa said. "It means I do."

"Anyway," Harrison's tone turned off hand. "You kissed Isabella."

"I had to," Pippa said. "I needed to get the press off your back."

"Did you like it?"

Pippa barked a laugh. "I didn't. Isabella seemed smitten, though."

"It was quite a kiss." Harrison cheered up a little. "A movie star quality kiss."

"Thank you." Pippa grinned. "It was the first time I kissed a girl. Glad you liked it."

"We're due to visit Isabella's house for a pre-wedding celebration dinner tomorrow."

"We?" Pippa arched an eyebrow.

"You."

"What's sort of do is it?"

"It's like a seated version of tonight. A few courses, drinks and conversation."

Pippa chewed her lip. "Do I get a plus one?"

Harrison shook his head. "Apart from your security detail, I suppose you could take an aide."

"You are my aide now, or had you forgotten?"

"I don't think I'll make a good aide in the real world!" Harrison's voice contained a dull sadness. "It's fine to keep us close here. Sorry. But you're not aide material."

"What does an aide do?"

"Tells you what you need to know."

"Do you know what I need to know to know what you know?"

Iain Benson — Royal Again

Harrison followed the words with his head tilting from side to side. "Well, yes."

"Then *you* make a good aide."

Harrison's balled fist rested on his nose. "I've nothing to wear."

Pippa burst out laughing. "No. I know you haven't. We'll have to get something in the daytime."

"It's the Hitchberg film premiere tomorrow."

"Afternoon?"

"Yes."

"What do I have on in the morning?" Ideas raced around Pippa's head.

"Breakfast, as usual, then the gym. Lunch will be at the palace."

Pippa's eyes lit up. "I'll skip the gym. We'll sneak out and get you some clothes. Maybe a haircut and a makeover."

"What?" Harrison scrambled to his feet, putting the sofa's scrolled arm between them.

"Do you know a great thing about being a woman is?"

"Short skirts and men's shirts?"

Pippa shook her head. "If you get a different hairstyle, a change of makeup and clothes, nobody recognises you."

"People will recognise me. You. Me."

Pippa returned to the *Daily Royal* webpage on her phone. The top story detailed the *Prince's Gallantry or Adultery*. The picture underneath showed both Harrison and Pippa, with a glaring contrast in quality. "I don't think anybody would recognise me, you, from that."

Harrison tapped the photo, making the grainy photocopy of Pippa's ID badge full screen. Either the photograph through Pippa's bedroom window had been unusable, or it had yet to reach the newspapers. "I see what you mean."

"Having you as my aide is the best disguise there is." Pippa's grin turned sneaky. "Who would think to look for my squeeze beside me on the red carpet?"

"Sounds risky." Harrison retook his seat. "Almost like you want me to get caught."

"I'm trying to make Dillon jealous."

Seeing Harrison's horrified face, Pippa laughed.

Harrison refused to look at her. "When we switch back, he's yours."

"But you enjoyed the kiss." Pippa's tiredness translated into playful needling. "You must *love* him."

At last, Harrison spotted the game and joined in. "I think it's your body reacting. You go weak at the knees every time he's near."

"You just *love* kissing boys."

Harrison's cheeks flushed, he turned away. "Do not."

Pippa arched an eyebrow and stood up. She held out her hand.

Harrison's eyes narrowed, but he took Pippa's hand.

She pulled, lifting her hand and spinning Harrison around like she had Isabella. She dipped Harrison, holding him there. She lowered her lips to Harrison's.

Part of her mind told her not to.

Harrison's eyes closed. His lips parted.

Those ideas that considered it a bad idea rounded up any objections, threw them out and replaced them with pure, red-tinted lust.

Pippa pressed her lips to Harrison's, lightly at first, but as he pressed back, more so, feeling the warmth spread around her, tingling in every finger.

Pippa couldn't say who broke first, but as their lips parted, she gasped. There had been definite stirrings down below. It had been an impromptu act, a bit of playful banter.

Testosterone curdled her brain. She could think of no other explanation for a sudden burst of feelings for him.

Harrison sounded breathless. "Let's definitely not do that again!"

"It didn't do anything for you?" Pippa's hope rose that she'd escaped without starting something she'd regret.

"Quite the opposite!"

Pippa straightened, allowing Harrison to come upright. "You're right. Isabella."

"Dillon."

Pippa's lips compressed. "I'm going to bed. Where have they put you up?"

"The Blue Suite."

"Ah, the Inappropriately Named Blue Suite Because It's Yellow."

Harrison smirked. "Once upon a time, it was blue. The name stuck more than the decor."

"I'll be back from breakfast by half nine. If I survive."

"Are you seriously considering risking being seen out with me?"

Pippa's smile spread slowly. "Trust me."

12
Harrison: Morning

The chance of a lie-in vanished as Harrison awoke far too early, hunger driving him from a fragmented dream.

Pippa's suitcase remained packed at the foot of his bed. If he wanted something to eat, he would have to get dressed. If he wanted to get dressed, he should shower. And to do that, he'd have to get up.

His problems started there. Tiredness kept him glued under the duvet.

It had taken a while to find sleep, with the feelings engendered by Pippa's kiss.

That kiss!

Even thinking about it made his body tingle.

He kept circling back to his feelings for Pippa.

He could envisage no situation where he could act on those feelings.

If they stayed swapped, Pippa would marry Isabella.

If they swapped back, he would marry Isabella.

Not to mention royalty did not date beneath their station.

"Duty sucks," he muttered and threw the sheets off to get a shower.

The water washed away some tiredness, but not completely. He finally cleaned his teeth using Pippa's toothbrush, before pulling out a pair of black leggings and a baggy green jumper to go over fresh underwear. He brushed out Pippa's hair, his mind returning to Pippa's idea of disguising him with a haircut. Staring into the dressing table mirror, he lifted his hair into an updo.

He still resembled Pippa, but with his hair up.

Rolling his eyes, Harrison brushed it smooth and put it into a soggy ponytail. He slipped on a pair of sandals and checked his appearance in the long, freestanding mirror. The mix of feelings hanging over from the night before seethed and mixed with the hunger to make him slightly nauseous. Perched with the clothes in the suitcase, Pippa's makeup bag mocked him.

"How hard can it be?" He unrolled it onto the dresser. Brushes and wands, creams and powders stared back in incomprehensible complexity.

Hard. Harrison rolled it up again and headed down to the cafeteria without makeup.

Royal Again   Iain Benson

Several staff members already occupied the tables. He greeted them as he went to the metal counter.

"Morning, Pippa! Are you feeling alright? You look pale." The man behind the counter went from chirpy to worried and straight back to chirpy, fixing into place a broad cheerful smile. His tufted blond hair peaked out from under his white cap. "What can I get you?"

The smells of food wafted up, making his stomach grumble, reminding of him of his enforced diet yesterday. "Scrambled eggs, bacon, sausage, and beans."

The chef grabbed a plate and gave Harrison a generous portion. "From the sounds your stomach is making, you need this."

Harrison agreed with an appreciative noise, moving to take the plate, but the chef held on for a moment.

"Is it true you slept with the prince? It's in the papers."

Harrison shook his head, the well-rehearsed story coming to his lips. "No. It's not true. He let me use his bed when I got stranded here, but he slept on the couch."

The chef released the plate. "The truth is always far duller than the papers, isn't it?"

"Oh, yes." Harrison gave a half-smile. *But not in this case.*

Rather than appear unsociable, Harrison put his plate down on the table with three other staff. By sheer coincidence, he sat opposite Dillon.

"Hey, Pip." Dillon's smile lit up his face, sending his eyes into twinkle mode.

"Dillon." Harrison replied with an equally broad smile. His kiss with Dillon crowded in on his memories. His smile faltered as he tried to wrestle with the feelings those memories brought.

Sitting beside Dillon, another man with shorn hair and piercing blue eyes leaned forward. From his black outfit, Harrison guessed he was a security team member. He did seem vaguely familiar and might have been one of his mother's team.

"Dillon said you didn't sleep with Harrison," he said.

"Dillon's right."

"Carl!" Dillon scowled at the security guard.

"So, why has he promoted you?" Carl stabbed the air with the tines of his fork, a triumphant grin on his face.

Everybody, it seemed, had no other business, leaning in to hear the answer whilst appearing nonchalant. A slight shake of his head betrayed

Harrison's perception of the staff's inept subterfuge.

"Two reasons," Harrison said, thinking on his feet and stabbing a sausage angrily. "First, if he'd not promoted me, I'd have got fired."

Harrison ate the sausage, desperately trying to conjure a second reason.

"And?" Carl was an expert in raising one eyebrow.

Harrison finished eating his sausage. He envied Pippa's quick thinking but gave the best second reason he'd come up with: "It was his fault I got in trouble in the first place."

"His fault you spent the night in his rooms?"

Harrison considered his reasons for the night. "He didn't want Isabella seeing a cleaner leaving, so I ended up in his changing room for five hours."

Carl sat back in his chair, folding his arms, both eyebrows raised. "God damn. He really is as big an ass as they say."

Harrison started to object but the man had him nailed. "I think he's realised."

"Getting somebody detained by the secret service is a definite wake-up call," Dillon said. "What did he promote you to? Valet?"

"Aide," Harrison said. "Though I don't know what an aide does."

"As little as possible!" Carl laughed loudly at his joke. "If you're not sleeping with the prince, how about the next best thing?"

Harrison chewed the inside of his cheek, his eyebrows colliding. "The next best thing?"

"I'm asking if you'd like to go out with me?" Both of Carl's thumbs pointed at his puffed-out chest.

Harrison shook his head slightly, a half-smile. He glanced at Dillon, seeing the driver's amused expression. "No. Thanks." He bit his lip, thinking of Pippa's future. "I'm possibly already spoken for."

Dillon's amused smile widened. He winked.

Harrison chuckled and pushed an empty plate away from him, immediately realising nobody would collect it, and took it to the silvery metal table beside the kitchen.

"Cheers!" somebody called from the kitchen's depths.

Harrison smiled his goodbyes, unintentionally lingering on Dillon.

"What is wrong with you, Harrison?" he muttered as he headed up the stairs. Dillon's kiss, Pippa's kiss. Had he *flirted* with Dillon?

He didn't have any answers by the time he reached his apartment.

Royal Again   Iain Benson

Pippa's apartment. No, *his* apartment. She hadn't yet returned from breakfast with his family. Hopefully, she'd survive a second encounter with his grandmother.

While he waited, Harrison watched some twenty-four-hour news.

Quite a lot focused on the upcoming wedding, but a grainy photograph of Pippa caught his attention. They'd used the same one that had already appeared in the paper. Where it came from, he didn't know. Thankfully, Pippa didn't use social media, so they'd not been able to lift a photo from that, and her friends and family were avoiding the press. Harrison silently thanked Pippa for sending the text to her mum. Her mum had texted the letter 'O' fifteen times followed by three blank lines and the words "I knee it want tree." He'd eventually translated that to "I knew it wasn't true." Either that or Pippa's mother ate a lot of hallucinogens.

As a story about the mystery woman finished, Pippa returned, leaning against the apartment door.

"Your grandmother is a force of nature," Pippa said. "Your dad is happy, though. The papers seem to have decided the Prince and the Maid is a non-story. Hopefully, it will die down soon."

"What's up with Grandmother?"

"She complimented me on the kiss, saying it quite surprised her at how well I'd done it, but she didn't think it was true love's kiss." Pippa frowned. "She knows something. She gave too many barbed comments for me to think otherwise."

"What did you say?"

"As little as possible." Shuddering, Pippa pulled herself together. "Anyway, as my new aide, could you give your boyfriend a bell to drive us into the city? It's time for you to take centre stage."

The ride into the city reeked of unbearable silence created by the passenger's twisted dynamics. Dillon constantly glanced at Harrison with those warm brown eyes of his. Pippa kept up her Harrison façade, for Dillon's sake. Adding to the twists and knots in his belly, the idea of Pippa's planned makeover jangled his nerves. It felt like the first day of boarding school. He didn't know what to expect but had prejudged it to be all bad.

Blithely missing the entire dynamic nuance in the car, Reece, his security chief, took the front passenger seat. Harrison had learned his name through listening, thinking if he'd had to pick a name to suit his personality, Reece would be it, but wishing he'd bothered to learn it before needing it.

Iain Benson   Royal Again

When he did manage to swap bodies back, he would make more of an effort to learn about who worked for his family. Starting with names. *Name badges would be useful.*

"Where are we heading, sir?" Dillon asked as they entered the hemmed in city streets.

"Head for Justine Hollywood's boutique," Pippa replied. Harrison noticed how she stayed leaning back in the seat and did not raise her voice. Exactly what he would have done. Although he also knew Dillon would struggle to hear.

The driver picked up enough, twisting and turning into a narrow road with imposing buildings on either side. Harrison knew the street well. His tailors had premises on the corner. It surprised him a little that Pippa knew the hairdresser was here. Expensive cars lined the street, the chauffeurs waiting for their employers to return from spending ridiculous money on clothes they would wear once. Having seen Pippa's life, the façade of money created glamourous people in the old meaning of glamour. A magical exterior covering a dark interior.

Dillon expertly slid the car into a gap outside a brightly lit brushed steel and glass frontage, the sign in a cursive font barely legible. Dillon showed his chauffer manners by coming to Harrison's side first, allowing the lady to alight. Opening the door for Pippa, Reece looked around, alert.

Harrison felt out of place; he still wore his baggy jumper and leggings.

"Wait here," Pippa instructed Dillon, gesturing for Harrison to go into the boutique.

Chewing the inside of his cheek and feeling a flush forming on his neck, Harrison pushed into a salon where he'd been many times before without any trepidation. This time, he didn't belong, and nerves almost got the better of him. The salon stretched deep into the building, with two banks of chairs, each in a discrete cubical. Of the six seats, two had occupants. A cherry-red reception desk protected a four-metre abstract canvas. Opposite, chrome chairs, low tables and low-hanging lights provided intimate seating for those waiting.

"I'm sorry, we have no appointments." The willowy receptionist with perfectly coiffed hair and immaculate makeup sneered at Harrison. He knew full well they had capacity. He could see it.

Before he could speak, Pippa entered, taking off her sunglasses and filling the doorway with a radiant personality like she had taken note of the

Royal Again   Iain Benson

way President Cruz occupied a space.

"Your highness!" The receptionist's manner changed like a light switch, from contemptuous scorn into sycophantic obsequiousness.

Pippa sauntered over, leaning casually on the sternum-high desk, sunglasses dangling from one hand, leaning to the receptionist.

"Is Justine available?"

"Sir, yes, sir." The receptionist's head bobbed up and down as though her neck attempted to curtsy independently of her body. She picked up the phone handset. "Justine? Prince Harrison is here!"

A door at the far end opened, admitting the larger-than-life personality of Justine Hollywood. Her teeth shone brilliant white; her thick blonde hair swept back revealing a sun-worn face that beamed geniality. She wore a flowing kaftan, her wrists packed with bangles.

"Sire, welcome back." The hairdresser gave a slight bow. She had an accent dulled by years away from her native Turkey. Harrison had heard her life story of where she heralded, with her name being neither Justine nor Hollywood. "What can I do for you today?"

Pippa indicated Harrison with her sunglasses. Harrison knew she'd planned the gesture, but it felt dismissive. "I need your discretion and amazing talent. You've seen the papers, I presume?"

"Your kiss of Lady Isabella is the only topic of conversation in my boutique today."

"The other news."

"Scurrilous rumours, sire. Not a word said near my ears."

"Quite," Pippa said, with a slightly sad smile. "This is the lady in question. I'm afraid for her safety. You know the press. Could you work your magic and transform her into the butterfly I'm sure she can be?"

Justine came over to Harrison. He flinched slightly as the hairdresser reached behind to pull the scrunchy out. She flicked through Harrison's hair, alternately sucking at her teeth and tutting. She stepped back, sniffing.

"This will be a challenge!"

Harrison saw Pippa's eyes wrinkle in annoyance. They'd both taken that as an insult.

"But?"

"For you sire, she will be unrecognisable!"

"Excellent. What are your intentions?"

"Her skin tone needs a deep chestnut colour, extensions to thicken. I think razor cut to frame her face, such a pretty face." Justine took a step back, using her fingers and thumbs to create a frame through which she examined Harrison. "I think with makeup, she could rival Isabella!"

Pippa gave a smile that reached no further than her lips.

Cupping the small of his back, Justine led Harrison towards a chair. As he left, he couldn't resist baiting the receptionist. "I think you had an appointment, after all."

The receptionist had the good grace to appear sheepish, masking it by turning to Pippa. "Would you like a coffee, sir?"

"I am afraid I have a small errand to run."

As he sat, Harrison saw Pippa leave, speaking briefly to Dillon, before he and Reece got back in the car. He wondered where they were going. Pippa had not told him she would leave. In the chrome chair, he froze, his eyes wide, pulse racing.

13
Harrison: Makeover

"I do not know what conditioner you are using, my dear," Justine said, breaking the spell of Pippa leaving. "When you return to your home, please destroy it all! With fire."

Justine began by washing Harrison's hair, massaging deep into his scalp. Her fingers created sensual waves, so deeply relaxing that Harrison almost drifted off to sleep. Other stylists came and went, bringing various tools that would be more at home in a DIY store than a hairdresser. Although he could see himself in the mirror, her long sleeves or heaving bosom kept obscuring his view. As she busied around him, her bangles jangled.

"My dear, this is wonderful! Beautiful. I respect the prince, those scurrilous rumours. Here, we know he is the most faithful for Isabella."

"Yes," Harrison supplied, although his input went unneeded and unheeded.

"When I have finished, you will turn his head, I am sure."

Did he want that? Harrison didn't know. Wanting and doing, they did not co-exist in his world. Isabella and a version of Harrison would wed by the weekend, regardless of his personal want. He didn't *want* to marry Isabella, but they would marry.

"Turn that frown upside down, my dear!" Justine said, fussing with his hair. "Even if Harrison you cannot have, any man will be yours for the having."

Hot hair with undertones of glue assailed his nostrils. Tugs and pulls on his scalp occasionally hurt, but mostly felt uncomfortable.

Justine stepped back. Harrison finally got to see what she had done to his hair. Justine had turned the sleek brown style Pippa favoured into a bird's nest of fluff and spikes with paler strands juxtaposed against his natural colour. However disastrous it appeared, she seemed satisfied.

"We will colour next, yes, colour. Can coffee or tea be brought for you while you wait? You have been a most patient girl. Indeed."

Harrison blinked. Realising amid the garbled verbal diatribe, she had asked him a question. "Oh, yes, please. A coffee would be wonderful."

"You take it how? I do a wonderful Turkish coffee. I know! I know! It is hard for all, but I like it!" She barked a laugh.

"Unsweetened black will be fine."

"Oh, my dear, just like Harrison himself. See, you two are matched in the stars. Or at least the espresso!"

"He is marrying Isabella," Harrison said, almost keeping the bitterness from his voice. "Our worlds are so far apart, whether he wants me or not, it's irrelevant. He has a duty."

"Duty, smooty." Justine turned to a passing assistant and ordered coffee. "The heart wants what the heart wants."

The aroma of coffee soon arrived; a solid mug placed on the counter by the mirror. Steam rose, creating a fogging on the glass in a heart-shaped pattern. Justine found an assistant to take the mass of hair he now sported and layer it in an acrid paste and silver foil. A tedious job she happily delegated.

"Now we are waiting." Justine took one of Harrison's hands in hers, turning it over. She stroked Harrison's palm. "A worker's hands, most definitely. Cocoa butter every night before bed. Your palm lines, they are interesting." Harrison felt a tingle as Justine's fingernail traced a square in his right palm. "Oh, such a cross I have not seen for many years. Interesting. Interesting."

Harrison wanted to ask what Justine meant, but before he could, she'd flipped his hand over and examined his nails. "This will never do. Never! I cannot have you leave here with hands that match not your hair."

Harrison examined his nails on his left with his right trapped in Justine's cupped hands. Pippa kept her nails short, unpolished. They had a rough texture. He'd never scrutinised them before. The phrase "knowing something like the back of your hand" did not apply here. He knew his original fingernails well: smooth, rounded, and buffed weekly. His next nail-buffing session scheduled for his wedding day.

Eventually, he managed to think of a response. "I keep them short, so they don't get damaged."

"Now, with the prince, you are. Beautiful, your nails will be for him."

She made it sound like he had started dating Pippa. Harrison didn't mind that allusion at all. "They're not going to grow in an hour."

Justine barked another laugh. "My sweet girl, of course they are!"

The stylist caught her assistant that had brought the coffee. Harrison estimated her to be in her late teens, though she dressed impeccably and had a bouffant style to her hair. He could tell she came from

Royal Again   Iain Benson

money and worked here for the prestige.

"Rosalind, be a dear and fetch the nail kit."

"Ma'am," Rosalind bobbed and vanished to the back room.

Justine's piercing glare returned to Harrison in the mirror, locking gazes. "What is your name, my girl?"

"Pippa." Harrison almost said his real name, wilting under the intense inspection.

"Phillipa or Penelope?" She pronounced Penelope like a song lyric.

"Penelope." Harrison wondered at Justine's conversational heading.

"Penelope is a beautiful name, too beautiful to be hidden under Pippa." Justine spat Pippa, as though expelling pips. "When you leave here, you will be a Penelope, not a Pippa."

Gulping, Harrison could only reply with a nod. The past two days had eroded his confident, self-assured demeanour, washed away in a tsunami of constant emotional action. Now, helpless and abducted by Justine, tied in place by a hairdresser's cape, he agreed.

A clanking, tinkling trolley announced Rosalind's reappearance.

Justine searched through the trolley. "Excellent. Most excellent. Rosalind, I am thinking of this deep pink. Her nails are shocking, but I know you are simply the best! Penelope, my dear, I shall be in repose while young Rosalind here, she will make your nails grow, as if by magic."

In a flounce of floral perfume, Justine vanished off down the aisle.

Rosalind took her place, pulling out a bar from the wall. Without the dramatics of Justine, she turned Harrison's chair and placed his hands on the bar.

"Hair and nails?" Harrison asked, more to make conversation than wanting to know. "I didn't know Justine Hollywood did nails."

"They're made from the same stuff," Rosalind's faint Irish accent told a story of moving to the big city some years ago. The capital's harsh accent slowly eroding the dulcet lilt of her homeland.

She lay various bottles and torture implements out on the bar and pulled up a stool to sit opposite.

"Justine was right. Your nails are atrocious. What is it you do for the prince?"

"It's embarrassing." Harrison realised how that sounded. "I used to be a cleaner. But when all the kerfuffle blew up, I nearly got sacked. Instead, he promoted me to his aide. However, I didn't look the part."

"Gosh." Rosalind, her mouth formed an O. "When the prince has come in before, he's always been so rude. The sort to let you get fired and disappear without a trace."

Harrison grunted a small chortle. He would have sacked Pippa immediately. Without even pausing. "People change."

With an industrial-grade sandpaper nail file, Rosalind began buffing and shaping what little nails Pippa had grown. "The papers said you slept with him, but you don't seem the type. Not to me, at least."

Harrison's slight head shake made the silver foil clash and rustle. "I was cleaning his apartment when Isabella came. Harrison didn't want her to see a maid still cleaning, so he put me in a closet."

"A closet?"

"Well, I call it that, but his closet is as big as my living room." Having seen Pippa's flat, Harrison knew that to be true.

"Still! See. Such a rude man."

"When he finished, I'd missed the bus back to town." Harrison had to concoct the story, but he'd told most of it so many times the lies came like truth. He lowered his voice to a conspiratorial whisper. "I think, what with the storm, what he didn't want was bad press. Cleaner forced to walk home through a storm after they kept me captive for six hours."

Rosalind's hand covered her mouth, her eyes wide. "Six?"

Harrison glanced surreptitiously from side to side and leaned forward a little. "He let me sleep in his bed, and he took the couch."

"That's something." Rosalind enjoyed the confessional, judging by her smile, as she began on Harrison's left hand. "He could have made you go on the couch. But why would you get fired for that?"

"It's less for that, and more for what happened yesterday." In truth, Harrison enjoyed the moment of intimacy, two young women chatting. Even if one took a metal spike and curved scissors to inflict maximum pain on Harrison's cuticles.

"What happened?"

"There was this enormous ball at the palace. President Cruz had come over for the wedding, so we, they, threw this lavish dance. I spent all morning polishing the floor. By the time the ball finished, it looked like I hadn't done it at all."

"I saw the President on the news. He's so dreamy. Did you meet him?"

Harrison shook his head, rustling again. "His security personnel noted that I had not signed out and back in. They stuck me in a bathroom!

Royal Again Iain Benson

Harrison had gone off to some opening or other, so he couldn't explain. I didn't know what to do." Those small words held a world of truth. He had been terrified and unable to explain the night's events, even slightly.

"You were so badly treated!"

"I know." Harrison winced as the cuticle came away on his left little finger. It seemed an odd place to have so many nerve endings. "Even though it wasn't my fault, I think I'd caused my supervisor too many problems or broken some rule or other, as I am positive she'd have fired me on the spot if it wasn't for Harrison."

"He promoted you?"

"To an aide," Harrison shrugged his free shoulder.

"Is it better paid?"

Harrison paused. He didn't know the staff salary structure. "I don't know yet. But so far, I'm in the most expensive salon in the country having my hair done by Justine Hollywood! Only days ago, I had my arm in a toilet!"

"That's why your nails are bad!" Rosalind laughed; a tinkling, pleasant sound filled with genuine warmth. "But you're here now. That must count for something."

She dunked Harrison's fingertips into a delicate blue liquid, which swilled an oily sensation deep into his nails.

"It's been a bit of a whirlwind."

Once dried, Rosalind coated Harrison's nails in a clear liquid, seeping a slight chill into his fingertips. Already the nails seemed longer, smoother and in a much better shape.

"Justine picked out this colour," Rosalind said, stroking a vibrant colour onto his little fingernail. "I think it's a lovely colour."

Harrison remembered the stylist describing it as pink, but that didn't come close to describing the deep colour. He supposed, at a push, pink described it, but there were tones of purples and maroon creating a lustrous sheen. If he'd had to name it, he'd call it enchanting.

"I think she picked well."

With a tight smile, Rosalind's head bent as she expertly stroked colour onto each nail. Once she'd finished his right hand, he lifted it to examine the hue as a total effect; the lights dancing along the liquid pigment, making his nails appear longer and luscious.

Rosalind finished up on his left hand, then began again on his right. She gave his nails three coats, finishing with a layer of clear liquid and a small box that emitted a high-pitched whine and a blue light. Finally, she rubbed his hands, pulling down from his wrist to the end of each finger. Strangely, that sent shivers down his whole body.

"Can I touch them?" He asked, unable to wrench his eyes away.

"Of course." Rosalind ran a finger along them before putting away her torture implements onto the trolley and sliding the bar back into the wall.

His nails slipped under his fingertips like oil, a tactile sensation he'd never experienced before. He ran his thumb over each nail slowly, enjoying their smooth surface. And, as promised, they appeared longer.

His genuine smile lit up his face. "Thank you, Rosalind."

"Any time." She picked up his empty mug. "Would you like another coffee?"

"Please. If I've got time."

Rosalind laughed. "Here, you always have time."

Justine reappeared in a riot of brightly coloured kaftan. She twisted Harrison's chair back to face the mirror and pulled off the silver paper, discarding them on the floor. Another assistant swept them up as soon as the glittery snow landed.

"I will have Beatrice wash this once more, and then we will begin."

Begin? I've been here ninety minutes already!

Begin they did. Beatrice, another elegantly dressed girl with Instagram makeup, led him to a sink, where she washed his hair. She seemed disinterested.

"Do you have any holidays planned?" Her question surprised Harrison. Everyone else had asked about the supposed affair.

It put him off guard. Harrison knew Pippa had told him. He searched his memory for the conversation, eventually remembering the destination.

"Albufeira, in Portugal." He desperately tried to remember all the details. "It's an all-inclusive hotel. I'm going with some girlfriends."

"That's nice," she said, absently, as though not hearing his answer. "Do you have conditioner?"

"Yes," he said, lapsing into silence.

When she'd finished and taken him back to the stylist's chair, he almost couldn't believe the transformation. The bird's nest had gone, as had the nondescript brown, replaced with a gorgeous chestnut that hung in rattails down past his shoulders. Justine grabbed a pair of scissors and started removing some of the length she had added in the first stage. Beatrice had gone from washing hair to sweeping hair, keeping the onyx

Royal Again
Iain Benson

floor spotless.

Voices from the shop front told Harrison of Pippa's return. Wherever she'd been, Harrison realised she'd had a better grasp on the time his hair would take than he had. She'd timed it perfectly, coinciding with Justine's ministrations with a hairdryer and finally a cutthroat razor.

Sniffing, Justine stepped back to admire her artistry. "Well, Penelope, my beautiful swan, you truly are taking breath in your beauty."

Harrison admired his reflection. The ponytail had gone, replaced with a volumized chestnut mane that framed his face. Bare of makeup, he realised Pippa's beauty, making his heart skip.

Justine removed the cape, revealing the baggy green sweater. She shuddered. "My advice to you, my girl, is to burn those clothes with your hair products."

Harrison had to agree. His hair turned the jumper into a shabby garment.

"Pippa," Pippa said as he came into reception. Her mouth dropped slightly, and her hands opened in admiration. "Wow."

"Shall we put this on your tab, sire?" the receptionist asked.

"Thank you." Pippa's dismissive wave matched Harrison's usual gesture perfectly. She took Harrison's arm and led him outside.

"Where have you been?" Harrison asked as they returned onto the street, the sudden chill a stark contrast to the salon's warmth.

"Here and there," Pippa replied enigmatically.

Harrison noticed a gap where Dillon's car should be. Reece stood by the door, falling in behind them as Pippa took Harrison's arm and steered her down the street. She saw Dillon's sleek saloon outside another shop.

"When I saw *Pretty Woman* as a girl," Pippa muttered, keeping her voice low so Reece couldn't hear, "I always wanted to be the girl who walked into a high-end boutique and told I couldn't afford it. Only to be able to pull out a wodge of cash and embarrass the sales assistant."

Harrison hadn't seen the film, but had a vague recollection of her description. He may have seen the scene. "I sense a 'but' coming."

"I thought I might be able to do it by proxy, but there's no point. Instead, I went to McNair and selected some clothes for you to try on."

Harrison started to ask how she'd know what would fit and suit but realised if anyone on the planet could do that, it would be Pippa herself.

They walked the four shops down to McNair's boutique, Harrison opening the door.

Hillary McNair herself waited; a rack of clothes selected and waiting. The clothes shop's interior smelled of sandalwood and incense, making Harrison momentarily lightheaded. Spotlights punctured the otherwise gloomy store, creating oases of brightness near the mirrors and clothes. What clothes Hillary had put on display adorned mannequins. Nobody came into her store on spec, but Pippa didn't fall into the classification of ordinary and the designer had accommodated royalty spectacularly.

Pippa handed Harrison a pantsuit in emerald green with a paler green leaf motif and nude courts. "Try these on."

"That will look stunning on you, my lovely," Hillary said, guiding him to a changing area at the back, pulling the clothes rack with her. Four walls of mirrors reflected infinite images at him. He felt ashamed seeing the clothing choice he'd made that morning. Hillary pursed her lips as she inspected the jumper.

"I take it you won't be wanting this," she waved dismissively, sneering, "*outfit* anymore?"

Harrison glanced at the door, wondering if Pippa would want it. He decided she wouldn't. "No."

Putting on the pantsuit, he discovered double-jointed acrobats designed women's clothing. However, it fit perfectly, except the leg length brushed the floor. He slipped into the heels, feeling the constriction around his toes.

Hillary gave Harrison a critical once over, satisfied. "Prince Harrison selected different shoes for each outfit. He seems remarkably knowledgeable about women's clothing."

"He's quite in touch with his feminine side." Harrison barely kept a straight face.

Swaying, he took a few tentative steps. Pippa only owned low heels. These higher heels wobbled more than he expected. Muscle memory kicked in, preventing him from twisting an ankle as he twisted to appraise the completed garment.

"Fabulous, my lovely, now take that off and let us try some more."

Harrison dressed and undressed into a score of different outfits, all elegantly cut. The designer tossed some into a corner, when they didn't work, others she rehung. After half an hour of dressing up, the rack contained ten dresses, a pantsuit, a skirt, four blouses and two pairs of trousers.

Harrison wondered if she would now have to pick. Hillary opened

Royal Again   Iain Benson

the mirrored door to allow Pippa to see the dress Harrison wore. Black strapped block heels completed the jasmine dress with a sunflower design, cut low in a vee at his neck. His chest shone, bare, in the light. He needed a necklace, but apart from the studs in his ears he'd never dared remove, Pippa didn't seem to wear jewellery.

"Is that the selection?" Pippa asked, pointing at the clothes rack.

"You have a good eye, sire," Hillary told him. "Most suited, but some would require a bit of alteration. You said you needed them today, though."

Pippa glanced briefly at the discard pile. "Don't immediately discount them. We'll come back and have some alterations done."

"As you wish," Hillary inclined her head.

More costs found their way onto the royal tab.

"I take it I'm wearing this now?" Harrison gestured up and down the dress. Inside the shop, he felt comfortable. The prospect of leaving a shop wearing a dress, however beautiful, flooded dread from his jaw to his toes. He hesitated by the door, controlling his breathing. In through his nose, out in a controlled stream through tightened lips.

Pippa stroked Harrison's arm. "You look amazing."

Harrison's arm tingled where she'd touched. A tracery of electricity. It gave him the strength and will to open the door and step out onto the street.

Nor had Pippa finished their morning outing. Dillon and Reece collected the bags and put them in the car as Pippa led Harrison across the road into Fleetwood, an unremarkable shop from the outside. Harrison had never heard of it. Inside, he paused and blinked. The riot of colour made him think of Jackson Pollock using David Hockney's palette.

A smiling woman with a broad face and masses of curls waited, expectantly.

"You must be Pippa!" She had a broad Jamaican accent. "My name is Femi." She lowered her voice theatrically. "Prince Harrison here has asked me to give you a makeover, and I'm so looking forward to it! This will be spectacular!"

She led him to a three-sided mirrored booth containing an infinitely reflected padded chair. Pippa had a wry smile as she leaned against the counter by the door. Stunned, Harrison allowed himself to be seated, watching Pippa. On either side, what Harrison initially saw as mechanic's toolboxes turned out to be containers for makeup.

Femi whistled as she slipped an Alice band into Harrison's new hairstyle, worrying him for a moment that she would undo the sculpture Justine had created for him.

"Oh! What a pretty face. Let's start by cleaning those pores!"

Potions and lotions, powders and creams came and went. Where Justine had been a sculptor of hair, Femi's skills lay as a portrait artist. In one hand, Harrison saw brushes protruding like tiger claws from her knuckles, pulled out and dabbed in assorted colours before Femi applied them to his face. The energetic beautician fussed and hummed, her tongue sticking from the corner of her mouth, her ample bosom banging into his face more than once. Occasionally she'd explain what she did, but Harrison found the words incomprehensible. Contours were on maps. Shadows and highlights were for paintings. As to feathering and blending, he had never encountered the concept before.

"Ta-dah!" Femi stepped back, removing the Alice band, her lips plumped in self-congratulation. "You are so beautiful. Please enjoy."

Harrison stepped back, stunned at his reflection.

Pippa had gone. In her place, Penelope. Pippa had been right. Nobody would think the woman standing here bore any relation to the maid.

He couldn't quite comprehend his feelings about the vision he saw. Stunning, yes; elegant, absolutely. He'd only started to become accustomed to seeing Pippa's face in the mirror, but the woman Pippa had been waiting to become left him speechless.

"Femi, you're a genius," Pippa said from the door, also admiring Harrison. "A makeup Michelangelo. Could you bag up all the products you used?"

"Certainly! Your Highness!" Femi bounced over to her makeup selection. "I think Pippa would really suit autumnal tones for her lips and eyes, so I'll throw in those colours as well."

Harrison heard the exchange but could not take his eyes off the mirror. With Pippa mentioning the scene from the movie, he wondered if her fantasy had been to go through this. And he had stolen it from her. That thought brought a prick of a tear to his eye.

A waft of cold air and a hubbub entered the shop with Reece.

"Sire," Reece muttered. "The press is here."

Pippa scratched her eyebrow, lips compressed. "They were bound to get wind eventually."

Royal Again   **Iain Benson**

"What do you want to do, sir?"

Tilting her head in consideration, Pippa surprised Harrison. "I guess I will need to answer some questions."

"Very good, sir." Reece slipped out again and gestured at the large group of people gathering outside the shop.

"I'll try and make sure they get a good shot of your frontage, Femi," Pippa said, smiling. "Pippa, shall we go?"

Harrison paused. "If they hear that name, it could turn ugly."

"Don't worry. I've got this."

14
Pippa: Lunch

She hoped her confident outward appearance would translate into inner confidence to help her get through the crowd outside.

Seeing Harrison made over gave her hope. If her mum saw her in those clothes, with that hair and makeup, Pippa doubted she'd recognise her; never mind the hordes waiting outside who didn't know the original Pippa or the elegant woman she'd become.

Pushing into the street, Pippa gave the press and paparazzi a smile. Photo flashes made vision difficult.

"Prince Harrison, who's the woman?" called one reporter.

Others followed with a barrage of questions from all sides. "Is she the maid you slept with? Did you sleep with a maid? Is the wedding still going ahead? What brings you into the city today?"

Holding up her hands, Pippa made a quietening gesture.

"The woman is my aide, Penelope. No, she's not a maid. Does she look like a maid? I did not and would not sleep with my maid, my aide, or any of my staff. The wedding is still going ahead. I'm deeply in love with Isabella."

In her peripheral vision, Harrison reacted as she said that. Disappointment flitted across his face. Perhaps she'd put a little too much gravitas into that statement. She wanted to comfort him, tell him she'd lied to the press, kept the myth alive. Or, she'd not seen disappointment, she'd seen realisation and Harrison *was* in love with Isabella, despite everything. The knowledge that the wedding would go ahead regardless of her personal feelings towards anybody kept her focused. A small knot of sadness hit her heart. If they didn't swap back, she knew Harrison would end up with Dillon.

Did the jealousy she felt come from Harrison being with Dillon, or Dillon being with Harrison?

She didn't know.

Harrison's vulnerable side had shown through. She didn't hate him anymore.

The storm of questions continued, her own circling emotions creating an extra dimension of turmoil.

Royal Again   Iain Benson

"No more questions," she said. "The only story here is my upcoming marriage. Now, if you'll excuse me, I have one more stop to make before lunch and the Hitchberg premiere this afternoon."

Questions answered, most reporters dispersed. Others, especially those with cameras, hung back, snapping more pictures, capturing Harrison as he accompanied Pippa down the street to the jewellers.

"Hopefully, they'll get bored," Pippa muttered, steering Harrison into the jewellers.

Upfront, Harrison questioned what she'd said. "I don't know how you can lie so easily. Neither of us love Isabella. I doubt she loves me, either. Or you."

Pippa shook her head. "It'd make the future easier, if I did."

Harrison lapsed into silence, but the angle of his lips told Pippa the future currently lacked appeal. For them both.

Pippa had already been into the jewellers. Two bags waited on the counter. Trying to dispel the impending doom the press had instilled in her, she forced a smile she didn't feel.

"There's some jewellery here, but I think in that dress you'll need a necklace and earrings." Pippa rested her hands on the jeweller's central glass counter, suspiciously watching the beefy security man by the door in his blue sweater with his shaved head and tattooed neck. She didn't belong in a place like this, but Harrison did, so she projected unfelt confidence.

Harrison leaned over and appraised the array of sparkling diamonds and coloured stones lit into a cascade of brilliance by the lighting in the box. On the case's far side, two attentive men waited, with broad grins plastered on their faces. They'd had their best day ever.

"How about those?" Harrison had a good eye, selecting dangling earrings with solitaires at the tips and a matching necklace.

"We'll take them. To wear now." Pippa waved a dismissive hand.

The sales assistant on the left leapt into action, unlocking the case and taking out the velvet display board. Nothing had a price tag. If you needed to ask, perhaps try a different shop.

Reverently, the assistant lifted the necklace, draping it around Harrison's neck. Harrison held his hair up and shivered as the cool metal created a sensuous electricity. The jeweller closed the fiddly clasp, letting the delicate strands of silver lie against Harrison's skin. With some difficulty, Harrison removed the gold studs from his ears, replacing them with sterilised dangling diamonds. Pippa had to admit they formed a finishing touch to Harrison's ensemble. The studs lay discarded on the counter. Pippa couldn't leave them there; her mum had given them to her. She slipped them into her jacket pocket.

Silently, the other assistant held up a mirror so Harrison could see how they set off the dress, the makeup and his hair.

"Perfect," Harrison breathed.

Nodding in approval, Pippa had to agree, though she wished she'd been in Harrison's place. The whole morning fulfilled a lifelong romantic fantasy for her. Ever since she'd seen Julia Roberts pampered by Hugh Grant, the idea of being the one treated like a princess had been her dream.

Once again, Reece took the bags acting as part security, part sherpa, to clear a path to Dillon's car.

The store security guard helped ensure Pippa had space amid the photographers and reporters. Stoically, she ignored them, allowing the car to finally shut them out.

Before Harrison joined her, she overheard Dillon. "You are stunning, Pip."

Harrison's head dipped, a strand of hair tucked shyly behind his ear, revealing his neck and the glinting diamond hanging from his earlobe. Pippa took a breath, smothering a sudden surge of testosterone that gave her an urge to cup Harrison's neck with one hand, and kiss him.

"I've booked a table at The Hedera," Pippa said, regaining her composure with some difficulty. "Strangely, they had a spare table."

"Weird that." Harrison's smile let Pippa know he understood. Harrison smoothed the folds of his dress.

Leaving the crowd of reporters behind, they drove the twenty minutes to the Art Deco-fronted restaurant near the parliament district. Pippa admired how Harrison turned gracefully in his seat and exited the vehicle, but almost lost her composure at the way Dillon helped him up.

"I'm not happy about this, sir," Reece said, sticking close behind as they crossed the wide pavement and up the two steps into the restaurant.

"Relax, Reece," Pippa told him, clasping the security man's arm. "This is totally impromptu. I doubt any assassin would have the time to organise a hit."

All around, tall Georgian buildings mixed with more modern white-clad skyscrapers. A pair of old Gothic theatres had pedestrians mingling outside, camera phones capturing the moment they saw the prince. At the door, an older gentleman with a top hat and forest green livery greeted

Royal Again   Iain Benson

them, tipping his hat to the prince and her guest.

A maître'd met them inside. Ramrod straight, his grey hair swept back from a haughty face.

"Good afternoon, your highness," the maître'd said, his accent identifying him most definitely as French. Pippa had to suppress a giggle. Harrison's father would have apoplexy if he discovered what she'd done this morning instead of going to the gym.

Two young servers arrived, a young man and a young woman, both in identical black and white uniforms with aprons around their waists. Dark, slicked-back hair and eager demeanours they gave the impression that anything Pippa asked for, they would somehow get. She wondered if she should ask for panda burgers.

She decided not to ask, in case a member of staff went to the city zoo.

A triangular, dark wooden bar filled the room's centre, surrounded by the lunchtime clientele, with a further ring of tables covered with white linen tablecloths. Each table had an ornate centrepiece floral arrangement, and every table held diners. Except for theirs in the wedge-shaped restaurant's narrowest corner. Lit on two sides by mullioned stained-glass windows that allowed in shafts of brilliant coloured light but obscured the outside world to create a rainbow effect striped across the table. Who had previously had this table when the crown prince rocked up for an impromptu meal? It didn't matter. *Rank hath privilege.* A slight dais raised the table slightly from the main dining area, partly cordoned off by a waist-high wooden balustrade.

Led through the restaurant, Pippa heard "Harrison" like a susurration rise from the hushed conversations, mingled with a few queries as to the woman accompanying her. Let them wonder.

The two servers pulled out the Rococo chairs with plump, red velvet seats.

"Today's fish special is pan-fried sea bass with lemon, whilst the soup is a thyme-infused chicken."

"Hmm," Pippa said, cupping her chin and tilting her head. "Penelope, when is the premier?"

Harrison made a show of checking his phone. "It's at three, sir."

Pippa twisted her wrist to look at Harrison's watch. They had about an hour to eat if they were to make it on time. "I do not believe we have time for both a soup and a fish course."

"Certainly not, sir." Harrison said, his eyes narrowing.

"Also, I do not think we should eat chicken before fish." Internally, Pippa convulsed with laughter at her preposterous pomposity; a playful smile the only betrayal of her fun.

"I will inform Chef," said the male server.

Still tempted to order something completely whacky, like a southern fried chicken, Pippa instead gestured to Harrison. Perfectly acceptable to ask the lady about her preference first.

"What would you like?"

Harrison turned to his server and asked her: "Does Chef have the Persian aubergine and poussin still available?"

"Yes, ma'am." The young woman gave a little bobbed curtsey.

"I'll have that."

"Make it two," Pippa said, glad Harrison had been before.

Both servers bobbed their heads, the young man also giving a curtsey.

Alone, Pippa finally allowed her giggle to surface. Harrison joined in.

"I never do this," Harrison whispered. "Pa will have a fit."

"Let him. In two days, I'll be married, and we still don't know how to switch back! It's a slightly more pressing priority."

"We've not had much time to figure that out," Harrison admitted, wearing a glum expression. "We'll have no time tonight, either."

"Ah, yes, we go to Isabella's for that dinner."

"I could research it while you're there." Harrison cupped his chin in his hand, Pippa able to fully admire his nails. "It's 'we' now, is it?"

"I can't do a dinner without you," Pippa admitted. She'd put off thinking about spending the night at Isabella's mansion. It left her wanting to sneak through the kitchens and vanish. "I don't know the first thing about what to wear, how to eat or even which spoon I need for the frothed cucumber coulis."

"Outside in," Harrison said. "Even if you take me, I won't be at the table."

"We'll need to figure something out. Do you know sign-language?"

"No. Do you?"

"Also no. But I need you to feed me lines. I don't know the names of anybody who will be there, other than Isabella. Who are her parents?"

"Frederick and Amestris."

"Weird name."

Royal Again — Iain Benson

"She's Greek. She's the Greek King's youngest daughter."

"I've got no chance of surviving the evening. They'll realise I'm an imposter immediately."

When Harrison said nothing immediately, she knew he agreed. "There is a *lot* of protocol. Amestris' parents will be there. They'll expect you to talk to them."

"The Greek king and queen? I can't speak Greek!"

"They speak English. Both have an Oxford education. Pavlos also went to Eton."

Pippa gestured in exasperation. "This is what I mean. You *know* all this stuff. All I know about Greece is what they taught us in school. I didn't even know they had a royal family! If I lasted ten minutes, it'd be a miracle."

Their servers returned, placing wide, oval dishes containing a small, whole chicken on sliced layers of aubergine, with some sauce and vegetables as an artistic accompaniment. Pippa didn't know if she'd like it or not.

Behind the servers appeared a rotund man, wearing a hairnet and chef's cap atop a bald head. He had the bushiest eyebrows Pippa had ever seen. In one hand, he had a bottle of red wine.

"Chef Andoni," whispered Harrison, barely moving his lips.

"Prince Harrison, your highness! Your visit here is of a most welcome surprise!" He had a bold Spanish accent, rolling each 'r' with accompanying hand gestures.

Smoothly, Pippa slipped into her role. "Sorry for the short notice, Andoni. I had business nearby, and your Persian aubergine is possibly the best dish in the city."

"You are too kind, sire, too kind!" He proffered the bottle, cradled in one hand like an infant. "May I suggest this two thousand and two Garnacha from my vineyard in Catalonia?"

Pippa gave a nod, the chef himself opening his wine with practised twists, pouring a little rich red into a wine glass already on the table.

He waited expectantly. Pippa mentally kicked herself when she realised he meant for her to taste it.

Swirling it around the glass, as she'd seen on television, she inhaled the aroma, putting her nose right inside, surprised at the perfumes it released, reminding her of blackberry picking. As it slowly crawled back down the sides, light from the windows sparkled through the ruby liquid. Something else she'd never seen. She'd previously drunk red wine in dark nightclubs. Usually under protest, suffering the vinegary concoction such venues sold. "The body is incredible, Andoni."

The chef made appreciative noises while she admired the wine. "It has clingy legs, sire!"

Pippa's usual wine drinking method involved glugging, but she suspected this would be indecorous. She recalled how she'd seen Harrison drinking wine the night before and took the glass stem between two fingers. She took a sip; the tannins caressing her tongue with explosions of berries.

"I'm getting forest fruits and wood smoke," she said, deliberately being preposterous. "Autumn days blackberry picking, a nearby cottage burning hickory."

"This is music to my ears," Andoni announced. "Your palette is, as ever, so sharp. The wood smoke, so few get. Dios Mio!"

Happy, Andoni filled their glasses and retreated to his kitchen.

"You handled that well," Harrison said, barely moving his lips.

"But I needed your help. It's why I need you tonight."

"We will have to work something out." Harrison's crooked smile made him cute.

"There's too much to do and no time to do it in," Pippa said, stirring her aubergine with a fork. She tried a slice. Her tongue exploded again. "Oh my god, this is delicious."

Harrison laughed.

15
Pippa: Premier

As the car stopped at the red carpet, the door perfectly aligned. Pippa's breath caught at the line of people hemmed in outside the thinnest of ropes. They made a gauntlet of well-wishers to run.

"That's quite a crowd." Pippa's imposter syndrome kicked in.

Ravishing, Harrison, walked a pace behind. He acted more at ease than Pippa could ever hope to achieve. She envied his social skills.

"It's fine, shake a few hands on the way up, don't give autographs, ignore the press and don't forget to smile!" Harrison stage whispered.

Plastering a rictus smile of fear on her face, Pippa took a deep breath and stepped onto the red carpet. She found it hard to believe that this time last week, she'd cleaned the palace wine glasses. All two hundred.

"Harrison! Harrison!" bayed the crowd. Pippa zigzagged up the carpet, shaking hands and greeting people.

"Where's Isabella?" yelled a woman from the crowd.

"Getting her dress fitted for Sunday," Pippa called back.

"I wish you could kiss me like you kissed her," said a girl of about fifteen in the front row. She had a dreamy, faraway expression, reminding Pippa of Harrison's popularity.

"My security team wouldn't approve, I'm afraid," Pippa said, leaning forward. She took the girl's hand and briefly brush the back of it with her lips.

The girl almost fainted, but her squealing kept her conscious.

"I'd say you were a natural," Harrison muttered as they reached the doors to the cinema. "But there's nothing natural about us."

"No, because if I were you and you were me, I'd consider it a fairy tale, but this situation is too stressful!"

"Fairy tales are meant to be Grimm."

The cinema had cordoned off certain sections to corral the visiting important people.

Pippa bit her lips at seeing the concessionary. "Do you think we're allowed popcorn?"

"I'm pretty sure you can have anything," Harrison replied. "You're a prince."

"Even a plate of nachos and cheese with a large diet Coke?"
"Diet Coke?"
"I've got to watch your figure."
"Thanks."

A friendly usher led them to a seat. "Can I take a drink or food order?"

"Unsweetened black coffee, please," Pippa asked.

"Same for me," Harrison added. "Please."

The usher inclined his head, disappearing off. Coming the other way, actors from the film and other various celebrities filed in, taking seats. The cinema filled up slowly.

The film's director came to stand in front of everybody. Danny Hitchberg's smiling face backdropped by the cinema screen.

"Ladies, gentlemen, thank you all for coming," he said, clasping his hands, head bowed. "This film is personal for me. My grandfather's cousin fought in this battle."

The director's speech made Pippa long for the adverts and trailers she'd normally have to endure. Fortunately, a coffee materialised, giving her something else to concentrate on until the lights dimmed and the film began.

Harrison enjoyed the film, but it left Pippa cold. Too much focus on war and death. Give her a rom-com over explosions any time.

Before they could leave the cinema, Pippa first had to go down the line of cast and crew. Hitchberg himself headed the queue up.

"Interesting film," Pippa told him, keeping her true opinion to herself. "It was very... accurate."

"I wanted accuracy," Hitchberg said, with a warm smile of all teeth and no eyes. "It tells the survivor's traumatic story."

"That really came through," Pippa said, shaking Hitchberg's hand, secretly amazed that *she* had shaken *Hitchberg's* hand. After that, she went down the line, briefly chatting with various movie stars. The cast reminded Pippa of the wives of Henry the Eighth. During the film, some actors died, some survived and at least one got beheaded.

At the end, after meeting everybody except the caterer, she got to leave.

"Argh!" she said as they came into weak sunlight. "Hated the film, the cast still look traumatised and I hate leaving the cinema in daylight. It feels wrong!"

Royal Again   Iain Benson

"All of that, plus smile for the cameras," Harrison said as they ran the gauntlet back to the car.

Pippa shook hands and posed for photographs with the people in the crowd who loved Harrison. The insignificant gesture enriched their lives for a moment of Pippa's. One little girl gave her a shy smile, whispering.

"Oh, I'm sorry," Pippa knelt, much to Reece's consternation. "Could you say that again? I couldn't quite hear."

"Your girlfriend is beautiful," the girl blushed and turned away.

"Thank-you, I'll be sure to tell her."

Pippa returned to stand beside Harrison, a few pictures and the breath-releasing safety the car offered.

The exchange with the girl intrigued Harrison. "What did the little girl say?"

"She said you were beautiful."

Harrison gave a slight smile and put on his seatbelt. "That's nice."

"Well, technically, she said my girlfriend. Which would be Isabella. But I think she *meant* you."

Dillon watched the exchange with a bemused expression. "Did you enjoy the film, sir?"

"I think they should have used actors who have actually lost a limb for the more traumatic scenes. It may have been less graphic."

"I might go and see that as well," Reece said to Dillon. "The trailers look amazing."

"Reece?" Harrison leant forward. Pippa saw Dillon's eyes flick to the mirror, glancing down Harrison's cleavage. She felt like cracking him over the back of his head.

"Pip?"

"Could you get me those little earpieces for two-way conversation?"

"Sure." Reece twisted in the seat. "Why?"

Pippa understood Harrison's plan. "I've got the dinner tonight and I've not been able to do all my usual research on the other guests. I don't want to accidentally think Isabella's uncle is a waiter."

Reece gave a sharp nod. His self-satisfied expression gave Pippa the impression he approved of wiring the prince up for sound. "When we get back to the palace, I'll sort you some comms."

16
Harrison: Revelation

At the main entrance, Pippa headed off inside with Reece. Being staff, Dillon drove Harrison to the rear entrance. As they walked back from the garage, Harrison discovered the little-known fact that a man must have designed gravel paths.

After stumbling a few times, his heels catching in the small stones, Dillon gallantly offered his arm, his other arm laden with half the bags from their shopping trip.

Not wishing to twist an ankle, Harrison took it, murmuring a grateful 'thanks'. He shifted his bags to his other hand. The support didn't prevent his heels from sticking, twisting, and pulling back, but it gave him the stability to make it to the paved steps up to the security lodge.

"Do you want a coffee before you go up?" Dillon asked.

"Sure," Harrison replied, placing his palm on the sign-in screen.

George had started on his night shift. He greeted them as they came in.

"Evening, Dillon," the security guard said in his friendly tone.

His gruff face creased in puzzlement at seeing Harrison. He checked the screen. "Pippa?"

Harrison gave him a broad smile. "I scrub up okay, don't I?"

"Aye, that you do." He let them both through with a cheery smile.

Instead of up to Harrison's room, they dropped by the cafeteria, filling two chunky mugs from the pot on the serving counter. Harrison gratefully took the weight off his feet. Dillon twisted his chair and leaned back, resting his head on the white-painted plaster.

"I find it weird." Dillon stared up at the bare fluorescent tube.

"What?"

"A few days ago, you were skirting termination and hated Harrison. And now. Not so much. In fact, you're basically inseparable."

Harrison propped his chin on clasped hands, elbows on the table, in direct contravention of every mealtime rule he'd ever had to observe. He gave Dillon his most level gaze. The sight of Dillon's stubble from the day made him, more attractive. *To my female hormones!* Harrison gave a little shake of his head at his errant thoughts.

"I think forced proximity has made us like each other a little more. Trust me! I would rather the world's press didn't treat me like a slut, even if it meant 'skirting termination'."

Dillon pressed his lips together tightly. "Yeah. You need to make sure they pay you more for being his aide, though. That's the top job you can get here. Don't let him palm you off with new clothes and stuff."

"You're right. I'll make sure Harrison knows what I'm worth."

"What hours do you do now?"

Harrison shrugged, still resting his chin on his hands. "Seems to be twenty-fours a day at the moment."

"I'm worried for you."

Harrison picked up his mug and sipped. "Don't be. I'm going to have to get a move on. I need to put together an overnight bag. Are you driving us there?"

"I'm finished for the night now. It'll probably be Olly."

Harrison could recognise three or four drivers for the family, but he thought there might be more. *I really should pay more attention!*

"Shame," Harrison gulped coffee and put the mug on the table to get to his feet.

Dillon's hand covered his. "I see how you look at him, you know. He'd never even consider one of us, no matter how well he's treating you now. I think you're blinded by all the pizzazz. He's never been a good guy."

Tilting his head, Harrison gave Dillon a skewed smile. He'd come to that conclusion himself. "Harrison will be married in a couple of days. And not to me."

"He has money, charm, and good looks." Dillon released her hand. "I could never compete."

Gathering the bags, Harrison blew Dillon a kiss. "Two out of three isn't bad, you know."

"I'm not that poor!"

"It's the good looks you're missing."

Harrison left Dillon chuckling.

How did Pippa see him? Did she like him? Her body certainly did!

Halfway up the staircase, he paused. Partly in introspection and partly with his calves screaming in agony. Deciding he could do nothing about neither Pippa's love life nor his calves, Harrison finished climbing up and headed to his room. He struggled inside and dropped the bags on the bed. The bed looked tempting. Lying back, arms spread, eyes closed.

Heaven. However, he firmly parked any notion of napping and lay the emerald-green shimmery dress on the bed, hanging the rest of his new possessions. A pair of black courts with an even higher heel than his current pair looked like they matched the best.

At which point had he crossed into thinking normality was wearing a dress?

He pulled the current dress over his head and hung it up.

A knock on the door made his heart leap into his mouth.

Thinking Pippa had come across, he called out: "Come in, it's open."

Reece opened the door.

Realising he only had on underwear, blood drained from Harrison's face.

"Sorry," Reece said. "Only you said come in."

A long heartbeat, and Harrison chose to style out the awkwardness. "It's fine." Harrison chuckled. "It's not like I'm completely naked."

Grabbing the dress, Harrison pulled it on. Although he had Pippa's shoulders, he had yet to master the art of double-jointed wiggling to reach the zip. After a few half-hearted attempts, he gave up.

"Could you do me up?" Harrison turned his back on the security man.

Reece entered the apartment and dropped some items on the bed next to the remaining bags. He zipped up the dress. "I can see why Dillon likes you."

"My sunny personality?"

"Yeah, that as well."

Harrison spent a moment admiring himself in the long mirror, smoothing down the wrinkles. "Have you found the earpiece?"

Giving Harrison a flicker of a smile, Reece took a small box from the paper bag. He opened the plastic case like an engagement ring. "Yes."

"You're supposed to kneel. And it's me that says 'yes'." Harrison's lopsided smile made Reece laugh.

He pulled at his nose with a subconscious gesture, his tone sardonic. "I'll bear it in mind if Zoe leaves me."

Putting the earpiece in his own ear, Reece handed him a second. Harrison slipped it in, feeling the slight pressure the plastic put on his ear canal.

"Can you hear me?" Harrison asked.

"I can see you as well. You're standing in front of me." Amused,

Reece shook his head. "I'll go in the bathroom."

Harrison sat on the bed, feet barely touching the floor.

Reece's voice came in his ear. "Testing."

"I can hear you."

"Fabulous. While I have you alone as well, I don't know what you've done to Harrison, but he's a changed guy."

Puzzled, Harrison had to find out more. What pounding would his ego get this time? "How do you mean?"

"He used my name for the first time, today. He's never been impromptu in his entire life and as well he has been a complete jerk about whatever appearances are on his schedule."

"That can't be down to me." Harrison realised his security chief's remarks hit home. He lowered his eyes.

"I don't know who else it could be." Reece left the bathroom, removing the earpiece. He wiped it with a sterilising cloth. "He likes you. It's a shame he's getting married."

"And he's a prince and I'm staff."

"True." Reece placed the earpiece back into its box. "There are stories. His family has a history with staff affairs. His grandmother had a fling with a stableboy, as well as Charlotte with my predecessor. Only stories. No proof. Though Charlotte got locked away before her wedding to Will. For over a week, as well. There must be a reason as well for that, doesn't there?"

"I." Harrison paused. It couldn't be true, could it? "I didn't know that."

"It's not widely talked about. I'm guessing the cleaning crew don't get the insider goss. Like I said as well. Only stories, but they sound common."

"Are you suggesting I try seducing Harrison?"

Reece's hands went up defensively. "I would never suggest anything like that. It's your heart that would be broken as well. He's always going to marry Isabella. As well, there's nothing you, me, or he can do about it. If we swapped places, I might give it a go, just for the giggles."

"No. Duty sucks sometimes." Harrison's feelings came through in his words.

Reece gave a self-satisfied laugh and a wink. "I knew you liked him. I can keep a secret as well as anybody. I won't tell Dillon he's the second choice. It's unlikely he'd keep his job having a fisticuff fight with the future king."

Images of Dillon and Pippa scrapping it out in a fountain crossed Harrison's mind. "Who said he was the second choice?"

Reece's eyebrows went up, his smile turned sardonic. "I can keep that a secret as well."

Harrison laughed. "And I'll never tell Zoe you proposed with an earpiece."

Reece clicked his tongue, making a gun sound. "I'll let you pack. We leave in thirty. You'll get thirty minutes on the earpieces and you'll need to recharge the case as well."

As the door closed, Harrison had a little practice in the higher heels, thinking about Reece's revelations. His mother having an affair shocked him. He wondered if Pa knew. And his grandmother! He believed that one. Even though they *might* have had an affair ahead of her marriage, it didn't mean they continued it after, or indeed that he should have one with Pippa. Also, he realised, he'd never really had a conversation with any of his staff. They seemed nice people. He'd not known Reece's wife's name, nor how easily he laughed.

He would ensure that changed if he ever found a way to switch back with Pippa.

Already, his calves complained at the heels and it had been a mere five minutes. He hunted through a bag for flats, when he caught sight of his bottom in the long mirror. Harrison gave his backside a lascivious once-over and slapped it, changing his mind about the ballet pumps. Giggling he emptied his little suitcase for refilling as an overnight bag.

Harrison got all the bathroom products he needed wherever he went. His suits magically appeared in any room where he stayed overnight. He'd never even had to take underwear. His aide wouldn't be so lucky.

17
Pippa: Dinner

"You look amazing." Pippa whispered as they walked from the car into the mansion's front entrance. "I didn't realise I could look quite that good."

"Thank you," Harrison replied. "I got donated good bone structure."

Isabella's mansion spread out on both sides. It had taken two minutes to drive from the road to the front door, through manicured gardens with ponds, copses and topiary, all designed and well-maintained. The Georgian-fronted property curved around the circular drive. A double-fronted door opened into a marble-clad hallway with a pair of wide curving staircases heading up to a gallery. Straight ahead, under the gallery, double doors opened onto the Main Hall.

Several people milled about. More through the bi-folding doors around a large table. Standing near the entrance to the Main Hall, Pippa identified Amestris, Isabella's mother, by her similarity to Isabella. The man with her had to be Frederick. An older couple would be Isabella's maternal grandparents. The Greek King sported a black suit, with a ruffled white shirt and a cummerbund in blue and white stripes. He'd slicked back his thinning, dark hair. In contrast, the Greek Queen had chosen a floor-length chiffon and lace gown in claret red, with her silver hair piled up to make her taller than her husband. Isabella's father wore a dark grey suit with a white shirt and jazzy yellow and black waistcoat. Isabella's mother's silvery cocktail dress came to her knee. She'd straightened her long, black hair giving it a lustrous sheen. Given both her parents had deep black hair, Pippa wondered if Isabella dyed her hair blonde.

Harrison confirmed their identities. "Pavlos and Katherine," he whispered. "I'll wait by the door, listening, prompting."

"Have you ever met them?"

"I've met Isabella's parents, obviously. Not her grandparents, no. But He went to the same college in Oxford I later attended. Magdalen. I did law, he did politics."

Suddenly alone, with Harrison heading in a different direction, Pippa's heart pounded. She put a smile on her face, opened her posture and made a beeline for her future family, while Isabella peeled away from another group, angling to arrive at her parents at the same time as Pippa.

Isabella had gone with a calf-length golden dress, two stripes of sequins running from her cuffs to the hem.

Pippa held both Isabella's hands and planting a chaste kiss on her lips. "Isabella! You are the very definition of beauty."

"Is that better than amazing?" Harrison asked in her ear. Pippa could almost hear the arched eyebrow.

Pippa turned to Isabella's parents.

"You call him Freddie," Harrison whispered into her ear.

"Freddie, Amestris. So nice to see you again."

Harrison kept talking. "You'll need to bow to Pavlos and Katherine. Feet together, from the waist, neck straight, arms by your side."

Keeping her smile in place, Pippa turned to the Greek royals. Harrison's words echoed around her head. Pippa put her feet together and bent from the waist, sure she'd forget something.

"That's enough." Harrison snapped.

As Pippa straightened, Pavlos stepped forward, his hand out. "My future grandson! It is fine to meet you finally!"

Pippa's hand got a thorough shaking, both of Pavlos's hands wrapped around hers, the King's cool, dry skin gripping like a newspaper bandage.

"It is good to finally meet you too," Pippa said, her mind racing, clashing ideas and desires causing her to stumble. She turned to the queen.

"Kiss the knuckles of her *left* hand."

Oddly specific. "And you, your majesty."

She took the queen's left hand and brushed her lips across Katherine's knuckles.

"Enchanted. I see why you like this boy," Katherine told Isabella, in quite a loud voice. "Manners and a handsome devil."

Isabella took Pippa's hand, pulling her towards the Main Hall. "There's dancing after dinner."

Pippa worked out from Isabella's incongruous shy smile that she had been thinking about the kiss. "You want another dance?"

"I think she wants another kiss." Harrison said. Pippa glanced over. Harrison's smirk was visible across the foyer. He waved at her with wriggling fingers.

"I do." Isabella followed Pippa's gaze, seeing Harrison. "Who's the woman you brought?"

"That's Penelope," Pippa said. "She's my aide."

"I've not seen her before. She's very glamorous."

"I decided she would fit in more easily without suspicion."

"Why do you need her?"

"She's primarily one of my researchers." Pippa leaned in closer to Isabella's ear. "I might appear I know everybody and have instant recall, but I don't."

"I did wonder." Isabella squeezed Pippa's fingers. "It's fine."

"Jealous?"

"You've brought a stunning woman with you to your fiancée's soiree, after news articles about sleeping with a maid." Isabella shook her head. "Not at all. I trust you."

"So you should."

Isabella snatched a champagne flute from a passing waiter. "Shall we go through?"

Passing Harrison by the door, Pippa felt a slight tug on her hand as Isabella dallied slightly to appraise Harrison. She glanced around, seeing Isabella and Harrison exchange looks. Harrison's surprise and Isabella's frosty glare.

Isabella sat to Pippa's left, her grandfather to Pippa's right.

Harrison filled Pippa in. "I don't think Isabella likes Penelope very much."

Pippa muttered under her breath: "She called you stunning."

Around the room, people took seats, Harrison filling Pippa in on various people. Pippa turned to Pavlos.

"I understand you went to Magdalen?"

"Ah, such fond memories," Pavlos turned his head to blast Pippa with a beaming smile, full of teeth and good humour at the memory.

"Tell him how you sat on the green, reading your books when the sun came out," Harrison whispered.

"Did you ever sit on the green?" Pippa asked. "I have fond memories of studying in the sunny weather, by the flower beds."

"Oh yes. Many times," Pavlos replied. "Did they still have the rose beds?"

"No." Harrison paused. "I think they were hydrangeas."

"The roses had gone by the time I arrived," Pippa said. "Replaced by hydrangeas. Enormous flowers filled with colour right through spring into summer."

"This must have been a sight." Pavlos picked up a knife and twizzled it in his fingers. "You missed a multi-sense treat as the roses bloomed, though. Sight and smell. Plus, we used to steal them and give them to the ladies, yes?"

Hors-d'oeuvres arrived. Two small pastry shells filled with a creamy filling, one pale yellow, the other having a pinkish hue.

"You pick these up with fingers to eat," Harrison whispered. "After this, from here on out, it's cutlery from the outside in."

"What can you do when they're gone, though?" Pippa asked, hoping Harrison would realise that she referred to the cutlery.

He did. "Top down, finishing with the cheese knife."

Her hand stayed as Harrison hissed "Wait!" into her ear. "Pavlos must begin as the elder statesman."

"I suppose the gardeners they know best." Pavlos delicately picked the pink hors-d'oeuvre. Pippa watched as he popped it into his mouth, barely chewing. "Were you a rower at all?"

Harrison's initial reply came immediately. "No."

"I'm afraid not," Pippa said.

"It took time away from my carousing," Harrison's comment held the warmth of a fond memory.

"Law studies are too involved," Pippa said instead. She doubted Isabella's grandfather would approve of a carouser marrying his granddaughter.

Seeing Isabella eat a shell, Pippa followed suit, popping it in whole. An explosion of flavours hit her tongue, a sweetness from the shell, a seafood taste from the filling, but not prawns. She knew what prawns tasted like.

"I'm hungry," Harrison complained.

"This is delicious." Pippa aimed her statement at Isabella, but both she and Harrison knew the real intended target.

As he didn't have food, Harrison's reply came first. "Tell me again why I like you."

Pippa almost turned at Harrison's remark, feeling her tummy flip-flop. Instead, to calm her sudden jump in heart rate, she concentrated on Isabella.

"It is." Isabella smiled. "Far easier to eat lobster this way than trying to open a claw with a hammer."

Around her place setting, Pippa counted six wine glasses and a stouter tumbler for water. Unlike the cutlery, having waiters fill the glasses

Royal Again   Iain Benson

told her which she should use. Should somebody get close to finishing a glass, a server magically appeared to refill it. Pippa now understood the idiom 'drunk as a lord'. Especially Isabella. She kept hitting the wine hard.

By the time the main course came, she'd already had four glasses, whilst Pippa had stuck to water, apart from an occasional sip for the appearance.

Katherine had leaned across her husband to rap Harrison's knuckle with a knife. "I understand you like horses," she said.

"I have three," Harrison said. "One for polo, one for riding, and a jumper."

"I adore horses," Pippa replied. "I have three."

"What are their names?" Katherine asked.

"Jazz," Harrison began, before a slight crackle and silence.

A cold bead of sweat pricked Pippa's forehead. "Jazz is my polo horse." Pippa managed, barely, to keep the quaver from her voice. She picked up the knife for the vine-wrapped lamb dish, twisting it as though it had a mark on, but actually searching for Harrison in the reflection. Harrison gave her a frantic cut-off signal, slicing his hand across his throat. Pippa knew they both had the problem.

"I've never heard you call Jasmine by a nickname before." Isabella gave Pippa a puzzled frown. "Is that knife clean?"

"I thought I saw a water mark, but it's only the lights reflecting." She hoped to answer Isabella's question before continuing with Katherine's, that she could buy time and change the subject.

No such luck. "Jasmine is a beautiful name," Katherine said. "Are the other horses so named?"

Pippa had no idea whether the other horses had names at all. She could feel a panic attack starting to build. She got a moment to think as a waiter took their plates whilst another refilled Isabella's red wine glass.

"Isabella," Pippa asked, turning. "Do you think my other horses are beautifully named?"

"Depends on if you gave Anise or Juniper nicknames or not."

New plates arrived. Pippa had run out of side cutlery, so took the small spoon from the top. "Anise and Juniper," she said to Katherine. "It seems your granddaughter is averse to my nicknaming horses."

Katherine gave a slight laugh and a small cough. "I am not averse. What nicknames did you give them?"

"Ani and Juniper."

Isabella pulled a face, her bottom lip sticking out. "Typical. Juniper has the nicest temperament, and you treat her like garbage."

Pippa frowned. "Are you feeling all right?"

Isabella shrugged like a petulant teen. "I've never felt better."

A definite sense of icy unease had come over Isabella's interactions with Pippa, growing as chilly as the ice-cream. Both her grandparents had picked up on this, their conversation drying up. Losing her wingman, made Pippa grip her cutlery and pray for the end of the meal.

The servers brought dessert wines. A young woman with dark hair in a braid filled the smallest glass with a sickly sweet-smelling liquor. Pippa sipped it, trying to hide her grimace at the burning confectionary taste, stripping a layer off her tongue. Isabella had no such compunction, downing the amber liquid like a free shot at a student bar. Spontaneous conversations broke out around the room.

Pavlos touched Pippa's arm lightly. "Tell me more about your alma mater. Reminiscing is good for my soul."

Isabella grunted and finished the shiraz from the cheese course.

"Excuse me, sire," Pippa said, inclining her head towards the Greek king. She couldn't begin to guess at 'alma mater'. It sounded Latin. Or Greek.

"Call me Pav," Pavlos said, winking.

"Pav." Pippa flashed a brief smile. "I promise to get back to you, but I fear I have been ignoring Isabella."

A slight harrumph from Isabella told Pippa she'd almost guessed correctly. Pavlos noticed his granddaughter's upset. His blue eyes twinkled. With a wry smile and a nod, he gave his permission.

Twisting, Pippa tilted her head slightly to appraise Isabella. She had the slightly glazed expression associated with approaching drunkenness.

"You're hitting the wine quite hard tonight." Pippa kept her tone light. She didn't want Isabella feeling chided.

"I've seen the pictures." Isabella drained her glass and gave Pippa a level stare. "Restaurant? Shopping? Cinema? It read like a first date! And it's that Penelope you've brought here!"

"What are you worried about?"

"I know you said the affair never happened, but with her here, it makes me wonder!"

Pippa gave a single nod. Other people drifted away from the table, giving her an opportunity. "Wait here for a moment. I'll bring her over."

"What?" Isabella half-rose.

"You can look her in the eyes and ask her if she's sleeping with me. You don't believe me when I say I'm not."

"There is something different about you." Isabella's eyes narrowed.

"I don't know what you think that would be." Pippa spread her hands.

"Nicknamed horses, that kiss at the dance. This Penelope coming from nowhere. Even the way you pay attention to me and consider my feelings."

"Wait here, for a minute." Pippa released her held breath as she moved away from Isabella. Her breathing came in short, ragged snatches, her senses felt magnified. She feared Isabella had started to guess something had happened.

Harrison remained by the door, leaning on the wall, near a servant.

"She knows something." Pippa sagged her shoulders a little.

"My feet hurt," Harrison replied. "What's wrong with the earpieces?"

"I'm guessing the battery ran out."

"What do we do?"

Pippa sighed. "Walk back with me, let Isabella interrogate you, then find somebody who might have batteries. Are they like wireless headphones?"

Harrison fell in beside Pippa, walking back. "No idea."

"Did they have a plastic case?"

"Yes."

"That's probably the recharging case." Pippa saw incomprehension on Harrison's face as if he'd never come across wireless headphones. "The case is a battery. You drop the earpieces in the slots, and they get recharged. There will be a small slot on the case. You can plug a USB into it in case that battery needs recharging as well."

"I'll sort that out." Harrison said. Pippa handed him her earpiece.

They had reached the table. Isabella held the table as she got to her feet to lock eyes with Harrison.

"Are you sleeping with my fiancé?"

18
Harrison: Dance

The accusation flattered Harrison. Isabella became more animated when demanding if the other woman had slept with him. He'd never seen this side of her.

Keeping his eyes locked on Isabella's, Harrison tried to sound as convincing as he could. "No."

"Do you want to?"

Slightly shakier ground. "No."

Although getting tipsy, Isabella picked up on his less than certain response. "That sounded less positive."

Harrison attempted a rescue. "He's an attractive man, but I know a more available one."

Pippa leaned into the conversation. "I think she and one of my drivers are a thing."

Puffing out her cheeks and glancing from Pippa to Harrison and back again, Isabella relaxed. "In that case, let's dance, and we'll see how much you have only eyes for me."

Hearing her, Harrison realised she'd gone beyond tipsy.

Cupping Isabella's arm, Pippa led her towards the ballroom. She turned slightly, trying to find Harrison, shrugging, unsure. Harrison hopefully gave her an encouraging smile, though his worries may have tainted it slightly.

From his bag, he took the case the earpieces had come in and laid it on the table. Closing his eyes and sighing, he sat. His feet made rhythmic throbs in time with his heart. He'd never had the ball of his foot burn with enough pain to make him want to curl up and sob in a corner. His whole body sagged into the seat and he had to find the motivation to examine the case. He turned it over, finding small lights and a slot. When he returned to his life, he made a mental note to be more attentive. Learning about Reece had been so interesting, he'd failed to pay full attention to the security chief's words or ask the right questions.

One light on the box flashed red. He stopped a passing server.

Harrison smiled at the young girl and showed her the box. "Hi, do you know what that flashing light might mean?"

Royal Again   Iain Benson

The girl tugged at her mousey-brown ponytail as she peered at the small plastic box. "If they were ear pods, I'd say the battery box needed recharging. I've not seen that make, so I'm not sure."

"Do you know where I could get a charger?"

The server took the box from Harrison's fingers and turned it over and around. "Oh, it's a USB micro. There might be one in the office you could use."

Her easy understanding rammed home how Harrison had almost zero knowledge of how the real world worked. "Where's the office?"

The server gave him directions before she carried on collecting wine glasses.

Producing a deep, heartfelt breath, Harrison forced himself back onto his feet. Unlike at the palace where they'd built the public areas around the staff area, allowing the staff easy unseen access to the entire palace, here, the staff access corridors wound around the public areas like an afterthought. Harrison found the staircase down to the office, gingerly placing each foot on the carpeted steps.

He found a breakroom but not the office.

"Can I help you?" a voice asked from behind.

Harrison turned. A tall woman filled the corridor with a rugby player's shoulders. She wore a pleated skirt and dark jacket to stamp her authority in an understated way. Her corkscrew curls sprung from her head to the width of her shoulders.

"I'm looking for a charging cable?"

"And you are?"

Harrison almost said "Pippa" but corrected himself. "Penelope, aide to Prince Harrison."

"I'm Ursula." Ursula rubbed her chin between her index finger and thumb. "House manager."

"Do you have a charging cable?"

Ursula tilted her head, judging Harrison from their minimal exchange and how he'd dressed.

He passed inspection, and she raised her chin in his direction. "Follow me."

The woman squeezed past, Harrison having to dance around to let her through. A wider section of the corridor contained a desk and chair. More of a niche than an office. Ursula sidled between the desk's edge and the wall to drop into the swivel chair. It tipped back alarmingly but her practised balance brought the chair under control and Ursula opened a drawer. Although the desk contained nothing but a closed laptop, the drawer disgorged cables and papers as though disembowelled.

Muttering about needing to tidy the drawer, she sorted out some cables.

"Do you know what sort?"

"USB," Harrison said.

Ursula rested her elbows on the desk and put her chin on her hands. She gave a sharp sigh. "This much I guessed. What kind? Micro? Mini? C?"

Harrison passed over the box. "To fit this."

"USB-micro. Old School." Ursula shook her head and put the box down. Harrison grabbed it quickly before the house manager swept it away with the junk. "No charger. But I do have a cable."

"Oh." Harrison didn't understand. "Can I use that to charge this?"

"You can connect it to a socket in a bedroom. Prince Harrison has a room for the night. All VIP rooms have USB charging sockets. Use that."

"What about my room?"

"You're in staff overnight dorm." Ursula shrugged with her lips. "There're no mod-cons there, I'm afraid."

A staff dorm sounded like the camp his parents had sent him on as a child to 'build character'. "How do I get to Harrison's room?"

Ursula's directions rapidly became overly complicated. Harrison concentrated hard, but by the sixth left and right, he shook his head.

"Where is it from the Main Hall?"

"That's public access, not staff. Not with the dinner on tonight."

"I'm a personal aide. I can be seen."

Ursula sniffed. "I've seen the news. You get seen. Take the first corridor on the left. It's the third door down."

Harrison gave the house manager a cheerful voice. "That's so much easier. Thank you."

Turning the light on in the room assigned over to Pippa for the night, Harrison hunted for a plug socket with any kind of hole he could jam the USB cable into, eventually finding it by the bed. A bed that almost filled the room. What little space remained contained a dresser to one side and a wardrobe to the other. It felt cramped. Quite a small room for a prince. At least the room had an ensuite bathroom. He bounced on the bed, checking the comfort level. It would do. As he bounced, his tired brain conjured up images of him and Pippa giving the bed a thorough workout. A tingle down

Royal Again   Iain Benson

below made him suck in a sudden gasp of air.

That came from nowhere!

He shook his head, removing the silly grin spreading across his lips.

"Business," he muttered. "I am an aide, after all."

The drawers contained a nightshirt and fresh underwear, whilst a wardrobe contained clothes for breakfast, shooting and opera. He gave a satisfied nod.

Having explored the room as much as possible, he returned to the charger. It remained stubbornly uncharged, only the first green light lit and flashing.

"Oh, come on," he muttered. "How long does it take?"

Charging batteries took longer than Harrison anticipated. He abandoned them to return to the ballroom in case Pippa needed him.

Negotiating the stairs gingerly made each tiptoed step a trial, partially supporting his weight by clutching the banister. He reached the bottom in time to be swept aside by Isabella stomping from the ballroom. In one hand, she clutched a mostly empty glass of wine.

"You can have him!" she said with feeling, using her free hand to waft Harrison away.

Harrison stared after his fiancée. What on earth had happened? He'd only been gone an hour.

He entered a ballroom filled with people all turning in his direction.

Pippa strode towards him, but looking past him.

Harrison caught her arm. "What happened?"

"They didn't play a waltz," Pippa sounded close to tears. "I started okay, but then realised I didn't recognise the music and it all went wrong."

"What did they play?"

"I need to go after her."

Harrison knew how to fix the problems. A Damascus moment of illumination flooded through him. "No. You don't. You need more dance lessons."

Pippa stared, incredulous. "You expect me to get lessons now?"

"I think your feet know." Harrison indicated the floor, other dancers choreographed in time with the music. "Besides. You are a prince. You absolutely do not run after a woman."

"I'm not a prince." Harrison could barely hear Pippa's whispered voice over the music.

"Unless we find some way of switching back in less than forty hours,

Iain Benson   Royal Again

I'm afraid you're a prince. I can't see any way of us ever getting together again after the wedding. I can't see Isabella wanting your floozy hanging around."

"I think you're right." Pippa's chest heaved. The longer she stayed as him, the more his duty sapped her will.

It seemed to go the other way for Harrison. The longer he spent as Pippa, the more circumstances required him to perform mental juggling on a scale he'd never experienced before.

Harrison laid his hand on her chest, seeing the dusky pink of his nails against her dark shirt. "Now, I think you can dance. You need to tap into that bit of me that lives outside the soul."

Slowly, Pippa acquiesced, taking his hand and leading him onto the floor, in front of dozens of important people. He spotted royalty from neighbouring countries and a few billionaires.

"This music is a foxtrot." Harrison clasped Pippa around the waist and took his hand. "Lead with a short step on the left and a long right. Bring Both feet together forward and left, then step back, half left full right."

Harrison kept up the verbalisation as Pippa followed them, easily picking them up, the legs making moves by habit.

"I'm doing it," she said, gasping a little.

"You need to focus on other things," Harrison told her. "Let your feet move automatically."

"What can I focus on?"

"Talk to me."

"About what?"

Harrison shrugged. "Anything."

"Like you and Dillon?"

Harrison stumbled. "What about that?"

"If we don't change back, would you and he get together?"

"I don't know," Harrison admitted, frowning. "I never imagined I might be gay, but there's something about him. I like *girls*."

"Me, my body. I'm not gay," Pippa said, stumbling over her words. "Like your feet are guiding me, my body's probably guiding you."

"I'd thought something similar." Harrison saw Isabella's parents surreptitiously approaching.

Frederick glided over with his wife. "Care to explain what happened and why you're dancing with your aide?"

Harrison saw Pippa wince. She recovered quickly. "She's upset with

Royal Again   Iain Benson

my dancing."

"It looks fine to me." Amestris said, with an amused glance.

"I feel it may be more to do with Penelope here," Pippa said, leaning slightly closer to Freddie. "She has nothing to worry about, but I fear she let the wine speak for her."

"And this dance?" Frederick asked.

"She fears losing me to my staff." Pippa slipped into her usual creative mindset. Harrison spotted her thinking on her feet. "I'm making her face her fear."

"I approve," Amestris said.

Isabella's parents glided away.

"You didn't notice that the music became a waltz and switched easily," Harrison said, enjoying the closeness of Pippa, the scent of her cologne filling his nose. "I think the trick is to think about anything other than dancing."

Pippa bit her lip. Harrison's eyes lingered on her mouth. Harrison thought of his conversation with Reece. Enforced proximity to one another had drawn them inevitably together. Pippa's beautiful soul enraptured him. Did she feel the same?

Before she could say anything, Isabella returned, alcohol-fuelled fire in her eyes. "You have my dance partner."

Harrison curtseyed unwillingly away. "He's all yours."

Like a wallflower, Harrison retreated to the wall to watch Pippa as she danced with Isabella. Though a part of him felt pleased to see Pippa execute the footwork with the practised ease of his childhood dance lessons growing up, envy consumed the rest of him. Isabella had rudely cut in and removed the crumb the moment had offered.

Controlling his breathing, Harrison seethed at the couple. Amestris gave him a pleased nod, as though thanking him for bringing her daughter back into the arms of Pippa in his place.

"Where is karma when you need it?" Harrison muttered, grabbing a wine from a passing server.

As though karma listened in on his innermost desire, Isabella stumbled. She went down awkwardly, Pippa unable to catch her as she crashed down to the floor with a mixture of mistimed dance steps and alcohol.

Across the room, music and dancing stopped in a stuttering wave around the stranded Isabella. Harrison's hand shot to his agape mouth, feeling irrationally responsible for the accident. Isabella's cry sounded loud amid the silence.

Pippa picked her fiancée up from the floor, lifting her like a mother lifting a baby, cradling Isabella in her arms. Isabella clasped her arms around Pippa's neck, burying her face in Pippa's shoulder. A brief whispered conversation took place.

"It's a twisted ankle," Pippa announced. "I'll take her to bed. Please, all carry on. It is nothing to worry about."

Striding purposefully, Pippa left the ballroom like some action hero rescuing a damsel. The knot of jealousy swung like a leaden weight in Harrison's midriff. A part of him would have loved to have Pippa carry him like that. He hung by the ballroom entrance, watching Pippa carry Isabella up the stairs. He imagined being in Pippa's arms and how it would feel.

He tilted his head. *Stop thinking anything can happen with Pippa!*

Pippa had Isabella.

She wouldn't need him.

A young man with a cravat, quiff, and trust fund approached. Harrison delved deep into his memory. Isabella's cousin? Tarquin, Quinn? Something pretentious.

"Would you like to dance?" His hopeful eyebrows tried to beckon Harrison onto the floor.

"I'd *like* another drink," he replied.

"You have one." The young man clinked his glass against Harrison's.

"So I do." Harrison drained it, grabbing another.

"I take it this is a no?"

"Quinn," Harrison remembered. "I'm Harrison's aide, not your fifth cousin twice removed."

"You know my name!"

Harrison gave a sad head shake. "I'm Harrison's aide. It's literally my job to know your name. It's a no."

"Such a shame. You're the most intriguing woman here tonight."

"If you knew the whole truth, you'd realise how absolutely correct that chat-up line is." Harrison wondered if deflecting amorous boys engendered quick thinking, or if some of Pippa's latent ability seeped into his own. "Please, leave me alone. I'm going to bed." He saw the reply coming before Quinn uttered it. "Alone."

19
Pippa: bedtime

Concerned, Pippa barely glanced at Harrison as she headed from the ballroom.

"I can walk," Isabella told Pippa as she carried her up the stairs, feeling Isabella's weight pulling Pippa's back muscles.

"Probably not a good idea," Pippa gently told her. "We need you able to walk down the aisle the day after tomorrow."

Saying the words created familiar anxiety in Pippa's stomach. "Day after tomorrow". Harrison's words echoed in her head: their last chance of switching back before the wedding. It added to the churning of her insides.

Isabella guided Pippa down the hall to her suite. Using her knee, Pippa opened the door.

"You're supposed to carry me over the threshold *after* we're married." Isabella gave a drunken giggle.

Despite the protests of her lower back, Pippa lowered Isabella onto her bed. Isabella refused to unlink her fingers, pulling Pippa onto her. She almost lost her balance to fall onto Isabella.

"You didn't give me my kiss." Isabella's words slurred with insobriety. "You're not going until I get it."

Pippa inwardly cringed. She lightly brushed her lips against Isabella's.

Standing up, Isabella lacked the strength to pull Harrison's body, but bent double, Pippa found herself pulled into a kiss with Isabella.

Isabella's tongue found its way between Pippa's slightly parted lips, flicking delicately over her tongue. Despite herself, she felt a stirring in little Harrison. As he'd said on the dancefloor, Harrison liked girls. His body responded as Isabella's fingers unlinked, running through Pippa's hair. She tasted of wine and smelled of lust.

Isabella broke off, her lips tracing a path across Pippa's cheek to her ear, Isabella's teeth delicately nibbling at Pippa's earlobe, her lips stroking across the sensitive skin. Pippa's breath fell on Isabella's neck. Pippa let her lips caress Isabella's pulse, eliciting a breathy gasp. Without volition, Pippa's hand moved sensuously down into the small of Isabella's back. She arched slightly.

"I want you," Isabella breathed into Pippa's ear.

Pippa gasped slightly. If she reacted honestly, she'd admit she wanted Isabella.

However, Pippa tenderly removed Isabella's hands, clasping them and kissing her fingertips.

"You're drunk." It sounded a hollow excuse to Pippa's ears, even as the words came out. However, completely true.

"I want to try you on for size." Her tilted smile had Pippa biting her bottom lip in indecision. "I never thought I would want that, but I do. There's something different about you."

With difficulty, Pippa straightened, smiling softly at Isabella gazing up with her downturned mouth, tears pricking her eyes. She needed to get out before Isabella stumbled across the truth. Or worse. Her own building lust made her do something she knew she'd regret.

"I don't think we'll have any issues on Sunday. In fact, I think we're quite compatible." Pippa hoped little Harrison would get the message that she didn't need him tonight.

Under no situation would little Harrison be doing anything tonight, not with Isabella one drink short of unconsciousness. Instead, to try and quell her desire, Pippa slipped each shoe from Isabella, rubbing her thumbs on the balls of her feet. The ecstatic moaning told Pippa she'd chosen right, but then she knew what heels did to feet and how good it felt having them rubbed before bed.

Softly, Pippa whispered, "You're in luck. I know where the g-spot is."

"Mm." Isabella's eyes closed, her mouth slightly open and her head tilted back.

Pippa reached behind Isabella and pulled down the long zip, helping her undress without needing to stand. *It's almost like I'm an expert at this.* The thought amused Pippa, seeing Isabella's lithe body clad only in expensive lingerie. The semi-conscious woman had a small butterfly tattoo with rainbow wings on her hip. Maybe, a life with Isabella would be bearable if the worst happened. She felt Isabella's hand on little Harrison, her thumb running up and down through the material. Pippa almost jumped back in surprise, regardless of how electric it felt. Pippa took Isabella's hand and placed it on her tummy. Isabella's flawless skin slipped under Pippa's fingers like silk as she released Isabella's hand.

Pulling the duvet from the other side, Pippa covered Isabella. Harrison's fiancée rolled over slightly and gave a contented grunt, her eyes closed. As she drifted off into sleep, Pippa bent, brushing her fringe to the side and kissing her forehead.

She knew she'd done the right thing. "Good night, Izzy."

Her voice laden with sleep, Isabella smiled. "Mm, Izzy, I like that."

Quietly, Pippa switched off the light and slipped from the room, pausing by the door to listen. Isabella's breathing suggested she slept.

The light in the hall caused Pippa to blink. She returned to the ballroom, though she felt tempted to go to bed and try and sleep away the desire Isabella had planted inside her.

Isabella's parents and guests deserved to know Isabella's state.

She noted Harrison had gone, giving a brief knot of panic that momentarily arrested her breathing. She would be somewhere. Probably sorting out the earpieces so Pippa could survive the evening.

Spotting Frederick and Amestris, Pippa angled in their direction.

Amestris reacted first, seeing Pippa's approach. "How is Isabella?"

Although she wanted to say *drunk and unconscious*, Pippa went with: "Sleeping peacefully. Hopefully, her ankle will be fine with a little rest."

"She has her final dress fitting tomorrow." Amestris's fingers tugged at the folds under her chin in nervous worry, wrinkles appearing around her eyes.

"I'm sure she'll be fine." Pippa hoped she gave a reassuring smile, but she didn't feel reassured.

"It's your last day of freedom tomorrow." Frederick clapped Pippa's arm. "I understand you're quite the shooter! I can't wait to see."

Desperately scrabbling through her mental diary, she recalled Harrison had an upper-class version of a bachelor party. She visualised the calendar. Her mouth dried as she recalled the attendees and events. "My father's coming," she said, through arid lips. "I dare not beat him, so expect my aim to be a little off."

Frederick gave a deep laugh that rose from his belly and erupted from his nose. "I am so happy you are joining our family!"

Conspiratorially, Amestris leaned in. "The first time he met you, he thought you were a stuffy aristocratic snob."

"I am. This friendliness is an act, so you don't call off the wedding."

"Never fear, my boy! I hope your aim is off enough that I can beat you!"

"I can but try to miss with every shot." Pippa knew if she hit anything, that would be a complete fluke. Compressing her lips to appear serious, she added. "I think I will retire. I will bid goodnight."

Pavlos and Katherine stopped by before Pippa could leave. "How is my granddaughter? Fine, I trust?"

"I think it is a sprain. She'll be up and running before Sunday. She seemed in high spirits before she fell asleep."

Katherine's eyebrow arched and one corner of her mouth raised. "A polite way of saying 'pissed as a fart'."

Pavlos scowled at Katherine before laughing. "Indeed."

"I'm afraid, I also must head to bed," Pippa said to Pavlos, inclining her head to give a half bow. "Thank you for an enjoyable conversation, Pav."

Pavlos scratched his nose, his eyes twinkling. "As long as it's your own room, you old dog!"

"Pav!" Katherine slapped her husband's arm.

"If you want great-grandchildren, Trina, they only arrive one way!"

Amestris buried her eyes in a hand, her shoulders shaking. She knew her father well.

"Katherine." Pippa lifted Katherine's left hand to her lips and brushed them. "It has been a pleasure."

Climbing the stairs, Pippa tried to push the evening's events from her mind. A warmth from Isabella's drunken fumble sent her mind towards her wedding night. Little Harrison's reaction told her she definitely perform on the night. *How do I feel about that?* Weirdly, okay. She imagined the act, feeling a little heat growing under her collar as she did. *No wonder men wanted sex all the time!* She could barely think of anything else.

Although they'd given her a cramped room, she felt emotionally drained and charged simultaneously. A good night's sleep seemed tantalising.

Pippa entered the bedroom to find Harrison fussing with the earpieces. He turned, slightly guilty.

"I think they're charged," he said, they dropped from limp fingers while gazing at Pippa's eyes.

The room faded away, leaving him all she could see in exquisite, beautiful detail.

Oh my god. Pippa's pulse seemed to stop. She took a deep breath.

After a mere moment's hesitation, Harrison crossed the few steps, wrapping his arms around her neck, and kicking the door closed.

Pippa leaned into the kiss, sweeping Harrison up into her arms.

Royal Again   Iain Benson

Harrison gave a blissful sigh, his tongue caressing Pippa's. She responded, eyes closed, feeling how his tongue entwined with hers. Pippa supported Harrison's neck with one hand, her other stroking his hair. He tasted of wine, but unlike Isabella, tantalising instead of overpowering. Her lips tingled desire, keeping him locked to her as she lowered him onto the bed.

Pain shot down her back, eliciting a wince and a gasp.

"Are you okay?" Harrison's hair fell across his face, sticking to his lipstick. He flicked away, catching Pippa's nose with the back of his hand, making her wince again. "Sorry!"

Pippa's deep giggle reverberated in her chest. "I think I've put my back out."

Harrison gulped. His bottom lip trembling. Pippa pressed her finger against on his lips. She smiled, feeling Harrison reciprocate. Her smile masked twinges. Perhaps if she ignored it, her back would loosen.

Harrison pushed himself up, hands behind him on the bed. Pippa noticed how the pose made his breasts push out, rekindling the desirous feeling finding him on the bed stirred. Yearning masked the pain. She knelt across him, cupping his head in her hands. Hungrily, their lips found each other. She could barely catch a breath as they drank deeply. Harrison fumbled with her belt, unable to unfasten it. Instead, he moved his hands up her back, the touch sending goosebumps racing across her body.

Sexily, he tried to slip her jacket off. Pippa released Harrison's head to help. The jacket wouldn't come down past her elbows, acting like a restraint. Pippa wriggled, but had to stop kissing Harrison's neck to take the jacket off. Shaking her arm to finally escape it, she tossed it across the room. It knocked the lamp off the bedside table. The crash startled Pippa, but Harrison pulled her back. His infectious mood brought back her own silly grin. She reached around Harrison to unzip his dress. She tugged, but the fastener refused to budge. Pippa had to stand, allowing Harrison to turn.

The zip slid open, the dress gaping revealing Harrison's slim neck, his spine creating tantalising bumps down to his bra strap. Pippa kissed the top one, Harrison sighing as his dress fell into a puddle around his feet. He turned, wrapping his hands around Pippa's neck, their mouths meeting, tongues tasting, teeth colliding, sounding loud in her head. They slowed, and Harrison undid the buttons on her shirt. With her chest exposed, Harrison's hands slid around her skin, electricity tracing the pattern he took. His manicured nails slowly sketched lines up and down her back.

Uncontrolled giggling made Harrison stop.

Pippa covered her mouth, trying to gulp away the giggles. "Sorry. That really tickles."

Harrison shrugged with a head tilt, his breasts raising in an alluring way. "I should have known."

Biting her top lip, Pippa traced a line down Harrison's throat, between his breasts to a spot above his navel. With a wicked smile, she tickled.

Harrison convulsed in a fit of giggles. "That's mean!"

Pippa made up for it, nibbling Harrison's neck in the exact right spot to bring out a long moan.

For the first time, she didn't feel in the wrong body. No bodies, only her and Harrison. She knew her own body well, easily finding those spots that she knew would send waves of ecstasy through Harrison's body. Harrison reciprocated, finally tackling her belt, allowing her trousers to fall to the floor. She shrugged out of her shirt, her feet tangling in the trouser legs around her ankles. Harrison gave her a little push, sending her collapsing back onto the bed.

Reversing their roles, Harrison straddled her.

She sneezed, trying to swallow it. The shudder almost threw Harrison off.

"Bless you," he automatically said.

"Sorry!"

He took each of her hands in his, pushing her willingly into a supine position. He bent, pressing into little Harrison to kiss her, and she responded with eager kisses of her own.

Rolling Harrison over, they went the wrong way, falling off the bed.

On the floor, Pippa once again on her back, she laughed. Harrison's breath was warm on her face. The fall had winded her and knocked some sense into her. She'd made Harrison's hair wild and smudged his makeup like he'd taken part in a kissing booth.

Little Harrison would never forgive her for what she needed to do. She didn't know if she *could* suppress the longing a second time.

She pushed herself into a seated position, her arms around Harrison's waist, licking her lips. Harrison leaned in and licked them, too. It almost made her change her mind as the electrical tingle coursed through her body.

"We can't do this," Pippa said.

Harrison lassoed her with his arms, leaning back, studying Pippa's

Royal Again   Iain Benson

face. "I want to."

"So do I," Pippa fervently replied. She wanted to make love with Harrison with every fibre of her soul.

"I can tell." Harrison's hands slid down between them.

Pippa's head tilted back, her eyes rolling as she felt a sensation she could best describe as chocolate-covered electricity. If he continued, she knew she'd capitulate. Harrison's rocking motions as he slowly licked his bottom lip almost seduced her.

"I am you. You are me," Pippa forced herself to say. "I feel weird."

"I feel the same way," Harrison admitted. "But this feeling of wanting you isn't something I've felt before. It's like my entire body wants you. Having you is crowding out other thoughts."

Lifting Harrison's hands out and putting them back over her head, Pippa feasted her eyes on her own body. Yes, her new body wanted her old body with a fire that burned in her loins, but her mind would hate her forever more. Little Harrison appeared to have a voice of his own, and he was all for sex. Pippa found his voice almost hypnotic.

"If we can swap back, then great. I'd love nothing more than a wild night of passion. But if we can't, then I need to get comfy looking at my sex face."

"Of course," Harrison bopped her on the nose, following it with a kiss to soften the blow. He suddenly brightened. "Sex might be the way we change back."

"That's a stretch and you know it."

Harrison wrinkled his nose, making him cuter than ever. A deep sigh welled up. Harrison's down-turned mouth told Pippa that he felt the same way she did about the decision.

"Change back or not." Harrison's gaze travelled down between their bodies, avoiding eye contact, but seeing the effect he had. "The day after tomorrow, Harrison and Isabella will be married. We may never get another chance."

Pippa considered that. "You know," she said. "It *might* be the way to switch back."

She put a hand on the bedpost and table, pulling herself to her feet, bringing Harrison with her, his legs wrapped around her waist.

Harrison giggled; a feminine sound that resonated in Pippa's masculine body. Her heart started pounding again. Harrison's pupils dilated as they delved into each other's souls.

Their skin pressed together as Pippa again lowered him onto the bed.

With a playful smile, Pippa slipped a strap from Harrison's shoulder. "Shall we start again?"

Harrison reached up and kissed Pippa, pulling her toward him. "Yes."

20
Harrison: The morning after

Yawning, Harrison stretched. The bed felt so comfortable he didn't want to get up.

Last night.

He rolled over to watch Pippa sleeping.

There had been moments when he felt weird seeing his face, but Pippa had known exactly what to do to make those feelings vanish in waves of ecstasy. Hopefully, he'd done the same for her. If he ever changed back, last night would remain as a memory. An amazing memory. If a male orgasm felt like Krakatoa exploding, a female one exploded like deccan traps forming, wave upon wave of world-changing euphoria. For one night only he'd wished to stay switched. Pippa slept, a slight smile on her face. Her eyes opened, catching him watching her.

"Morning," she said, her voice gruff with sleep.

Creases around her eyes deepened as she smiled. Harrison snuggled in, kissing her on the lips, his body responding with a tingle.

Checking her watch, Pippa gave a cheeky smile to Harrison. "What time do I need to get up?"

"You feel like you already are!" Harrison could feel the response to their closeness, pressing into his thigh. "Probably about eight."

With a sigh, Pippa rolled onto her back. "We've only got five minutes."

Harrison slipped from the bed and padded naked into the ensuite, watching in the mirror as Pippa watched him walk. He collected clothes on the way. He washed his face, wishing for makeup removal wipes. All the towels and flannels in the bathroom matched the bedroom's décor, coloured a deep teal. At least the colour muted the makeup on them. It took a few goes to work out the tangles in his hair. Yesterday's hairstyle had been obliterated in a mess of sleep and sex.

Memories of that danced across his lips in time with the recollection.

"Naughty girl, he gets married tomorrow," he said in a murmur to his reflection. *Pity there's no time to do it again, though!* He added as an afterthought.

No toothbrush, he realised, towelling dry. He squirted toothpaste onto his tongue and swilled it around as much as possible. Being unable to clean his teeth kept happening. *I should be used to it by now.* Picking through his clothes, he couldn't find his bra. He turned his knickers inside out and put them on, getting a vague waft from them that started a familiar feeling, making his breath catch.

Almost as though planned, the moment he headed back into the bedroom, Isabella knocked on the door.

"Harrison?" the door opened a crack.

Harrison froze. On the bed, Pippa's eyes widened, her hands half to her mouth. He watched as she glanced to the ceiling, composing herself. She quickly scanned around, spotting his bra on the floor and the makeup-covered pillow, panic etched across her face.

Flicking a palm towards him, telling him to stay there, she knocked the pillow off the bed and onto the bra, hiding both.

"I'm awake, come in." Harrison detected a tiny quaver in her voice.

Standing behind the ensuite door, she could see the bed through the crack at the hinges. Hopefully, Isabella would only stay a few minutes because Harrison desperately needed the toilet.

Patting the bed, Pippa gestured for Isabella to sit.

"Oh, this feels illicit." Isabella's tone sounded playful. Her nose wrinkled. "That smell? It's familiar."

She had already dressed, a simple lilac shift outfit with a low, scooped neck.

The scent. Pippa had hidden the makeup and bra, but the musk of sex lingered in the room. Unmistakable. Frowning, Harrison's confusion mounted. He'd never read of a tryst between Isabella and a man. In all the stories he'd read, she only had girls' nights.

Harrison returned his eye to his tiny viewpoint.

Pippa shrugged. "I had a bit of a sleepless night. It's probably me."

Leaning forward, Isabella theatrically sniffed Pippa's bare chest. "Yes. It's you."

"I'll shower," Pippa said, grinning.

Tracing a finger down Pippa's chest, Isabella shook her head. "It smells nice. You smell nice."

Seeing Harrison's fiancée intimate with Pippa stung Harrison. He wanted to open the door and claim his prize, but stayed hidden. The jealousy increased as she cheekily peered under the sheets.

Royal Again — Iain Benson

"Should you be seeing me today?" Pippa didn't stop Isabella's admiration.

"Mm? It's an old superstition. I'm checking out the merchandise."

"I'm glad to see you walking again," Pippa said. "You worried me last night."

Isabella let the sheet drop, her lips compressing. "Sorry about that. I got really drunk. Thanks for carrying me up to bed and being a gentleman about the whole thing. I don't know why I got jealous of Penelope. She is beautiful. With all the stories circulating. It got too much."

A warm glow came over Harrison, on hearing praise from Isabella.

"It doesn't matter," Pippa said, holding Isabella's bare arm.

"It does," she insisted. "I should know. I can trust you. You've been nothing but duty and grace since we our parents introduced us. The past couple of days, you have defrosted a little, but you're still a pure soul. You have revealed an intuitive feminine side I didn't know you had."

Behind the door, Harrison made a face. Had he been such a jerk around everybody?

Pippa removed a strand of hair from Isabella's face in a tender gesture. She leaned in and kissed Pippa. Harrison wondered if she could taste him on Pippa's lips.

"I should get a shower," Pippa said with a sad smile. "My family is coming soon."

"Oh." Isabella slid off the bed, almost dislodging the pillow on the floor. "About that. They're delayed. Breakfast will be at half nine now."

"Then I have time for a shower."

Isabella glanced around the room. Harrison realised she could see the dishevelled sheets and Pippa's clothing lying strewn around. "Yes, and when we're married, you may need to be a little tidier. I have a thing about messy spaces."

Pippa saluted with three fingers, like a scout. "Yes, ma'am."

Laughing, Isabella left, closing the door softly behind her.

Eyes wide, Pippa dropped back onto the pillows with a whoof. Harrison waited a moment, ensuring Isabella didn't immediately return.

"Wow! That was close." Pippa said, staring at the ceiling, eyes wide, relief erasing her crow's feet.

Giggling uncontrollably, Harrison came into the bedroom and straddled her legs, resting his hands on her chest.

"We've got a bit longer now!"

Lifting his hands easily, Pippa sat upright, their skin touching. He brushed aside his hair exactly how he'd hoped when he saw Pippa do the same to Isabella.

"I still need a shower."

"Let me use the toilet first."

Harrison bounced off the bed, enjoying the feeling of being a woman for the first time since the switch. As he washed his hands, Pippa opened the bathroom door, naked. Harrison's eyes flicked down at little Harrison, feeling a slight distaste at seeing his penis on her, but his revulsion lasted only until a need for her engulfed every sense.

"You can join me in the shower if you like." She opened the shower cubicle. "It's big enough for two."

"But is it strong enough?"

"Only one way to find out." Pippa lifted Harrison.

Harrison relaxed into Pippa. Would he ever be able to do to Pippa what he wanted her to do to him?

Dressed, but with wet hair, Harrison left Pippa to head to the staff quarters. Despite the early hour, the corridors buzzed with activity, staff clearing and cleaning from the night before. Dressed in last night's dress, makeup off, hair wet, Harrison could feel the stares follow him like a trailing cloud of steam, even though he tried to avoid them.

He could do nothing about it.

He found his room down in the basement in a row of several doors. Somebody had thoughtfully put "Penelope Palmer" on a plaque beside the door. Inside, he found a simple cot bed with his overnight bag sitting at the foot. A narrow walkway allowed him access to the mirror hanging on the far wall.

He messed up the sheets, and brushed his hair again, before tying it up and spreading makeup on the bed.

Such a lot of makeup.

His makeover had been yesterday, but it seemed a lifetime ago and he knew he'd never be able to produce the impeccable results Femi had achieved. He had tried paying attention as she fussed. His memory replayed her infectious Jamaican personality with exuberant gestures and flamboyant words.

"Foundation is the building block of all things." The mantra went through his mind as he searched for the right bottle.

Royal Again   Iain Benson

He squirted it onto a sponge and applied it. The shadows cast by the single energy-saving bulb made examining results difficult. He persevered, tracing cheekbones with highlighter and bronzer to define them as much as possible. Soon, every brush, vial and pot lay strewn across the bed. He ran the lip gloss wand over his lips, compressing them to disperse the colour. Forty minutes after starting, he'd finished.

"How I long for the days of brush and go." He blew a kiss at his reflection, a flashback of last night and this morning bringing forth a giggle and a blush the makeup couldn't hide.

He changed into the emerald green pantsuit with nude courts and put everything else back into his bag.

Dillon knocked. "Hey, Pip, you decent?"

Harrison dwelled on his overnight antics. "Depends on the definition."

His driver slouched into Harrison's room. Hunched together with his mouth downcast, dejection wrapped around him.

"What's up?"

"I've been told to drive you home. You've been fired."

21
Pippa: The morning after

In a mint green polo shirt and tan slacks, Pippa entered the breakfast room, seeing Frederick and Amestris already at the table's head, with Isabella to their left, a spare chair and Tiffany giving off sullen vibes. Opposite, William, Charlotte and Elizabeth. They'd all dressed immaculately, the King in a dark blue shirt, the Queen in a peacock green dress with a high neck and Isabella in a white chiffon blouse. Tiffany wore a vest top, her hair piled up.

Pippa joined them, greeting each in turn, her fingers tracing the neatly ironed creases on the tablecloth.

She noticed an iciness in the atmosphere as they returned her greetings.

"You're in trouble, dufus," Tiffany muttered gleefully.

"My apologies, we're late," William said, his voice holding a dark overtone. "We had some issues locating Tiffany."

"Sounds like you're in trouble," Pippa replied under her breath to Tiffany.

Her sullen expression cracked into an evil grin for a moment. "Just wait."

"We're all here now," Pippa said brightly, trying to hide her disquiet at Tiffany's words and William's expression.

Turning to Isabella, Pippa noticed how the young woman stared at the space on the table before her, unwilling to meet Pippa's gaze. She'd only seen her an hour ago. She couldn't begin to fathom what had happened in that time.

Servers came around pouring coffees into delicate cups and placing bowls of blueberries, raspberries, and granola. Isabella pushed hers away.

"I've sacked Pippa." William avoided preamble to get straight to the heart of what had caused the tension around the table.

It felt like Pippa's heart stopped beating on hearing those words, an icy cold filling her veins. "What? Why?"

"I received news that people saw her in the public corridors this morning. With wet hair and wearing the clothes she wore last night. Although you may have a perfectly rational explanation, with the wedding tomorrow, we cannot afford more rumours surrounding the pair of you."

Royal Again — Iain Benson

Pippa knew her face had drained of colour; she could feel the pinpricks of embarrassment bleach her cheeks.

"She came to tell me you'd be late." Pippa could think of nothing more reasonable as an excuse.

"I'd already told you that!" Isabella said, still staring ahead.

"That's what I told her," Pippa replied, taking Isabella's hand. "You were there. Tell them I was alone."

Isabella's eyes glistened. "You were."

"She came after that. Half an hour, at least."

Frederick and Amestris kept their counsel as the exchange unfolded. Elizabeth gave a slight cackle and threw her opinion into the mix with the abandon only the aged could supply.

"I don't care if you're sleeping with the help," she said. "It's the indiscretion."

Pippa weighed up outcomes from various avenues she could take, deciding on attacking, to mask the lies she would have to say. "You can treat me as guilty all you like. I am innocent."

"Why did you make her an aide?" William asked, his eyes narrowing. "Especially after the rumours? I saw you'd taken her to the premiere. You bought her clothes."

Pippa waved her hand. "When the press hounded her, I decided that the best way of keeping her safe was to disguise her. And I did a wonderful job. Making her my aide meant I could keep her safe."

William's lip turned up in disgust. "She'd have been safe at the palace."

"Would she? Really?" Pippa gave a sharp headshake. "The picture of her in the press came from *our* records. I've seen first-hand how the staff reacted when all this blew up."

"She would have been safe," William repeated, insistent. "Annalise would ensure that."

Annalise? It took Pippa a moment to realise he meant Annie. "I did what I thought was best. It was my fault in the first place she was in that position."

Tiffany snorted. "You? Taking personal responsibility for something? Who are you, and what did you do with my brother?"

"Tiffany!" Charlotte chided gently.

"What?" Tiffany demanded. "Am I the only one who can see how different he is since he met her?"

"That's rich coming from my gadabout sister," Pippa said, feeling anger replace embarrassment. She knew all about Tiffany's nocturnal outings. The canteen talked about little else some days. "Let me guess, Tiff? Nobody found you because you were out clubbing."

"At least I'm *honest* about it!"

Clinking her coffee cup back onto the saucer, Elizabeth raised an eyebrow. "It is a change for the better, I feel. Growth is important, this close to a union. Is that not true, Harry?"

Pippa felt under scrutiny from every member around the breakfast table, except Isabella, who had not moved.

"I've not changed." Pippa compressed her lips and folded her arms.

"You're still a jerk," Tiffany said. "But somehow, you're a more thoughtful jerk. That's a difficult feat to finesse. You'd impress, but you don't."

"Oh, you've changed, Harry. You've changed a lot." Elizabeth gave Pippa an amused glance over her coffee cup.

She couldn't put her finger on it, but Pippa *knew* the Queen's mother knew more than she let on. She'd known from that first morning. Now, it seemed, even Tiffany had picked up on whatever slip-ups she made trying to be Harrison in front of those who knew him best.

"Regardless," William said, bringing the conversation back to his original topic. "To avoid any *possible* incidents, Pippa has gone."

Keeping as much of her teeming emotions locked away from her face as her frayed nerves allowed, Pippa held the King's gaze. "Fine. Your actions absolve me of any responsibility. Perhaps we can get on with what's actually important."

Pippa picked up one of Isabella's hands in hers. She felt the trembling through her silken skin. Tears pricked the corners of Isabella's eyes, sending a wash of guilt through Pippa over what she'd done. She kept that carefully buried, wanting to reassure Isabella.

Keeping her voice soft and low, she kissed Isabella's fingertips and returned to gazing into Isabella's downy brown eyes. "Return to what's important. Us. Tomorrow and forever."

Deep inside her, bolted down and protected by an inner fortress, any future without Harrison created a swirling maelstrom of sadness and hurt.

Isabella gave a sad smile. "Do you still want to get married?"

Many answers passed through Pippa's head, including "no", but instead, she tried to placate Isabella. "Of course. You're getting your final fitting today. Flowers are filling the church as we speak."

"Besides." Frederick decided, with the worst over, that he could join the conversation. "It wouldn't matter even if you didn't want to. You're still getting married."

William agreed. "This is true."

Right now, she had limited options. The first hurdle would be facing a day with people Harrison knew, but she didn't.

That added to the feeling of dread building steadily.

Whether the words from the fathers or Pippa's reassurance, Isabella recovered enough to eat, even if her features displayed her dark emotions. By the time the meal had finished, she'd brightened enough to rub her bare foot up the inside of Pippa's trouser leg. Somehow, Pippa had rescued the situation. *Not that I really want to.* In some ways, having the whole event called off now, however late, would suit Pippa perfectly.

Breakfast's second course came as eggs on bacon and toast covered with a yellow sauce with the consistency of custard. Pippa had never seen asparagus in the flesh, but she recognised it crisscrossing the eggs Benedict. It tasted good; if a little sulphurous. The poached eggs had a perfectly runny yolk.

"How do you MC your way out of this crapola every time?" Tiffany whispered, nudging Pippa's other leg with her foot.

Pippa chose to ignore her.

After the meal, Tiffany followed Pippa back to her room.

"What?" Pippa asked, frowning.

"Who are you?"

"What are you talking about?"

Tiffany made an expansive gesture with her hands, waving them up and down Pippa. "I know I'm supposed to be the ditzy one, but this is seriously sketchy. Who are you? If you are Harrison, then how did I break my ankle, aged six?"

Wondering if she should close the door to end the interrogation, Pippa couldn't help herself but answer. She didn't recall the princess ever breaking a leg. "Have you actually lost your mind? You've never broken your leg."

Tiffany conceded that with a stuck out bottom lip and a head tilt. "What cartoon did I used to love?"

Weirdly, Pippa also knew that. When she first started working at the palace, Tiffany ran around dressed up as a member of *Paw Patrol*. However, she didn't really want to play twenty questions. Eventually, they'd reach a question she couldn't answer.

"Look at me. I am Harrison. Do you want to do a DNA test or something?"

"Answer the question."

"*Paw Patrol*."

Tiffany prodded Pippa's chest. "Ha! Right *and* wrong. It was *Paw Patrol*, but I called it *Puppy Pups*."

"That's not what you asked, and you know it."

The princess pushed into Pippa's room, wrinkling her nose at how untidy she'd left it. She sat on the bed.

Sighing, Pippa closed the door. "I've got to get ready for the shooting party."

"Uh, uh. I can't let you near Pa with a gun until I know what's going on."

There had to be some way to allay Tiffany's suspicions. "What makes you think I'm *not* your brother?"

"No. You hit different. You do stuff now you didn't do last week."

Pippa shrugged. "Like?"

Rolling her neck and examining the ceiling, she stabbed her finger toward Pippa. "Like saving that maid when she got detained."

"It was the right thing to do."

"No cap. Prince Harrison doesn't give a toss about right and wrong. He only cares how much it inconveniences him. You saved her twice. I bet you're trying to figure out how to save her right now."

Pippa had to hand it to Tiffany, for a self-confessed socialite, her perspicacity astounded her. "Save her? Pa saved her from the press. I'd sent her home."

"And you promoted her. What does she have on you, simp? How is she making you into somebody else?"

"I've got no time for this." Pippa opened the wardrobe to take out the tweed suit. It hung drably on the hanger. She could only hope it improved when she wore it.

"And why are you low key to Isabella suddenly?"

"Low key?"

"Getting all smoochy like." Tiffany made a kissing noise.

"I know what it means."

Royal Again — Iain Benson

"You never were before. Now you are."

Arching an eyebrow, Pippa wondered the direction of Tiffany questions. "Because, duh, we're getting married tomorrow."

She pulled the polo shirt off, folding it up and placing it over the chair back, followed by her slacks.

"Gross." Tiffany pretended to cover her eyes.

"Told you, no time. Somebody was late this morning. What was it? Jardins for cocktails, then Flamingo for dancing until meeting a hunk?"

Tiffany sneered. "Coco's, if you must know. Weird flex, but okay."

Pippa fastened up a pale yellow shirt before adding in the tweed waistcoat and matching suit. She fastened a red polka dot tie.

"You look awkward." Tiffany came over and adjusted his tie. "And that's a Half-Windsor knot. You're not my brother. He would never leave in anything less than a full Windsor. Preferably a Balthus for a shooting event."

"That's simply silly." Pippa shrugged into the jacket, slipping into green Wellingtons.

"If you don't tell me what's going on, I'm telling Pa you're not Harrison and you need a DNA test. He's found a look-a-like or something, so he doesn't have to marry Isabella."

"Are you still high?"

"I admit that scar on your right shoulder is a nice touch. Not many people know about me shooting you."

Pippa wondered if this could be another false story, but decided this time she'd played it straight. "Exactly."

"It's your left buttock, dummy. Gotcha. Though I did see the scar."

"I did wonder why you said shoulder."

"No, you didn't. Spill. If you're a look-a-like, you look identical. You have all his subconscious mannerisms. You walk like him, sound *almost* exactly like him."

Pippa gave Tiffany a dirty glare. "Almost?"

"Yeah, Harry would *never* say 'thank you' to *anybody*. I've heard you do it *twice!*"

When had she slipped up with that one? She tried maintaining aloofness in public.

Tiffany clicked her fingers as Pippa checked herself in the mirror. "Got it. You are a body double, and Pippa is your handler. That's why you have these earpieces."

"I'm not a body double, a look-a-like or an actor. If you did a DNA test, I'd still be your brother. More's the pity."

Tiffany bounded off the bed and pulled a hair from Pippa's head. "I will."

"Be my guest." Pippa wanted to leave. "You might struggle with one hair. A sudden gust of wind and it'll be gone."

"I'll guard it with my life." Tiffany held it up, only to discover it had gone. "Or not. Give me another."

Picking up the glass from the nightstand, she handed it to Tiffany. "This will be more useful."

"An empty glass?"

"It has my fingerprints and DNA."

"Thanks. I'll get it checked ASAP."

22
Harrison: Discarded

In the daylight, Pippa's flat might get mistaken for somewhere more affluent. The low bushes down the side added a splash of green against the yellow brick. Dillon pulled up to the front entrance. However, the board across the glass door's bottom half, the youths perching on the property's wall and the number of dying or dead plants dispelled any notion of wealth.

Harrison couldn't see any press, but they might be hiding.

Dillon had been silent for the entire journey. He'd held the door for the backseat and stared straight ahead, ignoring any attempts at conversation.

Harrison didn't move.

"We're here," Dillon announced.

Harrison admired his fabulous nails. While staying in the car.

Sighing, Dillon got in the back.

"Well, hi." Harrison gave him a smile that he didn't feel.

The journey had given him time to think about the future. A future in which he wouldn't see Pippa again, ever. Termination gave him no access to Pippa. She'd be marrying Isabella, further putting her out of reach. Unless something happened in the next thirty hours, his future was anticipating a trip to Portugal. An all-inclusive holiday to meet his new friends and family. He had to get a job, if he could find one. Harrison parked thinking about employment for the moment, as he'd never been for an interview and didn't even know Pippa's qualifications.

At some point, he and Pippa might meet, but they'd only get limited contact.

He had to make the best of what he had left. *I don't know how to live an actual real life.*

"Why aren't you getting out?"

"I want to know why I am getting the silent treatment."

Dillon shrugged. "I thought we had a chance."

Harrison knew the reason for the icy atmosphere in the car, chillier than any air-conditioning. He wanted Dillon to voice a confirmation.

"And now?"

"Twice, Pip? Twice?"

Puzzlement filled Harrison. How had the news got out that he'd had sex with Pippa twice?

"Twice?" he stumbled out.

"People say you slept with him a few days ago, and again last night."

"That's not true!" Harrison admitted that fifty percent untrue could be construed as not telling the truth at all.

"But it's following you around."

"Rumours do that." Harrison slumped. "I'm never getting away from it, am I? I'll always be the woman who slept with a prince. Even though it's untrue."

"Is it?"

"See," Harrison said. "If you won't believe me, who will?"

"Come on," Dillon said, climbing from the car and fetching her case. "Let's go inside."

Thoughtfully, Dillon carried her case and bag. It meant he came up to Pippa's flat. Harrison needed to get him back onside. He rationalised his intentions to ensure Pippa would have somebody after they swapped bodies back. Rationalised, but as he opened the door to the tiny flat, the thought they might not swap back struck him. Dillon carried the bags to the living room, putting them on the small couch.

"See you around, Pip." Dillon headed to leave.

Harrison knew if Dillon left, neither he nor Pippa would see him again.

He grabbed Dillon's arm, pulling him around so they faced one another. "Don't go."

His eyes searched Harrison's face, bewilderment furrowing his brow. "I don't know what to think, Pip."

Harrison wanted to tell him the truth. He couldn't find the words. "If I tell you that there is nothing between me and Harrison, can you believe me?"

"I want to." Dillon broke eye contact.

"There is nothing between me and Harrison," Harrison repeated, taking Dillon's cheeks in his hands and gazing into his eyes.

"Can there be something between us?"

His vulnerability caught Harrison off-guard. "Honestly? I don't know. I think I'd like to try."

With his foot, Dillon kicked the front door shut.

He kissed Harrison.

Royal Again   Iain Benson

Harrison didn't need protection from reporters this time, but he didn't stop the driver from kissing him.

Untangling his feelings would take some time, but Harrison kissed Dillon back and wanted to. He tasted of mints and smelled of a sweet musk Harrison liked. With Pippa, she was a woman, regardless that she inhabited a man's body. He knew he was male. They made sense, even without thinking about it.

But Dillon?

Harrison struggled to reconcile his feelings.

And he didn't care.

He could feel Dillon's hands, a warmth trailing where they caressed his body. His touch felt a hundred degrees. With Pippa, there had been electricity, a fire consuming him, pushing him deeper.

He felt differently towards Dillon.

Could it be better? Did the dimmer candle burn longer? Or was it friendship? Harrison had felt neither love, passion, nor friendship before.

They came apart. Harrison swallowed. The warmth continued, spreading throughout him.

He took Dillon's hand and led him to the sofa, moving the bags onto the floor.

"I should get back. In case I'm wanted." Dillon sat beside her anyway.

"They'll be shooting all morning. I don't want to be alone right now."

Competing worries and desires vied for attention in his head as Dillon's warmth seeped up through Harrison's thigh.

"I can understand that. They're going onto the next venue at lunchtime. I'll need to be back by then."

Harrison wriggled closer. "I don't have to be anywhere. I'm now jobless."

Dillon squeezed Harrison's hand. "I'm sure it's an overreaction. They'll have you back."

"I'm not sure that they will." A glum feeling settled over him.

"Perhaps Harrison will rescue you again." Dillon's bitterness seeped into his words.

"I don't know how to find another job." Harrison had never had to search for one. He didn't think Pippa would have become a cleaner if she had an alternative. "I've been at the palace for a long time."

I was born there, a wry part of his mind observed.

"What do you want to do? You can do anything, I'm sure."

"I've always fancied being a brain surgeon."

"Maybe not a brain surgeon."

"Tree surgeon?"

Dillon laughed. "Okay, you can't do anything. Wait, that sounded wrong. You will find something."

"I don't even know where to begin." Harrison put it down to Pippa's hormones, but he suddenly started sobbing. His shoulders shook and tears rolled down his cheeks. He leaned forward, trying to catch his breath. He couldn't.

"Oh, Pippa." Dillon's arm found its way around Harrison's shoulders.

Dillon pulled Harrison in close, Harrison's head resting on Dillon's shoulder. He stroked Harrison's hair, murmuring incomprehensible words that somehow calmed him.

The sobs slowed. Harrison pulled back. A dark tear stain on Dillon's suit shoulder. "Sorry."

Twisting his neck to examine the wet patch, Dillon shrugged. "It'll dry."

"I'd offer to make you lunch, but you helped me finish the soup, cheese and bread I was saving for a special occasion."

"That was a special occasion," Dillon replied, nudging her. "I was here."

Another problem. He had no experience in simple tasks, like shopping, cooking, cleaning and managing on almost zero money.

He took out Pippa's phone and turned it on, swiping through the apps until he found her banking app.

As he flicked through the options, he must have made a small noise. "What is it?"

"I might need to sell a kidney to pay rent and buy food."

Dillon tapped Harrison's earrings. "I don't know if he foresaw this outcome as a possibility, but the prince has given you a parting gift. You've got a couple of grand on your ears, and another round your neck."

Harrison reached up to touch the diamonds dangling from his ears. Had Pippa planned that? Given herself a nest egg if the worst happened? He knew how shrewd she had been so far. Harrison didn't consider it unreasonable.

The sadness welled up inside. She'd barely had anything, and what

Royal Again   Iain Benson

she had, his father had taken away. Living her life made him want to hide under the duvet and never emerge. Harrison's fingers traced the necklace's pendant's shape.

"Where can I sell them?"

"Have you never sold stuff before?" Dillon's surprise surprised Harrison.

He shrugged with a little shake of his head. "I worked. I didn't need to."

"You could sell them online, like *FleaMarket* or *x-change*." Dillon's wry smile suggested Dillon had these bookmarked. "But they can take a while for the money to come through. In town, you could try a pawn shop or cash-for-stuff store. There are a few. They're probably all pretty similar. They'd give you the money now, but you'll get less than online."

The world he now inhabited felt so alien to Harrison. Traps and pitfalls at every step, designed to keep people at their assigned level. He'd never stopped to think about how the staff *lived*. The conversations he'd overheard describing him as a jerk held a lot of truth. *I'm worse. I'm an entitled jerk.*

"Do you want me to drop you off in town?" Dillon's words snapped Harrison back to the present.

Pippa's phone bleeped. Harrison glanced at it, snatching it from the sofa arm. "It's a message from Harrison."

"You can't rely on him," Dillon squeezed Harrison's knee. "Where is my sharp-tongued sassy girl?"

Harrison's thumb hovered over the fingerprint scanner. "He might be telling me he got my job back."

Dillon shifted in his seat to see Harrison better. He took Harrison's hands in his. "I'll be honest. I'd like you to do the same."

Unsure of Dillon's direction, Harrison hesitated. "Sure."

Drawing in a deep, ragged breath, Dillon held Harrison's gaze. "I like you. A lot. This past couple of days, you've been acting weird. Out of character. It all started with that overnighter in Harrison's rooms. I can't help but feel that you somehow *connected* with him. I know you like him. You have no chance. Apart from the fact he gets married *tomorrow*, anything with him is like, what's the word?"

"Concubine," Harrison glumly supplied.

"Yeah. Even if you love each other, he's hardly going to give up the *throne* for you, is he?"

Would he give up the throne for Pippa? Could he? Harrison pulled from Dillon's grasp to go to the window, only so he could get a moment to think. "I'm not sure he could give up the throne." He watched the cars stream by on the road below. "Even if he wanted to."

"But you do like him?"

Harrison sighed. Currently, he didn't like himself. But Pippa? Yes. "Honestly? Yes. I like you too, though."

"I feel I am the second choice." She heard him stand. "When you sort your head out, give me a call. I can't play understudy to a Prince Not-So-Charming."

The urge to blurt out all the past week's events overcame Harrison. He needed somebody to confide in. If Dillon knew, he might have an insight, a way of getting his sharp-tongued sassy girl back so they could live happily ever after, and he could follow his duty into Isabella's wedding bed. But the driver vanished from the apartment before any words could form. If he could find a way back, he'd need to ensure Pippa and Dillon got back together. Admittedly, his destiny was a life of duty with Isabella, but Pippa seemed to have drawn a different side of Isabella out. She had a way of getting the best from people. Including him.

He watched from the window as Dillon got back into his car without looking back up to the window to see if Harrison watched.

Before embarking on a to-do list the length of his original arm, Harrison checked Pippa's message.

Working on it.

If he had to pick anybody to swim against the tide of duty, history and tradition, Harrison could think of nobody better than Pippa. He sat on the sofa.

Like a neon sign written on the wall, he came to a moment of clarity.

He liked Dillon.

But...

He loved Pippa.

23
Pippa: Bachelor Party

Standing behind King William with a fully loaded shotgun gave Pippa a wicked temptation.

Idly, she wondered what his security detail would do if she lifted both barrels up and blew the King's head off.

Would Reece protect her from them?

As she would instantly become King, what could they do? They'd work for her the instant William's head vanished. She remembered from school history lessons that the history books considered murder as natural causes for a monarch. The idea entertained her while other people took turns shooting poor, defenceless clay discs. As with dancing, if she let her body do its thing, she could hit the target with Harrison's reflexes and aim.

Several other people who greeted her like friends had joined the party. She spent most of her time trying to work out their names. Mostly they made up insults for one another like teenagers instead of grown men. She'd worked out the tallest might be Adrian, whilst the curly, dark-haired, loud-mouthed imbecile was Jack. Though Ass was now his middle name. The other two went by a variety of names, none of them pleasant. She guessed Ivor for the Slavic-featured man, judging by the number of joke names beginning with "I've". The final one had the same curl of russet hair as Adrian, telling Pippa they had to be related. Pippa worked out he was Michael for a similar joke around the name Mike.

Working out how Harrison had met them gave Pippa something to think about while letting her body take aim.

"I thought you'd be giving us a chance!" Frederick said. "What is your secret?"

"I don't think about it," Pippa told him truthfully.

"You are moping, Harry," William told him.

"Yeah," the one called Adrian said, leaning against a tree, trying to be casual whilst wearing a tweed suit and wellington boots. "You've been no fun at all this morning, H."

"You're getting married to Isabella freaking Eldridge, numb-nuts," Jack said. "Stop thinking about banging the hired help."

"Leave that to us," Mike said. "And that maid is quite bang-able,

Iain Benson   Royal Again

yeah?"

"Or, that Freedom Lunch thing your family does," Jack added. "Can we all share the bevvy of beauties they'll line up?"

The four laughed, leaving Pippa wondering which two to take out before she had to reload.

"That laughter should explain why I've sent her away, Harry." The King pointed to the laughter from Harrison's friends.

"But sacking her, Pa?" Pippa chewed her bottom lip. "She's done nothing wrong. If anybody is at fault, it's me."

"Irrelevant, Harry." The King waved his arm around, his breached shotgun dangling from it. "This is all about perception. We can't very well make a maid the next Queen, can we?"

I don't see why not.

"Tomorrow, you and my Isabella will be married, and you can put all of this nonsense from your mind." Frederick said. "Forget the maid. I believe you when you say nothing's happened, but I don't want anything overshadowing my daughter's big day. Let the world focus on that."

Constant scrutiny from friends and family stopped Pippa from ringing Harrison. Partly to check up on him, and partly to find out the names of his four friends. As she shot two clay pigeons perfectly, she wondered if he needed support, if he'd got back to her flat. What would he do without a job? How would he pay her rent?

Pippa didn't need his help, remembering what she had on her itinerary today. Harrison had mapped it out weeks ago, down to the minute.

"Your shooting was impeccable today." William clapped Pippa on the back in admiration. "Have you been practising?"

Biting her tongue, Pippa wondered how to respond and decided on how she actually felt. "I imagined the first clay was your decision to sack Pippa."

"And the other?" William took the comment in good grace.

"That one is you." Pippa's tone held no humour.

"That explains your perfect score today, Harry." The King laughed. "Do I need to be worried?"

"I feel it could put our security team in something of a quandary."

"Well done." Frederick defused the situation by clapping them both on the back. "With shooting like that, you could be on the Olympic team, Harry."

"I doubt I could fit it into my hectic schedule." Pippa sounded bitter, struggling to sound positive and disliking William more with each passing minute.

She removed herself from the temptation of regicide by standing by Harrison's friends. If anyone would call them real friends.

"Like on that rugger trip to France, yeah?" Mike stopped talking as Pippa came over. Inwardly, she sighed. From how they all fidgeted as she got within earshot, she knew they had planned something.

"The rugger trip in France?" Pippa scratched her ear and regarded them all with a faux-suspicious glare. "I'd have seen that coming."

"I doubt we'd have been able to get hold of a pig at this short notice," Adrian said, with a sniff.

The four snorted derisively and without any hint of irony at the porcine noises. Pippa wished she could be anywhere else but there.

"Man." Ivor clapped Pippa's shoulder. "I dunno how you do it. Isabella is like a ten. Hot and sexy. If I was in your place, I'd be all over that one."

"Forget that maid, H." Adrian sneered. "She's a four at best. Even when you took her to that Hitchberg prem. She'd have to be outstanding in the sack."

Pippa's tongue ran around her teeth. The urge to employ violence swamped her testosterone-soaked brain. With an effort the four would never know, Pippa suppressed her urge and gave a sarcastic half-grin. "One day, Ade, when you've had sex, you'll understand. I'm talking sex with an actual living woman. Not your dad's sock."

"Burn, dude!" Ivor flicked his fingers, trying to be gangsta, and managed a 'shaking soap suds off fingers' gesture.

"If I had a magic spell to trade places with you," Pippa told Ivor. "You could be the one to marry Isabella."

"No bad thing, man."

"Same woman for the rest of my life?" Pippa's insides sank at the prospect. "That's not me."

"Definitely not you." Jack's tongue flicked over his bottom lip lasciviously, nodding.

Not for the first time, Pippa wondered how Harrison had befriended these four. Something to do with rugby suggested Harrison's time at Magdalen. They seemed quite happy to fill in the blanks with a little prompting.

"Not you either." Mike punched Jack on the shoulder. "I still remember seeing you that first time. Walking in with H, six women between you."

"Benefits of knowing a prince, eh?" Pippa also punched Jack on the same shoulder, hoping it would bruise.

"About the only perk. Your security cramped my style some nights."

They lapsed into reminiscing about university days. Pippa stayed quiet. Listening. She had to remember every story facet in case she couldn't trade places back with Harrison. Regardless of how abhorrent she found the tales they told.

While half listening, she quickly sent a text to Harrison, telling him she hadn't abandoned him and that if she could find a solution, she would. With the focus on her, Pippa had to settle for three words.

Working on it.

An hour before lunch, they returned inside, leaving the groundskeepers to tidy away all the equipment. Pippa changed from the tweed suit into something a little more comfortable. She didn't know what to wear for an informal lunch in the city, but guessed informal to a royal meant a half-Windsor knot on a silk tie.

Dillon had returned by the time Pippa descended the stairs at Eldridge Manor. Reece held the door for him.

"Thanks." Pippa's mind was elsewhere.

"Three times," she heard him say as the door shut, perplexed at what he meant.

Pippa leaned forward. "How's Pippa?"

Dillon's eyebrows shot up in the mirror. "Upset, sir."

"The King fired her, not me." Pippa rubbed her temples. "I'm going to get it overturned."

"If I may be candid, sir?"

"Dillon, please do."

"I think you've broken her heart. She might not *want* to come back."

Pippa's heart skipped a beat, but she kept her placid Harrison face on. "I'd got the impression recently that the two of you were an item. Am I incorrect?"

Dillon's nostrils flared with a deep breath. "We could have been. I think she's in love with you."

"We both know that won't work." Pippa's mind gave a little leap of joy. "Perhaps after my wedding?"

Dillon gripped the steering wheel. "With all due respect, sir, I do not wish to be a consolation prize."

Wow. His passion surprised her. *Why didn't you say anything before I switched places?*

"Understandable." Pippa felt she needed to repair the bond between Dillon and Harrison, but at the same time, didn't want to. "If it's any consolation, the past few days have been quite stressful for her. It may have clouded her judgements."

"Sir."

Reece opened the door to allow Ivor and Jack entry. Pippa slid back into her seat, trying to appear aloof.

"Looking lit," Ivor waved vaguely at Pippa's suit. He'd changed into a dark blue shirt and charcoal slacks. Although designed to look simple, Pippa recognised from the cut that these were handmade. He may think he spoke like an inner-city youth but came from money. A lot of money. The *gangsta* style did not suit his appearance. It made him a bigger jerk than pre-switch Harrison.

The car pulled around the drive and made the long journey to the gate before heading into town.

Ivor and Jack played catch up on what they'd done since they last saw each other. Pippa listened with half an ear, lost in contemplation. Harrison's reflection was a ghost overlaid on the trees flashing past.

"You're quiet, H." Ivor nudged him.

"I've got less than twenty-four hours." Pippa continued to stare at the scenery, watching it change from trees to houses to apartments to offices.

"Tequila shots and strippers, man," Ivor said.

"Not tequila! Remember Alicante?" Jack laughed uproariously.

"I have no memory at all of Alicante," Pippa said, injecting laughter into her voice.

"I am totes unsurprised." Ivor punched Pippa's arm. "You monster!"

"No tequila and no strippers," Pippa said. "And absolutely no pigs."

"We'll stick to the plan," Jack said. "No diversions."

"There will be no diversions," Reece said from the front seat.

"Yes, sir! Scary dude, sir!" Ivor did a mock salute.

Pippa returned to watching the city pass by. She hoped Harrison would have time to work out how to change them back. She had less than twenty-four hours before the wedding and no time to herself.

What if they didn't make it?

Iain Benson   **Royal Again**

Then she'd marry Isabella.
She closed her eyes, trying to control her ragged breathing.
Maybe afterwards there would be enough time to work out how to change back.
The back of Dillon's head reminded her of that possibility.
If she swapped back, what of her and Dillon? Her job?
She had more problems than ideas on how to solve them.

At the Rocco-fronted restaurant on the corner opposite the park, Dillon stopped behind another long black limousine.

Hanging on after everybody else had entered the restaurant, Pippa leaned forward to Dillon. "Please don't give up on Pippa."

Dillon turned slightly. "It was a smart move giving her the jewellery. She can sell it to buy food."

Pippa mentally slapped her forehead. She'd only had unlimited wealth for a few days, but already she'd forgotten how hard it had been to manage on nothing. Payday was at month's end, with all her bills the day after. She didn't know how long it would take for money to come in from her termination, but she suspected the palace would hold on to the money until they had to release it. The same as they did with their other bills.

She paused by the double doors into the restaurant, scents of garlic entwining around her. Reece scowled, but waited, glancing in both directions down the street. Pippa wondered what he'd seen as his head movements paused. Police had cordoned off the road so nobody could get near them. Reece's constant alertness reassured her, despite not feeling in danger.

She texted quickly, double thumbs. *Send me my bank account details. I can't remember them. I'll send you some of your money.*

Technically true. The money belonged to Harrison.
To Reece's relief, she entered the restaurant.

24
Harrison: The night before

Relief flooded Harrison as he saw Pippa's bank account swell considerably.

He didn't need to sell Pippa's jewellery.

And he could still go shopping!

A small part of him anticipated this minor act of mundanity with joy. He'd never been supermarket shopping. The elation crashed around him. Last week, he'd never had to consider life's mundanities. Switching places and looking at his former life with unaccustomed eyes, gave him a perspective he'd never had the chance of before. He didn't like it.

In the mirror near the door, he checked nobody would point and laugh, getting a sudden sense of disconnect. He placed a hand on the wall, head bowed, feeling short of breath. He could make no connection to the face in the mirror. His maleness held no relation to the woman reflected. Although he needed the food, he suddenly wanted to stay inside and hide, to not let anybody see him. They'd see through the shell around him to the man underneath. Shame coloured his cheeks. He turned his back to the front door, sliding down into a sitting position.

Drawing his knees up and putting his head between them, Harrison's anxiety became a physical knot in his stomach, joining the gnawing emptiness of hunger. Voices yet to be heard crowded in, laughing, jeering, and pointing.

He had to go out.

"Nobody is going to know," he muttered, creating a mantra to drag his crumbling mind back from the abyss. "Even if they possibly could know, nobody would say anything, surely?"

Trans people go out. I'm not trans, but I guess it's similar. If a trans person can find the strength to leave their house, I can.

Taking a series of deepening breaths, Harrison lifted his head, sitting with his back to the apartment's front door. He took out Pippa's phone and searched for information on trans people. Nothing but procrastination. Putting off the inevitable.

"Dysphoria." Somehow, putting a word to his feelings helped.

While he had the phone in his hand, he searched for the nearest supermarket, discovering it did deliveries. He'd not had any food since lunch the day before. Though Pippa seemed able to go extended periods without eating, far longer than he'd ever managed, he now needed sustenance. Forcing himself to concentrate on the present, what he needed from the shop, and what he needed to take to the shop, he started to push the dysphoria aside. Nibbling at the inside of his cheek, Harrison forced himself to his feet, remaining leaning against the door. Having this safety barrier behind him couldn't restore his turmoil. Butterflies barely described the maelstrom swirling inside him each time his mind paused on leaving the flat. A tornado, a hurricane strong enough to lift Dorothy to Oz.

After some searching, he found a working pen and some paper. He located a drawer full of plastic shopping bags while searching, taking a handful.

Bread. Milk. Cheese.

He re-read the three words, adding eggs.

And tomato soup.

What do people buy? Food appeared on tables in front of him. Even in restaurants, he rarely got to choose.

Trying to work out what he needed gave him the distraction to squash the discordance currently crippling him. He grabbed Pippa's handbag, dropping in her phone, keys and the small scrap of an incomplete shopping list. According to the mapping app on Pippa's phone, he had to catch the number sixteen bus for two stops. That reminded him. He checked he had her bus pass and contactless card slotted into her phone case.

His next task: leaving.

Harrison regarded the exit to the apartment with trepidation. It swelled in size and importance, making him feel like Alice in Wonderland. Doors had two functions. They let you leave. They also, more importantly, kept the terrible things out.

Jaw clenched, he forced himself into the corridor. Two youths hung out by the stairwell. Harrison walked by them, feeling vulnerable. They didn't even glance at him until he got close.

"Suh, Pip." The one who spoke seemed harmless enough, despite wearing a slouch hat and baggy clothes. They both knew Pippa, so Harrison gave them a tight smile. Perhaps she'd babysat them as toddlers, or had coffee mornings with their mothers.

"Hey."

They parted to let him down the steps.

He found the bus stop: a glass wall and metal roof partially lit by a

Royal Again   Iain Benson

single fluorescent bulb. Two other people waited. Briefly exchanged nods passed for greetings among fellow travellers. Harrison pulled his coat closer against the chilled afternoon air. More rain threatened in the low, dark clouds.

After several minutes, the knot in his midriff slowly unwound, vanishing as the bus arrived. Keeping to himself, Harrison watched his phone until it told him to get off. He crossed the road and entered the supermarket. Blinding supermarket fluorescents replaced the dim afternoon light, reflecting off fruit and vegetables. He could smell air-conditioned air and oranges.

It took him all afternoon to do his shopping. He'd never visited a supermarket before. Except with a pair of scissors and a ribbon. He'd never been past the cut ribbon. Now, he traipsed up and down, wondering why any shop manager decided that bread and eggs belonged in the same section. Harrison also discovered he didn't know how to identify a raw aubergine. Very few fruits and vegetables resembled their prepared version. Eventually, with a half-full trolley, he reached the checkouts. He watched the person ahead in the queue load up the checkout. Another new skill. He also watched as they paid with their phone. He filed the idea away, as he didn't know Pippa's pin for her card.

The cashier greeted him with a friendly hello as he readied his bags to load up.

"Are you watching the wedding tomorrow?" The question seemed rhetorical, as she didn't wait for an answer. "We've all got the day off, so we're going to the pub. The Bricklayers? Do you know it? Anyway, there'll be a whole bunch of us watching all day!"

"I had hoped for an invitation." Harrison smiled to make clear he was joking, though he wished he had been invited. Had his father not sacked him, Pippa would have taken him.

"Well, you look a lot like that woman who's been in the papers," the cashier said, showing she had noticed Harrison's presence.

"I've been getting that a lot lately." Harrison suspected the cashier had merely drawn breath, but he took the break to contribute to the conversation.

"That's a thing, isn't it? Can you imagine if it's true, and he's having an affair with his maid *right before the wedding*? Me and our Derek, that's my husband, we can't believe it. Prince Harrison looks like such a gentleman. I think it's all made up by the press."

Iain Benson   Royal Again

He noticed nobody acted peculiarly toward him. With each exchange, he pushed lunchtime's meltdown further from his mind.

He had to admit, this could be his life now. He had to get used to it.

"Where are you watching the wedding from?"

He realised she'd stopped talking, expecting an answer. "I don't know yet. Probably TV."

Would he watch it? He had mixed feelings. It should have been him.

"It's like a fairy tale, isn't it? The prince and his bride. And she's so beautiful. And that Harrison is a bit of a dish. I tell our Derek, the prince has to work out every day. You don't get a body like sitting on a sofa watching sports." She broke off the small talk to tell Harrison the price.

He placed his phone on the reader and put his shopping back in the trolley.

"Have a lovely evening!" the cashier called.

"Thank you. You too."

Three bags became quite heavy by the time he reached the bus stop.

I made a mistake buying a big milk. Harrison placed the bags by his feet, waiting for the bus. *The two bottles of wine? They are my most important purchase.*

This waiting for buses and buying food felt unnatural, yet he knew most people did this every day. Paying for food! Cooking it himself! The concept pretzeled his brain. He didn't know how to cook. Budgeting. Another common task he had never considered before. As the bus hissed to a stop, he manhandled his bags onboard, the bus setting off before he'd reached a vacant seat, lurching and almost throwing him off balance.

I'm glad I didn't wear heels!

His reflection in the window showed him his grumpy visage.

"Smile love. It can't be that bad." said an older gentleman in a duffle coat walking to the rear to find a seat.

Harrison grimaced with a nervous tick in his eye. He could get no closer to a smile than that. The older man had no idea of Harrison's day.

Lost in reflection, he almost missed his stop, coming from a different direction this time. He dinged the bell and smashed bags against the seat backs and handrails to disembark.

"Thanks," he said to the driver. He'd meant it to sound sarcastic after the lurch at the journey's start. However, it came out grateful. The driver nodded pleasantly back.

Royal Again   Iain Benson

Weirdly, that gave him a small surge of elation. Making somebody else happy for a moment improved his mood.

By the time he put the bags down on the counter, the fleshy part of his fingers had red grooves where the handles had carved a crease. Harrison massaged feeling back into his hands. Most food went into the fridge. The can of soup went into a cupboard with Pippa's plates. Pippa didn't have a lot of space in her kitchen: two cupboards, a fridge, a sink, and an oven with a hob crammed into a line behind the sofa. As he put the milk in the fridge, the absurdity of his afternoon made him start to giggle.

"I went to a shop," he laughed. "Took milk out of a fridge, into a basket. Onto a conveyer and back into a basket until I could put it back in a fridge!"

Darkness had slid in through the windows by the time he'd cooked and eaten a ready meal. The lid pronounced it as spaghetti carbonara, but comparing it to the last carbonara he'd eaten, this lacked flavour, texture and any meat products.

"Who puts cream in carbonara?" he asked the packet. "Franco would have apoplexy."

The plastic and what he'd been unable to eat went in the bin. He washed the plate and fork. Even if he had to live out Pippa's life, he would never eat a ready meal carbonara again. He opened his laptop and searched for a recipe.

"Spaghetti, guanciale, pecorino and eggs. I don't think I'll get actual pork jowl at the supermarket." Harrison started to close the laptop lid, wondering if bacon would suffice when he remembered to search for a way to switch back. He still had twenty hours.

An hour down the rabbit hole, and he had nothing.

"This is ridiculous." Harrison closed the lid on the laptop and went to see if the wine had chilled enough.

Enough was a subjective measure. He poured a glass.

Sitting on the couch, he sipped, tapping on the laptop lid. He checked Pippa's phone. No messages from her. He contemplated ringing, but knew that would disrupt her evening festivities. Jack would notice Pippa taking a call, and his friends would know within seconds.

"I need a miracle."

He didn't get a miracle. He got a knock on his door.

Filled with trepidation, Harrison peered through the peephole, seeing Annie's mass of black curls. She glanced nervously from side to side.

Having been out there on his own, Harrison understood her worry.

"Annie!" Harrison ushered her inside.

"Pip! I'm so sorry. It wasn't up to me!" She came in, playing with the zip on her coat. She couldn't meet Harrison's eyes.

"Do you want some wine? I've just opened a bottle." Harrison figured this would be a good way to let her know he didn't blame her.

Annie finally met Harrison's gaze. "Oh, yes."

Taking her coat and hanging it on the pegs by the door, he led Pippa's former boss inside, sat her down and brought a glass of wine. He noticed she still wore her work clothes of a black skirt and pale green blouse.

"Sorry, it's not very chilled."

Annie gave a brief smile, accepting the glass with both hands. Harrison noticed the slight tremble.

Sitting perched and twisted slightly, Harrison could almost face Annie. She placed the glass on her knee. Both bobbed up and down as she fidgeted.

"I'm so sorry, Pippa."

Harrison laid a hand on Annie's knee. Stilling it. "It's not your fault."

"I got a message from King William telling me to end your employment, and I completed it. I had to revoke your clearance. You can't get back in to empty your locker. I'm sure we can sort something out."

She trailed off, sobbing.

Her reaction surprised Harrison. He'd assumed they had a working relationship and nothing more. With her sobbing, Harrison had to decide what Pippa would do. He knew what he'd do. He'd sit there, feeling awkward. Something he excelled at. Or he'd lacerate her with a barbed comment. Instead, he placed his glass on the floor and leaned forward to wrap Annie in a hug.

To his surprise, it worked.

"It is what it is." Harrison picked up his glass before he could knock it on the carpet.

"You're not upset?"

Harrison sat up straighter, almost choking on his sip of wine. "Oh, I'm really upset. I don't know how to find a job. I'm skint and feeling quite low at the moment."

"Didn't your sister get you the job at the palace? I think you told me that."

Royal Again   Iain Benson

Not knowing if Pippa's sister had got her the job or not, Harrison gave a noncommittal shrug. He couldn't remember Pippa's sister's name. He'd seen a picture of Pippa with two women she resembled. He'd assumed sister and mother, but he had no memory of her ever telling him.

"You could join an agency," Annie said. "It's not as steady as the work at the palace, but if you get an office block, you'd be set. I did that before I got the supervisor's role at the palace."

Thinking back to the week before, when hoping he had enough ties had been the worst problem he had, Harrison's heartfelt sigh accompanied the slump of his shoulders. "Could you help?"

"When I get home, I'll dig out the agency I used to work at and send you the details. Also. You're getting the *best* reference!"

"Thank you."

Annie told Harrison about cleaning jobs she'd done while working for the agency. It seemed, despite the long hours, she had fond memories of people she'd worked with.

Mood lifting, Harrison opened the second bottle. He didn't have to get up in the morning. He discarded his plan to drink the second bottle during Isabella and Harrison's wedding ceremony, toasting Pippa's new life. Blocking the pain with alcohol would be a pleasant side-effect. He made a mental note to get more in the morning.

His mood crashed down with the telephone ringing.

"Are you getting that?" Annie asked.

Harrison's hand hovered over the handset. The answerphone light flashed *full* at him. He hit the delete key instead of picking the handset from the cradle.

"All messages deleted." The machine announced before clicking through and answering the phone. "Hi, you're through to Pippa. I'm not in at the moment, you know the drill."

After the tone, a gruff, resigned voice spoke. "Ms Palmer, it's Mark Sporco again. I know you're there. Your light is on. Please pick up. Our offer is generous. Given what I've heard, you owe them nothing. Please, speak to us."

Mark pleaded a few more times, without any emotion in his voice. Harrison snarled at the phone. How did they get their information? Not that it mattered. It might be only a job and a story to the journalists, but for him and Pippa, salacious stories would alter their lives forever.

Harrison deleted the message immediately, stabbing at the button.

Iain Benson   Royal Again

He filled and emptied the wine glass before refilling it and Annie's. The room gave a little spin to let him know sobriety had left the building.

"What was that?" Annie asked.

"Reporters." Harrison glared at the phone. "And now I know they're watching my flat."

"They also know about your termination. Somebody's passing on messages to the press. They even had your staff photo at one point."

"My money's on Michael."

"Night security, slept with half the women on staff, Michael?"

Well, not my friend Michael. Pippa wouldn't know him!

He didn't know whether Night Security Michael bore any responsibility, but his brief encounter had left him wanting revenge; this provided a suitable way of doing it. "You know him, then?"

"I'll speak to him," Annie yawned. "How much did the papers offer?"

"Quarter of a mil." Harrison sighed. "I mean, for that sort of cash, given I'm out of work, giving the *Daily Royal* a Kiss and Tell tale is tempting. It might even be more now."

"I thought there was nothing to kiss and tell?" Annie straightened slightly, a slight shift of her shoulders. Harrison had gossip, and she wanted it.

"I suppose it doesn't matter now." Harrison leaned back into the couch, squishing into a comfortable corner. He drained his glass.

"Something happened?" Annie refilled Harrison's glass.

Memories of last night and the morning brought an involuntary smile to Harrison's lips. "Maybe."

Annie's mouth opened, but she brought it under control, biting her bottom lip and taking a sharp breath. "Maybe?"

"Nothing *would* have happened if there hadn't been that massive overreaction to me spending the night in Harrison's room. I swear. If I'd just got on with my job, nobody would care. The wedding would be tomorrow. Everybody would get on with their lives."

"What happened?"

"He'd just carried Isabella up to her room." Harrison's memory wrote across his face. "I was in his room trying to charge up some earpieces."

"I saw him carrying her on the news. So gallant. Sorry, go on."

"He doesn't want to marry Isabella, you know. He must."

Royal Again   Iain Benson

Annie blew air from inflated cheeks. "I don't blame him. But you must remember, life isn't a fairy tale. The maid only gets the prince in those. In real life, money marries money."

"There was a, a, I don't know, a spark when he came back to his room. I swear, I'd have gone straight back to the staff dorm, but something in his eye."

"He didn't take advantage of you, did he?"

Any notion of Pippa taking advantage made Harrison laugh. "There was a mutual feeling. I wanted to rip his clothes off. If there's a missing button on his dress shirt, that'll be me."

"Wow."

"And again in the morning." He giggled. He'd never giggled before the swap. It felt good.

Annie snorted a laugh. "I bet. What's his body like?"

Harrison pursed his lips and leaned forward. "Ripped."

"I bet!"

"You can't breathe a word of this to anybody," Harrison said, realising he'd probably said too much.

"My lips: sealed." Annie disproved that by unsealing them to drink more wine.

"I'm not telling the papers anything." Harrison gave a small head shake. "I don't want the entire world thinking I'm a marriage wrecker."

"I'm not saying you should, but you *could* point out to the King that you've been offered half a million by a tabloid." Annie waved her glass around. Her words slurred slightly. "You could ask how generous he's willing to be if you don't say anything."

"Half a million? They offered a quarter."

Annie wafted her glass around. "He doesn't know that."

Annie had started to go a little out of focus. "I don't think I'll tell anybody. It never should have happened."

"Anyway, I need to go," Annie emptied her glass. "My last bus is due soon."

After helping her into her coat, Harrison took her to the building entrance, making sure neither sustained injury on the steps. The sudden blast of chilly air heightened his drunkenness as Harrison let Annie out onto the path. He'd had the best part of two bottles of wine. He gave Annie a squeezy hug and she left. Harrison made sure she reached the street without falling into a bush. Before the door swung shut, a man in a long green coat put out his hand, preventing it from closing.

"Ms Palmer. Mark Sporco, *Daily Royal*. Do you have a few minutes?"

"No. Leave me alone."

The reporter kept his hand on the door. Harrison tried to close it, but Mark's strength prevented him. "I understand they sacked you. Surely you'd like to give your side? With good representation, you could make TV and radio appearances. It could make you wealthy. And famous."

"Please leave." Harrison's vulnerable anxiety ratcheted through several levels, especially as Mark stepped into Pippa's building. Harrison stepped back, trying to remember how to find the stairs.

"You'll be well known enough to get on a celebrity reality show." Mark advanced closer. Harrison had run out of places to go, the mailboxes pressing jaggedly into his back as he edged along. "We can make you. Or break you."

"Leave me alone!" Harrison felt the rough wall behind him as he placed his moist palms on it.

"I will write the story. You can make money from it or suffer from it."

"Hey, the lady said leave." The doorframe framed Dillon, with his head slightly lowered, his jaw and fists clenched, like an incensed bull.

Bowing his head in acquiescence, the reporter held up his hands and left, Dillon stepping aside to let him out. "If you change your mind, give me a ring. We can make you wealthy."

Dillon closed the door with a dramatic swing and slam, keeping his eyes on the reporter the whole time.

Harrison ran and hugged Dillon.

"Oof!" Harrison's momentum carried them into the door.

"Thank you!"

"I need to rescue damsels more often," Dillon said, returning the hug and wrapping Harrison in his muscular arms. He smelled of deodorant and him.

Dillon's warm hand clasped Harrison's as they returned to Pippa's flat. The safety Dillon gave Harrison made him once again question his sexuality.

Safely ensconced inside, Dillon tipped Harrison's chin up, kissing him lightly on the lips.

Comparing Dillon's kiss to Pippa's, Harrison got an answer to a question he didn't want to ask.

Royal Again   Iain Benson

Swallowing, he led Dillon into the living room, lightly holding his fingers.

"Dillon." Harrison faced Dillon, lightly holding both his hands. Dillon scanned Harrison's face, a slight smile on his lips.

"Yes?"

"I need to tell you something."

"You can tell me anything." Dillon's smile lit up his face.

"You might not feel that way in a minute."

Although Dillon maintained eye contact, a slight change in his breathing and how his eyebrows wrinkled together told Harrison of Dillon's puzzlement. The way his grip strengthened on Harrison's hands told him of Dillon's worry.

Did he want to do this?

The wine made him brave.

It's only fair. "I'm not Pippa."

25
Harrison: Truth

Dillon let Harrison's hands drop; he took a step back.

"What? I don't understand."

"Remember the storm earlier in the week?"

Dillon turned away, shaking his head. "I remember. No, you're Pippa."

"Have you ever seen the film *Manic Monday*? That happened."

"This isn't funny, Pip."

"I'm not joking, that's why."

"But." He started vocalising but stopped. "No."

"Yes." Harrison worked out what Dillon would have said had he dared think it. "I'm Prince Harrison."

"That. That makes no sense." Dillon's fingers went to his lips. "We kissed. More than once! *You* kissed *me*!"

"If it's any consolation, you and Pippa would have made a great couple. Physically, I want to drag you into my bedroom and have you now. Intellectually, I'm not feeling it. Sorry."

"If you're trying to let me down gently, this is not the way." Dillon's forehead wrinkles betrayed his hurt. "You could have said you were going to try to win Harrison's heart, or you didn't like me. Anything. But this lunacy is, is, *lunacy*!"

Harrison pressed on. He'd committed to telling Dillon he couldn't think of a reason to stop now. "Pippa and I have been attempting to find some way of switching back before she has to marry Isabella in my place."

"Stop it!" Dillon sat on the sofa, his head dropping into his hands. "No. You're Pippa."

Harrison joined him on the couch. Dillon responded by standing and heading for the door.

"Dillon. I need your help. Then you and Pippa can live happily ever after." Harrison forced the words through a tight chest. He wanted to be the one living happily ever after with Pippa. He couldn't relegate Pippa to concubine, his bit on the side. He wanted her to have a happy ever after. Knowing Pippa, she'd want that too. And that meant with Dillon. Not him.

Dillon paused by the door. "I don't understand why you're saying all

Royal Again   Iain Benson

this. I know you're drunk, but this is mean. You're going to end up alone. You know that, don't you? Harrison is not leaving Isabella for you."

His driver opened the door, breathing through his nose. "I'd say ring me tomorrow if you sober up. But no. Don't."

He walked out the door.

Tears rolled unchecked down Harrison's cheeks. His head hung down, his chin almost touching his chest, shoulders heaving with the sobs.

He'd handled that all wrong.

Darkness swirled around the flat, seeping into him.

A future exactly as Dillon described stretched out in lonely detail.

A knock had him rushing to fling open the door, expecting to see Dillon.

Instead of Dillon, he saw the journalist.

"I see your knight left. He didn't seem happy."

Harrison swallowed hard. His palms turning clammy. "If you don't leave, I'll call the police."

Mark rubbed his nose with his thumb, turning his head to the side. As though considering the chances of anybody ringing the police. "Go ahead. I'm not a danger to you. I don't plan on hurting you. It's going to be a hard sell. I only want to offer you three hundred thousand to dish the dirt on Harrison."

"I thought I told you to get lost." Dillon walked up the corridor, making Harrison's heart leap. "Are you particularly dense?"

"My mistake." Mark stepped back with his eyebrows raised. He gave them both long, steady looks and pushed aggressively past Dillon. Dillon held his ground, the reporter bouncing off him.

Dillon turned as Mark left, waiting until the stairwell door closed before he entered Pippa's apartment.

Harrison beamed at Dillon. "You came back!"

"I said I needed to rescue damsels more often."

"Consider me grateful."

Dillon made a beeline to the half a glass of wine Annie had left. He downed it in a single gulp. "You swapped bodies?"

Harrison leaned against the door. "Yes."

"Pippa is Harrison?"

Harrison shrugged a little. "That's right."

"What was the first thing Harrison said to me when I started as his driver?"

Iain Benson — Royal Again

Harrison searched his memory. He remembered seeing Dillon for the first time, pulling up outside a restaurant in the rain. "I think I asked you why you were late."

"Less polite, but that's right."

"I can only apologise. I'm coming to see what an arse I've been."

Pacing, Dillon kept pausing and glancing at Harrison, frowning, starting a gesticulation before wringing his hands.

Eventually, he stopped. "This explains a lot."

"Does it?" Harrison wondered what it explained.

"It explains Harrison." Dillon walked around the couch and dropped into it, rubbing his eyes. "You play Pippa far better than she plays you. Everybody is saying how much *nicer* Harrison is. Reece thinks it's because you're, she's, one of you is getting married. I thought hanging around Pippa rubbed off on you. Her. You."

"I am nice."

Scoffing, Dillon twisted towards Harrison. "No. You're not. Or at least you weren't."

"I'm nice now?"

Emotions flitted across Dillon's face. "Put it this way: I liked you. I mean, I thought you'd been a bit weird for the past few days. I understand that now. But we kissed."

"You're very good at that."

"Thanks. I think."

"Not many people have kissed their future monarch."

"Even fewer when they were temporarily a woman."

Harrison laughed. He realised he'd found more humour in situations while being Pippa than he had in all his time as himself. "You're probably unique in that case."

"Almost unique." Dillon wafted his hand toward the door. "I'm pretty certain you and Pippa have kissed."

Harrison held his hands up. "I'm not one to kiss and tell."

"The reporter found that out." Dillon's wry smile made Harrison laugh again. "Why did you decide to tell me? I'd never have known."

"You deserve to know. I've got to be married to Isabella, and Pippa deserves somebody who she can be with one hundred percent."

"Would you be together if you could?" Dillon spoke slowly.

"That would be up to Pippa."

"But you'd choose her over Isabella?"

Royal Again — Iain Benson

Harrison came slowly back to the sofa to delay answering. "Yes. If the world had different rules."

"You're in charge. You can set the rules."

"I'm bound by tradition." Harrison pressed his lips together. "Peer pressure from my ancestors. It's Pippa that's currently trapped in that cycle. I'm free, which is weirdly liberating. And simultaneously, terrifying."

"Have you found it difficult?" Dillon's puzzled expression stayed fixed on his face.

"Trying to go to the toilet when I'm wearing a pantsuit is difficult," Harrison said. "The rest of it seems straightforward after that. Except for mascara. That's also hard. As is eyeliner. It takes forty minutes to get up these days. And heels. I like them, but they hate me and can find the smallest crack on the floor. Sitting down to pee is okay, though." *And the orgasms!*

"I can't imagine coping." Dillon slumped forward. He stuttered a few times before eventually finding the words. "How did it happen?"

Wishing he still had wine left, Harrison told him about the stormy night and waking up as Pippa.

"We never really worked out the *how*." Harrison gave a brief sigh. "I wish I knew. Then we could recreate it and get on with our lives."

"Did you try electrocution again?"

Harrison clenched his hand in a mini fist pump. "That's what I suggested."

"What happens if you can't change back?"

Lapsing into silence, Harrison slumped back and stared at the ceiling. "I spend the rest of my life wondering where the next wage packet will come from. She has kids with Isabella, carrying on the royal line. We'll probably both be miserable. Now you know the truth. I can't see you wanting to be with me. I'm not sure I could do that to you either."

"I'm not sure it is an option anymore." Dillon's puzzlement morphed into glumness. "If I were in your place, I'd be trying to stop the wedding. Really, you and Harrison, sorry, you and Pippa need to be together. At least until you sort out who's in whose head. It's not fair to Isabella."

"Easier said than done," Harrison replied. "If it was a normal wedding, I could turn up at the church to explain why those two cannot wed."

Dillon gave a resigned shrug. "But it's a televised wedding being watched by half the world, with heads of state from dozens of countries and security so tight, they'll be able to tell who farted."

"Exactly."

"Pippa's currently at the palace. I dropped him, her, off before I came here." Dillon frowned. "We need to sneak you in so you can have one last go at switching back before tomorrow."

Laying his head back, Harrison knew how hopeless getting back into the palace would be. "My security clearance has been removed."

"If we can come up with a plan." Dillon spoke slowly. "I could go to the palace and brief Pippa."

"A plan for what? I think we need to be close to switch back."

"A plan for stopping the wedding."

"Pippa would know what to do." Harrison's voice dripped with the frustration and dismay bubbling through his veins.

"Call her."

Harrison picked up Pippa's phone. "Straight to voicemail."

Noticing the low charge on the phone, he took it to the kitchen and plugged it into the charger beside the microwave.

"I have an idea." Dillon's smile spread slowly across his face. "I can get you into the palace."

Harrison sat back beside his driver. "Only into the palace?"

"It's going to be manic tomorrow morning. They won't notice one more person."

"In the morning? That's cutting it fine!"

"Admittedly, it's the longest of long shots, but we're out of time."

"Okay, let me in on it."

"Well, the first part of this is we absolutely must keep Pippa in the dark. If she has any idea it's happening, it won't work. She'll try and help, and that'll alert security."

Harrison bit his lip. "This sounds risky!"

"The biggest rewards require the biggest risks." Dillon leaned forward. "Now, this is what we're going to do."

26
Pippa: The night before

When Dillon drove the car away, Pippa watched his car vanish, her hands hanging limply by her side. Possible alternate futures flitted across her tired mind.

She turned on her phone. He'd tried to call. She dialled back, getting her answerphone message.

"Call me when you get this Harrison," she told her phone. She bit her bottom lip, deep in thought, as she climbed the steps. She needed to know if he had any ideas. If he needed anything. That she missed him.

"Ciao, fratello." Tiffany bounded up the stairs, falling into step with her. She wore a multicoloured patchwork dress with a rustling skirt that created a wash of sound as they entered the bustling entrance hall.

"Tiff." Pippa wasn't in the mood for Harrison's sister. She kept walking.

"Come stai?"

Pippa knew enough Italian to spot Tiffany testing her. "Why do you suddenly care?"

She rattled through a complete sentence in Italian at speed. She might have asked about Pippa's celibacy, but Pippa couldn't follow her.

"I'm not playing, Tiff." Pippa gave Tiffany her best scowl. "Stop testing me. I'm not in the mood. The bachelor party was awful, and I want to go to bed."

"Hmm, so you understood me?"

"Either that or I got incredibly lucky," Pippa said, knowing she'd got lucky.

Staff opened doors as the pair went inside. Pippa fought down the urge to thank them. She put her phone away. She'd had to keep her phone off for the entire day. But now Harrison had his phone off. Pippa wondered if something had happened to him or if he'd got some food and gone to bed.

"Come on, Harpy. Who are you? Good job on the fingerprints, by the way. They convince the security scanner."

Halfway up the staircase, Pippa took a deep breath, releasing it slowly as she stopped and faced Harrison's sister. She sniffed, ensuring

Tiffany picked up on her displeasure.

"I really am too tired to get into this again, Tiff."

Tiffany wrinkled her nose and gave Pippa a cheeky grin. "Come on, you can tell me."

Pippa continued heading up to Harrison's room. Tiffany skipped along beside her, making Pippa think she might be high. She had form, although nobody had proved anything. She hooked arms with Pippa.

"There's only the two of us here. You can come clean."

Opening her apartment door, she extracted Tiffany from her arm. "Go to bed. We have a big day tomorrow."

Instead, Tiffany pushed through and bounced onto Harrison's sofa.

"Spill, and I'll go."

Pippa sat on a wingback chair to remove her shoes. "I'm an alien body snatcher. We ate Harrison and will rule this country, subjugating the entire population like cows for their alien overlords."

Tiffany tilted her head in both directions. "That sounds like a film. We could watch a film. Do you fancy watching *Wacky Wednesday*? *Large*? *He's Not Me*?"

Narrowing her eyes and folding her arms, Pippa waited a moment to get her churning emotions back under control. Keeping her voice steady and maintaining eye contact, she let herself relax. Naming three body swap films could be coincidental, but she doubted it. Tiffany knew. Or at least strongly suspected she knew. The public image of Tiffany being a flighty socialite seemed at odds with the person Pippa had come to know.

Sighing, Pippa got to her feet and took off her jacket. She draped it neatly over the chair back.

With a self-congratulatory 'Ha!', Tiffany pointed to this small act. "Harrison would never be that careful with his clothes to fold them up. He never did."

Biting her lip, Pippa turned to face Harrison's sister, leaning against the wall. The girl had a wry, playful smile with an expectant air, but still held her council.

"You get married *tomorrow*," Tiffany jabbed a finger in Pippa's direction.

With a deep, heartfelt sigh that expelled her doubts, Pippa decided to come clean. "I'm not Harrison."

"I know *that*!" Tiffany shrugged.

"I'm -" Pippa paused.

"You're Pippa!" Tiffany bounced off the bed and hugged Pippa.
Reluctantly, Pippa hugged Tiffany back. "Yes."
"I knew it!"
"How did you know?"
Tiffany laughed. "Loads of stuff. You'd be nice to people. You knew people's names! You didn't call me Whiffy *once*. You said I'd got high. I don't do drugs, Pippa. It's a front. H knows that. The socialite thing is to piss off Pa. God, this is *amazing*!"
"Not really. As you said, I get married tomorrow." Pippa rubbed her neck, frowning. "I've had no time to work out how to change back. And worse, Harrison's now back in my flat."
"Ring him."
Pippa took out Harrison's phone and rang her own again. "It's going straight to voice mail."
Although she suspected Harrison had gone to bed, the gnawing feeling of worry clenched her insides.
"That's a shame." Tiffany couldn't stay down for long. "I wanted to tease him about looking fabulous in a dress."
"Thanks," Pippa said.
Tiffany giggled. "Oh, yes! That's you being fabulous in a dress. Have you and he, you know?" Tiffany's gesture of her right index finger sliding in and out of her left fist made Pippa turn away, embarrassed. "You have! Oh! This is brilliant. Oh! I bet that's why you were late this morning."
With an ally, Pippa wondered if Harrison's sister's bouncy but sharp mind could help. "Do you have any ideas on how to turn back?"
"Have you tried rubbing a lamp? Ooh, touching a magical hourglass." Tiffany gave Pippa a playful punch on the arm. "Of course not. How did it happen?"
"You know the storm? He held my arm, and we both touched the doors, and all the lights went out. When we came to, he was me and I was him."
"Have you tried getting another shock?"
"I'd rather not risk electrocution." Pippa's head dropped. "It doesn't feel like the right answer. We weren't electrocuted."
"We need to go to the library!" Tiffany grabbed Pippa's hand, pulling her to the door.
"I really am tired." Pippa reluctantly allowed tiffany to drag her from the apartment. "What's in the library, anyway?"

"Books, dummy." Pippa found Tiffany's enthusiasm infectious. "The clue is in the name! From the Latin, *Libraria* or *Shop of Books*."

Deep within the house, Pippa heard a clock chime eleven. "Are you sure you don't do drugs? You're awfully bright for such a late hour."

"Nah. The night's just getting started. I'm only home because Pa told me he'd send me to a military academy in the Bahamas if I didn't make it to your wedding on time."

They crossed the landing from the suites towards the library, the hall a buzz of activity visible down the staircase. A team erected balloon arches, while another laid red carpet and a third put out floral displays, getting ready for the reception. Approaching from the other side, they met Harrison's grandmother dressed in a mint-green quilted dressing gown with a high neck.

"Lizzie!" Tiffany gave her grandmother a brief hug.

"Where are you two skulking off to at this hour?" Elizabeth asked, an odd twinkle in her eye.

"Library." Tiffany gave Elizabeth a broad smile and grabbed Pippa's sleeve.

"I've just come from there." Elizabeth bobbed her head. "I have left a couple of books out. You can leave them. I'll deal with them tomorrow. How are you feeling about tomorrow, *Harry*?"

The way she said Harrison's name only increased Pippa's suspicions over what Elizabeth knew. "A little nervous."

"I'm sure there will be a Happy Ever After," the older woman told them. She patted Pippa's arm. "Fairy tales tend to end that way."

"Unless they're written by the Brothers Grimm," Pippa replied.

"True, true," Elizabeth glanced around, lowering her voice. "Well, if you wonder at what big eyes I've got, you'll need to find a woodcutter, pronto."

"Come on!" Tiffany bounded away like an eager collie, before returning and grabbing Pippa's sleeve again.

"Goodnight," Pippa said as Elizabeth set off to bed.

She gave a half wave over her shoulder. Pippa heard Elizabeth say "Goodnight", but she could have testified under oath that the older woman also said "Pippa" not "Harry".

She had no time to ponder on what she'd heard, as Tiffany dragged her down the East Wing Gallery and into the Grand Library.

It had been a few years since Pippa had worked in the library. She had memories of traipsing up and down the movable stepladder to dust the acres of chestnut brown shelving. The cleaning staff considered it a punishment to be assigned to dust the books. Opposite the floor-to-ceiling bookcases, tall, mullioned windows overlooked the darkness beyond. The dark turned them into mirrors, reflecting lamps and reading desks. Near the main door, a pair of wingback chairs created a small nook, with an occasional table between them. On the table, Pippa spotted the books Elizabeth mentioned.

The number of books overwhelmed Pippa. "What book are we looking for?"

"We can ignore everything down that end," Tiffany said, waving her arm to the library's far end. "They're all *boring* law books."

"You want us to search all these books looking for a solution?" Pippa put her hands on her hips, feeling insignificant next to the mass of words facing her. "Can I wait for the movie?"

"Do you have a better idea?" Tiffany grabbed a thick, leather-bound book. It looked random but wasn't. She plonked herself down in a wingback chair. "We'll start with our family history. I'll take Pa's side, you take Ma's."

The family history had a second volume on the shelf. Shaking her head, Pippa pulled it off and sat opposite Harrison's sister. She desultorily flicked through. Words swam on the page. Only one page really caught her interest. It detailed how they'd locked Harrison's mother away in her room for a whole ten days before her wedding to the king, to the point where the press had started to speculate if she had been abducted.

"This is possibly the worst book I've ever read." Pippa barely took in a single word. "It needs more pictures."

"I've got an idea." Tiffany's head snapped up from her book.

A sense of excitement built in Pippa. "Go on?"

"When you do switch bodies back, you and I can have a girls' night!"

Tiffany's swerve threw Pippa a little bit. Hesitantly, she agreed. "Yes, okay."

Reading the family history almost put Pippa to sleep. Instead, her attention returned to the two books on the occasional table. Elizabeth's cryptic words echoed in her ears. Plus, the one on the top had pictures. Pippa picked it up to find it open on a fairy story about a witch's curse broken by True Love's kiss.

"That explains her infatuation with True Love's kiss," Pippa muttered.

"What was that?" Tiffany's head snapped up.

"Oh, it's this book your grandmother was reading." Pippa turned it so Tiffany could see. "A curse is broken by True Love's kiss."

Her face lit up, and Tiffany jumped to her feet. "That's it!"

"What?"

"True Love's kiss!"

Pippa shook her head. "Sorry, but we kissed this morning. And some other things."

"Oh." Tiffany folded back into the chair, her smile crumpling. She sat up straight. "And some other things. You two are so cute!"

Out of interest, Pippa swapped the fairy tale with the other book on the table. At some point, somebody had bound newspaper clippings into a scrapbook. Elizabeth had it open on the night before her wedding.

Pippa almost dropped the book. She blinked several times and re-read the story.

"You've got something?" Tiffany's eager tone almost dragged Pippa's eyes from the paper.

"Your grandmother did actually have an affair with a stable hand."

"Meh. I thought everybody knew that."

"They were inseparable for the days leading up to her wedding to your granddad, until her father, your great-granddad, had him deported."

"Oh! That is news. Hang on. I'm spotting parallels here."

Pippa agreed, putting the book back on the table and stabbing it. "I think this has happened before! We need to speak to Elizabeth."

"Gotta wait until morning for that."

"This is too important."

"Doesn't matter. She takes her hearing aids out and can't hear anything."

"The wedding morning?" Pippa entwined her fingers, blowing a stream of air towards the ceiling. "That's cutting it fine."

Tiffany bounded from her chair. "In that case, we'd best get some sleep."

A sentiment Pippa could get behind. She walked beside a skipping Tiffany who still had enough energy to power a small country. Tiffany linked arms with Pippa. "I'm going to show you some amazing clubs when you're free. I think we'll go to Coco's first."

Pippa scoffed. "I can't afford Coco's."

"I don't pay for anything!" Tiffany laughed. "Me being there makes

Royal Again   Iain Benson

Coco's popular. I'm like the ultimate influencer. Hey, I should get a social media channel!"

"Er, I suppose."

Stopping near the stairs, Tiffany frowned. "That bachelor party must have been ick for you."

"Yes. Harrison knows some awful people."

"How on Earth did you cope with Jack and co?"

Pippa shrugged. "How do you mean?"

"Jack's known you since you were both fifteen, the others since you were at uni."

"I let them fill in the details," Pippa said. "They're boys. They'll happily talk about themselves and the women who they claim to have been with."

"You don't think they have?"

"I wouldn't touch them if I wore a hazmat suit."

"Preach, girl." Tiffany flicked her fingers like a gangsta rapper. "You're right. I'd swerve, too."

"I used to think Harrison was like that." Pippa's voice softened.

"He's a stuffed suit," Tiffany said, starting walking again. "I think being you has been good for him. What do you think he'll do if you swap back?"

They'd nearly reached Harrison's apartment. Pippa paused, suddenly saddened. "I think he'll drop me in a hot second and marry Isabella. She's gorgeous, rich and will be queen."

"You might be right." Tiffany pulled a face. "Would you have him if he didn't?"

Pippa's microscopic shrug barely conveyed her indecision. "I don't know. Having been him, I know how important tradition is to him."

"Lizzie thinks you'll get a happy ever after. She said so. And she should know. I bet she's been where you and Harrison are now. Tomorrow, we'll find out."

Opening Harrison's door, Pippa gave Tiffany a confident smile. For once, she looked forward to the family breakfast with something approaching hope.

"I'll see you in the morning."

27
Pippa: Wedding morning

For the first time since the switch, Pippa couldn't wait to get down to breakfast. She put on a dark blue polo shirt and jeans without feeling the usual dread of the day.

Her eagerness translated into being the first one to the breakfast table, apart from the two butlers. Tim placed a coffee on the table. A neatly folded newspaper marked the King's place.

"Thanks, Tim."

"Sire." Tim's astonished intake of breath told Pippa she'd messed up again.

"Suh, fam." Tiffany bounded into the room. Her frivolous act slipped momentarily as she scrutinised the three empty chairs. "Are we first?"

"Looks like." Pippa sipped the coffee.

"I'm never first." Tiffany sat anyway, accepting her coffee with a smile to Tim.

"This is a surprise." William entered with Charlotte. "It is a long time since you *both* beat us to the table. Especially you, Tiffany."

She made a *whatever* gesture with her fingers to her father. "I seem to remember you telling me to be here. Here I am."

"Very good." The king took his place and unfolded his newspaper. The front page contained a huge photograph of Harrison carrying Isabella from a dance with the headline "Wedding of the Century" reminding Pippa of how little time remained.

"Did you sleep well, Harry?" Charlotte asked.

"Not really," Pippa replied.

Harrison's mother gave him a sympathetic smile. "Are you excited?"

Pippa's wry smile betrayed her genuine feelings. "Not excited, really. Anxious, terrified, overwhelmed."

"It's a big day."

"I was reading the family history last night." Pippa glanced at Tiffany, who blanched.

"Harry," Tiffany hissed.

Giving Harrison's sister a subtle wave, Pippa hoped Tiffany trusted

Royal Again   Iain Benson

her enough.

"You really couldn't sleep." Charlotte sounded amused.

"I wanted to read about the wedding of you and Pa."

A cloud crossed over Charlotte's face. Pippa wondered whether she could continue. She ploughed on. "Were you really locked away for over a week before the wedding?"

"My mother confined me to my suite for ten days." Charlotte gave a sad shrug. "I was to contemplate my future with William. I couldn't even see the people bringing me my food. Only on the wedding day did I see anybody, and they dressed me and did my hair."

Colliding eyebrows and a slight frown fleetingly crossed Tiffany's features. She and Pippa exchanged glances.

"Lizzie gaslit you?" Tiffany's slightly raised tone betrayed her disgust.

"Safety first," Elizabeth said, finally arriving. "I didn't want anything happening to Charlotte that close to the wedding."

"It was a different time," Charlotte said, her tone tinged with sadness. "A lot of trouble in the kingdom."

As Elizabeth sat, the butlers brought breakfast. Pippa detested granola and yoghurt. With each desultory spoonful, she resolved never to eat it again once she had her body back.

"Are you all prepared for the wedding?" William folded his newspaper to appraise Pippa.

"As I'll ever be," Pippa replied. "My schedule is tight leading up to the bridal march. I might at some point have a bit of time to think."

Elizabeth maintained her enigmatic approach to the breakfast conversation. "I think this will be a most memorable wedding."

"It's being broadcast to one hundred and fifty countries." William sounded quite proud of that. "They think a billion people might be watching."

"No pressure then." Pippa realised with a crushed heart that with the weight of so much expectation, she would be marrying Isabella. Even if Harrison swung in on a bell rope like a pirate.

The granola bowls became poached eggs on ciabatta without Pippa noticing. Each time she blinked, Isabella's face swam into view. How could Harrison get to her? More importantly, how could they change back? She needed to get Elizabeth alone. Jostling in the chair beside her, Tiffany obviously felt the same way.

"And Tiffany," William continued, dragging his daughter's attention from her untouched eggs. "I need you in your bridesmaid dress by ten. The makeup woman is arriving shortly after that."

Tiffany lowered her chin to stare at her father. "That dress is simply hideous. Purple? Nobody looks good in purple. I'd better not eat these eggs. Tight silk shows every centimetre of cellulite."

"I feel you are being overly dramatic." William tucked into his eggs, safe in the knowledge that his suit would have hidden the bulge from a breakfast pizza.

"I saw Isabella's dress yesterday." Charlotte tilted her head and smiled at the memory. "It will bowl you over."

"If there are another nine people beside Harry, she'll get a strike." Tiffany grinned and turned to Pippa, mouthing: "I'll talk to Lizzie."

The briefest of nods acknowledged Tiffany's surreptitious message.

"Tiffany, hardly the place for humour." Charlotte scolded her daughter, but only gently.

"Breakfast? Start the day with an egg and a giggle." Tiffany kept her twinkling eyes on her mother.

Charlotte had the grace to smile.

"I need to cut this short. I'm having my nails buffed." Pippa folded her napkin and placed it on the plate, her appetite gone, her mouth dry. Why she'd ever entertained the notion she would get to speak to Elizabeth alone, she didn't know.

"Drink plenty of fluids," Elizabeth said.

If any cryptic meaning existed in that statement, Pippa could not discern it. "Why?"

"We don't want you fainting in front of a billion viewers." Elizabeth's twinkling smile made her appear amused at the prospect.

"One more pressure to consider," Pippa muttered and returned to Harrison's suite.

With a towel wrapped around her waist, she emerged from the ensuite to discover Tiffany sitting on Harrison's bed, swinging her legs so they bounced off the base. She had earphones in, swaying her head. Seeing Pippa, she popped the earphones out and stopped the music on her phone.

"God! You take ages! Were you in there playing with your new limb?"

Pippa shuddered. "No. I try to avoid looking at it."

Royal Again   Iain Benson

"I'd definitely be playing with it." Tiffany bounded off the bed to examine Pippa's wedding suit, hanging up on a portable rail.

"I can kind of switch off that I'm a man," Pippa admitted. "That limb reminds me. Every time I see it, I get a sick feeling in my stomach."

"There's a girl I sometimes meet up with at Flamingos." Tiffany lifted the suit off the rack and held it up against herself in the mirror. "She feels the same. But Jessica has had a penis since she was born. You'd think she'd be used to seeing it by now."

"Hopefully, I won't have it much longer." Pippa let the towel drop and started dressing.

"Big yikes! That is so cringe."

"Tell me about it. I thought I'd over share." Her wedding suit had a few layers. Unless the cathedral's air held a deep chill, she would boil. "Also, tell me about what Lizzie said."

"Lizzie is a mardy cow. I told her you were Pippa."

"What did she say?"

"That she knew who you were." Tiffany handed Pippa the suit. "So, I'm like: How do we switch them back? And she comes back with 'I couldn't say'."

"Couldn't or wouldn't?"

"I guess both. She's being really sus about all this. She defo knows loads, but she's keeping it close." Tiffany screwed up her face and stomped off to the window to stare at the rain and wind lashing the courtyard below.

"Basically, we are where we were before." Pippa scowled as she tried to do the weird, thick tie. "She knows what's happened, which means she's seen this before. Yet she won't help. I mean, seriously? It's like she's taking a perverse pleasure in all this."

Tiffany saw Pippa struggling with the cravat. "Where's your valet to dress you?"

"Harrison sacked him."

Tiffany's lips pulled inside as she suppressed a giggle. "Typical. Here, let me. Don't they teach stuff like this at school?"

Pippa released the ends, allowing Tiffany to take over. "No. They teach us stuff like the exports of Norway and how many electrons a lithium atom has."

Tiffany wrinkled her nose. "Useful. How many?"

"How many what?"

"Electrons."

"I can't remember."

"Feels." Tiffany stepped back. "There. You'll pass. How did you know I liked *Paw Patrol*?"

The change in direction wrong-footed Pippa for a moment. "Er, you used to run around cosplaying the characters."

"Sweet. I wanted to be Chase when I grew up."

"Is that the police dog?"

"Yeah. Woof."

Pippa shrugged into the dark grey jacket. The smooth material slipped on easily, the silk lining felt sensual. She appreciated the man standing there.

"Your brother is really handsome." She twisted to check her sleek lines from several angles.

"If you like hunky guys, yeah, sure."

"You don't?"

"They're okay." Tiffany shrugged. "Pa will probs marry me off with one. But I like a pulse. Beyond that, not fussy. I draw the line at my brother! Even if you are someone else. Shudder!"

Pippa laughed. She liked Tiffany. "I think I'm done."

"I'm gonna miss you when Harrison comes back." Tiffany risked crumpling Pippa's tailcoat by hugging her. "He was a stuffy shirt. You're more fun. Can you stay?"

"I'd rather not." Pippa picked up a top hat and put it on her head. "I don't fancy Isabella."

"Don't wear the hat inside," Tiffany told her. "It's uncouth. You hold it under your left arm." Tiffany whipped the hat off Pippa's head. She rested the brim on her hip, her forearm resting on the top. "Like this, and only like this."

Pippa held the hat as instructed. "Like this."

"Yep. You look good."

Worried, Pippa checked the time. It had gone slightly past ten. "Don't you need to get ready?"

"Whatevs. It takes like five seconds to put on that stupid dress, and Femi will bitch and do my makeup anyway. Regardless of when she starts. What have you got next?"

"Photos."

Tiffany pretended to have a camera. "Shoulder to the camera! Chin up. Look over my shoulder. I want love, I want anger, I want camomile tea

Royal Again — Iain Benson

with three spoons of sugar. Mwah. You're gorgeous."

Laughing, Tiffany pirouetted and skipped from the apartment.

Pippa felt the momentary emptiness in the room that grew whenever Tiffany left a space.

With a final check in the mirror, Pippa headed down to the entrance hall. She spotted a pair of lawyers from the lunch she'd had. Their names escaped her.

Ivor, Mike, Adrian, and Jack formed a second knot of people she recognised. All six wore tailcoats, holding their top hats as she held hers. Their waistcoats differentiated their outfits. Where she wore a dark grey to match her jacket, their purple matched the bridesmaids. Pippa's groomsmen laughed and joked, nudging one another, but remained careful to keep their clothing pristine.

Sneaking up on them, she leaned into Jack's ear over his shoulder. "Oink."

Clasping his hand to his chest, Jack pretended Pippa has startled him. "I thought the ghost of Christmas pig had appeared to wreak his revenge."

It astounded Pippa that Harrison's friends couldn't spot the change in his behaviour.

"You're slapping," Ivor said, whistling as he surveyed Pippa's outfit.

"Have you been taking lessons off Tiff?" Pippa asked, raising an eyebrow.

"I'd like to," Ivor admitted lasciviously.

"She'd chew you up and spit you out," Mike said. "Now me, that's a different story."

"She'd probably ignore you," Pippa said.

"Moi?" Mike made a mock-offence pose, his free hand up by his head.

"She wants somebody with a pulse."

Mike simulated a heart attack, swaying and holding his chest. Pippa had picked up enough to understand about their interactions to play along, but she felt parts of her soul dying with every casual misogynistic comment they made.

Jack gave Pippa an appreciative nod. "You scrub up well. Nervous?"

"Freaking out."

"Freakout!" Adrian and Ivor said together, giving each other a high five.

"You'll be fine. Stiff upper lip and an even stiffer brandy." Jack clapped Pippa's shoulder.

Adrian clasped Pippa's other shoulder. "And if you faint, I'm recording the whole thing for TikTok."

"That's true friendship, right there." Pippa smiled at them.

"We got you, bro," Ivor said right before the photographer wanted them all to start gathering.

"Here we go," Pippa muttered, following Harrison's friends.

28
Harrison: Wedding morning

Temptation revealed itself in the form of Pippa's jeans in her tiny wardrobe.

Trousers.

Harrison took them from the hanger, holding them for several seconds. Dillon's plan centred around Harrison being able to get close to Pippa. Scruffy wouldn't allow that. He put the jeans back into the wardrobe and removed a designer dress from Hillary McNair's boutique, a luxurious dark blue knee-length. Harrison regarded the beautiful garment, but even now, trepidation flooded through him as he laid it on the bed. He pulled out a pair of nude courts with a three-inch heel, wincing as he recalled his previous dalliance with heels for an extended time. His toes still hated him.

Pulling off the oversized tee he slept in, he showered and washed his hair. Again. He needed to learn to style it without washing it first. As a man, he also showered and washed his hair daily, but he could use his two-in-one shampoo and body wash and it would be dry before he'd finished shaving. He'd also made do with one hairbrush. Pippa had four. When he'd first seen them, he'd laughed at the number, wondering at their uses. Now, he knew they all served a vital and different purpose, from untangling to adding body or shine. None of which had been an issue for him before.

Pippa had no dressing table. He had to make do with the bed, his legs dangling off the end. He spread Pippa's makeup on the chest of drawers. Slowly, he applied foundation and contouring before beginning the delicate operation of his eyes. Pippa had a steady hand, which helped. Especially with eyeliner.

Tapping the felt-tip pen against his reflection in the mirror, he wished that an easier way of applying eyeliner existed. With nothing materialising, he popped the lid, rested his elbow on the vanity and drew along his lashes.

"Oh!" He smiled. He'd got it right. He felt quite pleased with himself. It would require many years of mastery before he got to the level of applying it without a mirror or while on the bus. This notion, plus the further trials of blending eyeshadow colours and the risks of mascara, tempered his joy.

Halfway through, one eye done, one eye still to do, Dillon arrived.

"I'd hoped you'd be ready," he said.

"I nearly am."

"I might make a coffee while I wait." Dillon had a cheeky smile.

"I've only got one eye left to do!"

Dillon folded his arms and dramatically tapped his foot. "Exactly."

Muttering, Harrison returned to finish his other eye. He refused to let Dillon's arrival pressure him. The pressure would make him make a mistake and force him to start over.

He came out to discover Dillon had made them both a coffee.

"Wow." He put his coffee down and pushed a mug towards Harrison.

"Is that a 'wow' for my speed or how I look?"

"Both," Dillon said. "You look incredible. And you finished in under an hour."

Glancing at the microwave clock, Harrison kept quiet on how long ago he'd begun the process. "Shall we go?"

"We need to," Dillon said. He gulped a large glug of coffee, grimacing. "I'm not the driver today. They didn't give me Harrison's schedule. I got a sneak peek, and I think they're doing photos right now. After that, there will be a carriage ride to the cathedral."

"I remember." He'd read it so often that the schedule was burned in Harrison's brain.

Stopping short of slapping his forehead, Dillon still verbally scolded himself. "Yes, of course you do."

Harrison had never considered what kind of car Dillon might drive. A little black Mini would have been low on the list. Until his termination, he'd never sat shotgun with his driver, always in the back. Harrison added it to the list of things he would change. The sensation of Dillon speeding along the country lane towards the palace made Harrison's heart race. It had to be the speed and not the way Pippa's body reacted to Dillon's proximity, his smell, and the small noises he made as he changed gear.

"You suit my passenger seat." Dillon turned to Harrison as they waited at the traffic lights, the windscreen wipers squeaking with each swish.

Around them, Harrison noticed crowds with flags had started to gather in preparation for the wedding carriage, despite the rain.

Unsure how to take that, Harrison smiled. "Thanks. I think."

"I can't get my head around you not being Pippa." Dillon's returned

Royal Again   Iain Benson

smile turned sad. "Do you ever wish you'd done something sooner?"

"Most things," Harrison admitted. "Like what specifically?"

"Like ask you, Pippa, out months ago." Shifting gear, Dillon pulled away from the lights, taking the turn onto the road up to the palace.

They quickly caught up to the palace staff minibus, the white vehicle slowing their progress to a seeming crawl. Harrison's anxiety rose a notch. He wished he'd got up ten minutes earlier to be ready when Dillon arrived. He clasped his hands in his lap.

Sensing his tension, Dillon reached across and squeezed Harrison's hand. "We'll make it."

His strong grip eased some apprehension. Harrison squeezed back, releasing as Dillon shifted gears to overtake the slow-moving minibus. In the distance, the white marble palace created a misty mirage amid the rolling landscaped hills emerging from the rain. A lightning flash reflected off the dozens of windows. Dillon slowed at the entrance gates and security lodge.

"Hey Keith," Dillon passed over his pass.

Keith took the pass, pushing his hat up his bald head and scanning Dillon in. "Who's the lady, Dill?"

"She's my girlfriend." Dillon smiled.

"You're not scheduled to be in today." Keith's thick features glacially moved into concern.

"I promised Penelope she could see the wedding carriage before they reached the crowds. You should see town. It's already heaving."

Keith scratched his eyelid before rubbing his cheek. "It's unorthodox, mate. I can't really let you in."

Dillon spread his palms. "Mate, you're killing me. You know me! There must be some perks to this job. Surely?"

Keith switched from massaging his cheek to rubbing his chin with his thumb, but his dubious expression remained. "I know you. But the lady? She might have abducted you."

Harrison weighed up the options and leaned onto Dillon's knee so Keith could see him clearly, even though it meant the rain splattered her face. "Keith, it's me. Pippa."

"Pippa?" Keith's face lit up a little. "You not been sacked for sleeping with the prince?"

"They sacked me because the *press* said I'd slept with him. I'm with Dillon. I wouldn't sleep with that jackass if the press paid me to. Which they keep trying to do!"

"You and Dillon?" Keith gave a chortle. "You two kept that quiet."

Harrison flashed a smile. "You know how Annie is with staff hooking up. Now I'm sacked, we can be honest. Can't we Dillon?"

Dillon rode Harrison's ruse. "Absolutely."

Harrison pecked Dillon's lips. "It's okay if we can't see the carriage leaving the palace. We'll join the crowds in town."

Giving a friendly sigh, Keith returned Dillon's pass. "I know you both. Like you say. Got to have perks in this job. Don't go making me regret it, Pippa! Glad to see you happy."

"Thanks, Keith."

"Love to Jen," Dillon said, setting off with the barrier still rising. He glanced at Harrison, grinning. "Nice move."

"You just wanted a kiss." Harrison gave Dillon a playful nudge.

The staff drive curved around the palace to the back and into the staff carpark. Above them, the palace's staff entrance lacked the grandeur around the front. No marble like the façade, only red brick, the ground gravelled instead of flagged. Dillon negotiated the bends on autopilot. He'd driven this route many times. His familiarity almost caused him to rear-end the car parked in his usual spot. Tutting, Dillon reversed into a free space by the palace wall.

"You know the plan?" Dillon turned off the ignition and gave Harrison his full attention.

"Yes."

Dillon pulled his phone off the dash charger. "If they don't let you in, just come straight back out. I'll open the fire door in the stores."

Pippa discovered exiting a mini created a whole new set of problems he'd not yet had the fortune to experience. The low clearance combined with heels, rain and gravel almost caused the plan to fail before he'd completed the first part of getting into the palace.

"Are you okay?" Dillon reached across.

"Fine." Harrison took a deep breath and tried again, holding onto the seatbelt and car door. At least he'd remembered to swing his feet out first, so both feet connected with the uneven surface before he stood.

Feeling every stone beneath his soles, he reached the staff entrance with both ankles intact.

He'd half expected George to be on the security desk, but he came across a man he didn't recognise.

The security guard, however, recognised him. "Pippa. You can't be

Royal Again

Iain Benson

here."

"I need to clear out my locker. Give Annie a ring, she'll okay me." Harrison leaned on the security desk, aware the V-neck on his dress allowed the security guard a good leer at his cleavage.

He bent his head down, running long fingers through his buzz-cut and tutted. With a sniff, he picked up his phone handset and hit buttons. After a moment, Harrison heard it connect.

"Annie? Yeah. It's Simon on the staff desk." Simon gave Harrison a shrug that involved his whole body. "Yeah. Hi. Listen. Pippa's here. Yeah. Locker. Okay."

He hung up.

"Can I come in now?"

"Annie's coming down," Simon said.

"Thanks, Simon."

"Yeah. I feel for you." One corner of his mouth lifted. Harrison assumed he'd attempted sympathy, but it made him appear sardonic. "I heard nothing happened. They've treated you real shoddy like."

"Even the innocent get hung out to dry if it risks the family." Harrison had previously never cared, but having received that treatment, he mentally added it to his list of Things That Would Change.

"Yeah. True. True." Simon sniffed. "They shouldn't treat you like that, though."

Annie came bustling in. "Pippa! I wasn't expecting you!"

Harrison turned his full beam onto Pippa's former supervisor. "It's just you mentioned last night about my locker."

Annie pushed her glasses up into her thick hair, lifting her corkscrew fringe away from her forehead. "It's bad timing. You know Harrison's getting married? You're not here to do something stupid, are you? After what you said last night, it's crossing my mind."

"The wedding is front page news in every country." Harrison laughed. "I am here for my locker. I figured fewer people would be about."

"That is very true." Annie's smile faltered for a moment. "Simon, let her through."

The glass door buzzed. Harrison pushed through, his breath catching in his throat as he did so. "Thanks, Annie."

He accompanied Annie down the corridor towards the locker room.

"I'm not going to be able to help." Her eyes widened, and she threw her hands up. "There is so much to do today!"

"I understand. It's fine."

"I'd have brought it to you, you know?"

Harrison leaned in to hold Annie's arm. "You're welcome to pop over any time. You don't need an excuse. Bringing wine would be an acceptable reason."

Annie gave a tinkling laugh, suggesting that Pippa may well have a new friend. "I'll take you up on that. Was that Dillon's car outside?" Harrison's blush made Annie's eyebrows shoot up. "I think you've landed on your feet there, girl! He's *gorgeous*."

Unconsciously, Harrison's lips made a kissing motion. "He is."

Annie put her hand on the doorframe. "I need to get on. Ask the kitchen for a box if you need it. Take some fruit while you're at it."

"Thanks."

To complete the charade, Harrison opened Pippa's locker. He didn't need a box for a can of deodorant, a charging cable, and some nail polish. The spare apron could stay. All the items fit in his handbag. Harrison left the locker room and checked back down the corridor to Annie's office.

Annie had closed the door.

Aware of his heels clicking on the hard floor, Harrison headed away from the staff entrance towards the Entrance Hall.

He remembered the itinerary. They would gather everybody together for photographs.

At the T-junction, he paused, calming his breathing.

He closed his eyes. "Time for your grand entrance."

He rounded the corner straight into two security guards he didn't recognise. They wore identical black suits with white shirts of agency security. Both had earpieces and short hair.

"The Entrance Hall is off limits, miss." The left-hand one held up his hand, palm outward. "The pre-wedding photos are wrapping up."

"I need to get through." Harrison tried injecting as much of his royal authority as Pippa's voice could muster.

The security guard returned to his position, hands clasped in front of him. He'd said his piece.

"It's vital I get a message to the wedding party."

The slight shake of his head gave Harrison his answer. "Not happening."

"That's not Prince Harrison. It's an imposter."

The guard who hadn't spoken chortled. "Nice try, Ms Palmer. We know who you are. Please leave now, or we will physically escort you off the premises."

The first guard tilted his head and turned away, touching his ear. He used a muffled voice, but Harrison still made out his words. "They're heading for the secondary location."

"What?" Harrison turned and tried to head as fast down the corridor as he could without his heels skidding from under him.

On the way out, Harrison tapped on Annie's window and waved with, he hoped, a friendly smile. She waved back, currently on the phone.

"Bye, Simon," he said as the security guard let him out. "If I don't see you again, it's been fun."

"Stay safe, Pip."

He found Dillon leaning against the Mini. "What's happened?"

"They've got additional security for the event." Harrison felt breathless. "I couldn't get past."

"You told them it wasn't Harrison?"

"Of course! They laughed."

"Where are they now?" Dillon opened the door for Harrison, helping him in.

"They're heading to the secondary location."

"I don't know where that is." Dillon slumped.

"I do." Harrison clipped his seatbelt. "And we have a good chance of getting in front of Pippa."

29
Pippa: Wedding lunch

Waving to the crowd, William and Charlotte had their backs to the coach driver opposite Pippa and Jack. The horse-drawn carriage clopped down the road at a sedate pace, allowing the throng lining the streets to see the royal family as they passed.

Smiling and waving, Pippa tried to uphold the pomp and ceremony, but she wanted to climb down from the carriage and run and vanish into the crowd.

"This is an ego trip," Jack muttered out from the side of his mouth.

"I'd rather have arrived at the church on the back of a Vespa." Pippa's smile barely faltered. "This is interminable."

Jack's infectious laugh brought a genuine smile to Pippa's lips. "It's hardly royal, turning up like a food delivery, though, is it?"

Singing the popular jingle, Pippa grinned. "Did somebody say *'Just Married'*?"

"Prince Harrison, I love you!" shouted a young woman from the crowd. Pippa located her and blew a kiss.

"Don't pander to them, Harry," William scolded. "Smile, wave and repeat."

"The people in the crowd marry for love, Pa. They assume I love Isabella."

"Love is such a transient emotion." William spoke through his fake smile, not even glancing in Pippa's direction. "Your mother and I have something far deeper."

"The passwords for each other's bank accounts?" Jack asked.

Pippa and Charlotte laughed. William's amusement required more work. Pippa understood how Jack and Harrison had become lifelong friends. Away from Adrian, Mike, and Ivor, Jack became a congenial person.

William patted his wife's hand. "A mutual respect, Jack."

Charlotte waved her hand from side to side and winked at Pippa.

"Probably not something anybody ever asked their parents." Pippa kept waving and smiling. "But if you don't love each other, how do you have kids?"

"The traditional way, Harry," Charlotte said.

Royal Again — Iain Benson

Jack leaned over and stage-whispered in Pippa's ear. "Viagra and KY Jelly."

Charlotte's eyebrows rose as Pippa struggled to contain her laughter from bursting out.

"I hope your best man's speech is more family-friendly, Jack." William's smile faltered for a moment.

"I'm listing H's girlfriends in alphabetical order." Jack's lips twitched. "I've got the alphabet mostly covered. I need one for P."

The King's drawn eyebrows and narrowed eyes warned Pippa of a thunderstorm gathering inside the carriage to match the one outside. Jack had pushed a little too far.

"Probably best not lead with that one, Jack." Pippa nudged Harrison's friend.

Jack held up a single finger. "Someone vetted my speech. I solemnly swear to hold off the ad-libs."

"If you need a memory aid to that effect." William cocked his head to the side, amused. "Remember, every newspaper in the world will carry a transcript. Half the world will read your words."

Jack sniffed. "What I'm hearing is, this could really kick-start my comedy career."

William's smile touched on the sardonic. "It would end your oil business, so I hope the comedy is as lucrative."

"Point taken." Jack waved to some people in the crowd.

Turning into a tavern courtyard surprised Pippa. The cathedral loomed over the inn, but they stopped in a cobbled yard straight out of a period drama.

Hemmed in on all four sides by white stucco buildings, Pippa climbed from the carriage. An umbrella magically appeared, popping open for the short walk across the cobbles to a portico entrance. The narrow windows flanking the door let more light escape than they admitted. The building's interior washed warmth over them. Scents of cooking twined around her as she followed William and Charlotte deeper into the ancient building.

They reached a long room filled with a heavy wooden table, tall-backed chairs and Pippa's wedding party. Her groomsmen toasted her entrance with raised glasses. The terracotta tiled floor and glass droplet chandeliers would be a terrible chore to clean. Judging by the centuries of patina on the wooden panelled walls, nobody had bothered.

"Lunch?" Jack asked.

"This is an old family tradition," the King said. "Before the wedding of a crown prince, there is one last feast of freedom held in this venue."

Charlotte's eyes rolled. "There is normally a parade of wenches for the prince to select from."

"We have not done that for many generations," William pointed out. "The parade is merely ceremonial. Harry will pick one and kiss them so they can leave."

Jack and Pippa took adjacent chairs. He nudged Pippa. "You might get lucky, and that maid is up there."

"The only reason Pa would do that is to dare me to choose her."

"Call him out, kiss her like you mean it."

"Or just sweep her off her feet, leave the building, and vanish forever."

Jack laughed, punching Pippa's shoulder. "Now, *that* is a plan I can get behind."

"I'd have you found before you reached the street." William leaned between the pair. "I know I can't call for executions anymore, but I'd make an exception for that girl."

"It might be a fun game of hide and seek." Jack's attempts to force humour into William continued to fail.

The grandfather clock made a muted chime. Pippa idly noted the smears on the glass obscuring the numbers. "We've got two hours before we have to stand at the altar like good little church boys."

Jack winked. "Well, if you need me to source you fake IDs, I'll need a little more notice."

The servers saved Pippa from taking Jack up on his offer by bringing food. Jack turned to Adrian on the other side, with them soon degenerating into the banal banter that sent Jack's jackass meter rising rapidly. Pippa waited, watching the door. All the noise, the talking, banter and laughing washed around her and left her feeling strangely isolated. They all knew Harrison. They knew him better than she did. She didn't dare join in. She might slip up. They might uncover her subterfuge.

At that moment, in a room filled with people, Pippa had never felt so alone.

A loud crash echoed through the door to the kitchens. A small part of Pippa hoped Harrison caused it and would come bursting through the door to save her. She recognised the irony: a damsel rescuing the prince, but still with the prince rescuing the damsel.

"If I ever get through this, I'm making it into a movie."

"Make sure you include the spicy honeymoon scene at the end." Jack had overheard and nudged Pippa's ribs. "And change all the names."

"Is H making a film?" Adrian leaned forward. "I think that guy who played Thor should play me."

"Thor?" Pippa's tone rose from incredulous into amused.

"Why are you laughing?"

"Thor has biceps."

Adrian looked at his arms, flexing his right bicep and prodding it.

Food came from the kitchen. Pippa tried to see where the crash had come from, scanning each face to see if Harrison had a server's uniform on. She felt a little hope chip away with each server. A hunk of bread, cheese and pickle slid before her, accompanied by a floral scent from the server's perfume.

Maybe he'll be happy with Dillon. She pushed food around her plate.

"You need to eat." Elizabeth, on her feet behind Pippa, leaned in. "It's a bit late to figure a way out of this now."

Pippa wanted to stand up and demand what the older woman knew, but suddenly, the room had focused on their interaction. Instead, she had to be as cryptic as Elizabeth.

"Figuring a way out?" Pippa stabbed at the cheese with her fork and took a bite. "I'm out of ideas. If you can offer any advice, I'm all ears."

"A wedding ceremony ends with a kiss." Elizabeth touched her nose.

Lowering her voice, Pippa leaned back. "Any advice that didn't come from a fortune cookie?"

Elizabeth patted Pippa's shoulder. "You'll be fine. Pip-pip."

Startled, Pippa almost fell off her chair. The older woman headed back to her seat. Pip-pip? A casual farewell? She'd heard the royals use it before, always making her stop cleaning and check they hadn't called her. Or more? If more, of course, a wedding ended with a kiss. You may kiss the bride.

A billion people would watch, waiting, anticipating that kiss.

The room receded away; the food on her plate held no appeal. A sick twist in her stomach prevented her from swallowing the cheese she'd already chewed.

One billion people.

Iain Benson — Royal Again

A tinkling of a fork on glass snapped the world back into focus.

Harrison's father had got to his feet. "Family. Friends. This is my son's last hour of freedom. As is traditional in my family, we shall present twelve wenches unto him to see if any surpass his bride-to-be. When my father offered me this choice, I knew none could be more beautiful, nor radiant than Charlotte. She had truly ensnared me in her web and I chose her over them.

"Please, bring in the wenches."

The door opened and women filed in.

"Not very inclusive! Where are the guys?" Mike said, loud enough to extract a titter around the table.

Pippa ignored him.

"Come on Harrison," she muttered. "Where are you?"

30
Harrison: lunchtime

Harrison and Dillon drove back the way they'd come. Route after route had been closed to allow the royal carriage a smooth passage.

Harrison pulled out his phone and rang the Old Coach Inn. His toes waggled in his heels in time with the dialling tone.

"Old Coach Inn." The woman who answered sounded stressed.

"Hi, I'm with Italic, the agency supplying the wenches?"

"Oh, hi. What can I do for you?"

"Can you get the phone to a co-ordinator?" Harrison's knees joined his toes in wiggling.

"Sure. One minute." On the phone, the sound of rhythmic thumps and a muffled conversation told Harrison she'd found the co-ordinator.

A new voice came on the phone. "Hi! Hi! Gillian here, ha!"

Taking a beat, Harrison injected his own panic. Gillian, have all the girls arrived?"

"There's still three to come." Gillian snorted. "Ha! They're leaving it late."

"Who's missing?"

"Jilly, Sara and Kylie."

With a forced sigh that had Dillon muffling a snigger, Harrison launched into a rapid ad-lib. "Gillian! I'm not sure Kylie's going to make it. Can you get my Kylie's number?"

"Oh dear! Oh dear! Yes. Yes. Let me look."

Harrison repeated the number back after Gillian read it out.

They passed by the palace gatehouse, Keith's cheery wave following them on to the country lane.

"That's right. Ha! I hope everything's okay. What do we do?"

"Worse comes to worse," Harrison said, "send a server on. There absolutely must be twelve!"

"Yes! Oh! Jilly's here."

"Thank you, Gillian."

Harrison closed his eyes and took a breath. He dialled Kylie. "Yeah? Who's this?"

Harrison heard windscreen wipers squeaking. He guessed she was driving. "Sorry for the late notice, Kylie, dear."

"Oh! For f-"

"Kylie!"

"Sorry. What's up?"

Harrison tried to sound contrite. "You're not needed."

"I'd better still get paid!"

"You'll still get paid." Harrison knew she would. She would still be going.

"Well, that saves me sitting in this stupid traffic. Anybody would think it was somebody's wedding."

"Sorry again!"

The phone disconnected without a goodbye.

Dillon spotted traffic ahead and took a sharp turn down a back street. "It's easy to calculate a route when they close all the roads for you. It's a pain for the rest of us, though."

"It wouldn't do for the groom to be held up in traffic for this particular wedding." Harrison didn't know the route Dillon took. The wedding procession passed down the end of one closed street. Dillon reversed as though he'd robbed a bank and needed to escape the police.

"I suppose." Dillon pulled the wheel around and took a shortcut across a supermarket carpark. "And you're positive this freedom lunch thing is at the Old Coach Inn?"

"They've held it there for four hundred years, at least." Harrison now loved his regimented itinerary. It gave him the opening he needed. "I wish I'd thought of this before we went to the palace."

Dillon checked at a traffic light junction, seeing nothing in either direction. He drove through a red light. Even here, away from the parade route, bunting reminded Harrison the wedding started soon.

"Dillon." Harrison touched his hand on the gearstick briefly. "We won't get there if we hit anything or get stopped."

The prince's driver slowed his speed. "You're right."

Seeing the cathedral loom above the surrounding buildings allowed Harrison to feel calmer. They'd made it. With Dillon's driving, they'd beaten the wedding party by twenty minutes.

Dillon parked on a cobbled street next to the alley behind the inn. The front entrance had been swarming with security.

Although considered the city's old, traditional area, the hemmed in four-storey houses sold for several million, owned by the elite, firms and

Royal Again   Iain Benson

foreign investors. Immaculate frontages and no trace of grime like that surrounding Pippa's flat. Over them all, the cathedral cast a long shadow.

Harrison got out, the rain plastering his hair immediately, soaking through the thin material of his dress and adding a chill he didn't need. Where were the staff with umbrellas in this situation?

"Wait here." Harrison leaned down to speak into the car.

"Do you need an umbrella?" Dillon held out a compact umbrella.

"I needed one a minute ago." Harrison took it anyway. "I don't suppose you have a brush, hairdryer, and a fresh set of clothes?"

"Let me check my glove compartment." Dillon didn't move. "No. I'm fresh out of all of that."

Halfway down the alley, a gorilla in a drenched black suit told Harrison there had to be an entry down there. Splashing through the puddles in the alley, Harrison approached Gorilla.

"The inn is closed today," Gorilla told him, staring straight ahead. Harrison's presence was a mere footnote for him.

"I'm Kylie? A wench for the selection process?" Harrison tried to act apologetic. It didn't come naturally. "I got stuck in traffic, broke down and I've had to walk two miles in heels. Now I'm angry and soaking."

The guard's eyes took in the nice dress, the heels, plastered hair and smearing makeup. "You were supposed to be here an hour ago. Can I see your pass?"

"Nope. It's in my car. But ask yourself, how would I know about the wenches if I wasn't one?"

"It's a good point." Gorilla touched his earpiece. "I've a drenched wench here. Kylie, yeah. Are we expecting her?"

The rain continued to soak his dress to his legs. He shivered. "And?"

"Go through." He pointed through the gate and up a flagged path to a wooden door in the property's rear. "They told me they are expecting you and you're extremely late. They were going to put a member of the bar staff in the line-up. Rich people are weird."

"Tell me about it. I never realised how weird until recently."

Harrison started through, but Gorilla caught his arm. "You look familiar."

Harrison panicked. The security at the palace had also recognised him. His father. Harrison's eyes narrowed. *I bet all the security have seen my photo.*

Inspiration struck like a stray raindrop. "I'm an actor."

Iain Benson   Royal Again

"Oh, what have you been in?"

"Did you see the last series of *Hastings Road*?"

"Yeah. A school drama thing?"

"I was the chemistry teacher?"

"Oh, yeah." Gorilla wagged his finger at Harrison. "That's it. Must pay well getting a gig like that."

"Put it this way: I'm now doing wench line-ups for a Prince. Assuming I can get dry."

"Fair point." Gorilla scratched his chin, but let Harrison go.

Warmth enveloped him as he stepped over the threshold, straight into a kitchen. The chef, sporting a white cap, barked orders to dozens of cooks and servers. The scene looked like a chaotic black-and-white movie into which Harold Lloyd would fit right in, although the confusion felt more akin to the Marx Brothers.

The frantic air elevated Harrison's blood pressure, making it hard to think. He needed to find the restaurant and Pippa. He had no idea of which way to go, or who to ask.

A busty woman materialised. She wore dungarees, a headset and a pained expression, carrying a tablet and an air of barely controlled panic.

"Kylie! Kylie? Thank god. You are so late. You look a mess. Ha! I don't know if we have time, any time, to redo makeup and dry off. They're all here. They're about to start eating. Ha! Everybody else is ready. You're the last! Last! You're going to disappoint a young girl. She'd hoped to get a kiss! Ha!"

Gillian swung the tablet in a dramatic arc across the corridor filled with busy people carrying food on platters. The tablet connected to a silver tray, sending it and all the food on it crashing to the floor. Smears of pickle oozed lumps slowly down the wall. The server carrying the tray gave the woman with a tablet a dirty stare but got on with clearing up the mess in a calm manner.

"Sorry, sorry, sorry!" The woman grabbed Harrison's elbow and steered him to a steep set of stairs. "Oh, I'm Gillian, co-ordinator for this peculiar sideshow. Ha! Do you know your role?"

"I walk through a door, stand there and if Harrison picks me, let him kiss me."

"Pretty much. Pretty much." Gillian waved at Harrison's hair. "I hope he likes drowned rats. Ha!"

Gillian clattered up the stairs as though trying to do the percussion

Royal Again   Iain Benson

version of *Flight of the Bumblebee*. Heels, narrow wooden stairs and no handrail taxed Harrison. He trailed his hand up the rough plaster on the wall to keep his balance, emerging onto a wider landing. Opposite, a bright room held dozens of people fussing and primping. Gillian pushed Harrison inside.

"See if you can find what you need. If you can find what you need. Ha! If you need me, don't! Ha! So much to do, to do."

They'd cleared the room of furniture, except for some straight-back chairs around the perimeter for the women.

"Oh my!" Another woman appeared, swimming through the lianas of Harrison's fringe. "You must be Kylie. Oh, dear. Oh, dear. You are a mess."

"Thanks."

"I mean it in a nice way, but oh dear. I'm Kate. Take a seat. I need to find a hairdryer. Failing that, a brush!"

Harrison found himself plonked into a chair while Kate vanished to return a moment later with a hairdryer and a brush.

"Do you have a mirror?"

"Absolutely not!" Kate barked a laugh. "Do the best you can."

The noise in the room deafened him. Dozens of people talking simultaneously, hairdryers and scraping chairs all made thinking difficult. Harrison tried to find inner calm, blocking out the hubbub and chaos. So far, luck had been on his side. He took a few deep breaths, letting them out slowly, brushing his hair like raking a zen garden, tugging at the knots. The rain had undone all his styling. At least the warmth in the room gave his dress a chance to dry off and add to the general humidity fogging the windows.

With a whirlwind of rose petal scent, Gillian reappeared in the room. "Girls! Girls! Girls! I hope you're all totally ready! Ha! We need to get into position. Oh, Kylie! What did you do to your hair?"

It took Harrison a moment to realise Gillian meant him.

"Never mind! Never mind. Run a brush through it on your way downstairs. Go last. Ha! Right! Right! Everybody! Follow me!"

Rain-lashed windows provided a little in the way of reflection. Barely enough for Harrison to bring his hair under some control. He might have done better, but the condensation had steamed them into opaque panes. The room slowly emptied as each wench headed down the stairs with a clattering noise like thunder rolling in. Kate flanked the door, sending each down with a pat on their back like a parachute instructor. Harrison handed Kate her hairdryer and brush back.

"Not bad." Kate placed them on a chair. "You still look like a manic panda, but you'll do."

Joining the queue behind an athletic woman with big hair that sent wafts of floral hairspray in his direction, Harrison focused on the next few minutes. Get down the stairs without breaking an ankle, go into the restaurant and Pippa could... Pippa, could what?

He had no firm plan beyond reaching Pippa.

Get them to stop the wedding somehow?

Dillon's plan of telling security of Harrison's replacement didn't work.

He didn't have a better one.

Standing on the stage and announcing, "Harrison is an imposter!" was her only option.

Various safety and staff notices adorned the corridor, reminding the servers to be courteous and attentive to the customers. Harrison came to stop beside one that simply said: smile!

Fussing down the line, giving them all the once over, Gillian reached Harrison. She sighed. "Nobody said the wenches had to be perfect."

"Thanks," Harrison muttered.

"In you go!"

The line shuffled forward through an age-stained wooden door.

On the other side, Pippa waited.

"I'm coming, Pippa." Harrison neared his goal.

Four wenches away.

Three away.

Two.

A shout echoed down the corridor.

"There she is!"

Without looking, Harrison knew they'd discovered him. Gorilla pushed up past the tavern staff, flanked by two identical black-clad goons.

Harrison tried to push past the girl ahead of him.

"Hey!" The girl shoved him back, dislodging an inspirational poster that told him a clean table is a healthy table. Gillian watched on in horror. Her careful plans of a flawless execution of a centuries-old tradition unravelled as the three security people grabbed hold of Harrison and pulled him back up the corridor towards the kitchens. They knocked Kate aside as Harrison struggled to get free. Their grips on his arms bruised his skin.

Royal Again   Iain Benson

"Stop struggling!" Gorilla said. "We don't want to hurt you."

"Bring my girl back!" Gillian called. "She's on next!"

"She's not your girl!" Gorilla yelled back. "You'll have to run with one less."

"You don't understand!" Harrison struggled and got one arm free. The security operative stepped between Harrison and the restaurant.

"I understand you're familiar because you're the one person they told us to keep away from the prince. I didn't recognise you wet. It took a minute. Actor! I can't believe I fell for that. Now get lost."

They manhandled him to the back door and out into the yard.

"Can I at least have my umbrella?" Rain lashed down, immediately soaking through his dress. He shoved his fringe out of his eyes.

If I come out the other side of this without a cold, I'll be amazed.

31
Pippa: Church

Excitement mounted as the women came out. Pippa's breath caught as each emerged.

When nine stepped onto the raised stage, a kerfuffle raised Pippa's hopes. It sounded like the kind of scrambling that would occur if Harrison had arrived. However, two more girls came out, looking back over their shoulders and no sign of Harrison. Pippa scraped back her chair on the hard wooden floors.

"You're eager," Jack said. "They've not all come out yet."

Checking along the line, Pippa counted eleven.

"Isn't there meant to be twelve?" Pippa's confusion mounted. She had a strong suspicion that Harrison was the twelfth.

It explained the shouting and banging coming from the corridor.

A woman in her early twenties, wearing a server's uniform, emerged and joined the eleven on the raised dais. From her fidgeting and twiddling with her hair, Pippa suspected she'd replaced Harrison. Pippa checked down the corridor, hunting for any sign of him. The emanated calm down the white-painted corridor suggested earlier chaos. A dislodged picture frame lay shattered on the floor.

"There aren't any more, Harry." William gave a chortle. "Take your pick, give them a peck, and let's get over to the church."

The women on the dais had a dreamlike quality, with Pippa barely noticing them. Blondes, brunettes, redheads and raven-haired, nobody mattered because Harrison wasn't there.

Being the closest to him, the late addition to the line-up got Pippa's kiss on the lips. She made a slight gasp.

"Congratulations," Pippa muttered and returned to her seat, sinking into it.

A bleak future stretched out ahead of Pippa. Did Harrison have a plan?

Tradition had constricted her into a cycle of activities she'd been unable to break, but he'd been free to organise a rescue party. This line-up was his last chance. Maybe the security had been too much for him? He had such a privileged upbringing that when faced with an actual emergency,

Royal Again Iain Benson

he'd been unable to cope with the pressure. *I can't believe he'd give up easily. They got to him before he could get to me.*

"Don't get too comfortable." William came over and dropped a heavy hand on Pippa's shoulder. "We need to move across to the church."

Many historic reasons had gone into selecting this inn out of all those available, for the wedding party staging post. Mainly how it connected to the cloisters that ran into the cathedral. They left through a side entrance and straight into an arched and colonnaded cloister. Across the grassy courtyard, other guests milled, chatting. The wedding party ambled along at their slowest member's speed, Elizabeth. Wet soil scents assailed her, the air cool to her skin as the rain dripped off the cloisters' roofs, taking away any warmth. The old bricks in the walls crumbled in places, and the flagging on the floor wobbled slightly underfoot, but down this path, previous members of royalty had promenaded to their weddings. Including William.

An arched side door held open by a man in a long black cloak admitted them into the cathedral. His head bowed for each member of the party. A muttered "Sire" as William and Pippa passed him, but Pippa had the impression he'd been silent for the rest.

Odours of beeswax polish, incense and tallow swallowed the smell of damp earth as they cross the threshold into the church. Pippa's footsteps echoed back off the huge creamy stone blocks making up the walls, supporting a vaulted ceiling above them. Columns carved with fluted motifs added extra support around archways to either side. A sound like waves crashed down from the pews. Hundreds of dignitaries and family members found their seats, waiting for the big event. Stone flutes created an intricate array of arches to support a roof many metres above. Faced with this eternal space, her minuscule life held little importance.

The cathedral transept split the nave in two. Pippa and her entourage emerged in the middle. Pippa looked back at the exit, her pulse thudding in her ears. Jack led her to the pulpit and altar nestled against the apse, lit by vast stained glass windows. Big screens down the aisles displayed the wedding to those at the back. As they headed down the red carpet, Pippa spotted dozens of famous musicians, actors and television personalities in the congregation.

"What time is it?" Pippa asked Jack as they reached the altar, a simple stone table covered with a draped national flag. On it, a tall, imposing golden cross in the centre, flanked by two fat candles.

"Quarter to two." Jack gave Pippa a playful grin. "Nervous?"

Weirdly, Pippa had no nerves, only dread. "No. Bored."

Jack's laugh reverberated back off the walls causing others in the group to stare at him. He held up his hands. "Sorry, sorry."

An antique door, carved from a single piece of oak, opened in the apse wall, admitting the verger. The verger gave them all a broad smile as they filed into the antechamber.

"Everything is on schedule, sires," the verger said, inclining his head far enough for Pippa to wonder if the man's tonsure had been a deliberate choice or one forced upon him by an ironic nature.

The sounds from the main church increased in a flood as the remaining guests took their seats. In the transept, the orchestra and choir increased their volume to outdo the guests.

"How much do you remember from the rehearsals?" Jack corrected Pippa's position as the groomsmen fanned out on the groom's side.

"Absolutely nothing." With wedding stress, nobody would be surprised at her revelation. "Everything has gone from my head."

Awe filled Pippa as she gazed up and up into the distant ceiling and the frescoes painted by long-dead artists. Huge stained glass panes created a wash of colour over the congregation; men's grey suits created a backdrop for the bright women's dresses. Row after row of faces, all suddenly quietened as Pippa turned to stand before them. In the corners, she saw television cameras reminding her a billion people watched around the world on television. The more aware she became, the more cameras she saw.

The orchestral music increased in volume, sliding up the decibels in a practised fashion. Their music filled the space with a relaxing gentle rise and fall of notes. Harrison would recognise the piece, but Pippa had never heard it before.

Harrison's immediate family sat to the right, William and Charlotte beaming, turning and greeting those on the pew behind. On the cathedral's opposite side, Isabella's family. Amestris inclined her head towards Pippa when she saw Pippa's gaze land upon her. She wore a sensational ivory dress with a huge floral print and a disc of a hat fastened at a jaunty angle. Pavlos touched his forehead with an index finger. Like the men in Pippa's party, he wore a dark grey suit, though his waistcoat had a bold floral pattern echoing his daughter. Katherine had a nervous twitch, constantly aware of her surroundings, her own angled hat like a radar station.

Isabella's entire family held an expectant air. Their moment to shine

Royal Again — Iain Benson

had arrived. Somewhere, Isabella would be undergoing her last-second preparations. Tiffany would be there, with the other bridesmaids.

Beat by beat from the orchestra, the moment Isabella appeared drew closer.

With each percussive note, Pippa's blood drained slowly down to her ankles. Breathing seemed more laborious than ever. Her pulse raced, pounding in her ears, beginning to block out all the other sounds. Elizabeth, sitting in the centre on the front pew, gave a little cackle. It cut through the throbbing in Pippa's mind. Splashes of colour across the crowd made the scene into an impressionist painting. Her vision swam.

"Hey, H." Jack's palpable concern brought Pippa back to the here and now. "Are you okay, man?"

Barely able to raise her voice above a hoarse whisper, she fixed her eyes on his. "I'm not Harrison."

Jack's mouth twitched. "You've left it very late to plead insanity."

"This wedding." Pippa paused. "It can't go ahead."

A sudden change in music silenced Jack's response. Trumpets sounded. Blaring in a crescendo. A rustling wave of sound heralded the entire congregation turning as one to see the entrance. The imposing carved wooden doors opened as the music reached a high point.

Two young girls in flouncy purple dresses carrying flat-bottomed wicker baskets preceded Isabella. They created a fountain of pink petals for Isabella to glide through. Isabella herself appeared framed by the doors, flanked by purple-clad bridesmaids, tailed by four more bridesmaids and a long train. Holding her arm, Frederick exuded statesmanship. Isabella's white dress and veil created a shroud of chiffon and lace, sparkling with pearls and diamonds.

Step by stately step, Isabella advanced down the aisle. Triumphant trumpets gave a culminating counterpoint to her glide.

Had Pippa ever got married herself, wearing something so sensationally beautiful would have only been a dream. She might have gone for an off-the-shoulder, puffed chiffon sleeve, with a long dress and slight train, but she had to admire the strength Isabella showed in carrying the material's weight while wearing heels after twisting her ankle. Any wincing she did was hidden by the veil that fell to her waist.

Vaguely, Pippa heard the archbishop shuffling into place, but like a billion people around the world, she couldn't take her eyes off Isabella.

Stunning, beautiful, serene, the language barely had the

superlatives to do the future queen justice. Entire nations fell in love with her as she came down the aisle.

    Only one person watching did not.
    Pippa.
    She wanted to run.
    Forget the number of people watching, waiting, expectant.
    She wanted to shove the groomsmen aside and escape.
    Fear rooted her into inaction.

32
Harrison: Church

Two security people dumped Harrison outside the inn, back into the alley.

"Don't you know who I am?" Harrison regretted the words as they left his mouth.

"Yeah, Penelope Palmer," said one.

"That's why we're throwing you out," said the other.

"You two will regret ever making that decision!" Harrison screamed at the slammed door.

Uncaring about his dress sticking to his skin, his hair plastered or the difficulty of walking over slick cobbles in heels, Harrison returned to Dillon's car, wondering if he could get to Isabella as he couldn't get near Pippa.

He imagined stealing Isabella's dress and walking down the aisle towards Pippa, the veil down, everybody assuming his identity as Isabella until that moment as Pippa lifted the veil and saw him. She'd kiss him anyway. A small part of him wondered if that might work. A different, larger part wondered when the part thinking of wearing a dress had become so accustomed to the prospect.

Sneering and shaking his head. He didn't know where Isabella would be. Nor would her dress fit. She would have some security. And his sister would be there. He'd not seen her since the switch. If anybody would see through him, it would be her and she'd have a field day ridiculing him in a dress. The thought of replacing Isabella cheered him up momentarily, but he knew a non-starter when it derailed his thoughts.

The windows had steamed up as Harrison reached the Mini. He opened the door, his heart suddenly stopping as he saw Reece in the passenger seat.

"Jeeze," Reece climbed out and popped open an umbrella. "You're drenched."

"Where's my brolly?" Dillon called, leaning on the passenger seat to peer up at the drowned rat standing by his car.

"It got confiscated." Harrison sat in the passenger seat, his legs tucked up.

"Don't get my seat wet!"

"Too late," Harrison replied.

"I take it you didn't get to see him?" Dillon stroked Harrison's shoulder.

"I was close. Really close." Harrison's body slumped. "A metre away."

"You had no chance," Reece said. "Security is everywhere. We vetted everyone as well. I was patrolling the area when I found Dillon's car. He's damn lucky it was me that found him. Had it been anybody else, half of William's security force would have been here. With guns, as well."

"Have you told him?" Harrison asked Dillon.

"Told him what?" Dillon looked genuinely unsure.

"About Pippa and me."

"No." Dillon glanced nervously at Reece. "Of course not."

"Why not?" Harrison tutted.

"I can't out you." Dillon gestured to Reece, though a smile threatened to erupt onto his lips. "If you want somebody to know, you need to tell them."

"Ignore him, he told me." Reece scratched his chin, eyebrows colliding. "It's a bit different than coming out as gay."

Harrison got to his feet, standing close to his security chief under the umbrella. Although the rain had soaked him so much already, it made no difference.

"You know that I'm Harrison?"

"I have to admit, it made my mind dribble out my ears." Reece rubbed his forehead with his free hand. "Part of me thought Dillon was joking as well."

"Ask me anything only you and me would know."

Reece's eyes narrowed. "The only thing I've come up with is what did I say you shouldn't do, but you did anyway?"

"Visit the farmer's market?" Harrison guessed. He could think of dozens.

"What did you get?"

"Wensleydale with cranberry."

"Okay, that's pretty much what I remember as well." Reece prodded Harrison in his shoulder, checking he was real. "It explains a lot. You getting promoted, sticking to Harrison as well. Him suddenly knowing my name as well as thanking me. I've known *something* was up. Weird as it is, it makes sense."

"Pippa and I switched bodies five days ago. We were trying to find a way to switch back."

"It's like that film. *Supernatural Sunday.*"

Harrison didn't know the film. "Did two people swap bodies and have to live their lives as each other?"

"Yes."

"How did they swap back?"

Reece scratched his head. "I think the daughter makes the mother's boyfriend propose, and the mother passes the daughter's law exam, as well. I didn't really watch it. Zoe had it on."

"Well, this is like that, but when the lightning storm came, we swapped bodies."

Reece closed one eye. "Have you tried another shock?"

Harrison waved his hands in frustration. "That's what I suggested."

Reece's puzzled expression returned. "I guess you could have swapped. How are you planning on swapping back? I mean, Harrison gets married in fifteen minutes. What difference does it make? You can't change anything now."

Harrison peered through the rain at the cathedral. From his location, he could see Isabella's carriage arriving. Or rather, he could see the sudden cheering and flags telling him Isabella had arrived.

"Reece." Harrison gestured towards the cathedral. "I need you to get me in there."

Lightning split the sky to underline the drama of Harrison's words.

"I can't do that."

"You're my chief of security."

Reece's apologetic expression dropped into a saddened one. "Your dad has brought in additional security, as well as briefing the President's team. I'm not even your current personal security."

Harrison had forgotten the Presidential security team would still be around, bolstering his father's teams. "If anybody can get me in, you can."

Reece's glum expression brightened slightly, raising Harrison's hopes. "I could get in. Tell everybody that's not Harrison, halt the wedding and give you and him a chance to swap back."

"Work through how that plays out." Harrison's resigned tone made Reece think about it.

"They'd think I was unhinged as well as on drugs."

Harrison pointed to Reece. "I'm guessing you thought similar when Dillon told you."

"You're right. I thought you getting sacked had pushed him over the edge and you'd had a breakdown as well."

"But you believe me now?"

"Call me mostly convinced. Dillon believes it, and you seem genuine as well." Reece glanced over at the church. "Otherwise, I'd have walked away. You'd have never seen me again."

"Nice to know if Pippa does ever have a mental breakdown, her friends will help." Harrison accompanied his words with a soft, wry smile.

"Point taken," Reece pointed at the church. "If I can get you in. What then?"

"I'm hoping Pippa has figured out how to change us back."

"And if she hasn't?" Reece's set jaw caused his muscles to bulge a little. "If I get you in, and you can't change back, then I lose my job as well as get arrested. And probably Dillon as well, for helping."

"I get it." Harrison breathed in through his nose. "You're both risking a lot. I'll think of something that means you don't lose your job. Even if it's convincing my father of what's happened."

Reece rubbed his forehead with his index finger, concentrating on the issue. The time to the wedding ticked down as the number on Dillon's clock dash clicked up.

"Got it." Reece handed Harrison the umbrella. He leaned forward, holding the wet roof of Dillon's car. "Dillon, I'm going to call you in a few minutes. The only thing you need to say as well as answer the phone is 'I'll only talk to Pippa', got it?"

"I'll only talk to Pippa." Dillon nodded, confusion written across his features. "Got it."

"It's important. No matter what anybody says to you, that's your response. I'll only talk to Pippa."

Steering Harrison by his elbow, they headed for the security cordon at the church's rear.

"What's your plan?"

"I'm afraid we've got to unmask Pippa in front of a billion people." Reece kept staring straight ahead. "Assuming I can get you past the security. They told us to let you nowhere near the church."

"I've not been able to get to her yet."

"Unsurprising. We all saw your picture."

Taking him to a side entrance with only four armed security staff, Reece kept hold of Harrison's arm.

Royal Again   Iain Benson

"Grant," Reece greeted the one who stepped forward. "This is going to get weird."

"Reece." Grant grasped Harrison's free arm. "You know what the King said."

"Yeah, this woman, nowhere near the wedding." Reece released Harrison's arm, dialling Dillon. "Harrison is too far away to get here."

"No." Grant jerked his thumb over his shoulder. "He's at the front."

Harrison cottoned on. "That's an imposter. He's a look-a-like."

"You might have fooled Reece." Grant strengthened his grip on Harrison's arm, hurting him. "You're not getting in."

Reece dialled a number on his phone and passed the handset to Harrison as it connected.

"The real Harrison is on that phone." Reece kept his tone level. Harrison realised, as he held it, that Reece had spoken the truth.

Grant snatched it off Harrison. "Who is this?"

"I'll only speak to Pippa." Dillon played his role perfectly.

"You'll speak to me."

"I'll only speak to Pippa."

In disgust, Grant handed the phone to Pippa.

Reece opened his body language. "I was sceptical as well at first. I asked some questions. Pippa relayed them and all the answers were right."

"He won't trust anybody else but me," Harrison said, trying to sound innocent. "I've been trying to get through all day."

Grant ran his hand over his mouth. "I don't know the prince like you do, Reece. I don't have questions only he'd know. I don't know. Who are the groomsmen?"

Harrison held the phone up to his ear. "Who are Harrison's groomsmen?" After a moment, with Dillon not responding and confusion seeping from the handset, Harrison scowled at Grant. "Jack Menzies, Adrian and Mike Davis, Ivor Blanchet, Curtis and Alex Monroe."

"Who's the oldest?"

"Who's the oldest?" Harrison asked into the phone, already trying to work it out. He remembered after a few moments. "Jack's just had his twenty-eighth birthday. It's him."

"That's right." Grant's suspicion remained, but he no longer gripped Harrison's arm in a vice-like grip nor glared like he'd cheerfully throttle the prince. A narrow shaft of light had appeared in his armour of certainty. "It's all info on the internet, but you answered quicker than somebody searching for it."

From within the church, the sound of triumphant trumpets started up.

"Makes no odds anyway." Grant glanced at the doors. "That's the wedding march. Isabella's on her way down the aisle."

Heart leaping into his throat, Harrison pushed forward, caught by Grant. He wrapped Harrison up in muscular arms.

"I have to stop it!" The frigid grip of panic shut down Harrison's rational brain.

"You're too late."

Harrison stopped struggling. Grant let him go.

"Until she says 'I do', it's not too late." Before Grant reacted, Harrison pushed into the cathedral's vestibule.

The roof arced over a stone floor leading to the main church doors. At the join of each buttress, a delicately carved boss masked the join. Through the ancient doors, the trumpets stopped, and he heard the archbishop begin his speech to the congregation. Between him and the church, dozens of security and even more people, those not famous enough for inside seats.

"Penelope Palmer," Grant said from behind her. "Stop."

Harrison held up Grant's gun taken from his shoulder holster. Grant reached into his jacket and pulled out Reece's phone.

"Not this time." Harrison pushed at the nave doors.

33
Pippa: The ceremony

The archbishop's voice rang through the fabulous acoustics, each word reverberating and resounding.

Pippa held Isabella's hands. She wore delicate lace fingerless gloves. The openwork detail on her dress created a fabulous pattern, especially this close. Her many-layered veil provided a decorative voile, but Pippa could see Isabella's features through it, seeing her perfect makeup and her ruby lips in a broad smile. A small part of her had hoped that somehow Harrison had snuck in, replacing Isabella.

What would they do if I dropped Isabella's hands and walked away? Turn her around and put her right back here. She kept her face impassive as her emotions somersaulted and plummeted.

Behind her, Tiffany shuffled and fidgeted apprehensively, glancing back up the aisle.

In the front row, Frederick had joined his wife and Isabella's grandparents, attentively watching the proceedings.

The archbishop's words washed largely unheeded over Pippa. The scene's surrealness made it dreamlike. The archbishop's garments rivalled Isabella's dress; cream, satiny material with gold brocade and intricate embroidery covering every part down to his ankles. Even his felt slippers had gold embroidery. Voluminous sleeves created dark voids as the archbishop held up his hands to address the flock.

A sickening fear had grown in Pippa, cementing into a resigned dead lump filling her torso.

Even if Harrison had tried to reach her, he'd failed. Now, with the archbishop talking and a billion people watching, the time of rescue had passed. The weight of all those viewers pressed down on her like a winter blanket, stifling, keeping her in place with a suffocating comfort.

The archbishop paused, bringing all the eyes and ears in the room onto him. His tone changed as he started proceedings.

"I shall read from Corinthians thirteen, four to eight. Love is patient, love is kind. It does not envy, it does not boast, it is not proud." Pippa tuned out the sonorous voice, but the words in the passage snapped her attention back. "Where there are prophecies, they will cease; where there are tongues, they are stilled; where there is knowledge, it will pass away."

Lightning flashed, adding sparkles and splashes of brief colour to the air inside the church.

At the far end, the door banged open.

A rustle as two thousand people turned.

Harrison ran into the room, a gun in one hand.

More security tried to run up the aisle. Tiffany tripped one up, sending them sprawling, their gun clattering on the marble with a loud metallic rattle. Harrison skidded to a stop.

Water dripped from rattail hair onto a dress plastered with rainwater. A puddle had formed around his feet. His makeup, had it ever been good, was now smeared and smudged. From a side pew, a man in an army uniform tried to extricate himself from those sitting next to him. Harrison haphazardly waved the gun in the brigadier general's direction. Whether he feared for his safety or those around him, he returned to his pew.

A billion people watched as Harrison backed down the aisle, the gun wobbly in his grasp.

Additional security flooded in from the side aisles. So many doors, so little time. Harrison could never cover every angle. Red dots appeared on his dress, vivid against the wet material.

He reached the centre point where the transept widened the church. Here, galleries encircled the space above, supported by stout stone columns. All provided more cover than Harrison could simultaneously watch. The millions watching protected Harrison from the security simply gunning him down. However, he lost momentum by the transept, stumbling to a stop. Bedraggled and desperate.

Silence descended as two thousand congregation members held their breath.

At the front, William got to his feet, anger boiling into his cheeks. Pippa hoped he didn't give the order to fire.

"Drop the gun, Harrison," she whispered.

With metres between them, he could not have heard her. Harrison held the gun with one finger on the trigger guard. Pippa couldn't breathe. She knew they'd spirit Harrison away now, and she'd never see him again. Security with automatic machine guns moved through the pews, gun barrels never wavering from their target.

She had to act.

Royal Again   Iain Benson

"Wait!" Pippa's voice boomed down the church. She stepped off the dais onto the red carpet covering the nave's marble floor.

"Harrison," William's tone held a stern hint of menace.

Pippa stopped at the tone. "They'll take her away."

"So they should."

"You pushed her to this. I need to do something."

"This is unconscionable!" Although hissed, William's voice carried. "If you go down there, I will have to disavow you. The future monarch cannot be associated with this farce."

"Straight in there with the absolute threats." Pippa gave Harrison's father a sad head shake.

"I'm serious." William's tone held a steel edge. "This would be the most embarrassing event in our history."

"I don't care." Pippa took a step, her eyes flicking between William and Harrison.

"You will lose the throne, man!" the King's face turned purple.

Pippa came level with Harrison's father. "I never wanted it."

"Seriously, Harry." William faced her, breaking her eye line to Harrison and clasping her arms. "She is a cleaner. You'll learn to love Isabella."

"Not the point." Pippa shook herself free.

"One billion people are watching."

"Then one billion people can watch this."

Pippa brushed Harrison's father aside and ran down the church, the rustle of clothing on people turning, following like a wave rushing up a pebbled beach.

"You'll lose it all, boy!" William's plaintive voice reverberating in time with Pippa's thudding footsteps.

Lightning continued to punctuate the air, thunder sounding close.

Pippa reached Harrison, taking his hands in hers. "You made it."

Harrison's smile flew into his cheeks. "I didn't think I could, but yes."

In the wings, Reece and Dillon arrived. Reece pushed down a security guard's rifle barrel.

"Have you worked it out?" Pippa asked. "How do we change back?"

"I had hoped you had."

Pippa's heart sank but immediately buoyed back up. "I don't care. As long as we're together."

Harrison's eyes softened. "Maybe one day we can find a way to switch back, but I'm not in a hurry anymore."

    To a backdrop of crashing lightning, Pippa took Harrison's wet hair in her hands and bent to kiss him, smudging the rain-smeared lipstick even further.

    Every light, lamp, and candle in the nave extinguished simultaneously, plunging the room into darkness. A collective gasp added a counterpoint to the thunder.

34
Harrison: Decision

As the lights came back on, Harrison's eyes fluttered open.

Jack, of all people, had rushed over to see him, pushing through a crowd of concerned onlookers. The cathedral's distant wooden beams seemed to waver as Harrison's vision swam back into focus. He turned his head. Pippa lay beside him. She had a crowd of her own around her.

"Stand back. I'm a doctor." A familiar face drove through the crowd. Harrison recognised him as a television presenter of medical programmes. His thinning blond hair and smooth features made him appear perpetually young.

Harrison felt his wrist lifted, the doctor squeezing a spot and shining a bright light in his eyes.

William appeared. "You gave us all quite a shock there, Harry."

Pieces clicked together in Harrison's mind. William spoke directly to him. Not Pippa. Pippa had been Pippa lying next to him.

They'd switched back.

They'd switched back!

"I'm a royal again." Relief washed the shock from his system.

"Of course you are. You're fine." The doctor released his wrist and went over to Pippa.

Harrison pushed himself up onto his elbows. Instinctively, he went to brush long hair out of his face. It had gone.

Pippa!

The television doctor helped her into a sitting position. Around them, he could hear a buzz of concerned voices. Messages passed backwards through the crowd.

"I'm wet," she said, gesturing down at her clothes. Her voice sounded flat. Dillon elbowed his way through the circle of onlookers.

"You've been out in the rain." Dillon knelt and clasped her hands. "Did it work?"

Slowly, examining her hands still held by Dillon, she nodded. She raised her eyes to Harrison. His heart fluttered. He wanted to hold her hands, not Dillon, but he couldn't deny his driver the opportunity.

Harrison climbed to his feet, helped by Jack. His oldest friend headed to the altar where Harrison saw Isabella standing, her hands drooped by her side, head bowed. How must she be feeling? Indecision tore at Harrison. Moments before, he'd swore only Pippa mattered to him. She had said the same to him. She could have taken the throne, Isabella, and a luxurious life. As he swayed between the two, security came through the crowd of concerned onlookers and pulled Pippa roughly to her feet, tossing Dillon aside.

The guards may have sheathed their weapons, but strapped across backs or on a belt, they remained visible.

"Penelope Palmer, you're under arrest for treason."

"What?" Pippa struggled ineffectually, worry etched across her face.

"What?" Harrison echoed.

Starting towards her, he felt his father's hand on his arm.

"Let them take her." William's voice held no warmth.

"They're arresting her for treason." Harrison shook free, but didn't immediately move. "That's unfair. She's done nothing. All of this, it's on me."

Dillon appeared beside them, his face etched with concern. "You've got to fix this."

"The world has become mad," William said. "Impertinence all around me."

"You're the only one who can stop this, Pa." Harrison laid a hand on the King's shoulder, something he knew the King hated. "You made this. Now fix it."

"Easily done." William rapidly blinked in an otherwise impassive face. "Resume your wedding to Isabella. I'll ensure this is all forgotten."

The security had reached the door. Pippa worriedly tried to see him over her shoulder, with both her arms clamped in the tight clasp of the security officers. At the altar, Isabella turned her head in his direction.

Duty or love?

He admitted that he did love Pippa. With all his heart.

Duty had ruled his life since his earliest memories.

Dillon and the King waited expectantly.

Isabella waited.

Meanwhile, Pippa had vanished through the door with a last plaintive cry of his name.

He started after her. "I have to save her."

As Dillon stepped aside, the King stepped in his way. "She'll go down

Royal Again   Iain Benson

for treason."

"I'm a qualified lawyer, Pa. I'll defend her." Harrison out stared his father for the first time. "How's that going to look in your precious dynasty?"

William grabbed Harrison's arm. "Last chance, boy."

"Ironically, I was going to be the dutiful son until you ordered her taken away." He pulled his arm free. "I might love Pippa, but I'd have done my duty. As always. But I cannot stand by while they punish an innocent for my deeds. You brought this on yourself, *dad*."

Elizabeth tugged at the King's sleeve. "Don't be an ass, Willy. Harry, go save your girl."

Flashing a 'thank you' smile at his grandmother, Harry raced off down the aisle to the main entrance.

On the steps down to the street, an enormous crowd watched in a silence magnified by their number. Pippa had almost reached a waiting van. Surrounded by eight armed security men, they formed a shield around her. Tweedle Dumb and Tweedle Dumber held her arms. They relished the chance to grapple Pippa once more.

"Stop!" A small part of his mind wondered how dramatic he appeared, framed by the dark doorway in the centuries-old milky stonework rising in all its carved splendour behind him.

The security detail paused, confused. Harrison trotted down steps slick with rain. His expensive suit quickly turned from charcoal to black, the deluge soaking it. He felt his hair flatten, water dribbling past his eyebrows. *Surely eyebrows stop water from getting into your eyes?* He wiped the water away.

Reece appeared, clicking an umbrella above him.

"Sir?" Grant stepped forward. He'd taken great glee in being the one to take Pippa away.

"You can let her go. She's coming with me."

Grant adopted a military at-ease pose. "Your father gave strict instructions, sir."

"These instructions were to prevent this woman from disrupting the wedding?"

"Sir, yes, sir."

"There will be no wedding."

Pippa's face split into a massive smile.

"No wedding, sir?"

Harrison caught Pippa's eye, barely able to hide his returning smile while he dealt with Grant. "No. Nothing to disrupt."

Uncertainty flicked momentarily across Grant's face. "I'm afraid your father's instructions are clear."

As though summoned, William appeared. His security flanked him, Toby providing the umbrella. Behind him, Elizabeth, Tiffany and Charlotte came down, eliciting a moist, collective splatter of applause from the crowd, kept back by the metal fencing. The King raised a finger in Grant's direction, raising Harrison's hopes.

"Harry." William reached them.

"Pa." Harrison glanced at the rest of his family, hoping for a clue where this conversation would go. Tiffany gave him a "Whatever" sign and tried to appear bored, whilst desperate to hear everything.

"Would you give up the throne for this maid?" The King waved dismissively at Pippa. "Your home? Would you find work?"

Harrison had been thinking of nothing else. "Yes. I have a good law degree. I should be able to find work. I have friends who can help."

William turned to the security. "Let her go."

Pippa glared at Tweedle Dumb and Dumber, before running up into Harrison's waiting arms. Her kiss tasted of rain, but he didn't care.

"You'd really give up the throne for me?"

Harrison brought her into a hug, feeling how chilled she'd become. "Yes. If the past few days have taught me anything, it's that tradition is a chain that finding you broke."

"You need to go in there and tell Isabella, her family and then the billion people watching at home." William gestured towards the church. Harrison couldn't read his father's face.

"Can I watch?" Tiffany asked.

"You're going to have to." Harrison gave his sister a wry smile. "You're heir to the throne, Whiffy."

"Oh! Crap!" Tiffany's shocked face made Harrison laugh. His decision made him feel free. The air tasted sweeter as he breathed in deeply.

With a sideways glance at his father, Harrison gave Pippa another squeeze and headed back up the stairs.

Protected by the entrance, Pippa saw his grandmother and paused. "You and I need a talk. I need to know."

"I'll catch you up later." The Queen's mother gave a sparkling smile

Royal Again   Iain Benson

and raised her eyebrows.

After the weak sunlight outside, the interior felt dark. Sitting on a pew, being comforted by her father, Isabella shone in the darkness by the altar.

Acutely aware of all the eyes that followed him down the central aisle, Harrison went to Isabella, crouching in front of her.

"Isabella," he said.

The slap across his cheek echoed around the church.

He deserved that.

His hand rose involuntarily to the stinging mark she'd left behind.

"If you *knew* you weren't going ahead, you could have told me days ago."

"Until ten minutes ago, I didn't know." Harrison tried a placating gesture, but she wouldn't even face him. "Not that it matters."

"They will forever call me the queen that never was. Left at the altar." Isabella's clenched jaw pulsated. "Worse. Left *halfway* through the ceremony."

"There has been so much more going on than I can tell you." Harrison wondered how Isabella would take the news Pippa had wooed her, not him. The change from jackass to somebody Isabella could love came after Harrison became female. He barely believed it. Pippa came into the church, standing at the back.

Seeing her standing in the shadows by the door told Harrison he had made the right choice, however much Isabella hurt now, it had to be better than a lifetime of misery. He hoped Isabella felt the same way. *I hope Pippa feels the same way!*

"Like what?" Isabella dragged Harrison's attention back to her.

"You wouldn't believe me."

Isabella finally held his gaze. "Try me."

"Pippa and I switched places just after you left my rooms. We have spent the past five days trying to switch back. Ironically, so I could marry you. However, I love Pippa."

"Are you telling me that Pippa Kissed me and carried me from the dance floor? Pippa made me think you could be a person I could love?"

Mutely Harrison nodded.

After a moment's rumination, Isabella slowly nodded. "I believe you. You are still a jackass, Harry. Better than before. I hope you don't treat her like you treated me and she treats you like she treated me."

Iain Benson   **Royal Again**

    She gathered her frills and flounces in order to stand. Her family followed her to a side entrance so she wouldn't have to face the stunned crowd outside.
    At the door, she paused and turned. "Our marriage would have worked better with Pippa."
    Puzzled, Harrison asked: "Why?"
    "I'm bi, but prefer girls, you dummy. This was always about duty for me, too." She paused once more. "Pippa was twice the man you are."
    His mind stinging more than his cheek from that comment, Harrison left the church onto the steps, where the world's press had a thousand questions.

35
Pippa: Happy ever after

Harrison took Pippa's hand as he passed, leading her from the cathedral. William, Tiffany and Charlotte waited. Elizabeth had vanished. Pippa looked for her before they left the cathedral and onto the steps.

Although the rain had gone, the crowd had swelled, making it feel more oppressive. They'd opened the gates to allow the press through for a press conference. Initially there for the wedding photos, now for the scoop of a lifetime. Pippa felt her heart pound. She had left her comfort zone at the first breakfast with Harrison's family. She'd barely had time to think or plan. She'd stayed so Harrison could marry Isabella, and now? A smile tugged at the corner of her mouth.

Dozens of photographers took her photo holding Harrison's hand, her ghosting smile creating a mythos like the Mona Lisa. The facilities put in place for a brief wedding speech on the steps suddenly became Harrison's communication avenue with the world.

Questions barraged them, television cameras zooming in to capture the answers.

Harrison tried to quieten them with a gesture. "I am here to tell you that my wedding to Isabella Eldridge will not take place."

Many questions came firing back at them. Mostly "Why?"

"It is simple. I have chosen love over duty." Harrison squeezed Pippa's hand. "Recent events have taught me that love is more important than marrying somebody for tradition's sake. Isabella is a wonderful woman with no blame in any of this. My father kept Pippa and I apart, but they say love conquers all, and it has."

"Does this mean the maid will be queen?" shouted one reporter.

Harrison singled them out. "No. I have abdicated my place in succession for the throne. I will not be king."

That remark sent a palpable shockwave across the crowd.

The reporter who'd received the answer which would make his career tried his luck a second time. "Who is next in line?"

Harrison allowed his smile to play across his face. "Tiffany."

A second gasp passed through the crowd like gas at a bachelor party.

"Ms Palmer. Mark Sporco, *Daily Royal*." Harrison gasped at the name. She wondered what had happened between them for him to recognise the reporter. "How does it feel to have destroyed the monarchy?"

"He tried to get you to rat on us," Harrison whispered. "He even tried to get into your apartment."

Pippa stepped forward to the mic. "It is better to have an honest monarchy than one built on lies. Nothing is more honest than love."

"No more questions." Harrison started to turn away.

"Are you getting married?" Mark asked.

Pippa traded smiles with Harrison. She turned back to the mic. "Not today."

They headed up the stairs into the church. "You don't want to get married?"

"Not today," Pippa replied, squeezing his hand. "You might revert to being a jerk again. If that happens, you'll be gone. Giving up the throne for me or not."

"I'll bear that in mind."

William had a strange expression as they re-entered the gloomy cathedral interior. Pippa couldn't work it out. She glanced at Harrison.

"Pa?" Harrison's tone turned quizzical. He'd never come across this expression either.

"I didn't think you'd go through with it."

Pippa twigged. William felt proud of his son. She squeezed Harrison's hand. "He's stronger than you know."

William ignored Pippa. "You're welcome to keep your apartment until you can find a place to live."

"Thank you."

"She's not allowed." William didn't even glance at Pippa.

"Then I'll be staying with her." Pippa felt a warmth spread through her.

"I can't imagine you staying there." William dismissed the concept with a wave.

Harrison tilted his head and exchanged an amused glance with Pippa. "I might surprise you."

"You can bring her to the palace for the wedding meal."

"Is that still going ahead?" Harrison's dropped Pippa's hand in surprise.

"Of course," the King replied. "Everything is in place. However, we

Royal Again   **Iain Benson**

will now use it to celebrate Tiffany's ascension to next in line for the throne."

"Remind me, yeah?" Tiffany sighed and examined her nails. "Can't you like backtrack for once, Pa and have Pippa for Queen? She's cool, you know."

"You'll have to make your own way there." William ignored his daughter.

Charlotte looked about to say something, but William placed his hand on her shoulder, taking her deeper into the church towards the cloistered entrance Pippa had used.

Charlotte glanced back over her shoulder. Sadness etched lines into her face. William had kept her from providing her viewpoint. Tiffany, though, hung back, harder to control.

"Thanks, bro." She hugged Harrison. "I still had a few years of partying left before Pa married me off. Looks like that's cut short."

"I'm sure you'll find a way." Harrison hugged his sister back.

"Damn straight." Tiffany turned to Pippa. "I've not forgotten. I might be like a queen in waiting. You and me. We're going to have a blowout to end all blowouts."

Elizabeth reappeared. "Has Will gone?"

"Yes." Pippa scowled at the older woman. "Now. No more cagey remarks. What's going on?"

With a sneaky smile, Elizabeth motioned them to a pew. Most occupants in the nave had headed to the palace. Pippa spotted Reece, Dillon and a few stragglers, as well as Tiffany and Elizabeth's security detail. They all hung back while Elizabeth held court.

"People thought I had an affair before my marriage to your grandfather."

"A stableboy," Pippa said. "I read about it."

"We didn't have an affair," Elizabeth lowered her voice further. "We swapped places."

Tiffany gasped. "Wow. How did you change back in time?"

Elizabeth shrugged. "Who said we changed back? Elizabeth's father had Elizabeth deported. She joined the Foreign Legion and vanished. My name is Joseph." Elizabeth heaved a sad sigh. "It's been a long time since I uttered that name."

"Wow, Lizzie." Tiffany's mouth dropped open.

"I had some private security firm find her years later. She'd married a French woman and had two kids. I'm glad she found happiness. It's more than I did. I found out how painful childbirth is instead."

Pippa's incredulous voice rose in pitch. "You're kidding?"

"Trust me. It's painful."

Pippa glowered. "Not that. Never switching back!"

Elizabeth shook her head. "I found out years later about true love's kiss. That would have been all it took to break the curse."

"Er." Tiffany looked a little worried. "Curse?"

"We kissed before the wedding," Harrison said, ignoring his sister.

"You gave up everything in the church." Pippa slowly pieced the events together.

"As did you," Harrison pointed out. "If we'd not switched, would you have married Isabella?"

"Not when you made it inside."

Harrison's warm smile infected Pippa. "That's when the curse got broken."

Pippa nodded. "That must be it."

Tiffany shook her head incredulously and adopted a demanding pose. "Curse?"

Elizabeth held up her hand. "A long time ago, a witch cursed our family after one of our distant ancestors did not marry the witch's daughter."

"Sketchy vibes, gran." Tiffany folded her arms.

"The curse would switch the royal before the wedding, and only true love's kiss could undo it. It's why I had Lottie locked up for over a week when I realised she was having a fling with her security chief."

"Why not tell me?" Pippa gave the older woman her hardest stare.

"There is a story that if somebody tells you, while switched, the change is permanent." Elizabeth made an apologetic hand gesture. "I tried to give you clues."

"Never design a crossword," Pippa said, understanding dawning.

"Is the curse broken, though?" Tiffany had a reason to be worried.

Elizabeth grinned and shrugged. "Who knows?"

"It had better be." Tiffany narrowed her eyes.

"You might not need to worry," Elizabeth said. "William may backtrack and reinstate Harry. Harry can marry his true love, and that would end it. Maybe."

"I hope not." Harrison kissed Pippa's head. "I want to be plain old

Royal Again   Iain Benson

Harrison Rex."

"Pippa Rex? I'd sound like a dinosaur." Pippa shook her head. That name didn't suit. "You can be Harrison Palmer. That'll please my mum. She thought our name would end with Bex and me."

"At least your surname isn't Ford." Harrison's cheerfulness shone through.

"Small mercies." Pippa squeezed Harrison's hand. She could see Dillon trying to appear nonchalant by a side entrance. "I'll be back in a minute. You're not the only one who must let somebody down."

"Hey Pip," Dillon leant against the stone wall, one foot resting on it.

"I'm sorry, Dillon." Pippa hugged the driver. "Things might have been different."

"It's what it is, Pip." Dillon didn't hug Pippa back. "I realise it was Harrison I had feelings for. You and I, we never really talked. I should have asked you out back when I started. I think I got worried you'd turn that sharp tongue on me."

"Never. I should have asked you out. It's the twenty-first century, after all." Pippa paused. They'd done nothing before the switch, and he'd been with Harrison afterwards. The fates had different paths for them. "You made me flustered."

"It makes me question my sexuality."

"It shouldn't." Pippa punched him on the arm. "Harrison was a woman. And what a story as a chat-up line. Hey, I almost dated a prince."

"You think I'm ever telling anyone?" Dillon laughed. "Nobody would believe it."

"Anyway, could you give Harrison and me a ride back to my flat? I have a feeling the bus might be a little hazardous. I need to change out of these wet things."

Dillon's nod came slowly. "Of course."

Pippa signalled for Harrison to come over. She saw Jack talking to him. They shook hands, giving her hope. They'd be okay. Whatever happened next.

A happy ever after could be on the cards.

She smiled.

36
Tiffany: three years later

Jessica looked particularly hot as she gyrated under the rapidly spinning multicolour lights. Hot as in boiling *and* hot as in stunning. Tiffany joined her momentarily, a tall glass of something orange and bitter tasting in one hand.

She led Jessica from the dance floor to a side booth.

"I can't believe you're out dancing!" Jessica ran her fingers through her dyed red curls, producing a high ponytail she held above her head to let herself cool down.

Tiffany leaned into Jessica's armpit, tilting her head back to admire the pretty girl.

"This is my hen party," she said. "I'm not wasting my last week of freedom. Do you know how hard it is to slip my security these days?"

"I can believe it. How did you do it?"

"I gave my security head, um, head. He's mine for good now." Tiffany laughed. "I think he's at the bar getting stoked."

"Where's the princess tonight?"

"I'm here!"

"Not you, Pippa." Jessica kissed the top of Tiffany's head. "You're normally inseparable."

"She's six months pregnant. I'm going to be an aunt. Shouldn't stop her coming out, like. She's so dull now."

"She is not. She's cool."

"Not as cool as me."

Jessica switched topics. "What shall we do tonight, if it's just you and me?"

Tiffany reached up and traced the line of Jessica's nose. "I think you and me spending the night at your place. I'd take you back to mine, but there's less security at your flat."

Jessica smiled.

Tiffany turned in the seat. They kissed.

The lights flickered. Tiffany's heart skipped a beat. She quickly patted herself down, a heavy wash of relief at finding her body under her fingertips.

"Hey girls!" Pippa leaned against the booth, smirking.

Royal Again — Iain Benson

"Pip! You made it!"

"You'd think I'd let Bump keep me from your hen do?" Pippa mocked her affront. "I will be on Noseco, though."

"I nominate you the designated driver," Jessica said.

"Screw that," Pippa laughed. "I'll ring the palace and tell them I found Tiffany. They can lock her in the tower and I'll get a lift home."

"I've been growing my hair," Tiffany said. "I'll escape."

"I'm surprised you're out this close to your wedding," Pippa's eyes twinkled from more than the flashing disco lights. "What if the curse isn't broken?"

"Meh." She'd never admit the thought worried her a little. "I'm curse proof."

"Hey!" Jessica wriggled out from under Tiffany, giving Tiffany's backside a squeeze as she did so. "Let's dance."

Tiffany fell back onto the seat as Jessica escaped.

Pippa held her hand out to help Tiffany to her feet.

Clasping hands, all the lights went out to gasps, crashes and screams.

When Tiffany came round, she could smell toast. She felt a small kick inside her. *I'm pregnant! Aw, crap.* A worse thought appeared. *I'm married to my brother!*

Her own voice came from the floor beside her as Pippa regained consciousness. "Oh! No! Not again!"

Printed in Great Britain
by Amazon